Salt Redux

LUCINDA BRANT BOOKS

— Salt Hendon Books —
SALT BRIDE
SALT REDUX

— Alec Halsey Mysteries —
DEADLY ENGAGEMENT
DEADLY AFFAIR
DEADLY PERIL
DEADLY KIN

—The Roxton Family Saga —
NOBLE SATYR
MIDNIGHT MARRIAGE
AUTUMN DUCHESS
DAIR DEVIL
PROUD MARY
SATYR'S SON
ETERNALLY YOURS
FOREVER REMAIN

'Quizzing glass and quill, into my sedan chair and away —— the 1700s rock!'

Lucinda Brant is a *New York Times*, *USA Today*, and *Audible* bestselling author of award-winning Georgian historical romances and mysteries. Her books are renowned for wit, drama and a happily ever-after. She has a degree in history and political science from the Australian National University and a post-graduate degree in education from Bond University, where she was awarded the Frank Surman Medal.

Noble Satyr, Lucinda's first novel, was awarded the $10,000 Random House/Woman's Day Romantic Fiction Prize, and she has twice been a finalist for the Romance Writers' of Australia Romantic Book of the Year. All her novels have garnered multiple awards and become worldwide bestsellers.

Lucinda lives in the middle of a koala reserve, in a writing cave that is wall-to-wall books on all aspects of the Eighteenth Century, collected over 40 years—Heaven. She loves to hear from her readers (and she'll write back!).

lucindabrant@gmail.com	|	lucindabrant.com
pinterest.com/lucindabrant	|	twitter.com/lucindabrant
facebook.com/lucindabrantbooks	|	youtube.com/lucindabrantauthor

Salt Redux

SEQUEL TO SALT BRIDE

Salt Hendon Series Book Two

Lucinda Brant

A Sprigleaf Book
Published by Sprigleaf Pty. Ltd.

Salt Redux: Sequel to Salt Bride.

Editing: Martha Stites, Cathie Maud Cabot & Rob Van De Laak.
Art, design & photography: Sprigleaf & Larry Rostant.
Cover model: Aitor Manuel Alonso.

Typeset in Adobe Garamond Pro.

Also in ebook, audiobook and other languages.

ISBN 978-1-925614-20-6

10 9 8 7 6 5 4 3 Perfect Bound Paperback Edition (s.ii) I

for

Mirella

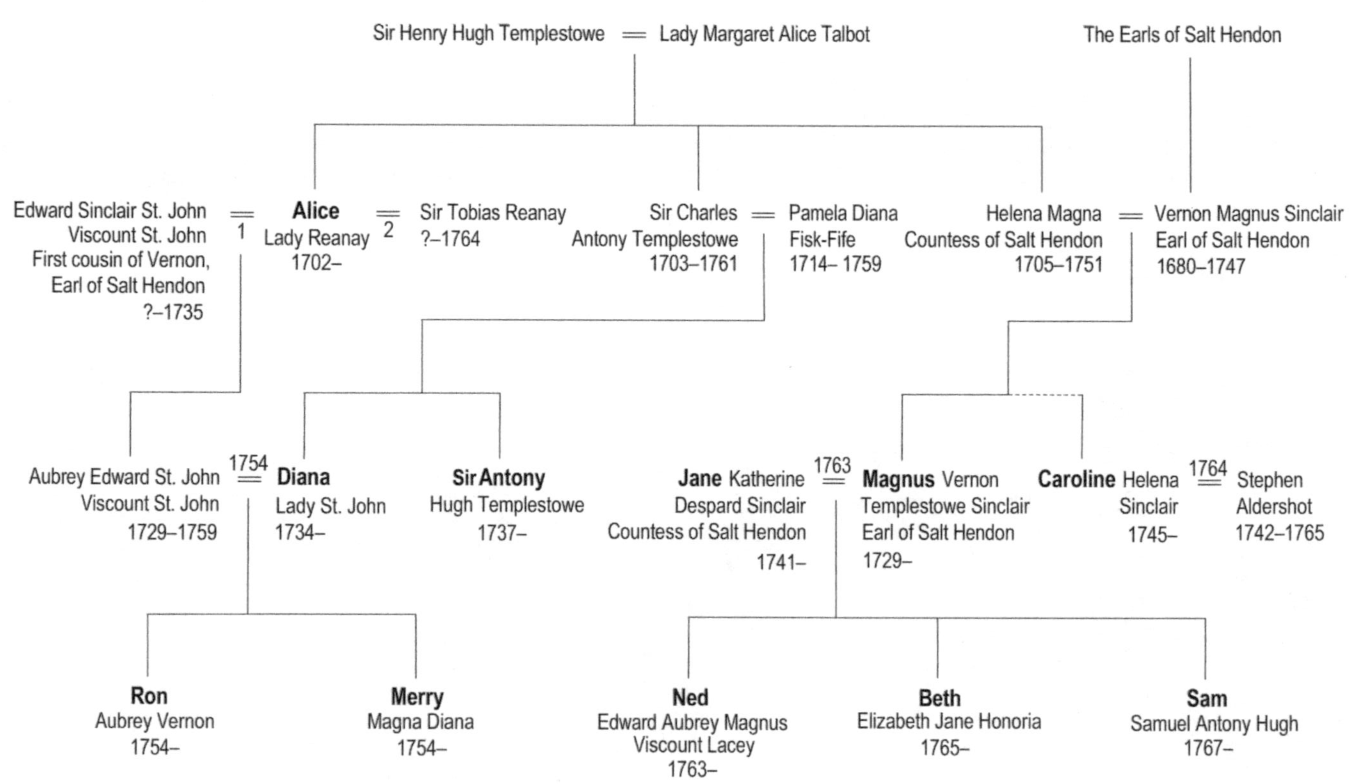

Sir Henry Hugh Templestowe = Lady Margaret Alice Talbot
The Earls of Salt Hendon
Edward Sinclair St. John Viscount St. John First cousin of Vernon, Earl of Salt Hendon ?–1735
1 = Alice Lady Reanay 1702– 2 =
Sir Tobias Reanay ?–1764
Sir Charles Antony Templestowe 1703–1761
= Pamela Diana Fisk-Fife 1714– 1759
Helena Magna Countess of Salt Hendon 1705–1751
= Vernon Magnus Sinclair Earl of Salt Hendon 1680–1747
Aubrey Edward St. John Viscount St. John 1729–1759
1754 = Diana Lady St. John 1734–
Sir Antony Hugh Templestowe 1737–
Jane Katherine Despard Sinclair Countess of Salt Hendon 1741–
1763 = Magnus Vernon Templestowe Sinclair Earl of Salt Hendon 1729–
Caroline Helena Sinclair 1745–
1764 = Stephen Aldershot 1742–1765
Ron Aubrey Vernon 1754–
Merry Magna Diana 1754–
Ned Edward Aubrey Magnus Viscount Lacey 1763–
Beth Elizabeth Jane Honoria 1765–
Sam Samuel Antony Hugh 1767–

PROLOGUE

Every month the guardian of the unnamed person of interest detained at Castle Harlech in remote north Wales sent a report to the Earl of Salt Hendon. A messenger delivered the report, always at night, into the hands of Mr. Rufus Willis, steward of the Earl's estate in Wiltshire. Mr. Willis then gave the report to his lordship when his employer was alone in the vastness of his library, and when there was no expectation of the Countess being present.

Mr. Willis caught the anguish on his lordship's face every time he handed over these reports. Upon one occasion, Mr. Willis offered to read the report to spare the Earl, but his noble employer declined saying it was his duty, however distasteful and difficult the task. Mr. Willis knew the Earl was punishing himself. The Earl believed the punishment justified. The monthly reports were a painful reminder that the unnamed person of interest had brought untold suffering on her own children and was a murderer of innocents. She had also caused the death of the Earl and Countess of Salt Hendon's first child while still in the womb. However, some comfort came from the reports. While his prisoner remained locked up, her children were safe, and so, too, were his. Although he did not need reminding of his good fortune, the Earl knew he was the luckiest of men and that nothing and no one was more important to him than his wife and family.

The guardian of the unnamed person of interest wrote much the same report every month. His "guest" was the model prisoner, afforded every comfort such a remote location could provide. The prisoner had maids to help her into velvet and satin petticoats and bodices, who dressed her waist-length auburn hair in the latest styles as remembered from her life in London, and who helped her choose what pieces of jewelry went best with each outfit. As befitting her exalted rank, she insisted on changing her gown three times a day. Servants waited on her at table as if she were queen of her own dominion and came swiftly in answer to the constant tinkling of her little hand bell. Her guardian accompanied her on walks about the parapets and courtyards of the castle, dined with her when invited, and over coffee and cake listened to her witty recollections about politicians and the esteemed persons of Polite Society, all known to her personally.

The unnamed person of interest spent most days reading the latest issues of *The Gentleman's Magazine*, particularly the reports of Parliamentary sittings, and wrote at her escritoire in her prettily-furnished drawing room, with its view of the sea. Her letters were sent but never delivered, and thus she never received a reply. These letters were sometimes ten pages in length and most were addressed to the Earl of Salt Hendon. Her guardian read these letters as part of his duties and found them full of advice for his lordship on all manner of topics political and domestic. The letters were then burned. While the guardian informed the Earl in general terms about these letters, he did not report what was most vital, though such information surely confirmed that the woman was indeed insane. Every letter was signed Diana, Countess of Salt Hendon.

She had one correspondent who wrote regularly and who did receive her letters of reply. There was a brother, a diplomat, who lived abroad. He wrote from St. Petersburg, long, detailed letters about the growing Russian capital and its environs, its people, and how he occupied his days as an assistant to the Ambassador. He often enclosed small gifts—a fan, a lace-bordered handkerchief, a pair of silk stockings, and for one of her birthdays he sent an embroidered silk shawl. His letters were also full of the latest Court gossip and palace intrigues, and sometimes he included clippings from months-old English newssheets dispatched to him in Russia.

The guardian knew this because his prisoner took great delight in reading these letters aloud. He soon realized that this brother was an astute gentleman because he never mentioned the Earl of Salt Hendon or any member of his family. What the brother knew from his sister's correspondence that the Earl and his family did not, and he, too, kept to himself, was that his sister signed her letters to him as if she was indeed the wife of the Earl of Salt Hendon.

After three years of incarceration, the unnamed person of interest no longer answered to her own name. Nor did she recognize the person she had once been when this person was described to her. She was the Countess of Salt Hendon, and Magnus Sinclair, the Earl of Salt Hendon was her dear husband. There was no persuading her otherwise. The guardian saw no harm in humoring her. After all, she was never to be released.

And so by her fourth year of imprisonment, the unnamed person of interest was in every way treated as if she were indeed the Countess of Salt Hendon. Her guardian, her apothecary, her personal maid, and her servants all addressed her by that title. So, too, did the local townspeople.

For her good behavior, and under strict supervision, she was eventually permitted visitors. Prominent members of the local town came to pay their respects and to see with their own eyes the beautiful noblewoman rumor said had been locked up by a brutish husband. The unnamed person of interest proved to be a gracious hostess, full of charm and grace, and possessing a noble bearing. It was an easy thing for the outsiders to believe they were indeed in the presence of English nobility. She was majestic in velvet and silks, with rubies about her throat and wrists. Her witty conversation was peppered with anecdotes of prominent politicians, exalted noblemen and their relatives, faraway marble palaces, and sleepless cities the local townspeople could only dream about. Soon her ladyship was holding court once a week to a room full of eager listeners.

This, too, the guardian withheld from his reports to his noble employer. Again, he reasoned there was little harm in his prisoner receiving a bunch of ignorant yokels to afternoon tea, who knew no one and were going nowhere. It kept her ladyship pacified, entertained and occupied, her thoughts on trivialities—a far cry from her disposition when first brought to the castle as a venomous abhorrent monster, whose every hate-filled word dripped vengeance and who vowed escape.

What the guardian failed to appreciate, what he could not know and never discovered, was that he was in the presence of a far superior and utterly malevolent intellect. In his confident conceit, that in four years he had tamed a monster and beaten down a beast, he remained ignorant, almost until the last breath left his body. He failed to grasp that just under the surface of her beautiful façade, the perfumed silks, the witty conversation, and the charming manners, the monster still lurked, biding its time, awaiting the perfect opportunity to escape and unleash its vengeance.

The horror of realization came the day the guardian was racked with stomach cramp and fell into a fever. The local apothecary thought it food poisoning and prescribed an emetic. A great favorite with her ladyship, whom he had treated for megrim for some months, the apothecary left the guardian in her capable hands. He advised he would return the following day. By nightfall, the guardian was dead. In his last conscious moments, he was blind and incapable of speech, but he could still hear. Her ladyship whispered at his ear as she gently tucked up his coverlet. The servants thought it a touching scene, an indication of her ladyship's high regard for her guardian.

In truth, she gleefully whispered she had poisoned him. Every speck of megrim powder the apothecary had prescribed she had carefully stored up until she had harvested enough to administer a lethal dose. She loathed him and she hoped he was in agony. Her greatest hatred she kept stored for the woman she believed falsely paraded about society as the wife and Countess of the Earl of Salt Hendon. She had spent four years devising her scheme for retribution and now, with freedom, she would put her plan into effect.

Upon the guardian's death, the unknown person of interest did not immediately flee. She mourned his passing, wearing dove gray petticoats and inviting the local townspeople to a dinner in his honor. Then, after the guardian's burial, a courier arrived in the dead of night. It was so late the horse's hooves on the cobblestones did not wake the servants. However, a restless maid heard voices echoing in the courtyard and was up, pressing her nose to the windowpane in time to see her ladyship in her nightgown and slippers, taper in hand, scurry under the arch and enter by the big oak door. She held a sealed packet.

The late-night letter was from the Earl begging her to return to him. He had been bewitched by a whore of a mistress, and with her death, so died her influence over him. To his shame, he now recognized his great wrongdoing in sending his devoted wife into exile. Could she forgive him? Would she come back to him? He could not wait to be reconciled and would ride to meet her at the Welsh border. She was to hurry with all speed.

The servants, the apothecary and, indeed, those prominent townspeople who counted themselves friends of the Countess of Salt Hendon, all knew word for word the contents of the Earl's letter, for she joyfully announced the news to them and showed them the letter. The apothecary did not doubt the seal and handwriting belonged to the illustrious Earl of Salt Hendon. There was much rejoicing, and the townspeople held a celebratory dinner to honor Lady Salt and wish her well, to which she wore her most magnificent gown and jewelry.

Holland covers draped furniture, and trunks and portmanteaux were packed to bursting. A splendid carriage pulled by four high-spirited grays took up Lady Salt and her personal maid, and her ladyship was farewelled with much fanfare. She was never seen again.

Two days following her departure a letter arrived. It was from Sir Antony Templestowe, and it had traveled all the way from St. Petersburg.

The apothecary, who had stayed on at the castle to settle her ladyship's small pile of accounts with money the dead guardian had for that purpose, did not know what was to be done with the letter. It was addressed to a Diana, Lady St. John, a person unknown to the apothecary, and yet the direction was correct.

Perhaps the correspondent did not personally know Lady Salt.

He had correctly identified her Christian name, but then become confused when writing her title. It was a mystery to the apothecary. Still, he would do his duty by her ladyship, and so he redirected the unopened letter to the Earl of Salt Hendon's estate, Salt Hall in Wiltshire, which he had heard Lady Salt talk of so many times he felt he had visited the grand Jacobean mansion and its spacious parkland.

As Sir Antony had provided his direction in St. Petersburg, the apothecary wrote him a civil letter. He explained what he had done with his letter and, presuming he knew Lady Salt because he had used her Christian name, he took the liberty of giving Sir Antony the good news: Her ladyship had departed Harlech Castle and was on her way to be reunited with her noble lord the Earl of Salt Hendon.

A month later, Sir Antony received the apothecary's letter. Upon reading it, he promptly threw up.

ONE

ST. PETERSBURG, RUSSIA, 1767

"Come back to bed, Tosha," a drowsy female voice coaxed from deep within the tumble of warm bedclothes.

Sir Antony Templestowe remained at the open bedchamber window, bare back to the darkened room. He was shaking, hard-gripping the painted sill, trying to bring the tremors under control. He leaned out the window to allow the icy breeze off the Neva River to flow across his colorless face. He had just thrown up onto the hewn granite pavement of the embankment below, and then promptly apologized to two Imperial palace guards who walked under the window minutes later. Singing a bawdy tavern song about a girl named Nina and her plump buttocks while propping each other up, the drunken guards failed to hear the apology. They staggered onwards into the fog as Sir Antony pulled the sash and sat on the sill with eyes closed.

"Tosha?"

The woman was now up on an elbow to see over the rumple of silken sheet, feather pillows, and damask coverlet. Eyes adjusting to the dim light, she smiled, gaze raking the length of her English lover's splendid physique silhouetted in the early morning glow filtering through the window at his back. From close-cropped auburn hair to hardened thigh muscles and down to his large bare feet, he was all male and all hers. She gave a little shudder of pleasure and was about to make a bawdy remark when she sensed all was not right. She sat up, brushed the mass of long honey curls from her face and slid the delicate silk nightgown up over her round shoulders to cover her breasts from the cold morning air.

"Tosha? *Antony?* Wh-what is it? What has happened?"

"Forgive me for waking you, Your Highness," Sir Antony replied placidly, a slight bow in the direction of the undraped alcove that housed his canopied bed and in it his lovely mistress, the Princess Ekaterina Knyazhevy-Yusupova. "I need—I need a moment alone…"

He scooped up the single-page parchment flung to the carpet in his haste to get to the window, and with another small bow strode through to his closet to swill ginger and cinnamon mouthwash. He dashed icy water over his face and hovered over the large patterned porcelain washbasin, gasping from the sudden cold, taking deep breaths, wishing the letter a bad dream. It was not. From the corner of his eye he looked at the parchment on the dressing table. Snatching up a porcelain jug, he poured the remaining icy water over his scalp until the jug ran dry.

He wrapped his nakedness in a green and gold silk damask banyan he found draped over the padded stool, slipped his bare feet into a pair of red Moroccan leather mules and sat before the spindle-legged dressing table towel-drying his hair. He then reread the letter from the unknown apothecary. Its contents filled him with overwhelming dread, and another wave of nausea fuelled by crippling anxiety flushed over him. He closed his eyes, willing the sickness away. Thankfully, the need to purge his stomach did not follow. He had not felt this ill since that fateful day in London, four years ago, when his beautiful only sister, one of Polite Society's bright shining lights, had been discovered as a terminating midwife; a murderer of innocents. Insane—there was no doubt. She had almost succeeded in killing her little son in her obsession to be the singular object of the Earl of Salt Hendon's affection. Delusional—most assuredly. Never to be released—without question.

Spirited away to a remote and undisclosed location before a whisper of scandal reached Polite Society, he knew this outcome for his sister was the right one. It spared the family, most importantly her son and daughter, and him, eternal ignominy. Family and friends believed Diana St. John had gone traveling on the Continent for her health; so, too, did Polite Society. As far as his cousin the Earl was concerned, Diana could have swung from a rope and suffered a slow death for her unspeakable crimes. He damned her to hell and Sir Antony could not blame him. His sister was a conscienceless monster. It was this realization and the knowledge of all she had done that had sent him spiraling into mindless oblivion the moment she was spirited out of London and his life forever—or so he thought.

He had not coped well. He drank to excess, and enough wine and spirits to drown thought. He neglected his family, most shamefully his now orphaned niece and nephew. He squandered his burgeoning career as a diplomat, and lost all pretension to one day being an ambassador. In an alcoholic haze, he staggered about society, making a fool of himself and becoming a nuisance. One day he went too far. To his eternal shame and the disgust of others, he arrived drunk at a recital hosted by the Earl and Countess of Salt Hendon. Before upwards of fifty people, he had a blazing row with the Earl's sister, the Lady Caroline, hurling accusations that were best left unsaid. He caused the sort of scandal his cousin the Earl abhorred and had avoided with Diana's banishment.

He wondered if the blood in his veins also coursed with insanity. He not only humiliated himself and Lord and Lady Salt, he devastated the hopes and dreams of the only woman to whom his heart truly belonged. For that he would never forgive himself. Could he blame Caroline for hating him? Was he surprised when she refused to see him before he set off for the Russian Imperial Court? Then one day, he discovered for himself, while reading a month old English newssheet, that the Lady Caroline Sinclair, only sister of the Earl of Salt Hendon had married The Right Honorable Stephen Aldershot. The love of his life was now Lady Caroline Aldershot and beyond his reach forever.

It was just as well he was sent packing to St. Petersburg. It was as far as the Earl of Salt Hendon could banish him without pushing him off the edge of the known world. True to type, he was drunk when he presented his diplomatic credentials as Minister Plenipotentiary at the Russian Imperial Court. If not for the friendship of Prince Mikhail (Misha) Ivan Knyazhevy-Yusupov and his lovely sister, the Princess Ekaterina (Katya), he might have stayed that way. If not for the princely couple, he was certain he would have drunk himself to death. What he owed Misha and Katya was immeasurable, for he literally owed them his life. With their support and encouragement, he picked himself up out of the cesspit of self-loathing and pity, sobered up, and now considered St. Petersburg his home. What did he have to go back to England for anyway?

The previous evening an Imperial serf delivered the fateful letter to his apartment.

He had returned from his fencing match with Misha to find Katya fanning herself with the sealed letter. She was sitting cross-legged in the middle of his bed, naked. He tossed the unopened letter aside, forgotten, until many hours later when he happened to find it amongst the crumple of bed sheets in the cold, dark hours of morning. He read the letter from the unknown apothecary unwittingly informing him that

"Lady Salt" had departed Castle Harlech and was on her way to reunite with her husband, the Earl of Salt Hendon.

His mad sister had escaped her fortress prison, and his life was again no longer his own.

He had no choice. He must leave St. Petersburg at once and return to London.

The squeak of a door hinge drew Sir Antony out of his thoughts on how best to break the news of his departure to Misha and Katya. The panel in the painted wall opened and his sleepy-eyed majordomo poked his head around the servant door.

"Is everything—I heard your lordship up and about…"

Sir Antony beckoned him into the room.

"Tea, Semper."

Semper peered keenly at his master. He asked the question, though he prayed he knew the answer. Sir Antony had not touched a drop of alcohol in two years. "Your lordship hasn't—You've not taken something stronger?"

Good God! How he wished to drink something stronger! If ever there was a time and a good reason to break his vow and return to the bottle, this was it. A bottle of claret and one of cognac and he would be well on his way to numbing his mind of his sister. But he shook his head and said evenly,

"No. Just tea. Perhaps bring some of those little macaroons Her Highness favors so much."

"Very good, my lord."

Master and servant locked eyes.

"If ever I lapse," Sir Antony said softly, "you know what to do."

"Yes, my lord, I do. I will not fail you."

Sir Antony briefly closed his eyes. "Thank you."

"I'll have the fires relit," Semper said to change the topic and to lighten the mood. "And have your bath drawn."

When his master nodded, Semper signaled to the open servant doorway and the serfs lingering in the darkened passageway scurried into the room. A dozen or more scattered soft-footed throughout the rooms of the apartment and went about their duties. The presence of so many servants had at first bothered Sir Antony upon his arrival in Russia. When he tried without success to decrease the number considered necessary for his comfort, the Princess enlightened him that serfs were owned body and soul; every one had a task, however menial, and to remove the task was to diminish the value of that serf.

Sir Antony said no more about it and left the battalion to Semper's organizational skills. His majordomo was directing them now. Two serfs to the fireplace, while another two padded into the bedchamber to see to the fire there. Three went through to the bathing room to ready his bath, while the rest disappeared back into the blackness of the servant passageway to fill the silver samovar full of boiling water, prepare the two porcelain teapots and return wheeling a trolley laden with all the necessary tea things for the English lord's morning tea ritual.

"Will your lordship be wanting to bathe first?"

"Tea first."

Semper bowed, and with a glance at the fireplace to see the serfs busy at the grate, and another glance into the bathing room, he turned to leave, but was called back.

"Semper…"

"Yes, my lord?"

Sir Antony tossed the folded letter amongst the clutter of crystal jars and silver and ivory personal grooming accoutrements on the dressing table. With a heavy sigh, he wrapped the silk banyan closer about his body as he rose and said,

"I recall that when I told you of my decision to remain in 'Petersburg you were not at all miserable at the prospect of never returning to England. In fact, you grinned."

"Yes, my lord, I did."

Sir Antony raised an eyebrow. "That grin had something to do with your sudden love of all things Russian and because you had formed a particular attachment to one of the Princess's serfs?"

"Yes, my lord. She's your serf now, a needlewoman, and takes care of your wardrobe."

"My serf? When did these servants become mine?"

"Her Highness gifted you fifty serfs at Christmastime."

"Gifted?" Sir Antony did not like the idea at all. He found human enslavement of any kind abhorrent.

"Yes, my lord. They belong to you now. Ten speak French as well as their native tongue, which has been a great help to me in managing their time."

"I had no idea you'd been put to so much bother."

"No bother at all, my lord."

"Remind me of my needlewoman's name."

"Nina. Her name is Nina."

"Not the possessor of the lovely posterior one hopes," murmured Sir Antony, recalling the bawdy tavern ditty, adding quickly at his majordomo's frown of incomprehension, "I suppose it would be a rhetorical question to ask if you love Nina?"

The valet smiled sheepishly. "It would, my lord…" Yet, when Sir Antony again sighed heavily, he gave a start. "She's not—She's not being sent back to the estate, is she, my lord?"

"I've no idea. No. Not that I am aware. Why would you think that? Didn't you say the Princess gifted me fifty serfs? If Nina is one of them, then is she not mine to do with as I wish?"

"That is true, my lord. But…"

Sir Antony waited for him to continue.

Semper glanced over his shoulder, at the serfs building a new fire and then at the open servant door, as if fearing to be overheard. It was an unnecessary action, because in these, the most intimate of Sir Antony's rooms, he had delegated the menial tasks to native speakers, ensuring his master's privacy. The only place he did not look was over Sir Antony's shoulder into the darkened bedchamber. This was noted.

"The Princess does not understand English," Sir Antony remarked with a wry smile. "Though I am very sure Her Highness is straining to hear every word of our conversation."

"It was some time ago, but I asked your lordship to have a word with Her Highness about Nina and me—the possibility of us marrying."

Sir Antony was grim faced and apologetic. "I did. Coward that I am, I hadn't the heart to tell you her response was to laugh in my face. It's beyond her comprehension why you, a free man and a foreigner, would want to lower yourself and be the object of ridicule by marrying one of her—um—slaves. It's just not done."

"I'm not lowering m'self and you know it, my lord!"

"Yes, you and I know that, Ralph," Sir Antony agreed calmly, "but we are Englishmen living in a foreign country. Russia, as we have discovered, is more foreign than most. 'Petersburg may appear a European capital, with all and sundry practicing their French language skills and aping French mannerisms to the point where if we blinked, we could very well think ourselves back at Versailles, but that's just a façade. So, too, is the unsettling fact that our Russian friends crave all things English, from our dogs to our coal! Yet, drive five miles out of the capital in any direction and it's beards, bare feet, and cabbage soup! And as much as it sets the hairs up on the back of our necks, slavery surrounds us. You know people are commodities, listed in an owner's inventory, just like that chair over there or that tapestry on the wall. You said yourself I was gifted fifty serfs at Christmastime, as easily as if you had said I'd been given fifty pairs of stockings. You might as well say you want to marry my settee, and you'd get the same laughing response, and not just from the Princess but from any Russian you cared to meet—low or highborn."

"Aye, I do know that, my lord," Semper grudgingly conceded. "I was just hoping Her Highness would be different from her kind because she shares your bed—"

"Steady, Semper," Sir Antony cut in very low.

"There's no harm in hoping, is there, my lord?" the majordomo continued to argue, mechanically scooping up discarded linen smalls, white stockings and diamond-buckled shoes from the night before. He dumped these into the arms of a passing serf with a sharp word that sent the staring servant scurrying away with a low bow and gaze to the floor. "Her Highness has an odd sense of morality, if you ask me!"

"I didn't ask you, Semper."

"Laughs at a free man wanting to do the honorable thing by a serf, *your* serf, my lord," the majordomo continued with an insolent grumble as he brushed down the sleeve of a midnight blue velvet frock coat embellished with silver embroidery on upturned cuffs and skirts. "And yet she has no compunction in sharing your—"

"*Enough.*"

Sir Antony flushed red and stared at the mulish Ralph Semper. The man had been in his employ for seven years, four as valet and then, since coming to Russia, had taken on the onerous task of majordomo of his considerable household. They had been through some tough times together—well, Semper had, dealing with a master who, at his most inebriated, had sunk lower than a sewer rat. But never had he been insolent. Sir Antony could only think Semper's deep-seated feelings for the serf Nina was the cause of such outrageous disrespect, and thus he would forgive him this insulting outburst. He ran a hand over his short-cropped hair and said in a low voice,

"Practice what you preach to my servants, Semper, and be as one blind to the presence of the Princess. If not, you are free to leave my service with a month's pay."

"My lord? Leave?" The majordomo's jaw fell open and it was his turn to color up. He bowed to his knees. "Forgive me. I was—I was—I have no wish to leave your service, my lord."

"Good. That makes two of us. So, for God's sake, have a care. If these lackeys understood English—if Her Highness did—you'd be strung up quicker than I could get an interview to plead your case. I can't save you from yourself, *dolt.* As for Nina, if she is one of the fifty serfs gifted to me by Her Highness, then it is for me to consent to you marrying her, or not. Am I in the right?"

"Yes, my lord," Semper agreed with a hesitant smile that grew into one of dawning wonder. "Yes! Yes, you are, my lord." He frowned. "Though it would be prudent to ask the permission of Her Highness as a matter of form…"

Sir Antony suppressed a smile. "Thank you, Semper. I will put your case to Her Highness today…"

"Thank you, my lord," Ralph Semper replied. "Again, I apologize. I don't know what came over me."

"I do," Sir Antony quipped.

Semper saw the Princess hovering in the bedchamber doorway and made certain to keep his gaze on his master's chiseled features, not least because every feminine curve and more was evident through the gossamer silk of her dressing gown and shift. He managed to flash a warning at Sir Antony by opening wide his eyes, which was noted.

Sir Antony strolled across the room towards his majordomo, hands deep in the pockets of his silk banyan, and said very quietly, so only Semper could hear,

"If Mr. Church is not up, rouse him. He has a long day of travel preparations ahead of him. We leave for London as soon as it can be arranged."

"London?" The majordomo blinked in surprise. He kept his voice to a whisper, despite the Princess being unable to decipher the English tongue. "Are we banished, my lord?"

Sir Antony's lips twitched at the use of the plural of the personal pronoun. Yet, there was no humor or warmth in his voice when he confided,

"No. We return to London because the lives of a little boy and his mother—perhaps others—are in danger. I only pray there is still suffi-cient time…"

"What do you mean to do when we get to London, my lord?"

Sir Antony was grim; his eyes, dull.

"To keep them from harm? Whatever it takes."

TWO

SALT HALL, WILTSHIRE, ENGLAND

Mr Rufus Willis, the Earl of Salt Hendon's estate steward, paced the cobbles under the arch that led to the stables. Twice he stepped out into the sunshine to look up at the large round clock face set in the arch and note the time, a pointless action. However, it calmed him knowing the Earl was returning to the house. An alert chimney sweep had spotted his lordship and his small party riding across the vast parkland in the direction of the house.

Pregnancy and birth scared the steward witless. Women died in childbirth and from its attendant complications all the time. His wife Anne had given him a healthy son and her second pregnancy was progressing just as smoothly. Yet, it was not Anne who set his heart racing, and taken him from his office in the main house to the stables in search of his employer, it was the Countess.

The Earl had set out very early, accompanied by his godson Ron St. John, Mr. Hoskins the head gamekeeper, and three of the assistant keepers. In the Earl's saddle, sitting up before him and holding the pommel with undisguised delight, was his lordship's pride and joy, Edward Aubrey Magnus Sinclair, Viscount Lacey, heir to the earldom of Salt Hendon—known by everyone as Ned.

The gamekeeper had promised Ned a look at a real live stag, and so when the opportunity arose, off they rode to the far wood to see this magnificent beast with its herd of deer. It was not the most convenient day, and the Earl was intent on postponing the half-day excursion, until the Countess said he could not disappoint their son by breaking his promise, whatever the circumstances. She assured him the pains she had been experiencing since the night before did not mean she was in labor. By her reckoning, there was still two weeks until that happy event. To satisfy the love of her life, and to ensure he took their son on the promised excursion, the Countess agreed to have the physician summoned, Lady Caroline woken early, and a footman sent to the gatehouse lodge to fetch Mrs. Willis. Two hours after the Earl reluctantly set off, Jane, Countess of Salt Hendon gave birth to a healthy child—her third.

To take his mind from the worry of the Countess and her newborn, Rufus Willis leaned against the smooth sandstone wall of the elegant arch and withdrew a letter from his frock coat pocket to reread it. The letter had accompanied a small parcel addressed to Diana, Lady St. John, at Harlech Castle and had been redirected to the Earl of Salt Hendon's estate. While it confused him as to why a parcel meant for the incarcerated Lady St. John had been forwarded to Salt Hall, it troubled the steward more that the accompanying letter was not from her guardian, but from an apothecary attached to the castle.

Willis had not received the monthly report on Lady St. John from her guardian and had yet to discover the reason for the man's tardiness. Perhaps the guardian had taken ill and the apothecary was writing on his behalf? But as no mention was made of the guardian, Willis was left none the wiser. He also wondered why the apothecary had forwarded on Sir Antony Templestowe's parcel, meant for his lordship's incarcerated sister. More perplexing was the fact the apothecary ended his letter by wishing Lord and Lady Salt all the very best in their reconciled happiness.

Reconciled happiness? What did it mean? Why had the apothecary written to the Countess as if she knew him when Willis would stake all that he held dear that the Countess had no idea the man existed? Why hadn't Sir Antony's parcel been delivered to his sister? Willis had more questions than answers. He also had a deep foreboding that there was more to the apothecary's letter than could be deduced from its contents. But Willis would not trouble his lordship with such a letter today. This of all days should be one of joy and celebration.

He slipped the letter into the pocket of his brown linen frock coat and thought of returning to the house to get on with ticking off his daily tasks. At the top of his list was awaiting the arrival of the newly-appointed nursery maid to join the growing number of servants employed in the nursery to cater to the needs and whims of a great nobleman's expanding young brood. With the arrival of the Countess's third child, the girl's timely arrival would be a godsend.

The welcome sound of horses' shoes clattering on the cobbles dragged the steward from his musings. He moved through the arch into the expansive stable yard as the Earl and his lively party walked their horses under the arch. Stable boys went to the horses' heads. The riders dismounted. Liveried footmen appeared from the kitchen courtyard with jugs of ale and one of cordial, crystal tumblers, bowls heavy with fruit, and a large basket of hot buttered bap rolls. Horses led away, leather riding gloves stripped off, riders' thirsts quenched and hunger sated, Willis came forward as the Earl, who was offering a bowl of strawberries to his young son, looked up and said with a wry smile,

"Mr. Willis! What taxing task are you performing on my behalf that it makes you look the gray cloud in an otherwise blue sky? Take that fat juicy one there, Ned," he coaxed his three-and-a-half-year-old son, whose little fingers hovered in indecision over the bowl his father patiently held out to him, "before Ron decides it has his name carved into it."

"Does it, Uncle Salt?" Ron St. John asked seriously, in on the ruse at the Earl's conspiratorial wink and peering over the bowl as if looking for the strawberry in question. "I should have it then, don't you think, Ned, if it's got my name on it?"

"No, Ron! It's *my* name on it! *Ned*," Ned protested, scowling. He grabbed the succulent strawberry pointed out to him by his father, as if his twelve-year-old cousin meant to steal it from him, and with a cheeky smile stuffed it whole into his mouth.

The Earl smiled at Ron, ruffled his son's mop of golden ringlets, and satisfied he was eating the entire strawberry, rose up from his haunches to look down at his steward, who was smiling at his tactics to get a little boy to eat fruit. He handed off the bowl to a hovering footman.

"So, Mr. Willis," Salt said to his steward, "have you come to tell me her ladyship is in labor?"

"No, my lord. That is… Approximately two hours after your departure her ladyship did go into labor. It was mercifully quick and her ladyship gave birth to a—"

"*No*! No, don't tell me! That's her ladyship's privilege," the Earl interrupted, and far from feeling the concern or alarm evident on his steward's face, he gave a shout of undisguised glee and slapped the man's back, adding with a grin, "Ha! I *knew* it! I knew the exact day with Ned and with Beth, so why not with number three? But would mamma listen to papa, Ned? No! She would not." He scooped up his little son and waited for Ron, who was politely offering thanks to the gamekeeper for showing them the stag. When the boy came over to him, he put an arm about his shoulders, saying in a low voice, "That was very well done, Ron. Thank you." Adding audibly as he set off across the courtyard, Mr. Willis and two footmen a step behind, "What is number three do you think, Ron? Ned? A brother or a sister?"

"Brother!" Ned was quick to offer.

"Yes. Please let it be a boy," Ron agreed with a solemn sigh of resignation. "There are too many females in this house as it is." Adding quickly, fearing his godfather might think him uncaring, "I love them, Uncle Salt, but their fripperies and conversation... If I have to listen to Merry describe her wedding dress... As if she's getting married tomorrow and not twelve years old like me, I think I'll cast up my accounts! Ugh. It turns a man's stomach."

"Then I shouldn't wonder you are eager to be off to Eton."

"Very! I must survive another month of stitchery and lace fichus first!"

This made the Earl laugh.

"One day, Ron, you will thank your sister," he said cryptically. "The understanding of such mysteries as embroidery and fichus will become inordinately important when you finally decide you do want to be around females and their conversations." He glanced over a shoulder at his steward. "Is that not so, Mr. Willis?"

"Very true, my lord. A keen interest in female accomplishments is particularly important when a young man turns his mind to courting."

Ron screwed up his face as if he had tasted something sour. "*Courting*? Ugh. *Never*."

With a grin, the Earl pulled Ron into an affectionate hug and then let him go to step off the courtyard onto the cool black and white marble flooring in the wide passageway. The smile died spying his butler in low conversation with the physician. Two footmen hovered at the butler's shoulder at the far end of the hallway where it opened out into the expansive entrance hall. With Ned still in his arms, he strode up to the physician, Willis and Ron quick to follow, trying to match the nobleman's long strides, and interrupted his butler.

"Well?" he demanded of the physician.

He noted the rotund man's greatcoat buttoned to his chins, and hanging at his side in one gloved hand was a black leather bag. He had no idea if the man was coming or going. When the physician's response was not immediate, his gaze snapped to his butler, who met his eye then looked away to the physician, waiting for him to speak first. The Earl's heart began to race and the blood to drain from his face.

"Speak!" he ordered the physician. "The Countess—"

The physician dared to cut him off. "I'm sorry, my lord, so very, very sorry. I was too late. I could do nothing—"

"Sweet Jes—Rufus! Take Ned!" Salt demanded, thinking the worst.

He handed Ned into his steward's arms with a perfunctory kiss to the little boy's forehead and strode away, leaving the party in the marble foyer gaping after him. The physician was still working his jaw to speak, but the moment was lost. Ron St. John nodded to Willis and silently took himself off to his rooms, following the Earl up the great staircase, but slowly, and with head bent lest a servant or worse, a member of his family, caught him with tears in his eyes.

The Earl went up the flight of marble stairs two at a time. He did not stop until he reached the second landing. Here he paused in the wide vestibule with its double-height windows that framed a picturesque view of lush rolling meadow, and beyond, the old stone bridge and the summerhouse by the lake. He drew breath, staring at the view without seeing it as he stripped out of his velvet riding frock coat and flung it away from him as if it had the plague. Two footmen opened the oak double doors that led into the private apartments he shared with the Countess, and closed them on their master's back, not a word, but with wide eyes and a knowing lift of their eyebrows.

Salt strode through the private dining room, not a glance at the two startled chambermaids who backed against the ebony table to get out of the Earl's way, or at a third chambermaid who was throwing wide the burgundy and gold curtains to allow light to stream across the polished floorboards.

He went through to the small antechamber with its two ornate doorways, one opening into his private rooms, the other onto a landing that crossed to the nursery rooms occupied by his children, and on into his wife's pretty sitting room with its chinoiserie wallpaper and matching curtains in soft pink and green pastels. It was such a feminine space and so very *Jane* that the room never failed to give him a warm glow, except today.

Today, the room could have been draped in Holland covers and he none the wiser as he flung wide the door that opened into his wife's dressing room. The door banged against the wallpapered wall and so loud that, despite the noise and activity within, the occupants stopped what they were doing and looked to the doorway. The room, from ornate dressing screen across to the cluttered dressing table, was full of women and industry. They curtsied as one, but as the Earl stared straight through them without acknowledgement they waited, as stone, for direction. A nod from Lady Caroline Aldershot to the Countess's head *femme de chambre* and the servants came to life and continued on with their tasks, gaze to the floor.

Salt would have walked on, but above the drumming in his ears he heard his name, and his head snapped to the left. Sitting on the pale blue damask chaise longue were his goddaughter Merry and his sister Caroline, and between them a nursery maid was gently rocking a snugly-wrapped newborn, to which all eyes on the sofa were pinned. That the newborn was not being cradled by its mother so soon after birth increased the Earl's fear that something was dreadfully wrong with his wife. Without a word to his sister, who rose with a shake of her silk flowered petticoats and went to meet him, he strode on to the bedchamber door.

Before he could open the door, a chubby two-year-old girl with tightly-sprung black curls and cherry-ripe cheeks ran across his path with a squeal of delight. She wrapped her arms tightly about his booted leg and did not let go. She demanded Papa take her for a ride like he always did. The Earl gently pried his little daughter from his jockey boot, scooped her up, gave her warm cheek a kiss, and handed her off to a hovering nursery maid, saying with none of his usual playfulness or smiles, and more sharply than intended,

"Mamma first. Then Beth."

"Salt, would you like to hold your—"

"Jane first," he stated to his sister Caroline without turning about and slipped into the bedchamber just as the Lady Elizabeth Jane Honoria Sinclair—Beth to all who knew her—burst into tears and called for her Mamma.

The Earl was at the four-poster bed before he realized he had not taken a breath since entering the room. He let out a sigh of relief as he wiped a cold hand over his face, then through his windswept chestnut hair, as the bed's occupant struggled to sit up against the mound of soft down pillows, her lady's maid quick to come to her aid.

"Salt? Magnus? What—what is it?" Jane, Countess of Salt Hendon, asked in alarm. "What's wrong? Not Ned? He didn't suffer a fall on your ride? Beth? She cried out just now. What's happened?"

She took the hand her husband held out to her as he went down on his knees beside the mattress, but when he did not respond immediately, just kissed her wrist and then lowered his head to touch their clasped hands to his warm forehead, as if in prayer, she became truly frightened.

"Not the—not the *baby*?" she asked in a fearful whisper.

He shook his head but did not look up. "No. No," he muttered. "All is as it should be…"

It was Jane's turn to sigh and she lay back against the pillows, a glance at the other occupants of the room. Without a word, her lady's maid ushered the two chambermaids with their pile of laundry from the bedchamber. Mrs. Willis placed a cup of tea on a tray within Jane's reach, and followed. The couple was alone. With the click of the bedchamber door, Salt looked up.

Through a film of tears he smiled at his wife. Her blue eyes were tired and her face lacked color. Yet, for all that, and all that she had just endured, she was utterly lovely and serene. Whatever troubled him, whenever he felt the weight of his responsibilities pressing on his shoulders, being with Jane never failed to lift him up and make him supremely contented with life; that all was right with the world. She seemed to read his thoughts, because as he propped himself on the mattress and faced her, she said brightly,

"I am not surprised you thought something was the matter. It all happened so quickly. This baby was determined to enter the world with least pain to its dear mamma, for which I will be forever grateful."

He handed her the cup of tea. "Did I not tell you today was the day?"

She dimpled and drank of the sweet tea and felt better for it.

"You did. But even you could not predict the baby would arrive before nuncheon! Mrs. Willis managed to be here in time to be of assistance, but Dr. Hume was no help at all. He is possibly still astride his horse."

"He's downstairs in the hall, still in his greatcoat."

"Well, he might as well leave it on!" Jane said with asperity. "I suppose it will make for a nice change that he does not have to deal with a woman in labor, screeching and cursing her husband for putting her through such a painful ordeal—"

"Did you curse me, Jane?"

"Oh, most assuredly. Mrs. Willis tells me that it is unnatural not to do so."

At that the Earl laughed. She held out her empty porcelain teacup on its saucer and he put it aside without taking his eyes from hers.

"As well as giving birth to a very healthy child, I have also managed to have the bedchamber set to rights, my face scrubbed and my hair brushed and braided, and all before the physician's arrival. Admittedly it is six hours since he was sent for, but he may be left wondering if I were indeed pregnant at all." She put out her hand to her husband, saying with a searching look, "When I am next pregnant, you had best send for Dr. Hume the moment you have one of your dreams. Last night you not only woke me, but obviously the baby had had enough of the disruption and wanted a cradle to sleep in."

When he huffed an apology and did not meet her gaze, it confirmed her suspicion that his dream had been in fact a nightmare, a regular occurrence over the past few weeks. She had no idea what was troubling him, and that troubled her.

"I wish you would confide what it is that is worrying you so. Please do not tell me it is a nothing or a trifle, or something that should not concern me. I have shared your bed every night for four years, and so I know when you are troubled beyond what is reasonably expected of a man in your position." She smiled into his brown eyes and said buoyantly, "If you cannot tell me, then whom can you tell—certainly not Willis. You and your steward share the same dour disposition, and I won't be called to account by Mrs. Willis for adding to her husband's worries."

When he smiled weakly and looked at their fingers entwined on the coverlet, she briefly closed her eyes, suddenly very tired and anxious to cradle her newborn again, and for her little son and baby daughter and their extended family to share with them in the birth of another Sinclair. Yet, as there was no wailing coming through the walls from her sitting room, she patiently waited, hoping she had coaxed her husband to confession.

"Dearest Jane, you have just given birth to our third child and I've not had the good manners to ask after the baby, and still your thoughts are all for me..." He suddenly pressed his lips to the back of her hand. "I don't deserve you..."

"Rot! Of course you do!"

"Jane... Without you... If I ever lost you, be it in childbirth, or in any other way... Without you, none of it matters... *None* of it."

She choked up and tenderly ran her fingers through his tussle of thick chestnut hair and said to his bowed head,

"My dear, dear man... I love you so very much..."

"And I you—beyond words..."

He could not bring himself to tell her the whole truth. Yes, he had worried about the impending birth of their third child. What husband was not terrified of childbirth and all its attendant calamities? He had kept those worries to himself. To his shame and guilt, the dreams that had disturbed his sleep over the past month were not filled with worry about his wife or children at all, but concerned another, a creature he so reviled that he reviled himself for allowing her to invade his thoughts at any time. It was the letter, or the lack of one, that had started the nightmares. He did not need his steward to tell him that the monthly letter from the guardian of the unnamed person of interest was overdue. He waited on those letters, as if with each letter he could breathe easy for another four weeks knowing the creature who had tried to kill his wife and was a murderer of the unborn remained locked up, away from Jane and his children and Ron and Merry; they were safe from harm, safe from evil for another month.

Over the past four years, he had often thought of ending the misery of the crippling apprehension that consumed him. With Diana St. John locked up for the rest of her natural life, stripped of her identity and referred to forever more as the unnamed person of interest, he presumed he would be free of her. He was not. He knew that release would only come with her death. Too many times to count he thought of having her poisoned, or orchestrate for her to have an accident—fall off a turret or break her neck on the stairs. It would be easy to arrange. Yet, that would make him a murderer, too, and no better than she. He could not have her murder on his conscience, for his children to one day discover that the father they loved and respected had been party to such a heinous crime, and against a creature who was clearly insane.

He sat up and mentally shook himself free of such melancholy thoughts. Jane's blue eyes were so full of concern that he knew himself for a selfish wretch. This should be a happy time, a time for celebration, for carefree laughter, and for family. He owed it to his two children, to the new little life just come into the world, to his extended family and retainers, to those who looked to him for guidance and to set the example, and most of all, he owed it to his wife, to Jane. Jane had not only given him three healthy children he adored, but given him a life worth leading.

He locked the dark thoughts away for another day as he kissed the back of her hand, and was about to offer her a garbled explanation for his frequent bouts of broken sleep over the past few weeks, when she gave him a plausible excuse, one he could readily agree to without the need to lie.

"Your problem is that your mind needs occupation. I don't mean counting sheep and fixing tenant fences. You need politics, papers and a hundred parliamentary annoyances to keep your thoughts away from petty domestic details. Willis has proved himself a marvelously competent estate steward, so competent that he leaves you little to do but say *yes* or *no* to his suggestions and advice." Jane squeezed his fingers.

"Willis can manage the estate without you needing to be here while Parliament is in session. He has proved himself more than capable, what with your frequent visits up to London in recent months on parliamentary business. Ned is in his fourth year. A month of lying-in, and the baby and I can travel. Please. Magnus. If you feel the time is right for you to return to the political arena, you must do so. Four years in the country seeing to your estates is time enough for a man with your abilities, and so the newssheets keep reminding me!"

Salt put up an eyebrow in surprise. "So her ladyship agrees with the editorial hacks who pepper their opinions with cries of "Recall Lord S from the country!" as if I am a salve to be applied and government will heal?"

"I don't know about you being a political salve," Jane said bluntly, "but I no longer want the Countess of S-H—not a subtle way of pointing the finger at me, I might add—being accused, in print, of holding you prisoner on your own estate with babies, babble and beauty!" She pouted and squeezed his hand. "Babies and beauty, mayhap, but *never* babble."

The Earl grinned and then became serious.

"You would readily return to London and the life of a politician's wife?"

"I would readily take the children and follow you to the ends of South America if it meant an unbroken night's sleep!"

At that, Salt gave a shout of laughter and hopped off the bed. He kissed her forehead and then made her an elegant bow.

"So be it, my love. Shall we tell the family the good news? Though, I doubt Caroline will be pleased at our decision to permanently reopen the house in Grosvenor Square. She enjoys living there with only Lady Reanay and Kitty Aldershot for company—"

"—and her menagerie of assorted feathered and furry friends!"

The Earl grinned and shook his head. "I do believe she enjoys their company more than ours." He frowned on a thought. "Does she mean to continue wallowing in self-recrimination now her mourning is over?"

Jane held his gaze. "There is only one person who has power over that."

The Earl knew she was referring to Sir Antony Templestowe, but he did not want to discuss his disgraced cousin today. So he refrained from answering her and went to the door, saying brightly, fingers curled about the ornate door handle, "Before I allow the family to descend upon you, and only for the briefest of visits, because you and the baby need to rest and recover, has my lady thought of names for the newest addition to our family?"

"Yes, my lord. Samuel. Sam."

Salt grinned with boyish pleasure. "Sam? A son, Jane?"

"Yes. Another boy. Your lordship now has an heir and a second. Though we shall never talk of Sam in such terms because he is as dear to us as Ned."

"Naturally. You know I would have been pleased with whatever you cared to give me, Jane."

"I know that, dearest," she replied, though they both knew the birth of a second son was what was needed to secure the earldom's future. "I hope you will be just as pleased with your son's second and third names: Antony Hugh."

This stopped the Earl from opening the door to his children, who could hear him through the slim crack where the door met the jamb and were calling to him, despite a nursery maid's best efforts to have them hush. He turned a shoulder to the bed, jaw clenched.

"I wish to call our son Samuel Antony Hugh Sinclair," Jane said placidly. "And for Antony to be Sam's godfather."

"When you have had time to rest and recover and reconsider—"

"Magnus, I have had nine months—longer—to consider names for our son. Had matters gone differently before Ned's birth, Antony would be Ned's godfather, too. Enough time has passed that not one eyebrow will be raised by such a gesture."

"And Caroline?" he asked with the raise of his eyebrow, as if highlighting the foolhardiness of her request. "I doubt she will see the matter as you do, my lady."

Jane sighed and briefly closed her eyes. She was exhausted and all she wanted was to sleep with her newborn son at her breast, but only after she had her husband's assent to her request. To leave it another day would see her husband and Caroline fanning the flame to each other's hurt pride, as they continued to be overly sensitive about an incident that had occurred four years ago. More than enough time had passed for brother and sister to put the past behind them and be reconciled to their cousin, Sir Antony Templestowe.

"I cannot refuse you," he said, after a small heavy silence between them. "I will write and ask him but there is the possibility he will refuse the honor."

"He won't. And Caroline cannot refuse to be Sam's godmother... If you ask her nicely."

"Jane. Do not play matchmaker. You are destined for disappointment. What's done cannot now be undone. Caroline has been married and widowed. And from what I hear from others, Antony spends more time between the sheets pleasuring a plump Russian princess than he does on diplomatic business!"

"Does he? Well, he has his mentor to thank for such diplomatic dexterity."

"I was his mentor!"

Jane snuggled under the silken coverlet, unable to stifle a giggle. "And what a wonderful mentor you proved to be."

Salt's face grew hot.

"Jane! This is no laughing matter! I won't have a lothario for a brother-in-law."

Jane did not state the obvious. Her husband had a past littered with beautiful mistresses and yet he was the most faithful and loving of husbands. She believed Sir Antony to be cut from the same uxorious cloth. Nor did she mention that Caroline's short-lived marriage to the young fortune-hunter Stephen Aldershot had been a disaster from day one, and for reasons she was not about to discuss with her husband; there were matters brothers did not need to know about their sisters. So, she said placidly,

"Of course I would not wish a lothario on Caroline. Now, please, my love, open that door before Ned and Beth scratch the paneling to wood shavings."

The Earl did as requested. With a beaming smile and lots of fuss, he scooped up his son and daughter, who ran into his open embrace. A nod to those crowded into the sitting room to follow, and he carried his children to the four-poster bed. Soon the bedchamber was over-flowing with family and favored retainers. The newest member of the noble Sinclair family, wrapped snugly in his blanket, was put into his mother's waiting arms and bravely slept through all the fuss.

With the apologetic physician satisfied with the health and well-being of both mother and baby, the Earl gave the order for the ringing of the church bells in the family chapel, the parish church, and in every church as far out into the county as his lands extended. The tolling of church bells was a public proclamation that the Countess had provided the earldom with a son—another heir. Jane drifted off to sleep to these pealing bells—the Honorable Samuel Antony Hugh Sinclair nestled at her breast—thoughts not on her newborn son, or her family or even her husband, but on a polite handsome gentleman a thousand miles away.

Had her noble husband been privy to her thoughts, he would have been alarmed and envious to discover the Countess was wondering how she could have Sir Antony Templestowe returned to England. She believed with all her heart that the love Sir Antony had for Caroline was enduring. The fire may appear to have died, but prod the log, feed the flame, and that love, she was utterly convinced, could be rekindled anew to burn as brightly as it had in the past. The love the Earl had for her was proof of that. She intended to prove the same was true for the two people, beyond her husband and three children, she loved most in the world.

THREE

LONDON, ENGLAND

SIR ANTONY TEMPLESTOWE WOULD HAVE BEEN GREATLY encouraged had he been privy to the Countess of Salt Hendon's thoughts. As he was not, he alighted from a dust-covered traveling coach laden with his personal luggage, weary, travel-worn and none the wiser that at least one family member had forgiven him for past indiscretions. He had not realized how much he missed his home city until now, standing on the pavement of South Audley Street looking down the row of Palladian terrace houses to the palace-sized mansions of Grosvenor Square. He stood as a statue for a moment, an ear to the discordant familiar sounds of the largest city in Europe: Horses' hooves clip-clopping; carriages lumbering over compacted earth; the lilting cadence of barrow sellers shouting out their wares, and loud enough to be heard over the constant din; the endless cacophony of building noise, hammering and banging and the general racket of industry.

He smiled, invigorated by it all, and finally went up the two shallow steps to the front door of his elegant double-fronted townhouse.

The townhouse, once occupied by his sister Diana, Lady St. John, had reverted to his possession upon her incarceration, whereupon he ordered the rooms stripped of every vestige of her existence. While he was in Russia, the rooms were freshly painted, wallpapered and furnished to suit his tastes. He was most looking forward to the Etruscan Saloon. Before his departure for St. Petersburg, he had had only time to consult with the architect and choose colors. From letters he was told the room was now furnished with deep-cushioned gilded sofas and spindle-legged tables, the sash windows draped with velvet curtains in hues of terracotta and chocolate brown to match the classical wallpaper of vases and ancient draped figures. It was the ideal space for his silver samovar and assorted teapots and Imperial tea service.

In his dressing room, there was a niche between the full-length window and the door into his closet, and this is where he would position the enormous Imperial copper bathtub with its canopy of diaphanous curtains to keep in the warmth while he soaked. Brought from Russia with great care and expense, it was a parting gift from his mentor, Prince Mikhail. He wondered if Semper had managed to have it positioned yet, and could think of nothing he wanted to do more than soak in scented water with a nice hot cup of caravan tea, perusing the latest edition of *The Gentleman's Magazine*.

He noticed the silver knocker was fixed to the black lacquered front door, signal he was at home to visitors, and reasoned Semper must have reinstated it knowing he was due to arrive any day. His majordomo, contingent of Russian servants, and personal effects he had sent on ahead by sail from Esjberg, while he traveled by carriage from Lubeck to The Hague to deliver diplomatic correspondence too sensitive to be trusted to a courier. More importantly, it allowed him to recover from the sea sickness suffered on the sea voyage from Helsinki to Lubeck. Stepping on to English soil after the final sea crossing, he was green but utterly relieved to be on *terra firma*.

The door opened and there was Boyle, his rake-thin butler, and behind him a footman who was quick to help him shrug out of his fitted greatcoat and divest him of ornate sword and tan leather kid gloves.

"So good to have you home at last, Sir Antony," Boyle said with a welcoming smile and short bow. "Mrs. Boyle and I have waited this day for a very long time." With a wave of a hand, he sent three hovering footmen out into the street to help offload the assortment of portmanteaux and parcels. "And may I say how well you're looking."

"You may, Boyle. Thank you. I trust Mr. Semper and my Russians have not disrupted your household routine to any great degree?"

"Not at all, sir," the butler replied, following Sir Antony into the black and white marble entrance foyer with its elegant Adam staircase.

"Mr. Semper found them all places to perch?"

When his lordship raised an eyebrow and waited, the old retainer said with a knowing smile, "There's no need for your lordship to concern yourself about the household staff. Mr. Semper has proved himself an excellent majordomo, and Mrs. Boyle couldn't be happier with the young Mrs. Semper. They are trying their best with a lingua franca, and Mrs. Boyle can't praise enough a more diligent seamstress and embroiderer as Mrs. Semper. Five of the Russians are quartered in the annex and been given odd jobs, and those who speak Frenchie have been put into footman's livery as requested. A more polite lot of foreigners I've yet to meet."

"Good."

At least his household was organized, which left him free of distraction to pursue the matter of getting his personal life in order. The thought of facing his cousin the Earl with the news his mad sister had broken free of her bonds and was lurking somewhere near—he did not doubt that for a moment—brought him out in a cold sweat.

Possibly, the Earl already knew. A month had come and gone since the apothecary's letter and no news of any kind from Salt. Admittedly, he had been traveling and not told his family of his intention to return, so letters could have crossed. But he did not think so. His sister was mad, that was indisputable, but she was also exceedingly intelligent and mind-bogglingly cunning and would wait for the most opportune moment to be *reunited* with the Earl, at a time and place that best suited her evil intent. As to how he was to find her and confine her before she could inflict harm to those he loved most in the world, he still had no clearer idea than he did before he set off from St. Petersburg. One thing he was very clear on. Once she was recaptured, he intended to have her transported to the furthest reaches of the Russian empire.

Diana running free was enough to dampen his enthusiasm for returning to the city of his birth, but there were also his strained relations with Lady Caroline Aldershot. If he had the choice between hacking off a limb or seeing her happily married to another, he'd choose the former any day! What was he to say to her? How could he congratulate her husband when he wanted to wring the life out of him? What was he to do…?

The butler repeating his question, a little louder than before, brought Sir Antony out of his reverie and he let go of the mahogany balustrade, suddenly aware he was gripping the polished wood.

"Would you care to change out of your travel clothes before joining the small party in the Saloon?"

Sir Antony stayed his jockey boot on the first step of the elegant staircase. His gaze traveled up the curved wall covered in gilt-framed ancestors and fixed on the first landing. "Small party…?"

"Yes, sir. Afternoon tea is being served in the Saloon before the party heads off to Vauxhall Gardens. I believe there is a recital this evening…"

Sir Antony looked over a shoulder. "Guests?"

"Lady Porter, Lady Dalrymple and a Mrs. Smith. Although, as Lady Dalrymple has come to stay and as Mrs. Smith is her ladyship's companion, there would in truth be only one guest: Lady Porter."

Sir Antony turned away from the staircase and faced his butler.

"I beg your pardon, Boyle. My brain is rather tired. All that traveling, you understand. You will need to enlighten me further."

"Her ladyship has taken to having a regular gathering on Thursdays. This being the third Thursday in a row, I would call it regular."

"And Lady Dalrymple has come to stay? *Here?*"

"Yes, sir. At her ladyship's invitation."

"And this other personage, this Mrs.—*Smith*, she also now resides under my roof?"

"As companion to her ladyship, Mrs. Smith is installed in the small apartment adjoining her ladyship's rooms, while Lady Dalrymple, after consultation with Mr. Semper, was given the second-best bedchamber, the one with the partial view of the garden that has a small adjoining sitting room, and is across the passageway from her ladyship. Lady Dalrymple's maid is being accommodated with the chambermaids and not wanting for anything. None of these arrangements, I assure you," the butler stressed, observing the blank look to his master's handsome features, "will affect your lordship's comfort in anyway. The ladies are ensconced on the south side of the staircase, while your lordship retains complete dominion of the north wing. On that, her ladyship, Mr. Semper, Mrs. Boyle *and* myself were in complete accord."

If Sir Antony was weary and wanting a bath when he alighted from his carriage, he was now in need of a nap to clear his mind, newly clouded with such assiduous household arrangements. One matter remained in complete fog. He realized later that there could be only one response to his question. Yet, at the time, the possibility remained so far removed from his consciousness that he never gave it a moment's consideration, despite it being the reason for his return to London. His complete and utter shock and failure to grasp what was staring him in the face exacerbated his reaction tenfold.

"Her ladyship…?"

The butler smiled in sympathy with his master's tiredness, for who else could her ladyship be if not his nearest and dearest? As if in response to his question, the door to the Etruscan Saloon opened and the noise of conversation and female laughter spilled onto the landing. Her ladyship, a clutch of talkative females at her back, peered over the balustrade, ivory lace fan gently waving across her low décolletage. Seeing who it was in the entrance foyer below, she let out a gasp of surprise and turned to the others to announce the master of the house was finally home safe. She came sailing down the stairs in a billow of brocaded yellow silk taffeta petticoats and matching mules that clack-clacked on the steps. Her arms, three tiers of delicate white lace cascading from the elbows of tight three-quarter length sleeves, were outstretched in welcome.

The butler grinned at such an effusive reconciliation and said with a sense of the grand occasion and sweep of an arm,

"Sir Antony, the Lady St. John."

Earlier, when outside his townhouse listening to the sounds of the city while admiring the view, and blissfully unaware of what awaited him indoors, Sir Antony was equally oblivious to the yellow-painted landau with its three female passengers that drew along-side the pavement. Had the female occupant on the house side of the landau extended her pretty silk parasol, she could have tapped Sir Antony on the shoulder. She did not. Her first reaction was to quickly avert her face lest he recognize her. But as he was in profile, gaze fixed on some distant point, there was little likelihood of him turning in any direction but the front door of his residence. He certainly would not want to front the congestion of a line of carriages that had come to a standstill because of a hold-up in the flow of traffic further down the street.

With this in mind, the female slowly turned to boldly stare at him. As she was wearing a very pretty straw Bergere with a wide brim and a string of blooms encircling its shallow crown, she had to move not only her head but also her shoulders, and tilt her chin up, so the brim did not obscure her view. Such was her shock at seeing Sir Antony returned from Russia, she was blind to the quizzical look of her sister-in-law sitting opposite, who stared openly from Lady Caroline to Sir Antony and back again. She was also deaf to her elderly aunt's monologue on the accident that had brought all traffic traveling north and south to a stop. Preoccupation with Sir Antony's profile also made Lady Caroline unaware her eccentric aunt had taken advantage of the stationary landau, and with the help of Kitty Aldershot, and the aid of her

Malacca cane, was up on her heels to have a clearer view of unfolding events.

"Oh dear! Oh dear! A sedan has overturned. The idiotic chairmen tried to outrun a wagon and mistimed their run. Dolts! The poor driver did his best to halt his beasts, but part of the load shifted in the attempt to avert a crisis. Now the tarpaulin is flapping about and disturbed whatever is in those crates… Fowl. Yes, fowl. And by the great to-do, I'd say geese. Who knows how many have been crushed and now roused by fear they'll flap each other to death! I wonder who the poor thing is in the sedan…? A female. Yes, a female. Her hat has come through the window with her hairpiece still attached and landed in the muck. Dear me! Those plumes will never look the same again. Foolish of her to have the glass down on such a dusty, hot day. Must've had her head out the window, barking orders, and got it snagged."

"Is it anyone we know, my lady?" Kitty Aldershot asked politely, only half-listening and briefly looking over her right shoulder. She quickly returned her gaze to her sister-in-law, wondering at the identity of the handsome gentleman who had all Lady Caroline's attention. "Perhaps Caroline will know who it is in the sedan chair? Her eyesight is vastly better than ours. My eyes are ruined through stitchery, which I know is Caroline's least favorite occupation. Caroline? Will you peek to allow us to know the identity of the unfortunate in the sedan chair? Caroline…?"

Her sister-in-law's unresponsiveness surprised Kitty. She might not listen to Lady Reanay's monologues, which were frequent and often delivered in lengths of a paragraph or two, but she could always rely on Caroline to be politely attentive to the elderly lady's speeches. This allowed Kitty to spend her time over her embroidery daydreaming. She had just been daydreaming about the need to visit Jackson's Habit Warehouse for the perfect costume for the Salt Masquerade Ball. But Lady Caroline's interest in the handsome stranger with the resolute chin and strong straight nose had Kitty sitting tall on the landau's velvet cushion, Lady Reanay and her observations of the traffic accident of no interest whatsoever.

Lady Caroline was doing the thing she was always telling Kitty never to do in public: Ogle.

But how could Lady Caroline help ogling a man who, in Kitty's opinion, was as close to male perfection as she had ever seen, dressed in his fitted traveling cloak and shiny jockey boots. Had she not been seated, she was very sure she would have swooned, just to give the handsome stranger the opportunity to catch her in his strong arms before her head hit the pavement. The prospect of being in the stranger's arms was so thrilling that it forced an involuntary giggle, and Kitty was quick to clap a gloved hand to her mouth to stop any further embarrassing outbursts.

Lady Caroline's preoccupation was such that she was deaf to Kitty's giggle. She had suffered a shock. Sir Antony Templestowe was the last person she expected to see in London. He was supposed to be fixed in St. Petersburg for a good many years yet, and as her brother had not told her otherwise, St. Petersburg was where he should still be. Not here in London—not outside his townhouse.

He was as tall as she remembered, his shoulders just as wide, but his stance, with back straight and chin up, was self-assured and proclaimed he was aware of his physicality. He gazed out on the world as if he knew his place in it, and others should know it too. This was in such marked contrast to the last time she had been in his company, when he had staggered about drunk at a musical recital and made a complete fool of himself, that she was forced to blink to make certain it was indeed him.

She did not hear the snap as her gloved thumb pressed too hard against the delicate ivory sticks of her gouache painted fan. Nor did she hear Kitty Aldershot's gasp as the fan fell limp in two parts. When Kitty touched her wrist to have her attention, Caroline turned and looked without seeing, thoughts still very much with the man on the pavement.

"Who is he, Caroline?" Kitty asked, a quick sidelong glance at Sir Antony just as he turned a shoulder on the street and went up the two shallow steps to the open front door.

Caroline felt the pressure on her wrist before she heard Kitty's question and instantly she felt her face grow hot.

"Who? Oh, he—It is not important," she muttered, coming out of her abstraction. She gave a start at the broken fan in her gloved hand and quickly shoved the pieces in her velvet reticule, glad to dip her head and thus her hat to hide her flushed cheeks from Kitty's inquisitive gaze.

"But you do know who he is, don't you?" Kitty persisted, watching three liveried footmen come out of the townhouse to offload a mountain of baggage from the carriage.

"Yes. Yes, I know," Caroline stated and turned to Lady Reanay, signaling discussion was at an end. She was surprised to see the elderly lady on her feet. "Aunt? Is there a possibility the obstruction to the traffic has cleared by now? Would you like me to help you sit? Your legs…"

Kitty's eyes narrowed. She may be just out of the schoolroom, but she knew the handsome stranger had greatly affected her sister-in-law. It heightened her curiosity and she said with that streak of inquisitiveness universal to females interested in a particular male, "Such a fine-looking gentleman arriving at this direction with so much luggage must have an equally fine name, mustn't he, Caroline?"

"The door won't open. One of the chairmen has fallen on his rump trying to tug it free. It's stuck tight," Lady Reanay announced evenly, still up on her heels, leaning on her cane with gaze on proceedings up ahead.

Yet, she had heard the exchange between her niece and Kitty Aldershot. She had also seen who had captured Caroline's attention and was not surprised the girl was flustered. She continued with her monologue about the traffic accident, to allow her niece time to regain her composure and to fill the awkward void of pleasant conversation in the landau.

"Perhaps, with her hairpiece missing, our lady of the sedan should sit tight and wait to be taken up again. I wouldn't come out in full view of the world with half my hair in the muck, all London looking on. A very handsome dark-haired young man, whose frock coat would match one of Salt's creations on theater night, has gone over to the sedan's window. He reminds me of Roxton's son, whom I met in Constantinople when his parents were—" She stopped abruptly and used the sticks of her fan to tap the knee of the liveried footman sitting at her back. "Barnes? Barnes! Be of assistance or we shall get nowhere fast and Lady Caroline and Miss Aldershot will fry like eggs in this noonday sun. At least try and rouse some of those fellows over there to set those crates upright before there are enough feathers flying about to stuff a pillow."

With a sigh of annoyance, she resettled herself on the cushioned seat and fluffed out her silk petticoats, Kitty Aldershot quick to offer assistance by pushing the padded footstool within range of her ladyship's walking shoes.

"Thank you, my dear. Oh, and, Barnes? Barnes. Don't *you* deal with the crates. You attend to the poor creature trapped in the sedan. It may be someone we know… Now, my dears," she continued brightly, looking from the wide-eyed Miss Aldershot to the flushed cheeks of Lady Caroline, "as soon as we are within doors you will apply wrapped ice to those heated complexions. Girls with such gloriously pearly skin should not be out-of-doors in the middle of the day. That is my fault. I would insist upon fresh air and a walk before nuncheon. We could very easily have had our usual promenade about the house, room to room, and received the same amount of exercise as we had walking the length and breadth of Hyde Park. But fresh air is best."

"Yes, my lady. And I do so enjoy promenading," Kitty agreed with a smile, and followed the old lady's gaze to Caroline, who was staring down at the velvet reticule in her silken lap, adding for her benefit, "Soon the Salt Hendons will be in town, and mayhap Lady Salt will permit us to take Miss Merry walking? In the morning, of course, because she is even younger than me! I have not seen her since my visit to Salt Hendon before Easter, and she is *such* an agreeable child. It would be a pity to keep her confined to the house, would it not, Caroline?"

"Yes, it would," Caroline agreed. "But we cannot go against Salt's edicts. The children—and that includes Ron and Merry—are not permitted beyond the walled garden. If the weather is inclement, there is always the royal tennis court to run about in. Salt will not have them exposed to the staring masses of a public park. He does not consider it *safe*."

Kitty knew this but she argued the point anyway.

"Walking Hyde Park is so agreeable and such a harmless diversion, surely with Miss Merry almost thirteen years of age there can be little harm in her accompanying us, particularly with Lady Reanay to watch over her?"

"It is not for us to question Salt," Caroline replied, though privately she agreed with Kitty. As a much older brother, Salt had been very protective of her. Indeed, she hardly ever came to London in her girl-hood. With his own children and the twins he was morbidly so. It was as if he feared to let them out of his sight, even for a moment, lest one or all of them be snatched from him. "He knows what is best for his own children, Kitty."

"Of-of course, Caroline, his-his lordship knows-knows what is best," Kitty stammered in apology. The Earl of Salt Hendon never ceased to make her nervous, despite his countess having a sweet nature and making her welcome.

Instantly repentant for her harsh tone, Caroline stretched out a gloved hand to her sister-in-law and said kindly, though she did not believe it for a moment, "Perhaps we can persuade him this spring..."

"Salt may change his mind if Antony were to accompany us. Merry is his niece, too," Lady Reanay added conversationally, not a look at

Caroline, whose jaw dropped at mention of Sir Antony, and addressed herself exclusively to Kitty. "Sir Antony Templestowe is my other nephew. His father, Lord Salt's mother and I were all siblings and Templestowes; not that *that* is of the slightest interest to you! What will be of interest, my dear, is the gentleman on the pavement you spied just now is that very Sir Antony—my nephew. Yes. He lives in that house," she added when Kitty turned to stare wide-eyed at the activity of servants going up and down the shallow steps of the South Audley street townhouse. "Such a handsome man and quite the athlete, so I am not surprised he caught your attention.

"One of the highlights of my visit to 'Petersburg to visit Antony was the privilege of watching a match on the newly-completed Imperial tennis court," she continued, ignoring Caroline who had sat up straight. "Antony and his playing partner, Prince Ivan-Something-or-Other... Do you know *everyone* at the Russian court is a Prince Something-or-Other so one just simply calls them *all* prince. Antony and Prince Ivan completely vanquished their opposition. It was only my second tournament of real tennis. I was present at a match at Fontainebleau. Fascinating. I never realized how compelling a sport it was until the Russian tournament, or how attractive men are in sweaty clothes—"

"Aunt Alice! You can't—you can't make such remarks about Antony in front of Kitty!"

"But I just have, my dear," Lady Reanay responded placidly with practiced vagueness. "It wasn't Antony I was referring to in the sweaty clothes, but now that you mention it, he, too, is swoon-worthy in a damp shirt and breeches."

She gave a little laugh, half giggle, as she unfurled her fan to stir the still city air across her painted face. The twinkle in her eyes she directed at Kitty, who was all wide-eyed attention now the handsome stranger had a name.

"You think because I am a gray-haired grandmother I no longer appreciate the male form, or feel any lust for the opposite gender? I'm *old*, not *cold*, child. Huzzah! Finally we are moving! And here is Barnes returned from playing the knight-errant," she proclaimed as the liveried footman hopped back up on the foot rail at her ladyship's back. "A moment longer and I was about to send poor Barnes to knock on Sir Antony's door for iced water. It is as well, though, that we leave the boy alone so soon upon his return. He does not need to see more of his relatives, not when his sister has made the decision to reside with *him*."

Lady Reanay could see by Kitty's wide-eyed look that the girl had no idea who she was talking about, so she said with a sigh and a smile,

"Sir Antony's sister Diana, who has come to stay with him, is not only my niece, she is also my daughter-in-law, as she was married to my dear son Aubrey St. John. As a consequence, she is the mother of my grandchildren Merry and Ron. More I could say on Diana, and an opinion of my daughter-in-law I certainly have, but it is not for me to comment beyond saying her residing with Antony is a grand presumption. The rest I will keep it to myself. Although—"

Kitty certainly had a clearer idea of whom Lady Reanay was talking about, but as her interest was in the nephew, and not the niece, and as the old lady never showed offence at having her conversation cut short in order for others to be able to speak, Kitty felt within her rights to ask abruptly,

"Will I—will *we* have the opportunity to become better acquainted with Sir Antony, my lady?" She could scarcely conceal her excitement, adding because she had just made an interesting connection, one she was sure would help her quest to accompany Lady Reanay on a visit to her nephew. "I would very much like to hear his tales of his time in Russia. I am aware of the precise location of 'Petersburg on the Globe because Miss Merry asked me to show her, and where Moscow is situated, too, because a mail service runs between the two Russian cities. And I helped Miss Merry calculate the distance her letters travel to reach her Uncle Antony. And we prepared scissor outlines for his birthday favor." Kitty looked at Caroline for confirmation, "Sir Antony is Miss Merry's Uncle Tony? And his birthday is in March?"

Caroline nodded, frowning. "Merry asked *your* help to construct a favor for Sir Antony's birthday?"

"Yes. She also shared with me one of his letters, in which he promised to send her a doll dressed in the latest fashions." Kitty suddenly had a frowning thought. "I do hope Miss Merry's birthday card arrived before Sir Antony departed 'Petersburg…"

Lady Caroline turned to her aunt, the increase in traffic noise as the horses picked up pace and drove past the squawking of distressed geese in crates stacked by the side of the road, forcing her to shout in her aunt's ear.

"Why wasn't I informed Diana had returned from her Continental wanderings?"

Lady Reanay pulled her niece close.

"Salt did not say a word to me, either. Lady Porter told me the news."

"Diana wouldn't dare return without Salt's blessing. Nor would Antony!"

Lady Reanay shrugged.

"Then Salt must have forgiven them both, because brother and sister are indeed returned to town." She smiled over at Kitty, who was as wide-eyed as ever to adult conversation, and said without raising her voice because the landau had come to a halt at the entrance to Grosvenor Square, "We can discover the answers to all our questions tomorrow. Lady St. John has invited us to afternoon tea. I, for one, cannot wait to be reacquainted with my dearest nephew, and you, dear Kitty, will have your opportunity of receiving Sir Antony's grateful thanks for helping Merry with her letters." She glanced at Caroline, the words on the tip of her tongue; *And you, my dear girl, if you know what is in your best interests, will swallow your pride, come to your senses and marry the man you love!*

But she did not say so. She sat back in silence, a satisfied smile hovering about her painted mouth. Caroline did not see the smile. She was wondering why Salt had failed to tell her that Diana, and more particularly Antony, was returned to London. As for Kitty, she had lost interest in everything but the picture in her mind's eye of the petticoats, bodice and shoes she intended to wear to afternoon tea to catch the eye of Sir Antony Templestowe.

FOUR

Inside the South Audley Street townhouse, Sir Antony stood transfixed, as if cemented to the base of the staircase, not even a facial muscle dared twitch as his sister swept down the staircase in greeting.

He had a second of joy. Her beauty had not diminished with time and she was just as radiant as ever. Her cosmetics had been carefully applied and her auburn hair dressed in the latest fashion, swept up off her neck, two fat auburn ringlets threaded with pearls and a pale ribbon caressing her bare neck. His instinct was to draw her close, to hug her to him, to feel the warmth of a sisterly embrace. It was a hollow expectation, and a foolish one. Not only had Diana never embraced him, but for all her outward beauty and appearance of goodness, she was as cold as the marble under his feet.

In his wildest imaginings he would never have supposed this outcome: That after escaping her castle incarceration she would dare to hide in plain sight. Yet, here she was, with her coterie of female friends, firmly fixed in his townhouse, her social calendar under full sail, and looking as sane as the next person.

What genius!

What supreme audacity!

What *ego*.

How was he to answer to it? What was he to say and do?

He was in the middle of a nightmare not of his making.

He knew that just below the surface of her beautiful façade there lurked a monster capable of great cunning—and great evil. Yet these women and the wider world, indeed most of her family, were ignorant of just whom they were dealing with. To limit family scandal and protect the innocent, the handful of people who did know the real Diana, and of what horrors she was capable, had taken a vow of silence. They also agreed on the fiction Salt concocted to explain Lady St. John's sudden disappearance from Polite Society and estrangement from her children. Her health had broken under the strain of Salt's marriage and she was sent to the Continent to recover. When she would return, no one knew and out of deference to the then newly-married Earl and Countess of Salt Hendon and their family, no one asked.

It was as if Diana St. John had vanished from the face of the earth…

Now, here she was! Such a healthy and lively Diana, Lady St. John, and such an implacable force that Sir Antony went cold and felt faint. His former self, the one who had found solace and oblivion in a bottle of good claret—the habitual drunkard—would have bowed to his sister's *force majeure*. The habitual drunkard could easily convince himself that such a vastly superior intellect, with all the cunning of a Machiavelli and the doggedness of a beagle with his snout in a rabbit hole, was beyond his derisory capabilities. Constant inebriation permitted him to absolve himself from care and responsibility. Others, meaning his cousin the Earl, more capable and determined than he, could better deal with the problem of his sister. This former self, this habitual drunkard, was a self-centered coward.

No more.

He had returned to London no longer a drunkard, determined to face up to his responsibilities. And his immediate responsibility was his sister Diana—discovering her evil intent and seeing her locked up more securely than before. To that end, he would play her at her own game. And so he did the most natural thing in the world, praying he was capable of matching her for deceit, and that her ego would blind her to his stratagem.

He greeted her as she did him, with a smile of warm welcome, bowing over her outstretched hand before drawing her close to lightly brush her rouged cheek with a kiss, careful not to crush the layers of her soft yellow taffeta petticoats. He caught the scent of her distinctive Floris perfume, and it brought with it a flood of unpleasant memories. Clamping his jaw shut and fixing his smile, he allowed her to return the kiss.

"Did I not tell you Antony was but a week or two behind me?"

Diana announced triumphantly, hooking her arm over his velvet sleeve, keeping him at her side. She looked up the stairs at the knot of females four steps above her. "Was it not you, dear Lady Dalrymple, who predicted my brother's return would be today?"

"Did I? Huzzah! Lady Porter, you owe me a guinea!" Lady Dalrymple exclaimed, tapping Lady Porter on the upper arm with the closed sticks of her fan before sweeping down the stairs to drop a curtsy before Sir Antony. "Then I am doubly pleased to see you home this day, Sir Antony!"

"Lady Dalrymple, you know; Lady Porter, too. And this is Mrs. Smith, who is my most stalwart companion," Diana St. John remarked, introducing the three women. She glanced at Sir Antony before saying to the tallest female in the group, "This, Mrs. Smith, is my dear brother, whom you have heard me speak so much about."

Mrs. Smith curtsied again and rose to fix her gaze upon Sir Antony. Unlike Lady Dalrymple and Lady Porter, she was not smiling, and there was nothing playful in her air. She disconcerted Sir Antony by staring him between the eyes. She was surprisingly tall for a female, and there was width in her shoulders and neck that he had only ever seen on the strongest of female farm workers. Instinctively, his gaze flickered to her wrists, but as she was wearing blue knitted mittens that covered the backs of her folded hands, he had no idea if she had the fingers of a farm laborer to match. He wondered where his sister had come by such a minder, for that was what she was, he had no doubt, and when she spoke, his acute linguistic ear was alerted to the soft burr of an unfamiliar county dialect.

"The pleasure to finally make your acquaintance, Sir Antony, is mine," Mrs. Smith said levelly, gaze never wavering. "Lady St. John has told me so much about you; I feel I know you. What her ladyship failed to tell me is how alike you are in form, if you'll pardon my forwardness."

"Alike? Are we?" Diana St. John showed surprise, a quick look up at her mute brother, before giving a tight smile. "Yes! I suppose we must, being brother and sister, although..." Again she looked at Sir Antony, but this time she let go of his arm and stepped back to stand by the three women to appraise him from forehead to foot. "There is something about you, dearest brother, that has changed since you left for 'Petersburg. Do you not agree, Lady Dalrymple? Lady Porter?"

"Most assuredly, my lady," Lady Dalrymple breathed, regarding Sir Antony over the top of her pleated fan.

"He's lost his fat," Lady Porter announced flatly. "It suits you. You'll have a dozen woolly-headed wenches clinging to both arms at your first soirée. What did it? The Russian winters? The Russian food? I hear they eat a lot of cabbage…"

"The Russian tea," Sir Antony murmured.

"Diana was just telling us all about their wretched winters," Lady Dalrymple added, eyes widening. "Shocking. Simply shocking. I have no idea how you both managed to keep yourselves warm. I dare say the bear skins helped."

"Of course they would help keep out the cold, Jenny, but bear skins hardly account for his loss of fat!" Lady Porter pointed out. "Besides, if that were the case, then dear Diana would not only have lost her fat but her looks. Gaunt men are still handsome; gaunt females are never beautiful. Scrawny chickens at best."

"Winters? Bear skins? Scrawny chickens?" Sir Antony forced himself to laugh and smile vacantly at his sister. He itched to hold aloft his quizzing glass but refrained from underscoring her lie. "What have you been telling dear Lady Porter and Lady Dalrymple, my dear?"

"All about 'Petersburg," Lady Dalrymple offered. "I can't wait to hear more about the Palace and the—"

"And so you shall, but not now," Diana St. John interrupted dismissively, signaling the butler, who was hovering dutifully in the background. "Boyle: Our cloaks. Is the carriage…?"

"Just pulled up at the door, my lady," the butler replied with a bow, and ushered forward two footmen holding various pieces of female outdoor attire, cloaks, muffs and shawls.

"Antony, you must be exhausted," Diana St. John continued, turning to her female companions as she slipped on yellow kid gloves before lightly placing a gloved hand on her brother's sleeve.

Sir Antony did not move a muscle.

"I'm sure he will be only too pleased to tell you all about 'Petersburg tomorrow. Won't you, Antony? Now we must be off to secure the best seats for Polly Young's performance. She has the most divine voice and is just seventeen years of age. Imagine!"

"Shall I see you all later this evening?" Sir Antony asked blandly. "Or at breakfast?"

"Not tonight; not me," Lady Porter volunteered. "But you will tomorrow, at the welcome-home afternoon tea."

"A welcome-home afternoon tea?" Sir Antony repeated, hoping his voice held the right note of joyful surprise. "How delightful! Will you be there, too, my lady? Mrs. Smith? Ah! I forget. Must be the exhaustion. Boyle tells me you are both *residing* under my roof…?"

"I cannot thank you enough for your generosity," Lady Dalrymple said as a footman placed a pink satin-lined velvet cloak about her shoulders. She looked up at Sir Antony with soulful brown eyes and said with a catch to her voice, "When Diana told me of your offer, I was so touched. I said to her at the time, did I not, Diana, how like you not to care a jot for the scandal of having a discarded wretch under your roof. And I repeat it here, now, before witnesses. If it were not for your kindness, and the kindness of Lady St. John—*such* a shoulder to cry on—I do believe I would have ended my days alone in a ditch!"

"Not a ditch, my dear," Diana St. John replied flatly and turned to the butler. "Boyle? I hope you sent word to Sir Antony's valet that his master is home, and that while we have been standing here, a bath is being drawn for his lordship?"

"Yes, my lady. And in the new Russian bathtub, too, my lady."

"A *Russian* bathtub?" Lady Dalrymple forgot her speech about her former lover's cruelty and her eyes widened with keen interest. "I don't believe I have ever seen a Russian bathtub. Are they any different from—"

"A bathtub is a bathtub, my dear. Now away you go with Mrs. Smith, who has been patiently waiting to take your arm," Lady Porter replied, a roll of her eyes at Sir Antony whose gaze had not left his sister. "Sad business," she told him quietly. "Dacre Wraxton. Philandering fiend. No better or worse than his kind, but Jenny Dalrymple made a fool of herself over the dratted man by being public about their affair. She hoped to force his hand to marriage. Of course, he immediately cast her off. We *all* told her what would happen. She did not listen. A man of his means and prospects isn't about to marry a widow toppled off the fence of thirty. He'll want something fresh and young. They all do." She smiled up at Sir Antony. "But how like *you* to care."

"Remind me, my lady. Is he brother or cousin of Hilary the poet?" Sir Antony asked casually, watching Mrs. Smith take Lady Dalrymple by the elbow and usher her across the wide foyer to the open front door, where the light town chaise could be seen waiting in the street. He had caught the swift glance that passed between his sister and her minder, which instantly set Mrs. Smith in motion. He decided the woman was dangerous and that she was aware, too, that her mistress was even more so.

"Elder brother. In expectation of inheriting his uncle's pile in the country and the title that goes with it," Lady Porter answered. "He's not on speaking terms with his milksop poet brother."

Sir Antony bowed her ladyship away and then met Diana's gaze, for she waited to take her leave of him. He kept his eyes focused on hers, expression suitably neutral, and waited for her to speak.

"You look tired, Antony. Traveling can be such a bore. I was certain you would make it back to London from 'Petersburg in record time. As it is, your effects and your foreign servants arrived before you. No wind to set sail?"

"I sent them on ahead while I delivered diplomatic correspondence to The Hague."

Diana St. John pouted. There was no sympathy in her voice. "Oh dear. The delay must have been *fretful* for you."

He smiled thinly. "Not at all." It was a lie, but only a very thin lie. Travel over land had been a relief. Arriving a week later than intended in London, *that* had made him fret. "It allowed me to forgo the wretched sea voyage from Denmark," he told her. "And to pick up a few gifts…"

"What a *dear* brother; *always* thinking of others," she remarked, a hand to the front of his velvet frock coat to feel the beat of his heart. What she felt was a small bump under the fabric. Surprise registered in the faint lift of her arched brows. "What have we here?" she purred, fingertips making out the shape of a brooch pinned out of sight to the front of his oyster silk waistcoat. Her gaze locked to her brother's blue eyes. "Your heart beats very strong and fast, Antony. I hope it is for the person whose miniature you have hidden here, rather than on my account?"

Sir Antony gently removed her hand and kept it in his, not a blink away from her gaze. With her yellow taffeta petticoats folded against his booted legs as she leaned in to speak softly, his nostrils filled with her pungent scent and he suddenly felt green again, but his expression did not change.

"If it does beat faster it is at the pleasure of seeing you looking so well after such an absence," he told her truthfully.

She cocked her head slightly, as if questioning his sincerity. Finally, she smiled and removed her hand from his to give him a perfunctory pat on the chest.

"Well, there's no reason for you to fret now. As you can see, I arrived safely in town and am in perfect health." She smiled up at him. "Don't wait up. After a good night's sleep, you will wake to find that our reconciliation is not a dream. I will still be here. I have no intention of ever leaving you. Your sister is here to stay. There is so much we have both missed—of London."

He waited by the stairwell watching through the open front door as a footman handed his sister up into the carriage with her female companions. With the carriage step folded away, the horses set to. The two footmen returned indoors and closed the front door. Hearing the latch shut fast woke Sir Antony from his trance, and before the butler could ask if his lordship required anything further of him, he fled up the curved staircase two steps at a time to his rooms.

He was inside and had crossed the sitting room before the sound of running water brought him up short. He strode through to the warmth of the dressing room, tugging at the complicated knot in his plain linen stock as he did so, and came to a halt just inside the curtained doorway. The big copper Russian bathtub with its linen inner skin was positioned precisely where he had instructed. It was full of hot steaming water; one of two bath stools was beside it and had upon its padded seat a tray of tea things and a folded newspaper. A fire roared in the grate. Two of his Russian servants waited silently by the window.

He wanted to shout with joy. He was so tired and so in need of a soothing bath, a cup of tea and nothing more mentally taxing than a perusal of *The Gentleman's Magazine*. Instead, he turned at footfall and said to Semper, who came into the room with a third Russian carrying bath sheets,

"Semper! Find me a thief-taker! And find me one *now*."

"You gave this thief-taker my instructions to the letter?"

Semper remained silent while he carefully pinned a pearl-headed gold stickpin into the soft folds of delicate lace at Sir Antony's throat. When he stepped back to view his handiwork, he nodded distractedly, then came forward again, not entirely happy, and fiddled with the folds of the cravat until Sir Antony had had enough preening and lightly slapped his hand away.

"I'm off downstairs to afternoon tea, not off to a coronation!" He addressed his majordomo's reflection. "This thief-taker understands precisely what is being asked of him?"

"Yes, my lord," Semper replied, returning to stand by the dressing table with a pair of black leather shoes. These he placed beside the padded swivel stool. "I went over your instructions to the letter with Mr.—"

"No! No names," Sir Antony interrupted, turning away from the looking glass. He slipped his large stockinged feet into the low-heeled shoes. "I don't want to know the fellow's name and I don't want him to know mine. This is one occasion where ignorance truly is for the best. If I don't know him and he doesn't know me then neither of us can be compromised."

"Yes, my lord. I've chosen the oval diamond buckles, if they meet with your approval?"

Sir Antony stared at the shoe buckles in the palm of Semper's hand and pondered. They did match the knee buckles, and were not as large as the diamond and sapphire buckles Misha and Katya had presented to him on his thirtieth birthday. *Look, Tosha! The stones match your eyes*, Katya had exclaimed playfully, the look in her own bright eyes he could only describe as one of loving friendship. He wondered if Caroline could ever look at him in that way again. But he wanted more than friendship, more than he could possibly hope for now she was married to another... He wiped a hand over his mouth, and came out of his abstraction, a nod to Semper, who silently threaded the latchets through the shoe buckles and fixed them firmly in place. When his majordomo was up off his knees, he said,

"Nor do I need to know what this thief-taker looks like. If I don't know him from Adam then I can't recognize him in a crowd. If I did, I'd be forever looking over my shoulder, and then the object of their shadowing is likely to discover the truth. We are dealing with a far superior intelligence to mine, Semper, remember that."

"Yes, my lord," the majordomo replied, though he was not entirely convinced. He knew Sir Antony had a remarkably keen mind. If Lady St. John possessed half his master's acuity, she was a formidable prospect indeed. "I did stress to Mr. T that he must keep his wits about him at all times."

"Good. And this Mr.—*T* is aware he is to be her ladyship's shadow every time she steps outside of this house?"

"Yes, my lord. Mr. T is very aware of that. He also knows to stay out of sight. And he has two of his associates helping him so that this house is under constant watch, as is her ladyship." Semper coughed into his fist, adding diffidently, "Begging your lordship's pardon, but Mr. T assured me that Lady St. John won't be able to use her *bourdaloue* without him knowing about it."

"Is that so? Then you have certainly hired the right man for the job. And he will report to you every other day?"

"Every other day, my lord," Semper repeated, holding wide a sky-blue silk frock coat. "Mr. T will see me in my office below stairs, where the personal maids do not trespass. Unless there is something untoward, and then he will send me word at once. I should also tell your lordship that I've taken the liberty of instructing the Russians that on no account is anyone in this household or out of it permitted entry to this wing without permission; that includes her ladyship."

Sir Antony allowed Semper to shrug him into the silk frock coat, and looked over a shoulder as the majordomo straightened the short skirts, saying quietly, "You understand I am having Lady St. John watched for her ladyship's own good, don't you, Semper?"

"Yes, my lord," the majordomo replied impassively and stepped back out of the way so his master could collect snuff box, etui and gold pocket watch from the orderly dressing table and drop them into a deep frock coat pocket. "Lady St. John appears well but her mind is unwell. You said she may do something to harm herself or others, and so we must be watchful at all times."

Sir Antony met his majordomo's gaze squarely.

"That's right, Semper. In much the same way as you watch out for me because I am—*unwell*. But we must keep a closer eye on Lady St. John because she is unaware she is unwell. I have come to terms with my addiction because I know the cause and how to deal with it. She does not and never will, because it is her mind that is broken and that cannot be repaired."

"Yes, my lord. I understand perfectly. Shall I tie on your quizzing glass?"

Sir Antony hesitated. He wondered if Semper did indeed understand. He had not confided the whole sordid story of his sister's murderous crimes and hideous misdemeanors, but his majordomo now knew more than anyone outside the small circle who did. One fact he was sure of: He trusted Ralph Semper with his life. He held out the gold quizzing glass with its black riband and allowed Semper to secure it about his neck and tuck the bow neatly around the inside collar of his frock coat.

"Is Mrs. Semper aware of the journey you must undertake and why?"

"She knew before we left 'Petersburg, my lord. I thought it only right to tell her—on the off chance I was only here for a short while before returning to Russia. I did not tell her why I had to return, only that I must, and that I would be back in London as soon as the job was done."

"I apologize for adding to your burden, Semper, but it cannot be helped. You need only escort my sister under guard of the five Russians as far as Lubeck, not 'Petersburg. I've arranged for an armed escort, with your Russian contingent, to take her from there to her final destination. The papers granting freedom for all those involved—all twenty serfs who volunteered for the mission—you are to give to Captain Vorlkonsy in Lubeck. He will see to it that once my sister is *settled* in her new lodgings, the men and their families are to have their freedom. You do not approve?" he added, catching his majordomo's frowning nod in the looking glass reflection.

"I approve of your plan, my lord; of course. I had thought I was to go as far as the final destination," Semper replied, disappointment evident in his tone. "To make absolutely certain the mission is carried out to your stipulations."

"Oh, don't misconstrue me!" Sir Antony replied with sincerity, turning to face Semper. "I have every confidence in your abilities, and I cannot tell you how grateful I am at your willingness to see this distasteful episode dealt with yourself. I just couldn't bear the thought of tearing you away from your bride for some considerable time. As a castle in the remoteness of Wales was unable to contain my sister, I have had to find a place that will, and for the rest of her natural life. So I am sending her to Beryozovo."

"Beryozovo…?"

"I'm not surprised you have not heard it spoken. It is not a place that comes up in conversation. Well, only in hushed tones. Even those who are sent there by Her Imperial Majesty read the name in the document of exile with disbelief, and so cannot bring themselves to speak it. Saying the name aloud makes their fate all that real, and finite. It is a *settlement* on the Ob River in Siberia."

The majordomo's face drained of color at mention of a region beyond the Ural mountains that was so far from civilized society of any sort, he had only ever heard it spoken once, and as his master said, in a whisper. He understood now why he was going only as far as the Prussian port. Traveling all the way to Beryozovo, even at this time of year, would be hazardous, arduous and more than a little dangerous; those who went there never returned, and not from want of trying.

"It's a settlement for those who are sentenced to *katorga*, my lord?"

"Penal servitude? Yes. And it is almost at the limits of the known world. I have heard it spoken of as an icy hell. People do freeze to death in the streets, if, indeed, they do have such amenities as streets. I have no idea…"

Sir Antony sighed heavily. It was not a fate he wished on anybody, yet knew there were few opportunities left to him where his sister's future was concerned, short of committing a heinous crime that would see him hang. He forced himself to rally, and said with a buoyancy he did not in the least feel,

"When this business is over with I will make it up to you—*both* of you," he told his majordomo. "You may take Mrs. Semper on the bridal trip you had to forgo to get me and my belongings back here with all speed."

"Thank you, my lord."

"At my expense, Semper. Wherever you wish."

"That is very generous of you, my lord."

"For a month."

"That is too generous."

"Rot! Any idea where you'll journey?"

"Dublin, my lord."

Sir Antony took up his quizzing glass and peered through the magnifying lens.

"Dublin? I didn't know you for an Irishman, Semper."

"I'm not, my lord. Nina—Mrs. Semper—her sister is married to a wool merchant. They have a small estate on the outskirts of Dublin, and two children."

Sir Antony let the quizzing glass drop on its black riband.

"Dear me, these Russians do get about!"

"Yes, sir. But it was Mr. Barry who went to Russia on business and met Sylvia—that's Mrs. Semper's sister." Semper followed Sir Antony across the dressing room and into his sitting room where two of the Russian servants in livery were standing either side of the double doors that lead out onto the passageway. "Barry paid for Mrs. Barry in wool bales. Said he would have paid twice what was asked for her."

Sir Antony paused, a frown between his brows. "She was a serf like her sister? Owned by the Yusupovs?"

It was Semper's turn to frown, and in surprise, that Sir Antony could think otherwise.

"Body and soul, my lord. Nina's family have been enslaved to the Yusupov princes for generations. She and her sister are the first in their family granted their freedom. For that alone my wife would let you send me to China, if the need arose. As for your Russian servants," he added, handing Sir Antony a lace-bordered handkerchief he had failed to slip into a deep pocket of his frock coat. "You can't be all that surprised twenty volunteered to go all the way to hell on earth; freedom is worth any price to the enslaved."

"Not surprised, Semper. I only wish they didn't need to travel to hell to get it!"

"Don't you concern yourself about that, my lord," Semper reassured him, a wave at the attendant footmen to open wide the double doors leading out onto the passageway. "There's plenty of serfs living in hell, and with no expectation of freedom or anything else from their masters. I don't mind telling you, my lord, that Nina and your Russians look upon you as their earthly savior. Candles are lighted every night and prayers said over them in your honor."

"Good Lord!"

Sir Antony shuddered his incredulity and left the room.

Two steps inside the crowded Etruscan Saloon and he caught the run of his sister's conversation as she mingled with the guests. It set the short hairs under his neat wig bristling. Had he heard correctly? Did she truly say: *When I was visiting Antony in 'Petersburg...?* He bowed to the perfumed and beribboned gathering as the butler announced his presence and was immediately sucked into the vortex of his sister's lies.

FIVE

"Here you are at last, Antony!" Diana St. John announced brightly, pulling him into a circle of bewigged gentlemen of which she was its center. "I was just explaining about the English Factory at 'Petersburg. Do you recall the gala evening? What a spectacle! I do believe I have not seen so many diamonds dripping from ears as I did that night." She turned to include several ladies hovering on the fringe of the small group and smiled at them. "And there was a dance—What was it called, Antony? Country *something*—"

"Bumpkin. Country *Bumpkin*."

"The very one! Country Bumpkin is danced by everyone. Antony and I danced the Country Bumpkin, and amongst all the merchants, which is the thing to do. There is no distinction amongst the English at such events, which vastly amuses the Russians," she continued, a hand pressed to her brother's close upturned cuff. In fact, she had hold of one of the three embroidered buttons, as if needing to anchor him to the spot. "Unlike the French and Austrian Courts, we don't have an embassy in Russia. Well, not in 'Petersburg, which is, for all intents and purposes, Russia, because that is where the Empress resides." She gave a little start, painted lace fan pressed to her low décolletage, as if to stress her next revelation. With wide eyes, gaze sweeping her rapt audience, she said, "I was never more surprised when I discovered that it is our merchants who are looked upon with more favor by the Russians, because of what they can supply to our foreign friends. Why, my poor brother here is treated as if he, too, were one of them. Imagine!

Tradesmen looked upon with as much favor as a first cousin of the Earl of Salt Hendon. Is that not so, Antony?"

"Yes," he replied evenly, because she had cunningly ended with a question to which he could reply without contradicting her.

There was a low rumble of shocked surprise at the very idea of the Russians showing favor to merchants of no particular family over persons of rank. Diana St. John was soon answering numerous questions that were directed at her brother, but which she was more than willing to answer in his stead. After all, as children, indeed well into adulthood, she was determined to outshine him, dominate him and show their father that she was by far the better choice of sibling to inherit the baronetcy, despite the insurmountable fact that as a female she could not inherit, no matter how superior her intelligence. At the time he had agreed with her, and was sympathetic she had not been born a man. Now, to his great sadness, he wished she had never been born at all.

As he listened to her erudite and very entertaining responses, shoulder slightly turned away, quizzing glass raised, searching out the one face he hoped to see above all others, Diana impressed and disturbed him in equal measure. The more questions she answered the more entrenched the idea became that she had indeed been to St. Petersburg. Her ability to recall details of places and persons entirely unknown to her was startling. That she was lying through her lovely teeth, and had drawn him into her web of deceit was appalling.

He had only himself to blame.

In St. Petersburg, sitting before the fire in his comfortable apartment with its view of the Neva River, he had written Diana beautifully detailed letters about St. Petersburg and his life there. He told her about its people, their customs, the places he visited and the happenings at court; he even told her about Misha and Katya, anything he thought would brighten her long, lonely days of captivity. And with these letters he sent gifts. She was displaying one now. A fan with intricately carved ivory sticks and leaf painted with a scene of the Neva in wintertime. He had not reckoned on her exceptional retentive memory. Then again, not in a month of Sundays had he ever expected she would escape her Welsh castle and he find himself standing beside her while she held court in his Etruscan saloon.

He calmed himself by staring out across the sea of faces. Even after a protracted absence from London's social scene, he could still put a name to many of the powdered faces within this crowded and noisy room. He had interacted with these people at a ball, recital, soirée or other function where Polite Society gathered in numbers. It was just that those standing about sipping champagne, eating strawberries dusted with sugar, and whispering the latest gossip behind their gossamer fans, were not his close friends but friends of his sister's set.

Why should he have expected her to invite his friends? Diana had always been of the opinion that her friends were the best sort of company and what few friends he had were of no importance, except for the Earl of Salt Hendon. He smiled to himself. What better way to proclaim her return to Society than with a select soirée for those dear friends who were sure to report the event and all that transpired by breakfast time.

She was well on her way to spinning her social web far and wide. The more she spun the more intricate her social web, she the big black spider at the center of it all. Try to sever a strand of her web, touch it even, and she was sure to come inching down it and strike. The wider her web was cast, the more difficult—dare he think stickier—the task of her removal from it.

Eliminate Diana from her web and all those ensnared by it would know instantly, and cause the sort of public scandal the Earl abhorred. He would not want Diana's crimes revealed to the world. While Salt's political career and reputation would never recover sufficiently to see him First Lord of the Treasury or any other post within government, the ramifications for the family would echo down the generations. When it suited the caprice of a public opponent or the family of a prospective suitor, old newssheets that carried the stories of Diana St. John's madness, her crimes and her incarceration, need only be aired as proof of the family insanity. It was no wonder Salt had had her bundled into a carriage and sent her off to Wales without thought or explanation to anyone. Yet, averting a public scandal four years ago by this method had now brought them to the precipice of another, and with Sir Antony none the wiser as to his sister's evil intent. Thus, Diana's removal from good society required not only the greatest of care, but timing was everything.

"You will be pleased to know our merchants residing in 'Petersburg give Antony and those of his station within the diplomatic corps the proper accord," Diana was saying to her rapt audience. "Which is only right and proper, even if the Russians do not feel the need to do so. Which, I can say here, but never dreamed of saying so before the Russians, shows a most shocking lack of manners." She looked to her brother, while signaling to a hovering footman holding a silver tray to step forward and offer champagne to those who did not have a glass.

"You were Envoy Extraordinary after Buckingham, were you not, Antony?"

"Envoy Extraordinary?" Lady Dalrymple echoed, turning her wide-eyed gaze on Sir Antony. "That sounds awfully important. Is it?"

Lady St. John watched her brother continue to sweep the room with his quizzing glass and knew who he was looking for, but did not offer to tell him Lady Caroline's whereabouts, saying brightly,

"It most certainly is, my dear Lady Dalrymple. An Envoy Extraordinary is one rank below ambassador and performs the duties of that post when an ambassador is not present. Lord Buckingham held the post of Ambassador to the court of 'Petersburg until '65, but of course, all the work, all the negotiation was left for poor Antony to shoulder. And now Antony has come home, we have no idea who will look after England's interests in that corner of the world."

"Mr. Hans Stanley has the post—" Sir Antony began and was interrupted by his sister.

"Stanley? But *he* has yet to leave English soil! Surely the Court of St. James's can do better than Hans Stanley?" She let her gaze sweep her audience and smiled sweetly. "Of course I don't need to tell you all that my little brother performed his duties with tact and aplomb." She let out a small sigh. "What a pity you were recalled home when you were just making inroads with the Russians…"

"Yes, a pity," he murmured, again unable to correct or contradict a word his sister spoke. He cursed the thoroughness and frequency of his letters.

When a tray of crystal champagne flutes was put under his nose, he waved aside the footman and dropped his quizzing glass on its silken black riband, looking about for his butler. What he wanted was a nice hot cup of tea, and he was certain the half a dozen turbaned dowagers in the room would prefer tea, too. Before he could ask the question, Diana thrust a champagne flute in his hand.

"I cannot perform a toast to our return if you do not have a glass of champagne. Besides, you have not sipped anything since you arrived. You must be parched."

"I am, for a cup of tea," he replied, a frown at the glass in his hand. He went to return it to the tray but Diana stayed his hand.

"I insist. Our guests insist." She leaned into him, and said, as if needing to remind him, "You, the most polite man I know, could never be bad-mannered and not raise your glass. You must, and join our friends in taking a sip or two at the very least."

He bit back a retort about sisterly interference and instantly reminded himself that the being inhabiting the beautiful outer shell of his sister was something else entirely, and he must not give himself away. Thankfully, into the tense moment stepped Lady Dalrymple, who held up her glass of champagne, and with a sweeping look at the assembled company, said with sincerity,

"I speak for everyone here when I say we are so very pleased our dear friend Lady St. John has returned from her Continental wanderings. We have greatly missed her company and the company of Sir Antony, and we hope they never need leave us again."

There was a general rumble of agreement and Sir Antony smiled and said no more.

Quiet was called for; a light tapping of gold quizzing glass rims against crystal set off a musical tinkle across the room. Conversations hushed then stopped. All powdered faces and coiffures turned to where Diana St. John stood beside her brother. No one thought it odd that Diana and not her brother should make a speech. As her friends, they knew she completely dominated him. She had led most of those in the crowd to believe her brother an ineffectual Merry Andrew of little consequence. Drunken episodes witnessed in Sir Antony's past did nothing to disabuse them of this belief.

Thus, when the tall, straight-backed Adonis with the piercing blue eyes had entered the room upon the butler's announcement, more than a few of the gentlemen and most of the ladies let their mouths drop to half-cock. The cold cruel Russian winters had certainly not done their friend's little brother any harm, and so a few of the guests murmured with approval to Diana St. John. One guest went so far as to congratulate her on recommending to the Earl of Salt Hendon that a post to St. Petersburg would do Sir Antony the world of good. Diana St. John inclined her auburn coiffure at the compliment and did nothing to dissuade her guests that this was indeed the truth of the matter.

Glasses raised, the toast was made, and champagne sipped then downed with relish.

Sir Antony followed the crowd and lifted the glass with a steady hand, but did not allow the rim to touch his mouth. His nostrils quivered when the enticing bitter sweetness of champagne bubbles tickled his nose. He breathed in and swallowed hard. He craved the taste of the golden fluid on his tongue and to feel its coldness slide down his throat and warm his blood. But he kept his mouth clamped before temptation overwhelmed good sense and he did the unthinkable.

There's no harm in one tiny sip. Drink and see for yourself you have the

willpower to resist the whole glass, coaxed the demon of temptation that sat on his shoulder.

No sooner had the demon posed the question than out of the corner of his eye he caught sight of one of his Russian servants. The man was standing tall and proud in his new livery, but startlingly incongruous was the growth of facial hair. Instantly, the demon of temptation vanished, replaced by a memory and words of encouragement from his good friend Prince Mikhail, who had noticed the signs of the habitual drunkard well before Sir Antony had admitted it to himself, for he, too, was one.

With a less-than-steady hand, he returned the untouched glass to a tray. He did not look at his sister, although he knew well enough that her gaze remained fixed on him the entire time he held the champagne flute. Instead, he pretended to make eye contact with someone at the opposite end of the room and hailed them with a raise of his quizzing glass.

It was an old trick, one he had employed often at dull embassy get-togethers or at the end of a long evening when he, Misha and Katya wished to slip away for a night of cards and easy conversation. With a heavy sigh of escape, he shouldered his way through the silken group as they devoured oysters, delicate fish tarts, and fruit of the season. He smiled at a middle-aged dowager here, saying a few words in reply to a *welcome home* from a familiar face from White's Club there, until he was at the open French windows that led out onto a balcony with a view of the orange trees in the courtyard garden below. Here, between the windows, perched on its inlaid cherrywood trolley was the welcoming sight of his ornate silver samovar.

Two footmen stood sentry either side of the trolley, while under the butler's watchful eye one of the Russian servants filled the samovar's drum with hot water. A second Russian carried a pail of hot coals necessary to fill the vertical pipe to keep the water at the correct temperature for tea drinking. A third Russian held to his chest a large polished rosewood box that had within it three ornate silver tea caddies. It was locked, and the key to it was dangling from Sir Antony's gold fob chain pinned to a waistcoat pocket, where also dangled a clutch of intricately carved intaglios.

Boyle sidled up to him, holding two teapots, and said confidentially at his shoulder,

"Unfortunately, Sir Antony, none of my fellows know what to do with that urn, and Mr. Semper says only the Russians are permitted to touch it. I should have had them organize the water and coal earlier, before the guests arrived, but her ladyship was unaware it would be needed."

"That's perfectly all right, Boyle," Sir Antony replied with a smile, handing him the key to the polished rosewood box. "Two scoops of the black tea from the middle caddy in the silver teapot, then just cover the tea leaves with hot water. The other teapot, fill three quarters with hot water. Set out the tea cups and I'll do the rest. I wonder if you might direct me to Lady Reanay; I was told she would be attending this afternoon…"

"Seated behind you, my lord. Lady Reanay, Lady Caroline Aldershot and a Miss Kitty Aldershot."

Sir Antony gave a little jump of surprise and instantly turned on a heel, feeling his face grow hot as he did so. He came face-to-face with three females perched on a chocolate-brown damask and gold leaf settee, straight-backed and silent. All three pairs of eyes locked to his tall frame, pretty gouache painted fans moving the breeze coming in off the balcony across their décolletages. It was the young woman with the blonde coiffure he glanced at first, as he straightened out of a bow of welcome.

He had heard much of Miss Kitty Aldershot from Tom Allenby's letters. She was pretty, but not to his taste, but he well understood Tom's infatuation. Next, he directed his gaze at his aunt at the other end of the settee because he couldn't yet bear to look at Caroline. He feared what he might find in her expression. His eyes might do as he ordered, but he could not stop his heart pounding hard in his chest. He was suddenly dizzy. Of course, he could be light-headed due to a lack of anything to eat or drink in many hours. Being romantically minded, he preferred to blame Caroline. His gaze disobeyed him and fixed on her as she rose with her companions, then curtsied at his bow of welcome.

He was not disappointed. Four years disappeared in an instant as her dark green eyes flickered up at him but did not hold his gaze. She was the same Caroline he had left behind. Same glorious sunset-red hair, same pert mouth that invited kissing. Her face had lost its plumpness, but the smattering of freckles to her cheeks and across her nose were just visible under the light dusting of powder, her only cosmetic.

Standing before him, she was a good half a head taller than his remembrance and it made him wonder if she had grown in his absence. He glanced at the polished parquetry floorboards and saw peeping out from under the hem of the light layers of silk petticoats the points of a pair of matching silk shoes. Well, there was something new! On his visits to Salt Hendon, she was always out and about the estate, riding, walking with her dogs, or taking care of her menagerie of animals, and thus was always in sturdy half-boots. The thought of her stockinged feet encased in a pair of very feminine shoes ripened the heat to his cheekbones, and he quickly took his thoughts elsewhere.

Why had he stupidly thought she would be unchanged? Naturally she would be wearing the latest fashion in footwear! It was London after all, and she was now a married woman. Why could she not look him in the eye? Where was her husband?

The last question brought him out of his reverie and landed him firmly in the reality of the here and now. He looked to his aunt, but before he could construct a coherent sentence of welcome, Lady Reanay was tugging his upturned cuff, brow furrowed with confusion.

"Antony? Why is Diana droning on about St. Petersburg when she has never been there a day in her life?"

SIX

"At least you're none the worse for your journey home.
But you must not lose any more weight, it's not good for a man of your
height and width," Lady Reanay continued, hardly drawing breath to
give Sir Antony a chance of reply to her first question, which was just
as well because he did not know what to tell her about Diana. "Perhaps
it is the trick of your tailor. That blue suits, not quite the color of your
eyes, but near enough. Why is Diana talking about St. Petersburg? You
never mentioned she had paid you a visit. I was with you a good six
months and departed just before the Russian winter set in. For her to
have traveled—Oh dear! There I go rattling on like a runaway carriage!
Caroline will scold me. Give your dearest aunt a kiss," she said, her
four feet eleven inches on tiptoe, rouged cheek presented. "It is good to
have you safe home and looking so well, my boy. We are *all* pleased to
see you."

Sir Antony lightly brushed her cheek, careful to avoid the dyed
ostrich plumes sprouting from her red silk turban, and before she could
continue, turned and bowed to Kitty Aldershot.

"I have not had the pleasure of an introduction, but I am very sure
you are Miss Aldershot?"

Kitty nodded, curtsied prettily, and bit her lower lip. She blushed
with delight that Sir Antony had chosen to introduce himself. He was
even more handsome at close quarters than she had anticipated, but
what tied her tongue was the soft timbre of his deep voice. It gave her
goose bumps. She went to speak, and was rudely cut off before uttering
a syllable.

Lady Reanay, thinking Kitty's hesitancy due to shyness, said, "Dear me! Yes! This is Kitty Aldershot, Poor Stephen's sister and Salt's ward. You may recall the Aldershots better than me. Their small estate was some five miles west of Hendon. Poor Stephen's father rode the hunt with Salt's papa. I remember *him* but not Poor Stephen's mamma. Diana would know. Which brings me back to her visit to St. Petersburg..."

"Tea? I'm sure we would all welcome a cup," Sir Antony said as his aunt paused for breath. He forced himself to look at Caroline, his well-practiced diplomatic smile fixed in place. "How thoughtless of Boyle not to see you had a glass of champagne. Would you like one fetched? Lady Aldershot? Miss Aldershot?"

"Thank you, Sir Antony, I will have champagne," Kitty Aldershot stated clearly, finding her voice and her bright smile.

"We will *all* have tea, thank you," Caroline enunciated, a quick warning glance at Kitty before turning to look at Sir Antony.

Yet, she could not bring herself to lift her gaze above his chin. She fixed on the pearl-headed gold pin nestled in the folds of soft lace at his throat. Such delicate lace, so white and finely wrought, and in such marked contrast to the ruggedness of his square heavy chin which, despite having been shaved earlier that day, was already showing a blue cast. There was something enticingly appealing in the juxtaposition of the feminine lace against the masculinity of that chin... She was very sure that if he rubbed his skin against hers it would be very rough indeed, the stubble chafe and redden her flesh. He would certainly leave his mark...

She sat heavily on the settee in a ripple of mauve silk and silver gauze petticoats, mortified. With mortification came the realization she had been deceiving herself for four years. She was not cured of her desire. She wanted Sir Antony Templestowe every bit as much as she had wanted him before his exile. It made her blurt out nervously, the public setting forgotten,

"It's Lady *Caroline* Aldershot. I'm still *Caroline*. I haven't altered in the slightest!"

"Yes, of course you are," Sir Antony replied placidly. "And no, you haven't." He made her a short bow. "Excuse me while I see to the tea."

He turned his shoulder, smile spreading into a grin, catching the following exchange,

"He has *such* a lovely voice. Caroline? Your face is quite red. Are you al—"

"*Hush*, Kitty!"

"You're as giddy as a one-winged beetle, Caroline! And there's no hushing the truth," Lady Reanay stated. "Be a good girl, Kitty, and wave air onto Caroline. Your face is an alarming shade of apple, my dear. A nice cup of tea will take the shock away."

"I'm not—I'm *not* in shock! I am—I was—*surprised.*"

"Shock. Surprise. 'Tis the same. I remember the shock I received when in Constantinople I was confronted with a splendid Turk, naked from the waist up. My knees were all atremble and gave out, and I…"

Sir Antony did not hear the rest of his aunt's startling monologue. A hand clamped his arm in welcome and a thin gentleman in a silk suit the color of stained grape pounced on him, much like an overeager puppy jumps at its master when he steps across the threshold after being away. Not only was the gentleman's entire ensemble a faded hue of purple, so too were his stockings, the enormous ribbon at his nape, and the bag into which his long queue was placed. The only article about the gentleman's person that was less startling and less colorful, and this in itself was a surprise, was his wig. It was plain, neat and powdered white. Such a wig on the head of the eccentric poet Hilary Wraxton Esquire was unusual indeed. Yet, upon closer inspection, as he shook hands with the poet, Sir Antony revised this opinion because the poet's wig was in fact made from the feathers of a white mallard, or were they goose feathers?

"Antony! What luck to see you here! Well, not here, not seeing you *here*, in your own home, seeing you *here*, back in England."

"What a pleasure to see you, dear fellow! I thought you fixed on the Continent for some time?"

The poet lost his smile.

"Was. *Was* fixed there. Having a jolly good time of it, too. Paris. Berne. Rome. Florence."

He followed Sir Antony to the tea trolley and watched him fiddle with the silver samovar and tea things, standing so close at his shoulder that more than once he was politely requested to stand aside while Sir Antony went through the precise steps of his tea-making ritual.

The ritual helped distract Sir Antony from temptation and kept the demon from his shoulder, for within arm's reach there were enough bottles of champagne and decanters of wine to feed his addiction and send him into blissful oblivion. The habitual drunkard in him held to the persuasive, but thoroughly deluded, line of argument that he had the willpower to drink one small glass of champagne without any ill effects. However, his tea-drinking self knew this for a lie. *Cured* of his addiction was in the realms of believing in fairy folk and pigs flying through the sky. Prince Mikhail had counseled him: Each step closer to the perfect cup of tea was another step away from the compulsive need for alcohol to get him through his day.

"Tea, Hilary?"

The poet waved a ruffle-covered hand in dismissal.

"Liked living in Florence; good for the creative juices. Then it all went sour!"

"What went sour?"

"Ha! Knew you'd understand. Always said you had more sentiment than wit."

"I'm not entirely sure that was complimentary. But, please, tell me before I rudely cut you off to take tea to three parched ladies."

"Well, there I was enjoying a lovely glass of *vino* in the sun on the Palazzo Saint Marco with Mann—that's Sir Horace Mann, our Resident in Florence, but I'm sure you know that—"

"I do."

"Yes, well, there was Mann and I having a tipple when Pascoe pounces on me with the most appalling news. Just like that! No warning. Nothing. Absolutely floored me. Pascoe said five months was time enough to get used to Lizzie's *interesting condition*. Couldn't imagine anything more hideous than Pascoe Church cooing over a brat. Took leave of the place, *subito*. No screaming brats for Hilary Wraxton!"

"Are you telling me the good news that Lady Church was delivered of an infant and that Pascoe is now the proud father of a son and heir?"

"Something like that. No! Not *something* like. *Precisely* like. Come to think on it, that's not what I wanted to tell you! That was the thought in my mind, to tell you about Pascoe's brat, but not what I wanted to tell you, if you get my drift."

Sir Antony removed the hot teapot off the samovar and poured a precise amount of the rich black tea into four lemon yellow porcelain cups, leaving room for the weaker tea from the second silver teapot. He replaced the teapot on its stand, saying casually,

"Sorry, Hilary, but you are drifting rather wide of the mark for me to *get* anything."

The poet looked up at Sir Antony, head tilted to one side. "I can confide in you, can't I, Antony?"

Sir Antony pressed his lips together to stifle a smile. With his absurd wig of white feathers and small black eyes blinking up at him, Hilary Wraxton was reminiscent of an enquiring pigeon. He half expected the poet to take a peck or two at the lumps of sugar in the silver sugar bowl he placed on the black lacquered chinoiserie tray.

"What is it you wish to confide in me, Hilary…?"

"Stopped in Hendon at the White Horse for a change of horses. Wish I hadn't. Wish I'd pushed on to the next town. But I dare say church bells were pealing there, too. Your cousin Salt owns most of Wiltshire, so stands to reason all the bells in the county were clanging loud and clear in congratulations of the Countess's safe delivery of a second son. But the clanging was enough to give me an infernal headache!"

"The church bells were ringing because the Countess of Salt Hendon was delivered of a healthy son?" When the poet nodded, Sir Antony was unable to hide his grin. "Well done Jane," he murmured to himself.

"Saw Lady St. John at Hendon—"

Sir Antony gave a start. "At *Hendon*? At the White Horse?"

"The very same. Waiting to be taken up by the Hendon-to-London stagecoach with her companion and a thin mop of a girl." He shuddered his distaste. "That companion… Shoulders wider than mine. Unpleasant. *Frightening*."

"Mrs. Smith?"

"Is she? Is she *Mrs*. Smith? I'm not convinced. Not convinced at all. Could very well be a man in petticoats. Turned me off m'steak and ale. Her ladyship said she'd just been visiting with Salt—"

"Diana was at the estate?" Sir Antony was so incredulous the poet took a step back. "Forgive me, Hilary. Do go on," he added in a soothing voice, which brought the poet back beside him.

"I offered her a seat in my carriage. It was the decent thing to do. Couldn't have her ladyship traveling with the mob on the common stage." His brow furrowed. "Don't know why Salt didn't offer her one of his carriages. Still, glad to be of service. There wasn't room for the Smith person or the girl inside the carriage. Sat them up with Parsons, m'driver. With her wrists, thought Smith could offer to take the reins and give Parsons a rest along the way. Strange…"

"Strange?" Sir Antony repeated, only half listening to the poet's prattle.

He arranged the tea things on the tray to his satisfaction waving away one of the footmen, who had come to do what he saw as his job, topped up the teacups from the weaker tea from the second teapot and handed the poet a teacup on its saucer. "There is sugar on the trolley."

Hilary Wraxton did his pigeon face again, and this time Sir Antony did smile. He jerked his feathered wig in the direction of a footman. "Lackeys not up to making a decent brew?"

"I prefer to make it myself."

"Do you? Do you indeed?" the poet muttered, sipping at the hot milky tea without comprehension.

He put the porcelain cup on its delicate saucer and followed Sir Antony the short distance to the settee. His conversation was unflagging, and for once, welcomed by the three ladies on the settee who, despite a room full of laughter and chatter, were all silent, but for very different reasons.

Lady Reanay was trying to fathom how her daughter-in-law Diana St. John had managed a visit to St. Petersburg, and why Sir Antony had failed to mention this to her.

Kitty Aldershot was wondering how to get her hands on a glass of champagne, and hoping Sir Antony would at least look at her long enough to notice how pretty she was in her brocade gown *à l'anglaise* with matching shoes and ribbons in her hair. After all, her effort was on his behalf.

Lady Caroline remained discomforted that within the blink of an eye in his company she was lusting after Sir Antony Templestowe like a frustrated widow from a Hogarth etching. And no longer being the naïve eighteen-year-old who had every expectation of marrying him, she was well aware where that lust could take her. Although, she was certain that when he knew the extent of her depravity while he was absent from England, he would be greatly relieved he had not married her.

Aware they were preoccupied with their own thoughts and wondering why they were suddenly sullen-faced, Sir Antony calmly distributed the tea with only one ear to Hilary Wraxton's prattle.

"I had to tell someone—tell *you*," the poet explained, following Sir Antony up and down the row as he offered tea, cream and sugar. "What happened to the mop girl?"

Sir Antony turned and handed off the empty tray to a po-faced footman, who was as startled as several of the guests at his master playing servant for the three ladies on the settee. The poet finally had his full attention again, though he had heard only one word in three.

"What mop, Hilary? You conveyed a mop to London?"

"No! No! *Not* a mop. A mop of a girl. Stick-thin and wearing one of those frilly white mobcaps that flap in the face. Noticed she had an overabundance of frizzy hair springing out in all directions. Looked like something you upend and mop the floor with."

"Hence the mop of a girl," confirmed Sir Antony, who was surprised the poet had any idea what such an aid to domestic tidiness looked like, but he did not dispute him. Perhaps he had taken notice of such mundane cleaning equipment as part of his keen poet's eye? He was known, after all, for poems on all manner of utilitarian subjects, from carriages to clocks to street sweepers, so why not an ode to mops? "What about this girl, Hilary?"

The poet sighed deeply.

"That's what I want to confide. Knew you were of keen mind, Antony. The girl who was with her ladyship and the Smith person at the White Horse Inn has vanished! She was no longer with us when we reached London."

"What happened to her?"

"That's what I want to know. It's not that I take an inordinate interest in servants but when one is strapped to the roof of one's carriage, it behooves one to want to know what happened if it disappears. Thought she must have fallen off the roof when we made a particularly bad lurch on our approach into the environs of Westminster. But no! My panic was all for naught." He leaned into Sir Antony's silken shoulder, eyes narrowed. "That man in a woman's skirt, that *Mrs.* Smith tried to tell me there was no such girl!" He tapped his thin, long nose, "But Hilary Wraxton Esquire has the eyes of a hawk and the brain to match! I saw her in their company and I offered her a seat up with my driver. So she does exist!"

"I'm sure she must, if you say so, Hilary."

"Good! Because I want *you* to find out what happened to her! I've dedicated a poem to her. And so I must have her name, or what's the point of the dedication, eh? The poem is called *Ode to a Lost Mop Girl.*"

Sir Antony bit back a retort about not resembling a Bow Street Runner in the least, and was about to suggest the poet seek out such individuals to find the mysterious mop girl when Hilary Wraxton gave the lace at his wrist a shake-down and began a recitation,

In white muslin mob cap, hidden away,
Flap, flap, flap, the frilly fringe would not obey!
A servant wench, abundant hair in disarray,
Her plight unfortunate, and gray...

Several of the guests gravitated from the four corners of the saloon to hear Hilary Wraxton recite his ode, while a handful were more interested in settling a wager as to the materials used to make the poet's wig. Under cover of Hilary's impromptu recital, Sir Antony drew up a ribbon-back chair beside his aunt, and with the delicate cup and saucer steady on a silken knee, leaned in to talk at her ear.

"Are you at home tomorrow? Shall I call on you?"

"In the morning. We will have time to talk. The Salt Hendons are due in the afternoon, which will see the house in a state of pandemonium. I do so love to see the children running about. I would say come then, too, but Salt—"

"—hasn't forgiven me? Or if he has, he isn't ready to receive me, yet."

"Antony..."

He smiled ruefully and held the mittened hand she put out to him in a comforting grasp. "It is perfectly all right, Aunt Alice. I understand. He'll come round in his own good time."

"Well, I don't!" Lady Reanay grumbled. "Enough time has passed for Salt to forgive and forget. Obstinate man! Just as I don't understand why he won't allow Diana to see her children. I admit I never warmed to Diana, but she was married to my son, and she is the mother of my grandchildren. No! Close your mouth and listen. I know what it is to be banished from one's family. St. John was taken from me when I ran off with Tobias, and even after we married, St. John was not permitted to visit his wicked mother for fear of being corrupted. Good God! *Corrupted.*

"If it hadn't been for dearest Jane, Salt would not have invited me to return to England. That I now have rooms in the house and regularly see my grandchildren is beyond my wildest expectations. Merry and Ron are such *dear* children. And because they are dear children, I believe they should see their mother, now she has returned from *her* exile. Do you know, my boy, she has not been permitted any contact with the twins since their ninth birthday? They are twelve and a half years old, Antony. And to see Salt with his own children... He is such a good papa that I simply do not understand his cruel actions toward his godchildren. They have no father and their only parent is refused permission to see them! It breaks my heart."

"Aunt Alice, I understand perfectly how you, as their grandmother, must feel for Ron and Merry's situation. On the surface, anyone would. I am very sure Diana pleaded her case with eloquence and passion, but there is far more to my sister's *circumstance* than you can possibly imagine." He gently squeezed his aunt's hand so she returned her attention to him from the sudden distraction of Hilary Wraxton's impromptu poetry recital. When she met his gaze he said, "I wish I could tell you more, but until I have spoken with Salt, I simply cannot. What I can tell you is that Diana is not in London under Salt's auspices. In fact, I am very sure he is unaware she is here."

Lady Reanay blinked at him. Raucous applause and movement within the semi-circle of persons listening to the poet allowed her to turn and stare across the room at Diana St. John entertaining a knot of gentlemen with what must be an amusing anecdote, given their laughter and animation. She was so beautiful in her brocade petticoats *à la française* that Lady Reanay gave a heavy sigh of sympathy. To Sir Antony's frustration, his aunt completely misread his intention, saying as she sat up tall, her voice full of indignation,

"Bravo for Diana, for having the courage to defy Salt for the sake of her children. I did not and I have regretted my cowardice every day of my life. Four years separated from her children is long enough, whatever her misconduct of the past. Which, I might add, Antony, no one has been willing or able to shine a candle's worth of light upon, not even Jane, who politely refers me to Salt if I dare mention the twins' mamma! Not even Caroline knows the reason for Diana's banishment. It is most irregular." It was Lady Reanay's turn to squeeze her nephew's hand. "I am very pleased you are taking up Diana's cause with Salt. Someone has to, and who better than her dearest brother and Ron and Merry's beloved uncle. Diana confided you are keeping a very close eye on her—"

"Did she?" he interrupted with a wry smile. "I am."

"Such a good and understanding brother."

"As to that…"

"She also told me *she* is the reason for your return from St. Petersburg."

"She was ever the cleverer of the two of us. That, too, is true."

Lady Reanay pouted and startled her nephew with an about-face.

"Making sacrifices for your sister is very admirable in a devoted brother, Antony, but not if it means the ruin of your career! I had hoped Diana was not the only reason for your return…"

She stopped, a swift glance over her left shoulder to see if Caroline was still seated beside her. She was not. Lady Caroline was by the French windows, where she was languidly fanning herself, a shoulder to the room, as if wanting the solitude that the open French window afforded. Lady Reanay realized at once that Caroline had strategically positioned herself close to where Kitty was in conversation with the darkly handsome Mr. Dacre Wraxton, a notorious flirt whose jaundiced eye lingered on girls enjoying their first Season. Kitty was showing the lothario her fan and he was showing her an inordinate amount of attention. When Caroline soon interrupted the pair, Lady Reanay breathed easy and returned her attention to Sir Antony, who had finished his tea and handed off the cup and saucer to a footman.

What she told him next could not have shocked him more had she slapped him hard across the face with a wet haddock, had such a fish been at her ladyship's disposal. Shock gave way to disbelief, which had him up off the chair. Disbelief gave way to possibility. A feeling he would later describe as a burst of sunshine consumed him, and he forgot his surroundings in the urgency of securing his future there and then. What was the point of procrastinating when he knew exactly what he wanted and it was within his grasp, just waiting for him to act? And so possibility was overrun by impetuousness.

In a move he later realized was reminiscent of his drunken behavior at the recital that caused his banishment, but which did not have the excuse of alcohol to blame, history, in an odd sort of way, repeated itself.

"Call me a romantic old fool, but I had hoped it was Caroline who had brought you home."

"Caroline?" Sir Antony frowned, a glance at Lady Caroline Aldershot framed in the window embrasure and now in close conversation with Mr. Dacre Wraxton. His throat went dry. "Why? Why would you think Caroline the catalyst for my homecoming?"

"You have no idea, have you?"

"I beg your pardon, Aunt. I must not."

"I will not take the blame for your ignorance because it happened after I had left you in St. Petersburg to travel on to Helsinki. And I did not discover it for myself until Paris, where a letter was waiting me, and by then, I assumed you would have discovered it for yourself through the English newssheets. Salt did not write you with the news?"

Sir Antony shook his head.

"Salt write to me with news? About *Caroline*? His occasional letters never mentioned Caroline. In fact, he seems to have been at pains to omit her from all correspondence. If there was anything in the English newssheets, it must have been in such fine print or tucked away in a back column that I missed it altogether."

Lady Reanay put up her penciled brows. "Not given to reading the births, deaths and marriages columns? Not even when supremely bored?"

Sir Antony gave a huff of laughter.

"No. Advertisements for James's Powders hold more fascination than those notices. Not since I read with horror Caroline married Aldershot. You've made me nervous."

He leaned in so only she could hear, although it was an unnecessary gesture because most of the guests had moved across the room to surround the clavichord and harp for an impromptu recital.

"You're not about to tell me she's going to give Aldershot a brat, are you? I have yet to come to terms with her marriage, so any further news in that quarter would surely shatter me. By the by, where is Aldershot? Shouldn't he be here at his wife's side? If she were *my* wife… God! There are some famous last words! Well, if she *were*, I certainly wouldn't want to be anywhere but at her side. What is it?" he asked, alarmed when his aunt's hand convulsed in his and tears filled her eyes. "Dear God, Aunt Alice, what did I say to bring this on?"

He made to rise, to fetch her a fresh cup of tea, water, anything to stop her tears, but she stayed him and he settled again and waited.

Lady Reanay thought it time to put her nephew out of his ignorant bewilderment.

"Twelve months and a little over two weeks ago, Poor Stephen—Aldershot—was tragically killed when he was thrown from his horse. He died almost instantly. Well, he certainly never opened his eyes again. He expired before a sawbones could attend. He was only three-and-twenty. A tragedy."

Sir Antony swallowed hard.

"Yes, a tragedy," Sir Antony replied soberly. "Poor fellow. And so young… What happened?"

"No one knows for certain. It is thought he tried to jump a particularly high dry stone wall and his mount shied at the last moment. He was thrown across the wall. The horse was found on one side of the field, Aldershot in a ditch on the other, the wall between them."

"Where did this happen?"

"At Salt Hendon."

Sir Antony nodded.

"Good. Not good he died. Good that Caroline was at home, with Salt and Jane, with family around at such a time." He wiped a hand over his mouth and shook his head. "Dear me, what an awful business, and she married not quite two years… Tragic." He glanced over at Kitty Aldershot who was talking with Diana and Lady Porter. "Is Miss Aldershot his only family?"

"Yes. She was orphaned at Poor Stephen's death. Salt took it upon himself to be her guardian. She is a sweet child, but penniless. I dare say Salt will be called upon to provide her with an adequate dowry should she receive an offer of marriage."

Sir Antony thought of Tom Allenby's letters and how he had once compared Miss Katherine "Kitty" Aldershot's blonde beauty to the Goddess Aphrodite walking amongst mere mortals. He smiled crookedly.

"Oh, Miss Aldershot will receive at least one excellent proposal of marriage before the season's end, I am sure of it..."

"Let us hope so. Should he prove worthy and she accept, that will be one less burden for Salt, and for Caroline. Since her mourning ended, she has chaperoned Kitty to functions where this old lady would feel exceedingly out of place."

Again Sir Antony nodded, and there was a faraway look in his eye.

"Since her mourning ended... Yes, of course. She should accompany Miss Aldershot to balls, and fetes and wherever there is dancing... She's too young to be a widow. Can't imagine her in widow's weeds, m'self. Miserable attire; miserable time of it I suspect. Caroline loves to dance..."

"My boy, I don't know what you've been told," she confided. "Indeed, I fear you've not been told much at all if you think Caroline has returned to her former self before she married Aldershot. She's not one for balls and fetes and dancing—"

"Caroline? Not *dance*? Not want to attend a ball?" Sir Antony blinked at his aunt with incomprehension.

Lady Reanay wondered if her nephew was suffering shock. He was distracted, and mumbling, almost to himself. His reaction to the news that his beloved Caroline was now a widow was not at all what she had expected. With the requisite period of mourning completed, Lady Caroline Aldershot was free to marry again—free to marry Sir Antony, and he was free to ask her to be his wife. Did he not see that? Did he not understand what this meant for him and for Caroline's future?

"You do understand what this means?" she added, peering at him closely. "Caroline is a widow... Antony?"

Suddenly he did understand. The dark clouds enveloping his private life parted to allow a bright sunlit moment, just as Lady Reanay asked the question of him. He was up off the seat, pulling at the points of his waistcoat, and hastily brushing the sleeves of his frock coat to be rid of imaginary creases. He straightened the sit of the pearl-headed pin in his cravat, leaned his head left then right while he cleared his throat. With a bow to his aunt, he politely excused himself, white in the face as if suddenly ill. He strode across to the French windows where Lady Caroline was admiring the view.

So intent was he, so full of purpose, that he was blind to everyone around him and deaf to his name.

The guests gathered about the clavichord appealed to him— everyone knew Sir Antony to be quite the musician. Their shouts of cajolery went unheeded. Lady St. John said she would rouse him. She would not play the harp unless her dear brother accompanied her on the clavichord. Taking up a handful of her embroidered petticoats, Diana St. John bustled across the room, determined to have her brother's attention. She appealed to Mr. Dacre Wraxton, who had just broken conversation with Lady Caroline, to add his entreaties to hers, and he willingly complied. She put out a hand to him, and he offered her the crook of his velvet sleeve.

Everyone watched and waited.

Sir Antony continued to ignore his sister and her champion.

Sir Antony was at Caroline's back before she sensed a presence at her shoulder. She heard the calls and pleas from across the room but had no idea what the commotion was about. All she wanted was to leave this gathering as soon as possible. Close conversation with Dacre Wraxton had drawn unwanted attention, and their association merely underscored her unworthiness. How could she hold up her head under the piercingly blue eyes of Sir Antony Templestowe, who knew nothing of her sordid past, and Cousin Diana's supercilious smile? According to Dacre Wraxton, her cousin Diana knew all there was to know about their affair. She did not doubt her cousin would use the information to her advantage. It was only a matter of time before Diana confided such shocking news in Salt, and worse, Sir Antony...

Two hours spent at an afternoon tea clearly designed as a self-congratulatory celebration of Diana St. John's return to London Society was time enough, and Caroline hoped Lady Reanay thought so, too. She craved the solitude of her rooms in her brother's Grosvenor Square mansion and the companionship of her menagerie. Her assortment of animals and birds loved her unconditionally. They never judged and they never failed to put her in a cheerful mood.

A clearing of the throat at her back intruded into these mental musings. Presuming it to be Dacre Wraxton intent on pressing his suit, she turned on a heel, snapping shut the sticks of her fan, which she then held across the lace gloved palm of her left hand, as one does a cudgel, and said with a sigh of exasperation,

"Wraxton, enough of your silly games. I will never share your bed again, married or unmarried, so it is pointless to—Oh! An—Antony!?"

He made her a formal bow and cleared his throat a second time.

He was so ashen-faced, the muscles in his face so tense that she instantly presumed Lady Reanay was unwell, and she put out a gloved hand, a glance past his silken shoulder to see if their aunt was perfectly well.

"What—What ever is the matter?"

He took her hand and instantly went down on silken bended knee.

"Lady Caroline… My lady, will you do me the supreme honor of becoming my wife?"

SEVEN

Fifteen minutes earlier, before Sir Antony's unrehearsed and very public marriage proposal, Lady Caroline Aldershot was staring down at the walled garden. Two hefty men, under direction of the head gardener, were engaged in moving tubs of orange trees into the sunshine. But her ear was to the inane conversation between Kitty Aldershot and Dacre Wraxton. Kitty's prattle was naturally all about herself. The time she had taken at her toilette to make certain everything from her curls to her clocked stockings were perfectly coordinated received only monosyllabic responses. Thankfully, Kitty was so naïve that not once did she pick up on Dacre Wraxton's attempts to engage her in serious flirtation. She answered all his remarks honestly and directly. When he made throwaway comments she did not understand, she pretended comprehension by replying with a silly comment of her own, ending her sentence with a giggle. When her giggles became louder, Caroline knew Kitty was growing increasingly nervous and finding it difficult to dig herself out of the attention hole created by Dacre Wraxton's singular notice.

Caroline knew this because Dacre Wraxton, debonair lothario, had played the same game with her when she was Kitty's age. She had responded to his advances in much the same manner as Kitty was doing now. Yet, whereas Kitty was hesitant and nervous, Caroline had enjoyed the attention and was flattered to be singled out by such a dangerously handsome man. She flirted outrageously with her admirer. Wraxton pursued her and singled her out at every public event. Caroline hoped his attentions would rouse Sir Antony Templestowe to jealousy. Her plan did not take.

The more she and Wraxton flirted under Sir Antony's fine nose, the more *her Antony* ignored her. In fact, he went out of his way to be blind to her behavior. Being ignored by the only man she truly cared about brought out the worst in her, and flirtation with Dacre Wraxton entered a dangerous phase. Her behavior became so outrageous Salt was on the brink of sending her back to the country when she had her very public spat with Antony at the Salt Hendon recital. That had changed everything.

That incident sent her spiraling out of control, and under the influence of too many glasses of champagne, she was brave and reckless in equal measure to allow matters with Dacre Wraxton to go beyond flirtation. She permitted him liberties from which there was no recover. Her only salvation was having the Earl of Salt Hendon for a brother. She doubted that even her dowry of thirty thousand pounds would have saved her from ruination, had Salt not intervened and married her off to Aldershot.

She was determined history would not repeat itself. Dacre Wraxton would not be the ruin of Kitty. Not only did Kitty lack the mental fortitude to recover from such a seduction, she did not have an earl for a brother or a substantial dowry, the prime factors that had allowed Caroline to avert open scandal and life-long recrimination.

So when the right moment presented itself, Caroline turned from the French window and said quietly but firmly as she slipped her fingers back into her delicate lace glove,

"Kitty, dear, be so kind as to fetch a glass of orange water. The warm air off the balcony has left me parched. Ask the footman over there for a fresh batch. I do believe all the jugs on the table are empty."

Kitty instantly closed her fan, bobbed a curtsy to Dacre Wraxton, and departed. If her sigh of relief was inaudible, the still air left by her immediate absence was enough to underscore her liberation. Dacre Wraxton moved into this space and with a shoulder against the painted window frame, looked down on Caroline with a rueful smile and a gleam in his dark eyes.

"Your charge is very pretty but she lacks your fire. I hope she finds a husband in her first season. Her blonde beauty will fade, and she'll become tedious before she gains the wisdom that comes with silence. She'll end her days on a shelf, gathering dust."

"Better a tedious beauty covered in dust than what you had in mind for her."

Dacre cocked his head with a twinge of a smile and his black eyes lost their cynical gleam.

"My dear Lady Caroline, I have nothing in mind for Miss Aldershot beyond mere flirtation in the here and now. I had hoped she would take the edge off my boredom. At the very least, take my mind off the fact my effete dolt of a brother is in the same room with me, spouting his poetical drivel. I applaud Lady St. John for orchestrating the family reunion. Let me not bore you with my family. I would prefer to hear all about yours. Other people's families are vastly more entertaining than one's own."

"There is nothing to tell."

He peered at her closely.

"Nothing? Ha! A nice try at nonchalance but I am not to be fooled, my dear. He's put you out of sorts, has he not, your blue-eyed baronet?" When she did not deny it and did not look up at him either, he smiled thinly. "Proximity has us both shivering—me with embarrassment for having such a brother, and you with renewed awakening for your baronet."

"Stop it, Dacre!"

"That's better. Call me by name. I much prefer you animated to maudlin, even if it is with anger. The latter complements your hair delightfully."

When he put out his hand, she lightly slapped his fingers with her fan and he took it from her, unfurled it and fluttered it like a woman.

"My dear, there really is no need to engage your scruples," he continued. "I find that to survive the rigors of this Society to which we belong, it is better to—pardon the cliché—lock away one's conscience and throw away the key."

At that, she did look up at him, face flushed with the embarrassment of memory.

"So you admit to having a conscience. How touching!"

For a moment, he lost his suave façade, dark brows contracting over his thin nose.

"If I was ever inconsiderate to your needs, at *any* time, my lady, I most sincerely apologize…"

"No. No. You need not apologize or think that," she confessed truthfully and swallowed. She bravely held his gaze. "You only did what I asked of you."

"I may now die a happy man," he drawled, and made her an elegant bow, lace ruffles at his wrists sweeping the floor.

When he straightened she tried to snatch back her fan.

"That was ill-judged, sir! Now half the room is looking this way."

He glanced over his shoulder and took in the fancifully painted walls with their Etruscan motifs of ancients in drapery, golden griffins and classical urns sprouting ivy foliage, and saw that indeed most eyes had turned in their direction. The guests were assembling around the gilded clavichord and footmen were arranging ribbon-back chairs in two rows. Thankfully, his brother had finished his recitation, and his discarded mistress, Lady Dalrymple, was no longer staring at him mournfully. He heard Diana St. John call to him, but he chose to ignore her, returning his attention to the deliciously curvaceous Lady Caroline—the only bright star in an otherwise dull affair.

"Only half?" he quipped. "Dear me. I must be losing my touch. I was hoping for all eyes."

"Pray be serious a moment."

"Must I? Why must I be serious, my sweet cheeks?"

"*Never* call me that," she demanded in a low voice, blushing.

"But you have the finest—"

"*Wraxton*," she hissed, face now the color of her hair. "*Your word.* You gave me your word you would never speak of our—of our —*encounter.*"

"Encounter?" he questioned. "I would prefer to hold to the memory as a most enjoyable *liaison.*"

"I'm surprised you can hold to a particular memory at all where women are concerned!"

His chuckle was low and full of amusement.

"I do miss you, spitfire. I miss your banter. To have you pretend to be disconsolate with me is such a refreshing change from doe-eyed ninnyhammers. Spitfire, you and I are cut from the same flawed cloth. We deserve each other. Admit to it! Now the boy is well-and-truly cold in his grave—"

"Don't talk of Aldershot with such disrespect. For all his faults, he was still my husband."

"Faults? He was a lily-livered, consumptive fortune hunter! He was undeserving of you. You are well rid of him, is the truth, and I'll say it, even if you and others cannot." He let the fan dip to her décolletage and ran its pleated edge along the little lace border of her chemise. "All I ask is that you give my offer serious consideration..."

"*Offer?* After a twelvemonth of marriage to you, if I should be so fortunate to receive your singular devotion for even that length of time, you'll return to your dissolute ways and I will be just one of many. Worse. I will be the wife you forsook for other women. Your callous treatment of the weaker sex is evident in poor crumpled Jenny Dalrymple. She may only have been your mistress, but she did not deserve to be summarily dismissed. I shudder at the prospect! No, I thank you."

He shrugged, a glance across at Sir Antony and Lady Reanay sipping tea. The large baronet was listening to the old lady as if her every word was coated in gold. It made him sneer.

"With the return of your blue-eyed baronet, you think you have a choice? Don't be fooled. A man like that has *scruples*. He'll accept a virtuous widow for a bride, but when he discovers you have a past, he'll have justifiable cause to cast you off before he marries you. Pardon me for mentioning it—but as the interested third party in your impending romantic imbroglio I do have a vested interest—what do you think will be his reaction when he learns the truth?"

Caroline suddenly felt faint.

"You would not stoop so low…"

He looked deep into her green eyes.

"For you I would stoop all the way to hell."

Caroline believed him. Such an earnest declaration from such a devilish handsome rogue would have had three quarters of London's females swooning at his boots. It did nothing but make her feel ill. *He* made her feel ill. She averted her face, and in so doing caught a glimpse of her big handsome *gentle* man. He had a delicate teacup and saucer balanced on his silken knee and was politely listening to one of Aunt Alice's monologues, as if she was telling him the most riveting piece of news. In all probability, she was giving him a medical inventory of her arthritis, and Antony was listening with all the assiduousness of an attending physician.

She swallowed back tears.

"He has the reputation of being a most chivalrous gentleman, and the most honorable," Dacre Wraxton said in a low voice near her ear, because there were calls coming from the other side of the room and his name was mentioned. He pressed home his advantage before being called away. "Four years ago you could have had your baronet, and yet you ruined your chances. Face the looking glass, my tiny spitfire. Even as a naïve innocent, you knew he was too good, too righteous, for the likes of you. What are the odds he will offer for you a second time once he discovers the truth? Your brother can have no objection to you marrying me, not after he married you off to a sot like Aldershot. One day I'll inherit title and wealth. I give you my word I'll be faithful after my own fashion. If I stray, I'll be discreet—"

"Discreet? Faithful? *Your word? You* face the looking glass, Wraxton!" Caroline replied, incredulous. "Such fine words are not in your lexicon." She took a step away and shook out her silk petticoats, rallying herself enough to say without emotion, "I am not the girl I was at that masquerade. What I did then was out of spite. Marriage to Aldershot—our-our *trifling* affair—has merely allowed me to gain clarity on what is truly important. Antony is worth a hundred—no—a *thousand* of you! I know precisely what I squandered. But you are wrong. He has never asked me to marry him."

Dacre Wraxton was genuinely surprised.

"It's not like Lady St. John to be wrong about such an important detail…"

"Lady St. John?" Caroline's eyes narrowed to slits. "How interesting. Time away from London society and Cousin Diana failed to learn her lesson to keep her nose out of other people's affairs—more precisely, my family's business!" She had a sudden, awful thought. "You couldn't—You wouldn't—You didn't tell *her*?"

Dacre Wraxton flicked shut her fan and lightly tapped the end of her nose before returning it to her.

"My dear spitfire, I own to being a complete rogue and a breaker of hearts, but I do not break confidences, particularly when shared in the bed of a lady." When Caroline closed her eyes with relief, he apologized. "I did not tell her, but she knows."

"How? How does she know?"

Dacre Wraxton smiled with sympathy that her anger should instantly turn to dread at this revelation. Unlike most of his peers, he was not pleased with Lady St. John's return to London. They shared a history in her late husband Aubrey St. John. He looked into Caroline's eyes and was not surprised she was fearful. Diana St. John was a force to be reckoned with. She had commanded Polite Society four years ago through force of personality and knowing other people's secrets. And by her forays into Society drawing rooms in recent weeks, was well on the way to regaining her pre-eminence, and by every means at her disposal.

"I do believe the saying *the walls have ears* apposite. Servants are everywhere and yet we see them nowhere. One can only assume a menial blabbed."

Caroline's gaze fixed on Diana St. John, the center of the gathering by the clavichord. She could well believe her cousin capable of paying servants to spy.

"One of yours or mine?"

He shrugged a shoulder, indifferent.

"My servants or yours, that is of no consequence. With your cousin, I would be more concerned about the *why* rather than the how. She stores away other people's secrets better than a squirrel does acorns for the winter! A circumstance I discovered too late for my own good, and so I dance to her tune when required. So now you must excuse me. I have been summoned." Across her shoulder he saw Sir Antony fast approaching and said at her ear, "When you're done playing silly games with honorable men, I'll be waiting."

Sir Antony's marriage proposal on bended knee caused such a cacophony of good-humored shouts of encouragement from the gentlemen, and exclamations of joy and sighs of happiness from the ladies, that Caroline felt she was at St. Bartholomew's Fair amongst the poor howling and squawking exotics of Pidcock's Wild Beast Show. Several of the ladies rushed forward in a rustle of petticoats so they could hear her reply to such a thoroughly romantic gesture. Lady St. John, on the arm of Mr. Dacre Wraxton, and Lady Reanay with Kitty holding her hand, waited at Sir Antony's back, eyes riveted to Lady Caroline's flushed countenance.

Still reeling from the revelation that Diana St. John knew about her past, and wondering what her cousin meant to do with such scandalous and damaging information—inform Salt was her first thought—Caroline could only stare at her gloved hand resting across Sir Antony's fingers. When she finally lifted her gaze to his pale face, the earnestness in his blue eyes formed an obstruction in her throat and she swallowed hard. She had not heard his words, but being on bended knee was indication enough of the question requiring her response. She had been waiting such a long time to hear him ask it, and had practically dreamed of this very moment on and off for so many years, that for him to make such a momentous declaration in public, and at such an inauspicious moment, terrified her to silence.

Joy. Elation. Supreme happiness. These were the feelings normally associated with a marriage proposal. Yet, her emotions were hopelessly tangled into knots. She believed herself thoroughly unworthy of Sir Antony's wildly romantic gesture. This handsome man who kneeled before her, who had opened his heart so publicly and so willingly, deserved better than her in a wife. He would think so, too, when he discovered her for what she truly was. Tears of self-pity welled up to be quickly blinked away. There was no point to feeling sorry for herself. She had made choices and now she must live with them. Antony had made choices, too, and now he must move on—move on without her. It was for the best. He would think so too when he finally knew the truth.

She mentally prepared herself to give him the answer she knew he did not want to hear. Removing her gloved hand from his, she took a deep breath and bravely met his gaze.

What she actually said and did was something altogether different. She blamed the look in his eyes—blue eyes that reflected an earnestness of purpose. How could she resist such honesty and such adoration? Her resolve, the guests and their surroundings, all melted away to leave just the two of them smiling at one another as if they were the only two people in the room. It was but a moment, not even a minute, but it was enough. Instead of her gloved hand dropping to her side, she lifted it to gently touch his face. Tracing the line of his strong jaw, her lace-covered fingertips caressed the roughness of stubble to cheek and chin. And when he briefly closed his eyes, turning his face into the palm of her hand, tears pricked her eyelids.

Without conscious volition she sniffed back tears and whispered, so that only he could hear, "Why ask me such a question in public, you *vexatious* man?"

Sir Antony smiled crookedly, kissed her hand and rose up to his full height. He was hurt that her response was not the spontaneous one he had hoped for, but it brought him to a sense of his surroundings and the realization that once again he had allowed his feelings for Caroline to get the better of him. In so doing, he had again placed her in a most awkward position, and he did not have the excuse of a drunken stupor to blame for his impetuosity! Still, she had not rejected him outright, and that gave him hope.

He had not let go of her gloved hand, and he took a step closer and bent to her ear, so that only she could hear him. To those watching on, it looked as if he was kissing her cheek.

"Because I love you, Caro," he replied softly. "I have never stopped loving you."

Overwhelmed and overcome, Caroline stifled a sob as she pulled her hand free. With one last look up at his flushed face, she snatched up a handful of her silk petticoats and fled the room, Kitty Aldershot quick to follow on her petticoat hems to a roar of applause.

. . .

LADY REANAY STOPPED SIR ANTONY FROM PURSUING CAROLINE, catching at the embroidered silk skirts of his frock coat and holding fast.

"Leave her, my boy. She's overwrought. A proposal from you was the last thing she expected. Best to wait until she can put a sentence together."

She smiled at his frown of confusion and was pleased when he heeded her advice with a nod and remained by her side. She was also relieved. In her present disordered state, there was every chance Caroline would refuse him, for all the wrong reasons, something she would later bitterly regret.

"You are calling on us tomorrow, so can talk with Caroline then," she added with forced brightness, and gave his silken arm a fond squeeze, turning to take her leave of her daughter-in-law before her nephew could ask any searching questions.

Diana St. John startled Lady Reanay by affectionately linking arms with her and walking her across the room and out onto the landing. She further surprised the old lady when she turned to face her, tears in her eyes,

"Thank you for accepting my invitation, my lady," Diana St. John said with a tremble in her voice. "We have not always been on the best of terms, but four years away, with only my thoughts for company, has given me time to reflect upon what is important in my life." She touched Lady Reanay's gloved arm. "Only you truly know what *agony* of thought I have been through, separated from my *dear* children. To be without their company... Not to see their dear little faces... I worried every day for their welfare. I worry now they will no longer know their own mother—"

"That is not true, my dear," Lady Reanay assured her, made uneasy by Diana St. John's melancholy tears. She had never seen her distressed. It was such a change from how she appeared in company. She was in total sympathy with her predicament. "Why, only the other day, Merry asked if you had received her latest letter." In truth it had been three months ago, but, under the circumstances, she thought a little latitude was required to alleviate a mother's distress. "Such a treasure. She is a credit to you, Diana."

Diana gasped. "Letter? My darling Magna wrote me a letter! Oh! If only I had known this while away, it would have given me *such* hope."

"Not just one letter, my dear, several letters. Merry is a very conscientious correspondent, to you, and to her Uncle Tony. She cherishes his replies and keeps all his letters tied up with ribbon and in a special box she decorated herself, with fabric and wallpaper strips cut into shapes. It is quite the most enchanting creation and the perfect place to put her keepsakes. She has an assortment of shells from our visit to the seashore, pressed flowers, and I think there is also—"

"How charming," Diana St. John interrupted, disinterested. She forced herself to smile and open wide her wet eyes in expectation. "Is that where she keeps my letters, too?"

Lady Reanay frowned in puzzlement. "Your letters? Forgive an old lady, my dear, but I do not understand."

"The many letters I wrote to my children while on my Continental wanderings," Diana St. John lied. She blinked at her mother-in-law's look of complete confusion and tilted her head to the side in question. "I wrote to my darlings every week. I made a habit of making Tuesday writing day. No matter where I was, I always found the time to write to my two little ones. I understand letters can and do go astray... But it did not stop me from writing to them." She pressed Lady Reanay's gloved hand. "You see, I remember St. John telling me once how much he valued your letters to him while you were traveling abroad. He said they made him feel close to you, even though he knew there was no opportunity of ever seeing you again." This, too, was a lie and it achieved its object when the old lady's eyes filled with tears at mention of her son. Diana sighed her sadness, while inwardly congratulating herself on her best performance yet. "That is the excuse I told myself, that their letters to me had gone astray, as to why I never heard from them in all the time I was away."

"Are you saying you never received one of Merry's or Ron's letters? Not one?" When Diana nodded sadly and dropped her lashes, Lady Reanay was appalled. "How can that be? Why, even when Sir Tobias and I were literally at the ends of the earth in Oslo, I still received Aubrey's weekly letter. Of course, at times, four weekly letters would arrive at once... Not one letter?"

"Not one. I thought—I thought they wished to forget me," Diana replied in a small, weak voice and dabbed carefully at her eyes with her kerchief. She sniffed. "Of course it is not for me to say, but perhaps there were others—others who wished my darlings to forget their dear mother..."

"Oh! I cannot believe Salt would... That dearest Jane could..." She shook her powdered coiffure, saying more to convince herself than Diana St. John, "No. No. They could not withhold the letters of a mother to her children... Not the letters Ron and Merry wrote you... I cannot believe—"

"Can't you?" Diana snarled through her teeth, unable to help herself. She instantly pulled herself up, covering her involuntary outburst with a dry sob, hands to her face, the façade of sorrowful parent masking her true feelings and intent. She looked up when the old lady laid a gloved hand on her arm. "You are Ron and Merry's grandmamma, you know—in your heart—you know that it is indeed true. Just as it is true my dearest darlings have been kept from me! And you will be shocked when I tell you, but I must, that Salt's decision to keep them from me is not his own..." Over the top of her mother-in-law's plumed turban she saw a footman coming up the stairs and added with a trembling smile, "I have detained you far too long," she apologized. "Caroline and her sweet blonde companion are waiting for you..."

The old lady met Diana's sad smile, a frown between her brows.

"But Jane would never... She has been so good and kind to Ron and Merry... I cannot believe... My dear, if there is anything I can do for you...?"

Diana hesitated, hands clasped together. As if she had little hope of having her wishes fulfilled, she said heavily, "I dare not impose on your good offices, as I fear it is too much to ask..."

This prompted Lady Reanay to take hold of both her hands.

"You *must* allow me to help you in some small way. You are the mother of my grandchildren, and they are most dear to me, more than anything or anyone else."

"Very well then," Diana responded, gaze lifting from the old lady's gloved hands about hers. "My dearest wish is to hold my children in my arms. It has been such a long time since I felt the warmth of them... To hold them... To know they are well and happy..."

"Consider it done, my dear," Lady Reanay stated. "I shall arrange it. The Earl and Countess need not know... You are the twins' mother after all... Now you must return to your guests, my dear," she added, giving Diana's hands a quick squeeze. "Dry your eyes. You shall see your darlings. That I promise!"

With that reassurance, Lady Reanay sailed off down the Adam staircase to join Caroline and Kitty in the carriage for home. From the landing, Diana watched with a smile of satisfaction as her gullible fool of a mother-in-law disappeared out into the late afternoon light. What tears she had shed were all to good purpose. She fully expected to have her son and daughter returned to her by the end of the week, and then she would discover for herself how much they had missed their dearest mamma. No doubt, that she-devil who shared the Earl's bed had corrupted their minds, but she would soon disabuse them of false notions and correct their faults. It was her duty as their mother, and their duty as her children to obey.

She bustled back to her waiting guests, invigorated that her plans were coming to fruition. It was a stroke of luck—or mayhap it was ordained that her plans be given a helping hand—that Salt was hosting a masquerade ball at the end of the sennight. The day after the masquerade, all her troubles would be over. The Earl would again be hers alone. There would be nothing left in his life to distract him from his purpose. He would be able to focus exclusively on becoming First Lord of the Treasury and she would be there beside him, basking in his glory as she had done before.

While incarcerated in her Welsh prison, she had racked her brain to find a means of being reunited with the Earl, a means that would forever bind him to her. Every day she dreamed of being Countess of Salt Hendon, and every day she permitted the ignorant yokels to think of her as such. Parading about Harlech Castle as if she were in truth Lady Salt fed her addiction and focused her mind. It helped her realize that her dream was not an impossible one. One day she would be Countess of Salt Hendon.

And then, as if by divine providence, the answer came to her in a dream. Sorrow. Not just grief, but unimaginable sorrow. Only with unimaginable sorrow would the Earl be hers again.

She truly was a genius.

The death of her husband from smallpox showed her the way forward and out of her present predicament.

She recalled the Earl's devastation at the loss of his closest cousin and best friend to smallpox. The Earl's best friend, Aubrey St. John, had been her husband. Far from being a grieving widow, she had been relieved at his passing. But she had hidden her relief with a mask of sorrow to match the grief experienced by the Earl. In mourning the loss of Aubrey St. John together, they had never been closer. It was only in a state of grief-stricken distraction that the Earl fully appreciated what she meant to him. Everything and everyone else in his life was reduced to little or no consequence. Only the here and now had mattered; *she* had mattered. So it would be again between them.

There was no better way for them to bond than through the Earl's unimaginable sorrow. Mutual grief and loss would unite them, this time forever. He would welcome her comfort and counsel with open arms. She would make certain there was no chance of him ever making a recovery. No one recovered from the loss of one's entire family. There would be no hope left to him other than the hope she provided. He would see that her devotion was constant and unflagging, and she would again be the singular focus of his attention. He would need her to prop him up, to show him that he could overcome his loss for the greater good. To be great, he had to forgo the ordinary; sacrifices were required if he was to be immortalized. No one entered the pages of history as a consequence of being a family man. The thought was a ludicrous one, and he would come to realize this once he reached his potential as the political leader of his country.

Her plans were in place. She was counting the days with barely-disguised glee. What remained for her to do was to discover the depths of her brother's ignorance, and deal with him accordingly. She smiled to herself. Such a kind-hearted blockhead as her brother was the least of her worries.

EIGHT

THE SHORT CARRIAGE RIDE TO GROSVENOR SQUARE WAS accomplished in silence. Lady Reanay and Kitty Aldershot, sitting opposite Lady Caroline, were tearfully ordered by her to make no comment. And so they remained silent and glanced at one another from time to time, while looking mutely on as Caroline averted her face, desolate—view blinded by tears, unaware of her shudders of misery.

Such was her distress that upon returning to Salt House, she failed to notice the mud-spattered carriage, with the family coat of arms on the black lacquered doors, in the street outside the main entrance. Once indoors, she fled up the main stairs without a second glance at the hive of officious activity that accompanies the arrival of the master of the house and his family.

Lady Reanay and Kitty Aldershot were more leisurely in alighting the carriage.

Despite the well-ordered pandemonium in the entrance hall, they were shown every courtesy by the butler, who appeared as if from nowhere to take their cloaks and tell them the happy news that the Countess and her young family had arrived safely, and with everyone in good health and the best of spirits.

Immediately, Lady Reanay and Kitty rushed to the nursery to meet the newest member of the family, whom they found sleeping peacefully in his cradle. A young nursery maid was gently rocking the cradle of the six-week-old Samuel Antony Hugh Sinclair, and obliged their curiosity by lightly pulling back the soft woolen coverlet so they could clearly see his chubby little face. There was much whispered cooing, and Lady Reanay declared the baby to be the spitting image of his handsome papa. The nursery maid volunteered the children had slept a good deal on the journey, so were much too excited to go to their beds. They could be found across the hall in the nursery's playroom with her ladyship and Miss Merry.

Here, Lady Reanay and Kitty Aldershot were greeted with such enthusiasm that they quite forgot Lady Caroline's misery while everyone became reacquainted over tea and macaroons. That is, until Miss Merry asked after her cousin, which soon had Lady Reanay whispering in a corner with the Countess, advising Jane that it was best she speak to Caroline directly. She would not tell her more. She would leave that to Caroline. If anyone could make the poor misguided girl see sense, it was Jane.

And so Lady Caroline found her desolation interrupted when her personal maid, who was ordered not to answer the outer door to anyone, not even if it was Lord Salt himself, opened the door without hesitation to the Countess's soft insistent scratching.

The Countess was taken into the pretty sitting room, where she discovered Caroline prostrate on the chaise longue by the fire, still dressed in her mauve and silver petticoats, still wearing her lace mittens and with a heeled mule kicked off to the Turkey rug. Her face was pressed into the softness of an embroidered pillow and upon hearing footfall she muttered something unintelligible into this pillow. It was only when Jane brushed aside the layers of crumpled silk so she could perch on the chaise longue's damask cushion, and put a hand to her sister-in-law's disordered coiffure, that Caroline realized it was not her maid but a visitor.

Jane did not wait for Caroline to decide whether to ignore her or satisfy her curiosity and sit up, saying evenly,

"Poor Aunt Alice cannot understand why you are so unhappy. That's all she would tell me. She said you must tell me your news yourself. So here I am. Of course, you do not have to tell me anything if you don't wish to, but if you do decide to confide in a sympathetic ear, sooner would be best, as Sam will be demanding my breast on the hour and he has no tolerance for my tardiness." She gave a little sigh, adding, as Caroline's tearstained face slowly turned on the pillow to regard her through a muss of red silken locks, "And while I am here, perhaps you can advise me if I am being selfish to employ a wet nurse so soon. Salt says I should have done so a fortnight ago, Sam is such a greedy little boy and bigger than Ned and Beth were at the same age. If not for the upcoming masquerade and all the organization that requires, and the night itself, I had meant to persist for another month, if only to absolve my guilt. I nursed Ned until he was a year old, and Beth was nine months before I handed her over to Nanny Browne. Poor Sam is to be denied such comfort much sooner than I had anticipated... Tell me what that says about my chances of suckling Baby Four at all when he arrives?"

At that, Caroline tossed aside the pillow and scrambled up to fling herself into Jane's embrace.

"Oh, Jane, as if *you* could ever be selfish! I should have stayed at Salt Hendon to be of some use to you. I should have been there instead of coming up to London before the family. If I'd stayed, I could have overseen the packing, taken on the children's supervision, anything—at least offered Merry some companionship if it had allowed you some respite. And I'd have told Salt what I thought of his *advice*. What does he know of a baby's needs?

"What do men know about—about *anything*," Caroline continued, warming to her topic. "They are such self-centered, self-absorbed creatures! They expect females to fall in with *their* plans, as if *they* know what is best for us, when they haven't an ounce of insight. They say and do things that make it impossible for us not to do as they wish. Even when it is our freely expressed desire to fall in with those plans, we should have the-the—*choice* to say yes of our own accord and in our own good time. Our choice should not be taken for granted by them, should it? Salt is selfish and unreasonable. He has no right to take *you* for granted, to expect *you* to give up suckling Sam so you can fall pregnant with Baby Four all the sooner because *he* wishes a dozen children! And so I will tell him when—"

"Dearest, I fell pregnant with Beth while still suckling Ned," Jane said quietly, gently brushing the hair from Caroline's flushed cheek, a heightened color to her own at sharing such a confidence. But she and Caroline had always been candid with one another and so she wasn't about to dissimulate now. She also suspected that much of Caroline's emotional diatribe was not about men in general, her dead husband or Salt, but about one man in particular. "You know your brother has never taken me for granted... When I fall pregnant with Baby Four it will be a blessing, not a burden, and that is entirely in His hands."

"Yes, yes, of course," Caroline replied, much subdued. She sat back and accepted the fresh linen handkerchief Caroline's personal maid had handed to Jane, and patted her blotchy, tearstained face. She blew her little nose and felt better for it, and with the handkerchief scrunched up in her hand met Jane's patient blue eyes.

"It wasn't my place to say what I did. Forgive me."

"No, it wasn't, but it hasn't stopped you in the past!" Jane quipped, and kissed Caroline's cheek when her sister-in-law's green eyes opened wide and she frowned with mortification. "Your brother would blush to hear our conversation. His ears are possibly burning brightly this very minute. But I do love that we can be candid with one another, always…"

She paused, allowing Caroline the opportunity to confide in her, and was rewarded when her sister-in-law shuddered in a great breath and nodded her agreement.

"I'm the one who's selfish and unreasonable," Caroline confessed. "And I know I'm miserable for its own sake. I should be the happiest girl alive. I'd dreamed of that moment for many years, and then when I married Aldershot, I never again dreamed of it happening. Well, how could it? And then Aldershot died and, oh Jane! You will think me the most horrid creature alive when I tell you my first thought after we buried Aldershot was that I was free, free to marry Antony! And now Antony has asked me to marry him, what do I say? I ask him why he has asked me."

"Antony? Sir Antony asked you to marry him?" Jane blinked and sat up very tall, incredulous.

Caroline grabbed Jane's hand. "Oh, Jane, I could not say yes even if I wanted to. But I could not bring myself to say no to him either because I desperately want to say yes! But when he discovers the truth… When Antony knows me for what I truly am, he will not want this Caroline at all, will he? He won't care for this Caroline. Will he, Jane? *Will he?*"

Jane blinked at her. It was as if the Antony Caroline was talking about was not real, but a conjured being from her imagination. It was not that she disbelieved Caroline that Sir Antony Templestowe had asked her to marry him, it was the fact the baronet was returned to London and without warning or notice. She tried to steady her voice.

"Where did you see him, Caro? When? I thought—"

"—he was in 'Petersburg?" Caroline interrupted. "So did we all until yesterday when I happened to see him. We traveled up Audley Street, and whom should I spy on the pavement outside his town-house? Antony! I was as shocked then as you look now. I had no idea at all. Did you know he was returning? Salt must have had a letter. Did he not tell you? And as if that weren't enough of a shock, today Aunt

Alice, Kitty and I attended a welcome home soirée for Antony *and* Diana—"

"*Diana?*"

"Yes."

The way in which Jane breathed the name told Caroline Cousin Diana's return from exile on the Continent was also news to the Countess. Did her brother keep everything to himself these days? She enlightened her sister-in-law.

"I have no idea why she invited Aunt Alice and me, when the last time we were in each other's company I wanted to strangle the life out of her for daring to presume she had the right to manage the teapot and dish out cups of tea in *your* sitting room. I dare her to try that today!"

"A soirée…?"

"Yes. All the guests are connected to the government or politically important enough for Diana to think them worthy of her attention." Caroline rolled her eyes, unimpressed. "Salt would know them all, of course, and that's why Diana invited them, to reacquaint herself with who's important. Someone—I would wager it was Dacre Wraxton— must have written and told her of Salt's decision to resume his government posts, and so she's come home to interfere and meddle in his political life, as she always did in the past. But if she thinks she can—"

"Did—Did she appear—*well?*"

"Diana is always at her best when surrounded by toadies," Caroline complained, but then instantly apologized. "Forgive me. That was uncharitable. She looked very well indeed and as beautiful as ever. Her gown was stare-worthy, all silver thread with sparkly sequined embroidery on the bodice and hem, and she wore a pair of matching mules. I think she wore diamonds, or was it a strand of pearls? Perhaps it was both." Caroline shrugged a shoulder and smiled crookedly. "Aunt Alice could tell you more. You know me, Jane. I prefer a redingote and a comfortable pair of walking half-boots." She stuck out her left foot and wriggled her toes out of the mule so that both her stockinged feet were bereft of shoes. "Heels make my arches ache… Strange that it took me three London seasons and two dozen pairs of high-heeled shoes to know myself better!"

"And it was at this soirée Sir Antony proposed…?"

Caroline nodded.

"Before Diana and the guests, he came straight up to me and without warning, without having said more than *two* words to me, he makes an exhibition of himself, as only he can, by dropping on one knee and asking me to marry him! Foolish man! As if I would say yes just like that!"

"And you did not...?" Jane was surprised.

"How can you think I could? It was a most romantic gesture, I agree, but... Jane, it's been four years since he went away and so much has happened to me... I've changed, and when he discovers just how much I have changed, he will be relieved I did not say yes." She pouted and looked at the crumpled handkerchief crushed in one hand. "Not that I said no," she admitted reluctantly. "I could not disappoint him then and there... Jane, I so dread him finding out—of seeing his disappointment... He won't want me then. He—"

Caroline stopped abruptly, realizing Jane was not listening. The Countess had a faraway look in her eye, but more disturbing, her hands were clasped so tightly together that the whites of her knuckles were showing through her translucent skin. It was Caroline's turn to put her hand out to the Countess, and was alarmed, not only by how cold were her fingers, but how her hands shook. In fact, Jane was doing her best to stop her whole body from trembling.

"Jane! Oh, Jane, why did you let me chatter on when you're not well?" Caroline called for her maid. "Elspeth! Cordial. Quickly!" When it came she put the tumbler into Jane's hands and had her drink. "You need to be put to bed with a mug of hot milk and have a good night's sleep. The journey from Hendon has exhausted you. And I have only added to your burden. Perhaps more fluids would help, what with feeding the baby..."

"Yes. Yes, that must be it," Jane murmured and handed off the glass tumbler, only having tasted a few sips of the bittersweet lemon water. What she wanted was a hot cup of tea in bed and that would come soon enough, but first she needed to find out what she could about Diana St. John's return. She waited until the maid had set the tray on the low table by the chaise longue, bobbed a curtsy and left the room, before she forced herself to say calmly, "So Di-Diana returned from the Continent a fortnight ago...?"

Caroline frowned.

"Didn't Salt tell you she was coming home? He must have pardoned her for her atrocious jealousy all those years ago... I don't know how he could! I don't know what persuasive argument she used, but Diana has always had a way of getting what she wants, particularly with my brother. You only have to watch how she treats Antony, as if he is her lackey! Hideous creature. But I suspect he allows her to have her own way with matters of no consequence to him." She peered at

Jane. "Are you any better for the cordial?" When the Countess nodded, she was not convinced but asked, "Is this truly the first you have heard mention of Diana's return?"

"Oh, I'm sure your brother must have told me, I'd just forgotten," Jane replied airily and hated herself for lying.

She was sick to her stomach at the thought of such an evil creature as Diana St. John again roaming free, and worse, in such close proximity as to be living just a street away. She could hardly believe it true. Salt had assured her his cousin was forever banished, that never again would she need to worry for her personal safety, or his, or that of their children. Diana's twins Ron and Merry would also be safe from their mother's evil. She had never enquired where Diana was incarcerated; she did not want to know. She only asked that she be treated humanely, but locked away from good society forever more. She had an irresistible and quite irrational need to run to the nursery to see with her own eyes her three children and Merry all safe and well and sleeping peacefully in their beds. At least with Ron away at Eton, he was out of his mother's evil orbit.

But Caroline, along with Lady Reanay and the majority of Society, had no inkling of the truth behind Diana's banishment, and there had never been a need to enlighten them. Not for one moment did Jane believe Salt had sanctioned Diana's release. She wondered if in fact he knew, and would spend a sleepless night wondering because he had yet to arrive in town, breaking his journey with her and the children to accompany Ron to Windsor, and see him settled in at Eton.

She curbed her instincts, forcing herself to be calm, to wait, to put wild imaginings about Diana to the back of her thoughts so she could concentrate on Caroline's news and why her sister-in-law felt unequal to accepting Sir Antony Templestowe's marriage proposal.

Simply knowing Antony had returned to London was a comfort and did much to lift her spirits. As did the news he had asked Caroline to marry him. She had prayed for this outcome since Caroline was made a widow. That it had finally happened was cause for celebration, not misery, and she had a sneaking suspicion as to why her sister-in-law was miserable, but she needed to hear her say why before she could offer a solution she hoped she could accept.

"Salt possibly told me about Antony returning to London, too, but again, I'm certain I am at fault for being so forgetful," she explained to Caroline. She tried her best to sound offhand. "No doubt I was in some nether world while Sam was feeding. The past six weeks have gone by so quickly, most of it in a blur, which is quite usual for a mother with a newborn." She patted Caroline's hand. "No matter. I shall ask Salt to repeat it all to me tomorrow. He should be home before nuncheon." She cocked her head at Caroline. "But I interrupted you telling me about Antony and his very romantic proposal..."

Caroline plucked at a silken thread of the intricate embroidery that bordered the hem of her silk petticoats. "It was everything a girl could ask for... Why, I think I even dreamed of him on bended knee asking me to marry him! But you, more than any other, know why I must decline, why I cannot marry him."

"No. I do not," Jane said bluntly. "Not if you love him..."

"But you know, Jane. *You know* why I can't be his wife."

Jane regarded her sister-in-law with a sad smile. Yes, she did know to what she alluded and understood Caroline's distress, but she had a solution that would help ease Caroline's conscience. It was not something she would ever have contemplated suggesting before her own marriage, but an absurdly happy marriage, and now being the mother of three thriving children had given her latitude to be more pragmatic.

She knew very well that Salt had been compelled to marry his sister off to a fortune hunter to save her honor and the family from unwanted gossip, but her noble husband remained ignorant of the true nature of events of that fateful night of the masquerade, and to Jane's mind that was not a bad thing. She doubted Salt would cope well with the truth. He had not coped well with the fiction told to him about his sister and Stephen Aldershot, but it was easier for him to believe that the two young people had been so caught up in the passionate moment as to forget themselves. He had never shown his true feelings about his sister's marriage to anybody, only to her, and Jane knew he was devastated by it. She also knew he blamed the events leading up to Caroline's marriage, and the marriage itself, on Sir Antony Templestowe, and that there was nothing Jane could say to dissuade him otherwise.

"You need not tell Antony about your marriage; any of it. There is no reason you should."

Caroline blinked at Jane, shocked.

"Jane? Are *you* telling me to-to *lie*? To *Antony*?"

"Not at all. All I am saying is that you need not tell him. There is a difference."

"And if I do not tell him, he will never know?"

"You have never told Salt, and as I will never tell him, he will never know. Why should Antony be any different? Even if he does find out far into the future, or you decide you must tell him—though why you would do so after years of being married to Antony I know not—when you start a family of your own, do you think what happened before you married Antony, before you became one, will hold any significance for him when he loves you so very dearly?"

When Caroline looked unconvinced, Jane took hold of her hand with a smile of reassurance.

"Many years ago, before your brother and I were married, when I was at a very low place in my thoughts, my nurse gave me a wonderful piece of advice. She told me to always look to the future, not to look back, not to dwell in the past. And that is what you must do, Caro, so that you and Antony can have a future together."

"Your nurse was a wise woman."

"Yes. And if she were here today, she would tell you that if Antony cares about the past and not his future with you, then he was never the man for you. Of course, it is my considered opinion that the moment he discovered you were no longer married, all he has been thinking about is the future, a future he can share with you."

Caroline smiled askance.

"It is all very well for you to consign a bride's virginity to the dust of least consequence, dearest Jane, when you were as white and as pure as a falling snowflake on your wedding night."

"I was no such thing!" Jane retorted, startling Caroline into shocked disbelief.

"Jane! No. Not *you*."

"Whether I was a-a *snowflake* or not, is neither here nor there to your predicament," Jane managed to say with head held high, though her throat had stained red with the embarrassment of blunt confession. She added in a rush, because her sister-in-law was staring at her as if she had run mad, "You are not to breathe that revelation to another living soul, particularly not to your brother."

"Of course not, Jane. Never." Caroline inched closer to Jane, green eyes very wide. "Was it your nurse who told you not to tell Salt?"

Jane blinked at the question, and then put a hand to her mouth to stifle a giggle.

"Oh, Caro! No. No. Silly me! I gave you the wrong impression altogether, for which I apologize. There has never been any other man but Magnus, so banish those evil thoughts about me, wicked sister. But he would be furiously embarrassed, and very disappointed in me, if he ever discovered his little sister knew we had made love before going up before parson."

"He is such a stick in the mud!" Caroline complained good-naturedly. "And become so stuffy since marrying you, that it is hard to believe he ever had a mistress in his past, least of all dozens of them!"

"Thank you, Caro, I believe we will keep your brother's past where it belongs."

"Yes, of course," Caroline murmured, though she could not help adding cheekily, "But I always knew him to have a soft center, and where you are concerned his heart has always ruled his stuffy head. Which is no bad thing." She squeezed Jane's hand. "Thank you for taking me into your confidence."

Jane smiled and returned the pressure on Caroline's fingers.

"I confided this in you so you are aware you're not the only member of this family to have allowed lust to overrule good sense—"

"But you and Salt were in love," Caroline argued. "What happened at the masquerade had nothing to do with love! And my absurd marriage to Aldershot—"

"As for your marriage to Aldershot," Jane repeated, cutting Caroline off before she could spiral away into another episode of self-recrimination, "you were married for two years. So unless Antony is a complete simpleton, he is not expecting you to be a snowflake on your wedding night, is he?"

"No, no, he is not," Caroline murmured and blushed, not because the thought had never occurred to her, but because there was a matter of a more serious nature, one that crippled her with guilt and made her so ashamed that she had never been able to bring herself to confide this in Jane. She wondered what Sir Antony would think of her should he ever discover her shameful secret? Would he forgive her? Would he ever trust her? Would he ever want such a woman as his wife? She thought not. Better she lose his love than his respect. She shuddered at the prospect.

"So you have nothing to tell him, have you?" Jane reasoned as she stood and shook out her glazed cotton petticoats.

"No. No. I do not," Caroline murmured, up on her stocking feet. She smiled, not because she was any less miserable, but because she did not want to add to Jane's burden. What was the point of ruminating further on a future with Sir Antony she knew was impossible?

"Now you must excuse me." Jane kissed her sister-in-law's forehead. "Sam will be wailing by this hour and I dare not leave him with his nursery maid much longer. The girl is young and quite new to the household. Salt scares the poor creature witless."

"He scares everyone witless," Caroline replied good-naturedly, following her to the outer door. "If not for you, dearest Jane, the servants would be dropping with fright on a regular basis."

Both women parted with an affectionate kiss, but Jane's smile died the moment a liveried footman closed the door to Lady Caroline's apartment. She hurried to the nursery, an unreasonable dread pressing on her chest. Until she saw her children safely tucked up in their little beds and the baby in his cradle, her thudding heart would not quiet.

NINE

JANE TOOK THE STAIRCASE CONNECTING HER PRIVATE ROOMS with the nursery directly above on the third floor. She found Nanny Browne supervising the nursery maids setting to rights the toys and furniture in the playroom, and went through to the spacious bedchamber occupied by her two eldest children. The room had no doors, but was kept warm by a velvet portière pulled across the doorway at sleep times, and a constant coal fire in the grate of a large fireplace. Its warm, orange glow illuminated the polished brass back of a tapestry fire screen that provided a comforting light should the children wake in the night.

Her heart slowed and swelled with love seeing Ned and Beth deep asleep in their beds, tired-out little bodies tucked up under soft coverlets. Her son clutched his favorite toy, a much-loved cloth monkey stitched by his Aunt Caro, while her daughter had a chubby arm flung above her head of black curls tucked up in a lace nightcap, face turned on the down pillow towards the wallpaper. Satisfied, she went through to the baby's room. Here her infant son spent his sleeping hours during the day, watched over by the new nursery maid. He would be spending more of his time here, now they were in London and she was required to fulfill her duties as countess and attend and host dinner parties, something she was sure would be a regular occurrence with Salt returning to his government posts. A second cradle remained in her bedchamber and she had been reluctant to have it removed until the wet nurse was installed. Caroline's news of Diana's return from exile decided her: Sam would continue to spend his nights in her bedchamber until she was convinced her children were safe from harm.

Her expression must have given away her deep anxiety, because the new nursery maid so far forgot herself as to address Jane before she herself was addressed, saying with concern as she bobbed a curtsy,

"Forgive me, my lady. I only picked him up the once. He'd been fretting. He's ever so hungry—"

"Betsy! Mind your manners!" said a clipped voice at the Countess's shoulder, Nanny Browne stepping forward to take the wailing baby from the nursery maid. "Her ladyship didn't address you, nor does her ladyship wish to hear what you have to say."

"Oh, but I do, Nanny, if it has anything to do with my children," Jane said pleasantly, a smile at the new nursery maid who had dropped her gaze to the floor the moment Nanny Browne walked into the room. "I'm not surprised Sam is fretting. He must be very hungry by now. But Mamma will soon have you content," she said in soothing accents as she peered down at her wailing son squirming in Nanny Browne's arms. "If I am not in the way, I shall feed Sam here..."

Instantly, the servants went into action. A footman positioned the wingchair and footstool not too near the warmth radiating from the small fireplace, then promptly left the room to have an upstairs maid fetch her ladyship a pot of tea and a plate with bread and butter. A now-screaming Samuel was handed back to the new nursery maid so Nanny Browne could assist with untying the ribbons either side of her ladyship's quilted jumps. Jane, once seated comfortably in the wingchair, her feet upon the padded stool and a cushion placed under her elbow, deftly unhooked the front of her maternity stays, allowing her infant son access to what he most desired. All this was accomplished with the greatest speed, and within minutes the Countess's youngest son was no longer distressed, and the room was again at peace.

"Come along, Betsy," Nanny Browne ordered the new nursery maid, who was staring at the Countess suckling her infant, "I'll find you something to do."

Jane looked up from admiring her son, who had his tiny chubby fingers clamped hard about her index finger.

"Nanny, be good enough to have a maid look in on Miss Merry. She is in the habit of taking Viscount Fourpaws to bed with her, but since Dr. Barlow tells us it is his fur that causes her sneezing, his fluffy lordship is relegated to his basket by the fire in my sitting room."

"Very good, my lady."

When Nanny Browne jerked her head at the new nursery maid, signal for her to leave the room with her, Jane said, "If you do not have need of Betsy she may remain here, and when the teapot arrives, make herself useful in that way."

The head of the nursery closed her mouth, bobbed another curtsy, and with a warning look at Betsy, which went unnoticed because Jane's attention had returned to her feeding infant, she left the new nursery maid alone with the Countess of Salt Hendon.

Being alone with her ladyship was a novel experience for Betsy. She had never been alone with anyone higher on the social register in the Earl's household than his steward, and she had hardly been able to form a sentence in that officious gentleman's presence. That was just as well, because had Mr. Willis probed her responses a little deeper, he would have discovered that Betsy Smith was not all she said she was, nor were her impressive references genuine. The only details that were true about Betsy Smith were her name and, being the eldest of fourteen children, her experience with infants and very young children. What her ladyship could possibly have to say to her, Betsy had no idea, but what she did know was that this beautiful lady could have no inkling of what was in store for her and her children.

Betsy had no real idea either, but she had an awful feeling in her gut that whatever it was, it was bad. Aunt Smith, who was not in truth her aunt but a long-time family friend who happened to have the same surname, confided that the woman parading about Polite Society as the Countess of Salt Hendon was not a countess at all, and thus not the true wife of the Earl, but his harlot, who had stolen the Earl from his true wife. The Earl had banished his true wife and entered into an unnatural marriage with his mistress. Aunt Smith said the Earl was bewitched by the harlot's beauty, which, gazing at her feeding her infant, Betsy could readily believe. Aunt Smith was helping the true countess regain what was rightfully hers, and if Betsy's father wanted his debts paid and release from Bridewell House on Pinfold Street— Birmingham's overcrowded and filthy jail and debtors prison—then all George Smith had to do was give Betsy into the care of Bertha Smith.

George Smith readily complied. He did more than that. He told Betsy to do whatever was necessary to help Aunt Smith, short of murder, which would see Betsy hang and what was the use of a dead daughter to him? He certainly wouldn't be released and Betsy had to remember to put her father and her thirteen brothers and sisters before herself; it's what her dead ma would expect.

Betsy was a good, obedient daughter, and off she went with Aunt Smith and onto the Birmingham-to-Hendon stagecoach. It was on the stagecoach that Aunt Smith told her she was to be a nursery maid in the Earl of Salt Hendon's household, and when called upon, she was to do precisely as Aunt Smith instructed. Besides obtaining the coin necessary to get her father released from Bridewell House, she would be helping a great lady regain what was rightfully hers, which was surely the right thing to do.

To her great surprise and trepidation, before entering the stagecoach for the journey to Hendon, she was brought before the true Countess of Salt Hendon. She had never been in the presence of nobility before, and she was so frightened and awed by the grand lady in the magnificently embroidered velvet gown that she was sick to her stomach. The true Countess of Salt Hendon was everything she dreamed a great lady would be: Beautiful, richly attired, and coldly disdaining of everyone who fell under her gaze.

Betsy was not surprised when the great lady looked at her with disapproval, commented that her hair reminded her of an untrimmed gooseberry bush, and sniffed when Aunt Smith apologized that Betsy had suffered a bout of cowpox but was not, as her ladyship had hoped, suffering with the smallpox—a consequence the true Countess of Salt Hendon had lamented. It was a pity Betsy wasn't riddled with the smallpox, because the contagion was just what she needed to wipe clean the present scourge from the Earl's household, to which Aunt Smith had said "Amen".

Betsy was given a clean linen gown, a pair of stockings, and secondhand leather shoes that pinched her little toes. She was also provided with an excellent character reference from a previous employer, whose name Betsy had never heard but was assured a copy of the reference had done the trick in gaining her employment in the Salt Hendon household. Mr. Willis had immediately employed Betsy on the strength of that reference. Joining the ranks of the Earl's battalion of servants could not have been easier.

What was easier were her daily duties, Betsy thought with a smile. She was given a warm roof over her head and kept fed, and all to care for the most beautiful baby boy she had ever set eyes on. He was no trouble at all. He cried only when he was hungry, and who could blame him for that? Her brothers and sisters had done it often enough, but once weaned from their mother's breast they had often gone hungry. This baby boy would never face a hungry day in his life, and at his rate of growth, Betsy reckoned he was going to grow into a big handsome lad just like his noble father.

"Mr. Willis tells me you are not from Wiltshire… Betsy?"

Betsy bobbed a curtsy and dropped her trance-like gaze from the suckling infant to the floor, face aglow at such thoughts being interrupted by the nobleman's false wife.

"No, my lady. Birmingham."

"You are permitted to look at me, Betsy. In fact, I would prefer that you do. It makes for more pleasant conversation."

"Yes, my lady," Betsy murmured, praying the conversation did not turn to questions about her previous employment. Her prayer went unanswered.

"Your position before this one was in the nursery of Lady Elizabeth Sedley…? When she was staying in Bath…?"

"Yes, my lady," Betsy lied. "But I never seen her ladyship." Which was the truth, and at the Countess's quizzical frown, lied again for good measure. "She never visited the nursery."

Knowing her friend well, and that she, too, was very much a hands-on mother like Jane, she was surprised by this, but did not contradict the girl. Before putting her contented son to her other breast, she held him to her shoulder to let his stomach settle, saying as she gently rubbed his back,

"I know it's only been a few months since you assisted in the Sedley nursery, so you will be pleased to know you will have the opportunity to become reacquainted with your Sedley babies. Lady Elizabeth and her three children will be here for an afternoon tea and a play next week. They are all eager to make Sam's acquaintance. And you, my darling," she said, holding her gurgling son up to her smiling face and rubbing her nose against his before kissing his ripe cheek, "will be on your best behavior. Unlike your brother, who is an outrageous show-off, and Beth, who is feeling less special because she is no longer the baby of the family, so will no doubt test Mamma's patience with her demands."

She moved the cushion to the other arm of the wingchair, Betsy quick to come to her aid, and with her baby son again settled at her breast, looked up with a smile.

"Perhaps we shall dress Beth in new petticoats and ribands for her hair so she feels special for our guests. What do you think, Betsy?"

Startled to be asked her opinion, Betsy nodded her agreement and as a maid had arrived with the tea tray, was relieved to have something to do that she hoped would preclude more questions being asked by the Earl's false wife.

With the tea poured, sugar and a slice of lemon added, and this and the plate of bread and butter slices put within the Countess's reach, Betsy retreated to stand by the cradle where she went about neatly tucking the sheets and coverlet, anything to avoid being asked questions she could not answer. It worked for a time, but when Sam was replete, Jane had Betsy cradle him while she readjusted her clothing.

"When you have changed him into clean linens and a nightgown, please bring him down to my rooms."

Betsy's eyes went very wide, and in her panic she so far forgot herself as to be unintentionally rude.

"I've never been downstairs! I wouldn't know where to find—"

"Have Nanny show you. You need to know where Sam sleeps when he is not with you. That way, if I need you, if Sam needs me, you will know where to come." When Betsy continued to frown, though she bobbed a curtsy and nodded her understanding, Jane came over to her. "I am certain Mr. Willis and Nanny both explained everything you needed to know about your position in his lordship's household...?"

"Yes, my lady, they did."

"Good. And if you have any questions or need assistance, you go to Nanny without hesitation?"

"Yes, my lady. Nanny Browne treats me fair."

"I am pleased to hear it, Betsy."

"I like my work, my lady," Betsy blurted out and bobbed another curtsy, a glance down at the sleeping infant in her arms. "Sam's a bonny baby—I mean—Beggin' your ladyship's pardon—Samuel."

"Sam is best, Betsy. Always Sam."

"Yes, my lady."

"I wanted to speak to you myself, because now we are in London, I will be spending more time away from my baby, which means he will be spending more time with you. Nanny tells me you take very good care of Sam and are also very patient with Ned and Beth, too, who both like you. Nothing is more important to his lordship and to me than our children, Betsy. That means who takes care of them and how they are cared for is of supreme importance. Do you understand?"

Awed by her ladyship's words, Betsy nodded. To her way of thinking, she spoke exactly as she imagined a great lady would speak, and acted like one, too. And she was very pretty and wore the most beautiful clothes, all satins and silks with wondrous embroidery. And she was kind. Come to think on it, in the six weeks she had been part of the Salt Hendon household, not one servant had an unkind word to say about her ladyship. The other nursery maids only said good things about the Earl's false wife, and when Nanny Browne mentioned her ladyship it was as if she worshipped the ground she walked on! She certainly did not appear or act the bad person Aunt Smith said she was. For the first time since becoming part of the Salt Hendon household the thought occurred to Betsy that Aunt Smith may have spun her a web of lies. But how could that be, and to what purpose? Although, watching the Earl's false wife suckling her infant, it occurred to Betsy that a true lady and a countess, would not stoop to suckling. A nobleman's true wife gave her infant over to a wet nurse to feed; everyone knew that.

As if reading her mind, the Countess said,

"Because I will be spending time away from my baby, most reluctantly I am forced to employ a wet nurse to cater to Sam's needs." Her ladyship smiled down at her son in Betsy's arms and gently caressed his smooth brow with one long finger. "But I don't want her arrival to stop you giving my darling little boy lots of cuddles. That's what he needs most when I cannot be with him." She looked at Betsy. "I want you to go on holding him whenever you please. Babies cannot be spoiled enough. Do you understand me, Betsy?"

"Yes, my lady."

"I am pleased we understand one another. The cradle is in my bedchamber. Dicken—you are acquainted with my personal maid—will show you if I am indisposed. And if I am not there, please wait until I return. Sam is never to be left alone, Betsy. Ever."

Betsy audibly gulped and far from making her ladyship angry, Jane laughed behind her hand, remembering what Caroline had said about Salt scaring the servants witless.

"You have nothing to fear by coming downstairs to our rooms," she assured her. "I trust you with Sam, Betsy. I trust *you*. And if I trust you, then so does Lord Salt."

"Thank you, my lady," Betsy said in an awed whisper, holding her precious bundle wrapped in his soft baby blanket a little closer. No one in her young life had ever trusted her with anything before, or spoken to her with such kindness.

Having her ladyship's trust made her feel her life was worth something after all; that she had a purpose and it was important, *she* was important. Never mind that if she did Aunt Smith's bidding, her father would be released from Bridewell House and her brothers and sisters not be forced to beg on the streets. Helping her family was expected and retribution threatened if she failed them, not least a good beating from her unforgiving father. Betsy so wanted to believe in her heart of hearts that this beautiful kind creature was indeed the real countess. She wished, too, that she could help her avoid what Aunt Smith said was her due for her wickedness in stealing away the Earl from his true wife.

She had no idea what reckoning was planned for the Earl's false wife, and even if she did, what could she, a lowly nursery maid do to prevent it?

It was not the specter of Aunt Smith's anger that kept Betsy silent and biddable, it was the frightening image of the true Countess of Salt Hendon. She might not be able to put a stop to whatever was planned for the false wife, but there was one thing she knew she could do. She vowed with every fiber of her being not to allow harm to come to the baby cradled in her arms. And as if hearing her silent vow, Samuel Antony Hugh Sinclair, second in line to an ancient earldom, turned his head to the warmth of Betsy's body and gave a contented milk-drugged sigh.

TEN

WITH LADY REANAY SAFELY OUT OF THE HOUSE, DIANA ST. JOHN re-entered the salon with a self-satisfied smile. She swept up to her brother, who was being showered with good wishes upon his engagement to Lady Caroline Aldershot, and led him away, to the clavichord, with the pretext of wanting a private word. In truth, she was unhappy the focus of her little gathering had shifted from her successful return to society's bosom to her sentimental brother's maudlin and very public proposal of marriage.

Still numb and feeling as if he had just lived through a dream, Sir Antony acquiesced to his sister's request, hearing only one word in ten of the guests' congratulatory good wishes. He was still dazed by his outlandish behavior, given what had occurred the last time he and Lady Caroline were together in company, and because Caroline had hesitated to say yes. He had expected, naively in hindsight, she would be elated he had finally proposed, and would accept without hesitation. After all, it was what they both wanted, wasn't it?

When he realized Diana had brought him to stand before the clavichord, he mentally shook his thoughts free of Caroline. It did not do to cloud his mind in a mental fog around his sister. With supreme effort of will, he turned his attention to her.

Diana sat beside him on the padded music stool, back to the clavichord's ivory keys, and said with a tight smile, "Well, brother dear, you have done what I thought impossible! You have surprised me. Twice in two days, in fact."

"How so?" he asked mildly, setting the score sheet on the music stand and staring, not at her, but at the crotchets and quavers in front of him. He hoped his voice held a note of disinterest.

"I never thought to see *you* lean and sober." She cocked her head, studying his profile. "I am undecided if I like you this way…"

"When you have made up your mind, I am sure you will let me know."

She gave a huff of harsh laughter. "That I will!"

"And the second?"

"Your impetuous proposal to Caroline."

"Impetuous?"

"Dear me, Antony, I knew she had a girlish infatuation for you, and you indulged her, but to offer her your name…?" She leaned against his silken shoulder. "But perhaps you truly are ignorant, or allowed yourself to be deluded into ignorance? What a shame your declaration was so public, you cannot now retract your offer…"

It took all his self-control not to move away from her proximity. Yet, for one moment, he allowed himself to believe his sister capable of normal emotion and he dropped his guard. "I love Caroline. I have wanted to marry her since I can remember. That's all there is to it, Di."

"Love her? How quaint," she responded dismissively and sighed her resignation. "But you were ever the romantic, and that is why you will never rise to the dizzying heights of the Privy Council. Unlike Salt, you are incapable of detaching your feelings when making a decision. In politics, the end always justifies the means, as it does in war. Do you know the gentleman seated in conversation with Mr. Wraxton?"

Sir Antony was in no mood for one of Diana's lectures on his lack of political acumen, nor did he know where his sister's thoughts were leading, but he humored her by glancing across the clavichord to just beyond the harp to the row of chairs set up for the recital. Mr. Dacre Wraxton was in deep conversation with a gentleman of middling years and upright posture, in full military uniform that was as bright as his expression was dour. He did not know the man personally, but he knew Sir Jeffrey Amherst had been stationed in the American Colonies for some years. Lady Reanay confided this over her teacup, and that Sir Jeffrey had recently married for the second time, a much younger woman, the daughter of a General, whose name Sir Antony had not bothered to remember.

"That's Amherst. Not even a nodding acquaintance, I'm not sorry to say. Military types don't interest me. Aunt Alice tells me he recently married the daughter of a brother officer…"

Diana gave a snort of dismissal.

"Your reply illustrates my point! You remember what is unimportant, when others—*Salt*—would be able to tell you, as I can, all about Sir Jeffrey's illustrious military career. We have been correspondents for years," she informed him with a self-satisfied smile and pulled a face. "Of what importance is his remarriage, if you do not know Amherst's bride is the daughter of General Cary; the only reason a man like Amherst would look at such an insipid creature twice! What you should know, and need to remember is, it is these *military types* who allow us to live civilized lives. Amherst fought in the French and Indian War and was instrumental in not only defeating those savages fighting for the French, but he managed to have such native brutes and their tribes wiped from the face of the earth."

"I beg your pardon, he did *what?*"

Diana St. John misread her brother's mood, mistaking his startled horror for appreciative amazement.

"The colonists have always been plagued by savages; those on the frontiers even more so. What to do about them has been a constant headache for the colonial administration, and the government here at home. I cannot tell you if it was Amherst who had the clever idea or one of his subordinates. Whatever, that is unimportant. What is important is that it was dear Sir Jeffrey who approved the scheme."

"Scheme?"

"He gave them the smallpox."

"He gave them *what?*"

"Oh do listen, Antony! Smallpox. Not personally." She sighed her annoyance with her brother's total lack of comprehension, adding in a voice used with a small child, "When the savages came to parley, soldiers from our fort gave them blankets taken from the military smallpox hospital. The blankets were polluted with smallpox, and when the savages took them back to their camp, they infected not only themselves, but the tribe and anyone else they came into contact with."

Sir Antony felt queasy and he dared to ask, though he was certain he knew the answer,

"Men, women *and* children?"

Diana St. John could hardly contain her enthusiasm. "Of course, men, women and children. It wiped out their entire tribe; every last savage. You must admit," she added gleefully, "Amherst is a genius. To rid oneself of an enemy without that enemy ever knowing what hit them, without the need to shed a drop of English blood, is worthy of a medal!"

Sir Antony felt physically ill and wished himself a thousand miles from his sister. He stared at Sir Jeffrey Amherst with unconcealed loathing.

"A man who can inflict such suffering on the defenseless, the helpless and the young is nothing less than a monster; his method, monstrous. I won't listen to you sing his praises. In fact, I don't want him in my drawing room!" Sir Antony growled, buttocks up off the music stool.

Diana St. John pushed him down again, an elbow to his shoulder, and kept it there.

"Remember we are not alone, little brother," she cautioned and made a display of rustling her petticoats, a sweeping glance with fixed smile at her guests, who were entertaining themselves taking wagers as to the possible date for Sir Antony and Lady Caroline's nuptials. She returned her gaze to her brother, saying matter-of-factly, "You always did allow emotion to rule good sense. Amherst did what he had to do for the good of the kingdom. Nothing more. Nothing less. In war, all actions are justifiable."

"Any action can be justified but that doesn't make it ethical or-or *right*. Murdering women and children is never justifiable, in war, or anywhere else! I won't have it, Di!"

"And I won't have you interfering in my plans for Salt's political rehabilitation."

Sir Antony blinked. Mention of the Earl of Salt Hendon knocked the sense back into him. He could have kicked his own stockinged shin for letting down his guard. What was the point in arguing with his sister? She was not a rational human being. She lacked empathy and had no conscience, her admiration for Amherst underscored that. Why had he stupidly thought he could make her see his point of view? Subdued, he asked her mildly,

"What plans are they, Di?"

"I have returned to London at the perfect time for Salt to re-enter the political fray," she replied with a confident smile. "He is on his way to London, and due to arrive in town tomorrow for this very reason. The newssheets cannot waste enough ink on speculation as to Salt's intentions. The government is in disarray. Not Grafton, Newcastle, nor Bute can agree on appropriate measures, and the House remains crippled by division. It is the perfect scenario for Salt to step up and take control, and I am here to see he finally achieves his political potential."

Sir Antony hesitated to respond. He did not doubt she truly believed what she was saying, which was further evidence of her unsound mind. He wondered how she knew the Earl's movements, but then Aunt Alice could have told her, or perhaps Dacre Wraxton, as a Member of Parliament and one of Salt's factional supporters, had dropped the news in his conversation. For the moment, he decided to play along with his sister's delusions—it might be the only way of discovering exactly how she planned to help Salt achieve his political ambitions.

With this in mind, he faced her and forced himself to take hold of her hand. He just prayed his voice remained as steady as his fingers.

"I would hate to interfere with your plans for Salt, so perhaps it would be wise to let me know your intentions... I may be able to help...?"

Diana smiled at her brother's long fingers about her hand and then raised her gaze to his blue eyes, face devoid of her thoughts. Sir Antony hoped his features remained composed, though his heart thudded against his chest and he half-expected the demon within to break through his sister's lovely form and take him by the throat. It did not, and she remained poised, though he detected a gleam in her eye when she said silkily,

"Always good. Always honorable. But what has goodness and honor got you, Antony? Thirty years of age and still not an ambassador. Though... Mr. Wraxton did confide a piece of news about you which did surprise me, and gives me hope you will make something of yourself of which I can finally be proud. But I shan't tell you. No! Don't ask. Salt must be the one to tell you, not I," she demanded when he went to speak, and put a finger to his parted lips. When he closed his mouth she removed her finger to tap his clean-shaven cheek annoyingly. "You were the only one to care; the only one to write; the only one I will spare... Come! We have neglected our guests long enough, and now we must not talk of politics, but play," she insisted, coming to a sense of her surroundings and the noise of uncontrolled chatter from restless guests waiting for the performance to begin.

She was up off the music stool, and would have gone over to the harp but Sir Antony grabbed her wrist. He knew his efforts would be in vain—How did one reason with a heartless serpent?—but he still had to try and reach within the recesses of his sister's mind for that speck of humanity he prayed still functioned.

"Di! *Listen*. I do care. I care very much. I *want* to help. I *can* help you, if you will let me."

"Help me?" she echoed, momentarily taken aback. "How can you help me?"

"I know what it's like to be so consumed by something or someone that nothing and no one else matters."

"I have no idea—"

"You must. We are brother and sister. We share more than a bond. We have the same blood running through our veins. We also have the same demon—"

"Demon?"

Hopeful he had connected with her rational self, he nodded, "Yes. That's right, Di. I fight the demon every day. You can, too. It's an obsession, a-a compulsion we—"

"Obsession? Compulsion? Really, Antony, I have no idea what you are driveling on about!"

"*Listen*, Di. If you let the demon control you, it will kill you…"

"Kill me? How?"

"The only way to control the demon is to stay away from Salt. You *must* stay away from him and his countess."

At the mention of the Countess of Salt Hendon, Diana St. John wrenched her wrist free with a snarl, the veil of rationality, of caring older sister and of gracious hostess, slipping for the merest of moments before being quickly reinstated with a forced laugh and flutter of her fan. She tapped her brother playfully on the wrist and said loudly, so the others could hear,

"Of course you are capable of playing the piece, Antony! No one will think less of you should your fingers trip up once or twice. For luck," she added, leaning in to kiss his cheek.

"No good will come of your return to London, Di," Sir Antony whispered in a rush.

She kissed his cheek and said at his ear, "I mean to spare you, dearest brother, but I insist that *you* stay out of *my* way."

"What of Ron and Merry? Shall they be spared, too?"

"Ron and Merry?" Diana St. John blinked with incomprehension. "Why do you evoke their names?"

"They are your children, Di. They—"

"—will be returned to me, have no fear of that!" she spat. "*She* took them from me! *She* poisoned their minds against me. They've been bewitched by that *she-devil* to *hate* me but I shall soon have them good, obedient children again."

"Nonsense. Ron and Merry are still your children. They will always love you. You will always be their mother. Yet, you cannot want them going through life suffering ridicule and shame? That is precisely what will happen to them if you do not give up these schemes and plans while there is still time—"

"*Fool.* My plans were well underway before I arrived in London!"

Her smile was smug. As his eyes went wide with new knowledge, she leaned across him, as if to correct the sit of the sheets of music on the stand. In fact, what she did was slide a hand between the silk lining of his frock coat and the embroidered front of his waistcoat, to the place over his heart where he kept pinned the small gold brooch containing the miniature of Lady Caroline bordered by a tiny plait of her strawberry blonde hair.

Sir Antony wondered what she was about when she pressed her palm to his chest, and reasoned if she wanted a true measure of his anxiety then it could be found in the hard elevated beat of his heart. What she did next startled him to immobility by its very viciousness. Her fingers found the catch to the brooch. She twisted it open and tore it free from his waistcoat. Brooch in her fist, she shoved her hand through the slit in the layers of her petticoats and dropped it into her concealed pocket. It all happened so quickly Sir Antony had no time to react to the theft.

"I shall keep your devotional token for now, dear brother. Its loss will be a reminder not to interfere in my plans or you stand to lose what you cherish most."

ELEVEN

The following morning, Sir Antony spent more time than was necessary in his dressing room brooding over what to wear. In fact, it was not his clothes but his sister and her machinations that preoccupied his thoughts. With depressing certainty, he knew she'd had ample time since escaping her incarceration to set any number of plans in motion. What those plans were, he had no idea.

To watch her play the harp at their impromptu recital the night before, and then act as hostess to a small dinner party was to marvel at her ability to maintain the appearance of the well-bred hostess without revealing the demon within. He felt compelled to keep an eye on her and wait for her to make a mistake or for something or someone—for she could not act alone—to give her game away. He hoped it was sooner rather than later, particularly with the Salt Hendons returned to London.

Dinner had stretched to cards and charades in his book room until the early hours of the morning, and he had forced himself to remain until the last of the guests—Mr. Dacre Wraxton—took his leave. That gentleman had shaken his hand upon departure, congratulating him on his engagement to the lovely Lady Caroline, whom he called *a rare and fascinating jewel*. Sir Antony wasn't sure what he disliked more—the sneering hint of laughter in the man's tone, or his use of the word *fascinating* to describe Caroline, with all that word's implied nuances. It made him uncomfortable and he was glad to see the back of the man.

Throughout dinner, he had marveled at the gentleman's immense sangfroid in ignoring his cast-off mistress, not once looking her way, even when the poor wretch made every effort to catch his eye. But what brought the bile up into his throat was Diana's callous indifference to Jenny Dalrymple's feelings. She had offered the woman sanctuary in his house and yet, throughout dinner and later, while in the book room, his sister flirted outrageously with Jenny Dalrymple's ex-lover under her friend's tear-filled gaze.

Diana's cruel indifference did not surprise him, and as she never did anything without good reason, taking in Jenny Dalrymple must have served some purpose. He realized what that purpose was during dinner whilst engaging her in conversation as a distraction from her morbidity. The woman had stored away, in what he had always considered a rather pretty but vacant head, an infinite supply of social minutiae about people, places and events. During twelve courses she entertained him with a précis of the social happenings during his absence from London. Just as Diana had memorized the contents of the letters he had sent her from Russia, and then used it to her advantage by telling all and sundry she had visited him in St. Petersburg, he was certain she had taken all the social gossip Jenny Dalrymple could supply her with and used this in some way to further her plans.

As he sipped his tea and watched her act out charades with her guests, he took stock of her attire and accoutrements. His sister always had an exquisite dress sense, and a very expensive one. He noted the pearl and diamond choker about her slender throat, the matching three-strand pearl bracelet about her wrist, and a coiffure sparkling with gold pins and satin bows, and he wondered—not surprisingly—where she had come by such sumptuous gowns and jewelry. He was certain Salt had not provided her with enough pin money to purchase such magnificence in her confinement, nor would she need it locked up in a remote castle. He speculated how his sister had financed her life since her escape, not only the clothes on her back, but a horse and carriage for travel, lodgings, the upkeep of her companion, not to mention such banal items as food, toiletries and servant hire. He did not need to sleep on the question because he was given the answer when, with the street door locked and bolted on a cold dark early morning, Diana led him back to the book room and to the leather top desk by the fireplace.

She took the greatest delight in showing him four neat piles of accounts, each secured with a black riband. All were sorted, she told him with satisfaction, and all remained unpaid. She had no idea as to the exact amount when all the notes of credit, bills from tradesmen, dressmakers, milliners, shoemakers, and the like, were totaled together, but she was very sure it could be no less than two thousand pounds. He should be pleased that she had accumulated most of the bills in Birmingham, where goods, particularly the cost of fabric and dress-makers, were much cheaper to be had than they were in London. She advised, for the sake of his good name and the family's reputation, he pay his debts swiftly—most accounts were thirty days or more outstanding. It was all very well for Salt to be tardy with paying his bills, if he ever was—their first cousin was a nobleman and so exempt from debtors' prison—but as a baronet, Sir Antony was not exempt. She was quite sure Salt would not sanction his sister's engagement to an inmate of Fleet Street prison, or perhaps he would be conveyed to Birmingham's debtor's prison; best to settle his accounts at once. Oh, and there were more to come…

Two *thousand* pounds.

His sister had spent in two months more than he had in a year on the upkeep of an entire household: Servants, carriages and horses, wax and other general living expenses! The amount had thundered about in his head as he kept his thoughts and feelings well in check as Diana bid him a goodnight and airily told him not to expect her down to break-fast. She and Jenny Dalrymple were driving out to spend the day at Horace Walpole's fanciful Gothic retreat Strawberry Hill, but would be home in time to dine. Sir Antony had no doubts she was telling him the truth, but having Mr. Thief-taker as her shadow gave him an odd sense of comfort, if not satisfaction. He could at least make his visit to the Salt Hendon household without worrying about her whereabouts.

Two *thousand* pounds.

The sum haunted his sleep and left him with the makings of a megrim when he awoke. It was still knocking about at the back of his eyelids as he sat at his dressing table with a copper silk banyan thrown over his shirt and smalls, while Semper and two attendants came and went with suitable outfits. Finally, two silk ensembles in a long line of exquisitely embroidered frock coats, waistcoats and pairs of breeches were mulled over and then rejected as unsatisfactory for the impending visit to Salt House in Grosvenor Square.

Back Semper went to the closet, features devoid of his mounting frustration. He had not seen his master so preoccupied since dressing him for a private audience with the Russian Empress. He returned with a matching frock coat and waistcoat in contrasting striped silk in shades of lavender and plum with a soft drape to the skirts, the breeches of plain cream silk.

It was dressed in this ensemble Sir Antony entered Salt House and offloaded greatcoat, hat, kid gloves and ornate sword to an attendant footman.

Nervous with anticipation, his head swiveled left and right and up and down as he followed the under butler across the wide expanse of the black and white marbled tiled entrance foyer, the grand entrance bespeaking great wealth and restrained elegance. From the Robert Adam double staircase that curved up to the heavens of a stained glass oculus from which was suspended an enormous chandelier of cut crystal, wood gleamed and crystal winked, polished to a high brilliance for the Earl and Countess's return.

An interview with the noble owner of such a grand establishment would cause the uninitiated to quake in their stockings and shoes, opined Sir Antony, who, as favored cousin and one-time regular visitor under this roof, had not given these surroundings a moment's notice. In disfavor and absent for many years, his eyes were opened anew to the symbolic significance such a grand house and its appointments must have on lesser mortals, particularly those currying the Earl's favor.

"Poor wretches," he muttered to himself, as the under-butler came to a halt at a set of double doors flanked by two liveried footmen standing to attention. When the under-butler faced him he said audibly, "You're new, aren't you?"

"Four years new, my lord."

"And Jenkins? Where is he lurking?"

The under-butler smiled thinly, catching the slight nervous edge to the tall handsome visitor's voice rather than at the inference that any of the Earl's servants would lurk. The previous butler he did not know personally, only by reputation, and said so, adding,

"Mr. Miller has been butler to his lordship for as long as I have been under-butler, my lord. Feeling a bit on in years to keep up the running of such a large establishment, Mr. Jenkins has taken on the role of butler at the Arlington Street townhouse.

"His lordship still use that address?"

At Sir Antony's surprise, the under-butler replied with emphasis, "Yes, my lord, upon occasion, usually during parliamentary sittings. But now with this house reopened I suspect—"

"No one is interested in your speculations, Pratt," said a deep voice full of foreboding that instantly closed the under-butler's mouth and sent him into a bow. "I apologize for my absence, Sir Antony," Miller said, glancing at the under-butler's back as that servant scurried off across the hall. "His lordship is usually at home to visitors on a Tuesday, but this being the first Tuesday, and with his lordship's family just returned to the city late yesterday, the house is not open to receiving at this time. I therefore respectfully request you forgive Pratt his lapse, and ask that you kindly return—"

"Miller isn't it? Well, Miller, his lordship will see me because I am not a visitor, I am family. So you can announce me or not, but I intend to see his lordship today."

The butler paused and took a longer raking look at Sir Antony. The expensive cloth and tailoring, not to mention exquisite embroidery work of his ensemble, was starkly evident, and the stones in the shoe buckles were very possibly real diamonds, not paste. His upright posture, the deep smooth voice and the unblinking handsome blue-eyed gaze proclaimed the gentleman, not a parvenu. Additionally, the butler realized he could not afford to offend either this gentleman, if he were indeed a blood relative of the Earl, or offend his noble employer by turning away one of his kin, despite never having set eyes on this gentleman before. Sir Antony's next sentence settled the matter.

"I've just returned from a posting to 'Petersburg and the four crates out in the entrance hall are filled with gifts. Have the servants take extra care with the largest crate as it is for her ladyship and contains a porcelain tea service from the Russian Imperial Manufactory. That and the three others I would rather you squirreled away somewhere for safe-keeping before Miss Merry, Master Ron and the children see them and demand to know their contents. I will not be the one to deny them their gifts, but perhaps it would be best for Lady Salt to decide when my largesse should be distributed? What do you think, Miller?"

"Yes, sir, of course. I will see to it at once the crates are carefully stored out of harm's way until I hear from her ladyship what is to be done with them." He signaled to the footmen to open the double doors and then sent one off to stand guard over Sir Antony's crates until such time as he could arrange and supervise their careful removal to his butler's pantry. "Please step into the anteroom and wait here while I inform his lordship of your arrival. I do apologize for the fire—"

"Ha! No apology necessary, Miller," Sir Antony replied cheerfully, yet shuddered as if suddenly faced with a chilled wind. "As I recall, the temperature in the anteroom could freeze water!"

The anteroom off the Earl's book room was one room Sir Antony did remember well, and not fondly, precisely because it never had a fire in the grate and thus was always chilly. The marble floor, lack of adequate furniture and blue painted walls without decoration added to its unwelcoming coldness. Even when crowded with strangers armed with petitions, proposals and paper seeking the Earl of Salt Hendon's patronage for this, that and every other thing imaginable, the room's temperature never rose above freezing. It was a ploy to ensure only the most dedicated petitioner sought an audience with his lordship; the less hardy and half-hearted inclined to slink away before their bones seized up with cold and well before their name was called for their five minutes of the Earl's precious time. Still, Sir Antony had considered such measures at crowd control draconian, and was always full of sympathy for the frozen wretches whenever he slipped into the warmth of the book room, unannounced and as often as he liked—one of the privileged few given unrestricted access.

How times had changed, he sighed with sadness. Now he, too, required permission to see his first cousin and former best friend. Looking neither left nor right but gaze locked between the butler's shoulder blades, he followed the servant across the anteroom to another set of double doors and another pair of liveried footmen standing as sentries.

"If you will remain here, Sir Antony, I will inquire of Lord Salt if he is at home to—um—family." The butler dared to give the hint of a smile, saying before disappearing into the book room, "Should you feel cold, my lord, one of the footmen will oblige by having a maid fetched to place more coal in the grate to make a more sizeable fire."

It was only with the door shut on the butler's back that Sir Antony realized he was not the least bit cold, and a look over at the large fireplace with its smoldering fire made him take a step backward. But what dropped his jaw and had him looking about in wonder was the anteroom itself. His first thought was that Miller had brought him to the wrong room entirely, but the layout, with two French windows overlooking the expansive Square and, on the opposite wall, the large fireplace with its carved overmantel, were both familiar. Everything else had changed, and for the better.

The walls had been repainted a pale yellow, the ceiling with its plaster molding, an eggshell white. A massive mirror in an ornate gilt frame hung above the overmantel, reflecting light from the floor-to-ceiling windows opposite. Framed by blue and gold damask curtains tied back by heavy gold and dark blue velvet rope, the midmorning sun stretched out across the two blocks of ladder-back chairs arranged in neat rows and facing the double doors of the Earl's book room. A walnut sideboard stood between the windows, and had upon it two large silver ewers and matching silver candelabras at either end. Above the sideboard was a portrait and it was the portrait Sir Antony was admiring when into the room stepped the Earl's secretary, Mr. Arthur Ellis.

It was a full-length portrait of the Countess of Salt Hendon, dressed in a deep blue velvet riding habit, the outer layer of petticoats bunched to show the embroidered underskirt and a hint of a riding boot; the jacket, embroidered on pockets and lapel with small yellow and blue flowers, had a mannish cut that molded to her upper torso and long slender arms. Her coal-black hair was teased full in the latest fashion and swept up, atop which sat a narrow-brimmed hat at a rakish angle. She carried a riding crop in one gloved hand, while the other held the reins to her mount, a sleek bay with white tipped ears. In the distance was the Jacobean palace, Salt Hall, ancestral home of the Earls of Salt Hendon.

Sir Antony peered closer to see the name of the painter who had managed in his deft brushstrokes to capture to the life the beautiful Countess, and had the answer given to him.

"It's by a new painter, a Mr. George Romney. He's gifted, you'd agree, Sir Antony."

Sir Antony gave a little jump at having his reverie broken so abruptly, but made an immediate recover, delighted to see a familiar face. He stuck out his hand in greeting.

"Mr. Ellis! How good to see you!" he said shaking the younger man's hand vigorously. "Yes, gifted, and with such subject matter, no real effort required. I see you are ready to do battle with all petitioners," he added, a glance at the familiar black leather bound appointment book hugged to the front of Arthur Ellis's fine wool waistcoat, much like a shield. Some things never changed and it was comforting.

"Thankfully, not today," the secretary replied with a smile, holding the Earl's diary a little tighter. "This room must have been a surprise to you, sir."

"Surprise? Ha! An understatement. Thought I'd been brought to the wrong room." Sir Antony glanced up at the portrait. "No wagers need be made to guess under whose influence the anteroom has a far cheerier aspect, eh, Ellis?"

"Very true, sir." The secretary adding with a hint of sad apology, "You will find there have been a great many changes to Lord Salt's household since your untimely departure..."

"All for the better, I'm certain," Sir Antony replied with a bright smile, hiding his own sadness that time had gone on without him in this noble household, but not wishing to pursue the matter further, despite the secretary's obvious sympathy for his cause. He caught sight of the unfamiliar and pointed it out for something to say, "So what's under here, Ellis?" he asked, stepping across to the opposite corner by the fireplace. "A cage methinks? What sort of beast hides beneath the cloth? Is it feathered or furred?"

Leaving his appointment book on the sideboard, Arthur Ellis joined Sir Antony by the large square cage on its pedestal and covered by a sheet.

"Feathered, my lord."

The secretary took out his pocket watch, noted the time and pushed it back in his waistcoat pocket.

"In fact," he continued, "I am surprised to see the cage under covers at this late hour. But perhaps, in the hubbub of arrival, it was for the best. It is time for Peter's fruit, but the cover will remain until Miss Aldershot arrives, or Peter's squawking may be the death of him." He grinned sheepishly. "Lord Salt is not enamored of the bird, I'm afraid, and has, on more than one occasion, threatened to have poor Peter stuffed and mounted, which he says would afford those waiting an audience with his lordship just as much pleasure as seeing a live macaw. Oh! I did not mention that Miss Aldershot is his lordship's ward and— Ah! Here is Miss Aldershot now," he added with a nervous smile and beckoned the two footmen to come forward to remove the sheet covering the cage.

"Miss Aldershot and I have been introduced," Sir Antony said and suppressed a grin when the secretary merely nodded in an absent sort of way, seemingly having lost the ability to hear with Kitty Aldershot in the room.

Kitty Aldershot crossed the anteroom carrying a large porcelain bowl covered by a linen napkin. She was dressed in a pretty pink-patterned gown *à l'anglaise* with a matching colored ribbon about her throat and several bows in her fair hair. She was humming to herself and, removing the linen napkin, peered at the contents of the bowl, oblivious to the gentlemen by the cage. That is, until the two footmen holding the cover between them knocked the cage, causing it to swing on its ornate brass pedestal and its occupant to give a loud squawk in protest.

The secretary stepped forward to take the bowl from her and so Kitty saw him first.

"Has Peter been misbehaving himself, Mr. Ellis?" she asked, smiling brightly, causing Arthur Ellis to choke back his reply at such a smile being bestowed upon him. "I have his fruit and nuts and if you wish to help me feed—Sir Antony! Oh! What a pleasure it is to see you again so soon, sir!" she exclaimed, shoving the bowl of fruit at the secretary and dropping a quick curtsy as she brushed down the transparent linen apron tied about her waist. "I mean... It is *very* pleasant to see you again! This is Mr. Ellis, his lordship's secretary. But you would know that..."

She gave a nervous little laugh and turned to the secretary expecting him to say something, but Arthur Ellis was staring into the bowl, trying to bring his features under control, not wishing to alert Sir Antony to the true nature of his feelings for Kitty Aldershot.

Too late for that, reasoned Sir Antony. He also now knew why Arthur Ellis happened to be lurking in the anteroom when there was no likelihood of petitioners that day and should be engaged elsewhere. All three were relieved when Peter the Macaw let them know what he thought of being ignored by a dramatic display of rustling feathers, followed by a loud screeching that would surely have brought on a heart attack in an elderly petitioner.

"That's enough, Peter!" Kitty Aldershot scolded the bird affectionately, selecting a segment of orange from the bowl. She passed it through two brass ribs of the cage. "Be a good boy and you may even be permitted to take a walk when her ladyship arrives."

Sir Antony moved closer to the ornate cage of polished brass to better observe the large bird. Its plumage was magnificently colored, with vivid blue wings and a long luxuriant tail, golden yellow breast and under parts, and a powerful black beak. The macaw's forehead was covered in bright green feathers, its chin had feathers of deepest blue, and its large claws were black like its beak. And as if its coloring weren't enough to attract attention, there were the mesmerizing black and white markings circling its small inquisitive eyes.

Sir Antony had seen illustrations of such exotic creatures and been in the presence of a scarlet parrot, but they were as nothing compared to being up close to this magnificent creature that now danced up and down on its sturdy perch in greeting.

The macaw also rocked back and forth when spoken to, and whenever a piece of fruit was passed through the brass rungs, it took it in its claw, almost gently, and delicately savored the succulent fruit. When Arthur Ellis provided Peter with a walnut to crack, the bird grasped the nut in one claw and broke open the walnut's hard outer-casing with its strong beak, giving a gurgling, almost self-satisfied sound at its own cleverness at revealing the soft inner kernel of the nut. Sir Antony received the strongest impression Peter was well aware of his status as pampered main attraction and was only too willing to dance on his perch and climb up and down the brass ribs of his cage for as long as he was given tasty morsels to devour.

"What an extraordinary creature," Sir Antony exclaimed, voicing his delight. "May I be permitted to offer Peter some fruit?"

Kitty Aldershot handed him a large slice of apple to give the macaw, and he did so, timidly. Yet, the second piece of apple he passed through the cage into Peter's claw with more confidence and was rewarded with what sounded like a garbled *thank you* in French.

"Did he just say *merci beaucoup*?" he gasped, and when Kitty nodded, he laughed and addressed the bird, "You cheeky show-off!"

"He is that, Sir Antony," Arthur Ellis agreed, feeling he should say something to regain Miss Aldershot's attention because she was looking up at Sir Antony with what he could only depressingly describe as veneration. "And the bigger the audience, the more Peter likes to perform. Is that not so, Miss Aldershot? I recall the time when this room was overflowing with petitioners, and Peter was in fine form, dancing up and down his perch for a lady who took it upon herself to have a conversation with him. Do you remember, Miss Aldershot? Unfortunately, she made the mistake of leaning in too close to the cage and her hat poked through the bars and—"

"—Peter pulled the hat off her head with his beak and shredded it within seconds! Oh, yes! I do remember, Mr. Ellis." She glanced up at Sir Antony, whose focus remained on Peter. "The lady's hat was of blond straw with a small crown but a wide brim, and had the prettiest green sash—"

"Not after Peter had finished with it," Arthur Ellis quipped.

Kitty Aldershot giggled and Arthur Ellis laughed, and Sir Antony, feeling the interloper, offered the macaw one of the two walnuts he was holding in the awkward silence that followed once the couple's laughter died away. All three were unaware they were being observed from the doorway.

"Does Peter have anything else to say in French?" Sir Antony asked casually in the silence, addressing the bird. He glanced at the couple. "Why Peter? Why not Pierre? Or Francois? An odd name, or should I say, *specific* name, for a bird, isn't it—Peter?"

"As to that, my lord, you would need to inquire of Lady Caroline, to whom the macaw belongs," the secretary informed him. He shrugged his shoulders and deferred to Kitty Aldershot. "Perhaps Miss Aldershot knows the origin of Peter's name?"

"That I do, Mr. Ellis," Kitty volunteered excitedly with a bright smile and moved closer to Sir Antony to place her hand on his upturned embroidered cuff. She smiled up at him and dropped her voice. "If I tell you, you must not repeat it…" She took Sir Antony's frowning silence for assent, blind that the familiarity of her hand on his arm had not only unsettled him, but Arthur Ellis. "I thought it an odd name, too, for a bird. And once I came upon Lady Caroline alone with Peter and talking to him in French. I had little idea birds could speak! So imagine my surprise when Peter did so, and in French, of all the tongues God put on this earth. He says more than *merci beaucoup*, too, but you need to know the right phrase, and say it in French, for Peter to respond…" She leaned in to Sir Antony, her excitement at divulging what she knew and anticipating his reaction making her a little breathless. Deliberately, Sir Antony leaned away as Arthur Ellis unconsciously leaned toward her. "It's Peter for 'Peter*sburg*. I am very sure she named the bird after—"

The name was left unsaid as Kitty gave a jump of fright because the macaw had gone into a frenzy of squawking and bright-colored flapping of wings in excited recognition of Lady Caroline, who came further into the room and within Peter's line of sight.

"Thank you for feeding Peter, Kitty. Ned would not hear of me leaving the nursery until I had played a third game of skittles. And Beth was determined to join in. How do you do, Sir Antony?"

She said this as she swept up to them, all three persons gathered about Peter's cage stepping aside to allow her access to her over-excited pet. She did not make eye contact with Sir Antony, nor did she pay much attention to the warm faces of Kitty and Arthur Ellis.

Lady Caroline's attention was all for the macaw.

TWELVE

From a heavy gold and enameled chatelaine, Lady Caroline opened an etui that contained tweezers, scissors and the brass key to unlock the door of the birdcage. She closed the etui and let the chatelaine dangle on its chain amongst the soft folds of her floral sack-back gown. She then swung wide the cage door, all the while speaking soothingly in French, which soon had the macaw behaving and watching her intently.

Four liveried footmen followed Lady Caroline into the anteroom. One carried an intricately carved and gilded tall wooden stand that had rungs attached to it at intervals, and this was placed by the second window on a square of carpet laid upon the polished floorboards by a second footman. A third affixed a length of chain to the perch closest to the ground. A porcelain bowl holding fresh water was placed on the square of carpet and then all four footmen silently departed, leaving Lady Caroline to coax Peter from his cage to step up onto the leading edge of her proffered hand.

Secure, the macaw nestled in, head against Lady Caroline's shoulder. At her soft-spoken encouragement, Peter became the most docile of creatures, perfectly content to be petted and talked to by his mistress, who, ignoring her audience of three, walked the length of the room to the undraped windows, where the sun filtered across the square of carpet. Here she remained by Peter's perch.

The Earl's secretary came to a sense of his surroundings, and realizing the serious lapse in his duties, made a short bow to Sir Antony and Miss Aldershot. Without a glance at the fair Kitty, he quietly excused himself, scooped up the appointment diary off the sideboard, and marched from the anteroom out into the hall, not into the book room as Sir Antony had presumed was his original destination. Kitty Aldershot, her cheeks flushed with the guilt of being caught out sharing confidences in close proximity with Sir Antony, bobbed a curtsy to Lady Caroline's back, mumbled her excuses at needing to be elsewhere, and scurried away. Sir Antony was now alone with only the two wooden-faced footmen guarding the entrance to the Earl's book room and Lady Caroline on the far side of the anteroom, continuing to croon to Peter the Macaw.

Inexplicably, for the first time in his life he was overcome with apprehension and awkwardness in Caroline's company. Not from her girlhood through to her growing into a beautiful young woman had he ever experienced the feeling of intense unease and clumsiness that he did at that moment. His large feet fixed to the polished floorboards and kept him lingering by the empty cage. Here was his opportunity to march up to Caroline, to take her in his arms and kiss her, and tell her that if she accepted his proposal of marriage, she would not only make him the happiest of men, but he would strive for the rest of his days to make her just as happy. Yet, he did not do so. He could not move and he did not speak. He was the best-dressed clod in all London!

It did not take him many minutes to realize why he was being ridiculously gauche in Caroline's company. Thinking about it, he was confident his was not an unusual case. Many men on the precipice of becoming engaged to be married must feel as he did. It's just that he had never expected it to happen to him—to be paralyzed with the uncertainty that the woman he had chosen to spend the rest of his life with did, indeed, love him as immutably as he did her.

When she was fifteen years old, Caroline had told him with all the naïve confidence of youth that she loved him and intended to marry him when she left the nursery. He had been shocked, disbelieving even, but it had not taken many hours before it dawned on him that he reciprocated her feelings. From that day forward he wanted no other but her as his wife. He had waited for her to grow out of her girlhood, content to share their similar interests in a love of animals, dancing and music, and a loathing of the hunting and shooting seasons. This latter he had confided in no one but her, and she promised never to tell the Earl, for it was most unmanly to have an aversion for blood sports. Sir Antony sympathized with the fox, admiring its cunning and determination in the face of implacable odds, nor could he see the fairness in beating pheasants out of a bush into the open air, only to shoot them dead.

Before today, more precisely before last night when he had asked her to marry him, he had continued to look upon Caroline as his best friend's little sister, to be admired from afar, off-limits until she came of age and the Earl gave their marriage his blessing. And now here she was, at two-and-twenty, a young widow and almost his betrothed. So why couldn't he move his feet, go to her, and tell her how he felt?

What a complete and utter dolt!

Finally, Peter the Macaw was placed on his elaborately carved and gilded perch before the window, Caroline saying a few words to him as she secured the long length of chain to the gold band about his left foot, the chain permitting free movement up and down the rungs of the perch. Caroline then stroked the side of Peter's face lovingly and he responded by giving her finger a nudge. Sir Antony found himself smiling at this play between them, and wishing it were his cheek being stroked.

"Once a week I take Peter to the royal tennis court so he has somewhere to fly about freely," Caroline said conversationally as she turned away from the macaw to face Sir Antony, but kept distance between them by remaining at the window, where the sun warmed the hem of her silk petticoats. "I wish I could return him to his natural home, but that is not possible. So Salt's tennis court it is, where he flies about and roosts on one of the high window sills and will not be caught until he is hungry." She smiled at a memory as she unconsciously brushed a long wisp of bright strawberry blonde hair from her flushed cheek. "Peter senses Salt's disapproval and acts accordingly. Salt cannot walk into a room without Peter screeching loud and long at him. But the petitioners like him. He gives them something to focus on while they idle away the hours awaiting Salt's pleasure. Jane approves, so what can Salt do?"

Take action in any number of ways if the bird truly annoyed him, Sir Antony thought grimly, but did not say so. Her casual conversation unstuck his black leather shoes from the floor and he slowly came across the room.

"From where was he rescued? Some flea-ridden animal bazaar I presume?"

"Murdoch's Animal Menagerie. Horrid place." She gave an involuntary shudder at a memory that still had the power to make her tear up. "Most animals were starved, and those exotics still alive amounted to a margay with mange and a marmoset monkey that died soon after I took him into care, poor little creature. All the songbirds were infested, had lost feathers and were near death. Poor Peter was kept in a cage much too small for him that was constantly under a tarpaulin, so he rarely saw light. I had Salt have the place closed down and Murdoch prosecuted."

"Of course you did."

She cocked her head. "How did you know I had rescued Peter?"

"You said yourself you would rather he be in his natural home than caged. And for as long as I have known you, you've nursed injured animals on the estate, set birds free from cages, Salt's prize kestrel one year, and told Salt in no uncertain terms your thoughts on the shooting of pheasants." He smiled at a memory. "I think you used the words *unmitigated slaughter*, if I am not mistaken." He glanced at Peter perched on the edge of the porcelain bowl, dipping to drink the cool water, then looked down into Caroline's green eyes. "That is one supremely fortunate bird, and I am honored you named him for me."

For a fraction of a second she thought of denying the truth, but what was the point? She *had* named the macaw after him, not because of the bird's magnificently vibrant plumage or the way its raucous behavior set her brother's teeth on edge, it was the look in the macaw's eye. It was hard to explain, and she did not dare voice it aloud, but the bird looked at her with unconditional love in the same way Sir Antony was looking down at her now. She didn't deserve to be so loved, not by the macaw, because she could not set it free from captivity, and not by Sir Antony, because her behavior while he was in Russia had made her thoroughly unworthy of him. She needed him to see that—for him to know she was not the same person he had fallen in love with all those years ago.

She took a step closer to him and demanded with a frown, "Why? Why did you ask me to marry you?"

"For the same reason you will say yes," he answered calmly, all mental clumsiness and uncertainty evaporating with her frowning question. "Because we love each other. We have been friends for a dozen years or more and have loved each other for at least half of those years, and—marriage is what we both want, is it not? You told me so yourself when you were fifteen."

"Yes. Yes, I remember. But... Even if I did still want to marry you... My life... Life for me is very different now from what it once was."

She swallowed and looked up into his blue eyes, eyes that were full of trust and love, and which reflected the confidence he had in his own feelings in wanting to marry her. And she knew that because they were friends and because she did love him, she could not leave him in ignorance of her past and marry him in good conscience, whatever Jane's sage advice.

"Everything changed when you went away," she added quietly. "Even before I married Aldershot."

"That was my fault."

"No. No, that is not true!"

"Thank you for saying so, but you know the fault is mine," he said gently. "My actions at your coming-out recital were reprehensible. I have no excuse and I should have known better. I was drunk beyond saving and it made me say things, deeply regrettable things..." He lowered his chin into the lacey folds of his cravat. "I ruined your come-out and I fear I ruined your life thereafter..."

"Please, I don't want to relive that night," Caroline pleaded. "It's not that I haven't, a hundred times over! It's just that I realized a long time ago that wishing the outcome had been different won't make it so. We both behaved appallingly. But I was little more than a child..." She managed to hold his gaze. "So if you want to take the blame for the ruin of what should have been a perfectly heavenly evening for both of us, then I shall let you."

"Thank you."

"But I will not allow you to shoulder the blame for what occurred once you left for the Continent. What I did—No one is to blame for the consequences but myself. Salt would agree with me. My marriage to Aldershot is a shining example of my folly." She glanced down at her tightly clasped hands and then back up at him. "I am a sad disappointment to my brother. Imagine! He kept me away from London Society until my eighteenth birthday, fearing I would run off with the first fortune hunter who made up to me, and what did I do? I end up married to one!"

"If I had been here to protect you, that would not have happened."

"No. You are wrong," she responded simply. "Four years ago I did not appreciate what I had. I was a silly little girl, a-a spoiled child, who believed the world—*you*—were at my feet and I acted accordingly. Do I regret what I did? Yes. Do I wish I had never been married? Yes. But what is done, cannot now be undone." She sighed. "Love won't be enough for you, *for us*, not when you know-know—*everything*."

"I don't need to know—*everything*, Caro," he replied calmly.

He was quite content to leave the young man dead and buried and ask no questions, if that was what she wanted. But he could not fathom why she assumed her disappointing first marriage would bother him or why it was an impediment to their marital happiness; now *that* did bother him. Still, he managed to smile and add gently,

"I am content to start our lives today and move forward and not look back."

Caroline knew Jane would say this was precisely the response she needed from him, and she should accept his offer and go with him into the future, closing the door on her past. And yet, Caroline's conscience again held her in check and the door on her past remained wide-open, inviting confession, urging her to reveal all or she would not be able to live with herself, least of all as wife of Sir Antony Templestowe.

"You say that now," she countered, hovering between indecision and confession. "But if you ever found out... If someone told you other than me..."

"Then you tell me whatever it is you want to tell me, in your own good time—or not."

"Why do you *always* have to be so-so *conciliatory*?" she demanded, bunching her silk petticoats in balled fists of mild frustration. "Why are you always so—so *affable*?"

"Not always."

Wrapped up in the misery of indecision, she failed to hear the edge to his voice.

"Well, I very much doubt you would be at all affable if you discovered people whispering about your wife behind your back!"

"No. I would not be *affable*, far from it."

"There you are then," she stated, as if they were in accord. Opening her fists, she shook her petticoats with a satisfied sigh.

But as she had not confided in him what it was that was bothering her, the matter, whatever it was, was far from resolved. He wondered if she would feel more at ease if he shared a confidence with her. It was one he had every intention of disclosing, but had hardly expected to do so in an anteroom on his way in to have, what would be, in all probability, a highly unpleasant interview with her brother. But before he could offer her any insight into these thoughts, she grabbed hold of his hand and led him across the room, down the aisle that divided the arrangement of chairs, away from the double doors and out of earshot of the two footmen, who remained wooden-faced and stared into the middle distance but who undoubtedly had their ears wide-open.

Sir Antony wondered what she was about until her gaze darted in warning to the double doors. It brought him to a sense of his surroundings and the realization that the servants understood every word of their conversation, unlike in Russia, where their counterparts were considered part of the furniture, so after a time became invisible. As if to underscore that servants in England were sentient beings, Caroline lowered her voice, which also added emphasis to her argument.

"And what if these whispers reached the ears of some important men in the government, men of influence that make the decisions on who will be elevated to ambassador and who won't? Having a wife who is whispered about—who has a-a *past*—could affect your chances of being an ambassador one day, could it not?"

"Caro, *darling*, most ministers within the Foreign Department begin to worry for their careers if they are *not* whispered about."

Caroline did not see the humor in this quip. His good-natured responses, far from making her at ease, only served to increase her anxiety and the belief she was unworthy to be his wife. She let go of his hand and clasped hers together, fingers tightly entwined.

"But not whispers about their wives... No man wants his wife spoken about, for others to believe him a-a *cuckold*, even if it is in word only. Rumors don't have to be true for some of the-the *muck* to stick, do they?"

Sir Antony lost his smile. He could see she was on the verge of tears, and all that his easygoing reassurances had achieved was to increase her apprehension. There was some monumental struggle going on inside her beautiful head, and he felt an ass for making light of her anxiety. There was only one way to alleviate her doubts and help her over the abyss of indecision, so he said gently,

"What is it you would have me do, Caro? Just ask it of me and I will do it, whatever it is. But there is one thing I will not do, and that is falter in my determination to marry you."

"Don't tell Salt you proposed. Don't ask him. Not today. Please."

He was surprised by her quick bluntness, and by the request. Still, he remained calm and inclined his head.

"Very well, I will delay the formality of seeking Salt's permission to marry you, if that is your wish."

When she visibly sighed her relief, he was hurt. He wasn't sure if she wanted to delay for her own reasons or if she lacked the confidence in his ability to convince Salt to give his permission. He pretended an interest in his quizzing glass, polishing the lens with the folds of intricate lace at his wrist, though his attention did not waver from her for a moment.

"Do you have any notion when would be an appropriate time for me to broach the subject of our betrothal with your brother?" he asked calmly. "Or is something required of me before I may do so?"

"Oh, I knew you would understand!" Caroline declared with a smile of relief, the dark cloud lifting from her brow.

He returned her smile, no clearer idea what she was talking about, but thankful for small mercies because it was the first time she had smiled at him since they came face-to-face the previous evening at Diana's soirée. He let the quizzing glass suspend on its riband and swept her a majestic bow.

"Make your request of me, my lady," he said with playful grandiloquence, "and I will do my utmost to please you. Walk backwards to Bristol; storm the doors of some mismanaged menagerie; take up Peter's cause against Salt's displeasure; you name it. All I ask is that you are there beside me."

What she proposed startled him, and while Caroline had always been forthright and frank in her opinions with him, he would never have imagined the Caroline he knew before his exile to Russia ever offering up such an outrageous suggestion. Ultimately, it was her emotional speech of halting, half-finished sentences leading up to her request, a speech full of raw honesty and filled with self-doubt, coupled with what she required of him before she would be willing to marry him, that had him reeling and reaching for the back of the nearest chair.

THIRTEEN

IT WAS IN THAT SMALL HESITANT MOMENT BEFORE MAKING HER request that Caroline truly saw him for the first time since finding him in easy conversation with Kitty and Mr. Ellis. She hardly noticed his suit, that he was wearing her favorite color; or anything else about his person. She was too annoyed with Kitty for having her hand on Antony's close cuff. It was enough to blind her to all other considerations, which was a childish reaction. If she were honest with herself, it had little to do with her harmless sister-in-law and everything to do with her feelings for Sir Antony.

With her request on the tip of her tongue, and clasped hands pressed to her mouth in anticipation of his response, she allowed her green eyes to flicker across the lean contours of his handsome face to his square heavy chin, and all the way down to the hardened muscle of his large calves encased in white silk stockings. And for the umpteenth time since spying him outside his townhouse, she wondered what such well-exercised masculinity must look like stripped of all those exquisitely embroidered silk layers.

The thought of him naked was not new. As a maiden, she had often speculated what it would be like to share the bed of Sir Antony Templestowe. What was new was the uncertainty and dread that accompanied this speculation, because at two-and-twenty, she was now well aware of what it was like to be desired and ignored in equal measure.

She wondered if Antony would still desire her without her feminine protective outer shell of layered petticoats, buckram stays, and shapeless chemise. Would he find her rounded breasts and silken thighs to his liking, or would her female curves in all their naked glory fail to arouse him, as had happened with her unresponsive husband? She was no svelte nymph, no sylph beauty like Jane—Jane, whom Antony had held up—thrown in her face more belike—in a drunken stupor at the disastrous recital, as the epitome of feminine beauty.

It was this need to know and a determination that Antony should have his eyes wide-open to her shame that made her hesitate to accept his offer of marriage. Dacre Wraxton was right. Antony was a man of scruples, and she admired him all the more for it, but it also meant that he was unlikely to accept anything less than a virtuous widow for a bride. Despite what Jane had counseled, she believed she must air her past history. Only then could there be no surprises or disappointment and she could marry Antony with a clear conscience...

With this in mind, she took a deep breath and let the fears and doubts swirling about her subconscious spill forth with little regard of their effect on her receptive audience of one.

"I hardly recognized you in the street yesterday. You are quite transformed. Oh, I very much like the way you are now, but you must know it would not have mattered a jot to me had you returned unchanged. And there is something—something about you that has changed in here," she added, placing her flattened palm to the front of his silken waistcoat where his heart beat. "But when I look in your eyes, it is you I see—the friend of my girlhood, and it is such a relief to know you are still *you*. I just wish..." She became misty-eyed and put her hands behind her back. "When I think of all that has happened to me since you went away... I dreaded you finding out about my marriage... That I was no longer a—"

She baulked at the word *virgin*, saying it in her head. It made her anxious every time she ruminated on what would be his reaction when he discovered just how she had lost her virginity. Yet, it wasn't just him finding out the circumstances of that fateful night, it was what he would think of her, and if he would still want her.

"Of course I realize you are aware I am no longer an innocent. I was married for two years." She met Sir Antony's unwavering blue eyes with a wan smile. "I am certain you have been told, or you may have guessed, that it was not a happy marriage by any means. In truth, we were both wretched. He-he did not care for me in that way," she confessed. "I thought there was something wrong with me. But I was shown differently, so I do know how it is meant to be when a couple are-are—*physically intimate*—" She pulled herself up when he grabbed for the back of the nearest chair, as if needing to steady himself, reasoning she had made enough of a startling admission for now. She took a deep breath. "Which brings me to my request… I think it prudent—in fact, it is most important to me—that we share a bed *before* we are married. It is all very well that you say you love me, but if we don't share a bed before we are married we won't-won't—*know* if we are-are—*right* for each other *in that way*. If we are to spend the rest of our lives together, we need to be physically compatible, don't you agree?"

There was a moment of complete silence between them, the only sound in the room being the tinkling of Peter the Macaw's chain. It rattled against the carved pedestal as the bird climbed from one rung to the next in the warmth of the sun.

Sir Antony attempted to clear his throat, fist up to his closed mouth, though he did not let go of the chair back.

"I cannot fault your reasoning, Caro," he managed to say in a tone he hoped was neutral.

Mentally, he was frantically wondering what she had endured in the bed shared with her husband that she required physical confirmation he was able to perform in the bedchamber before she was prepared to accept his offer of marriage. And what did she mean when she said she was *shown differently*, and by whom? He stored that startling disclosure away for another day, and continued in a voice that was at odds with his frenetic thoughts.

"Physical compatibility is exceedingly important in a marriage based on love, I agree," he continued levelly. "I would be telling an untruth if I said otherwise. And although I have no firsthand experience of the institution of marriage, arranged for convenience or for love, the single most important ingredient for me is love. All else can be worked through. Friendship, mutual respect and shared interests, these, too, are very important. But I would hate myself forevermore if I thought you married me with unresolved doubts of any kind. And so I am willing to accept your proposal that we share a bed before marriage. I understand it is only in this way that you can assure yourself that I measure up as a lover—that I am more than capable of *pleasing* you."

"Oh! You must not think it is you!" she blurted out, suddenly shy and awkward under his unblinking gaze. "I do not doubt you will please me—*exceedingly*. You have experience. All men must… But that was a *naïve* assumption. But I know you have had your-your—*share* of of affairs. You possibly had a mistress or two in Russia—"

"One," he confessed, his cravat suddenly inexplicably tight. "I had one mistress while in Russia. It was not a tawdry affair, Caro. You must understand, once I discovered you were married, I lost all hope. Your husband was a very young man. There was every expectation your marriage would last for at least twenty years, perhaps thirty. I had to get on with my life or go mad. I allowed myself to care—to care very deeply—for Katya…"

"Katya…?"

"The Princess Ekaterina Naryshkina Knyazhevy-Yusupova."

"A princess?"

"Yes."

"A Russian princess?"

"Yes." Sir Antony heard the edge to her voice and couldn't be happier that she might be jealous. He suppressed a smile, adding seriously, "Katya is the sister of Misha, more formally Prince Mikhail Ivan Knyazhevy-Yusupov, Russian minister for trade. Both Katya and her brother Misha were—are—my very good friends. If not for them, I doubt I would be the man you see standing before you."

"The sister was your mistress, and the brother and his sister are your good friends?" Caroline frowned at his nod. She did not like such an arrangement at all. "Did this Prince Mikhail know you were bedding his sister?"

"Katya and I would not have become lovers had her brother been unhappy with the arrangement."

"Naturally," Caroline murmured, thinking the customs of the Russian nobility odd indeed; knowing Salt would never have countenanced such an arrangement.

For some inexplicable reason, such a civilized understanding between brother, sister, and lover only increased her jealousy for this unknown princess, as did Sir Antony's affront that she would dare suggest he would act less than honorably in the matter. Of course he had asked permission of the brother, Caroline thought with a mental twinge of annoyance. No doubt he and the Prince came to some sort of gentlemanly arrangement. It would not have surprised her to learn that Antony had not touched a hair on the head of the precious princess until her brother had given his consent. She knew it was not in his nature to be deceitful. What deceit and cunning there was in his family had all gone to Diana.

Knowing all this, then why, she wondered, did it hurt her heart he had conducted his affair, as he did everything in his life, in a gentlemanly manner? Why would her feelings not have been so bruised had he cavorted in the beds of any number of Russian females with no thought to their brothers, or even their husbands?

She did not need to look for answers. She knew. He had said it himself. He cared deeply for this Russian princess and their affair had been conducted honorably, if such unions could be called thus. Whereas, her behavior before and after her marriage had been anything but honorable. She was quite certain she knew the answer to her next question, but she asked it anyway.

"Do you—Do you still care—*deeply*—for your Russian princess?"

He could not lie to her. It was no way for them to begin again.

"Yes. But not in the way you think," he added in a rush watching her porcelain cheeks flood with heat. He smiled crookedly. "You said yourself love won't be enough for me, for us, when I know everything. I believe you will be proved wrong. I, too, don't want to hide anything from you. You need to know that the moment I found out you were a widow, my hope returned. I want us to marry and spend the rest of our lives into old age *together*... Do you understand, Caro? Just the two of us. I do not now have a mistress and it is my heartfelt wish that I never shall again. But that depends on you..."

"Oh? Oh!" Caroline could not suppress her delight at his emphatic confession and she blushed, quickly lowering her lashes when he raised one eyebrow, as if to quell any doubt she might have as to his sincerity. Finally, she looked up at him again. "You must be satisfied that I please you too. It is only fair, is it not, that we please each other?"

"Yes. But I fail to understand why you would harbor doubts that you would be a disappointment to me in any way."

Caroline moved closer, so close that her petticoats brushed against his long legs, and he straightened and let go of the chair back.

"It is because I do have firsthand experience of the institution of marriage, not a love match, but a marriage nonetheless," she explained, "that I am very aware there are expectations on both sides. If the husband fails to provide... If the wife is not what the husband expects... Then there will be disappointment. I do not believe my *feelings* for you have changed and my skin remains the same. What you see before you is the Caroline you knew. I am no taller, no prettier, and still have the same wretched red hair and freckles I have always had. Stripped of this shell I am no different, either. But what would you know of that? But—I *have* changed, Antony. *Under* my skin, I am not the same female you knew before you went to 'Petersburg. And because I am not the same, I fear that when you know me better as I am now, you will not want me in that way as you once did..."

When he remained silent, she gave a little sigh of defeat and fiddled with the gold chains of her chatelaine before looking up at him again.

"Not that I am at all certain you ever wanted me *in that way* before you left for 'Petersburg! You say you love me, have always loved me, but you have never—in all the years we have known one another—ever tried to kiss me. So how do I know that you truly *want* me? Those pecks on the cheek at birthdays and Christmases I dismiss!"

"Not want you?" he repeated in a whisper. "Not *want* to kiss you?"

Later, he was to wonder what prompted him into action: How bravely she looked directly into his eyes as she voiced her doubts about his desire for her, or Peter the Macaw's loud attention-seeking screech. Whatever it was, something triggered deep within him and it gave him the strength and purpose to vault the high mental wall, built many years ago to keep his desire prisoner until Caroline had grown to womanhood. One word—*want*—was all it took for that wall to crumble.

One moment she was explaining her feelings to him and he was patiently listening, a hand in the pocket of his lavender silk frock coat, the other fiddling with the gold-rimmed quizzing glass dangling on a silken riband about his neck. In the next he shoved aside a chair, and so violently it collided with another and toppled, and pulled Caroline into his arms to press his mouth to hers, stopping her words and sweeping aside years spent in purgatorial circumspection.

"Want you? How could you doubt it?" he asked huskily, keeping her within the circle of his embrace, face poised over hers.

Her green eyes looked up at him without guile and there was a light there, something he had never seen, or failed to see because he had never taken the liberty of holding her in his arms before: *Desire.* He saw that she desired him as much as he did her, and he wanted to lift her up and twirl her about in his arms in celebration.

"I can't wait to show you just how much I *want* you, my doubting beauty. Truth be told, I have wanted to kiss you since you were fifteen years old, when you so confidently announced we would marry on your eighteenth birthday. I want to kiss you all over; every strand of your glorious golden hair, every enticing curve—*everything.*"

His words were wondrously reassuring, as was his kiss. The long line of his hard body pressed against her, the masculine traces of sandalwood cologne, and the roughness of his skin as his mouth met hers were all so intoxicating. *He* was intoxicating. She held on tightly to the open front of his frock coat as if she feared drowning. And she was drowning, in wanting more of him. She *needed* more. She needed a proper kiss, a kiss that would forever remove the memories of a puerile husband and the attentions of a lover that left her feeling nothing but bitter regret. She needed a loving, giving kiss from the one man who truly loved her.

So when he followed up his gentle kiss to her mouth with words of reassurance, then kissed her forehead and apologized for taking a liberty, unfolding his arms from about her waist as he did so, Caroline would not let go of him. She had spent too many sleepless nights to count, imagining this moment and wondering if it would ever come to pass. Now, with such doubts cast like dust to the four winds, she wasn't about to let it end before she was satisfied. She put her arms up to his wide shoulders and held fast. On tiptoe, she kissed his mouth, and as she did so a silk-covered mule slid from her stockinged foot. The shoe clattered to the polished floor, and it was this that had Antony's arms securely about her waist once again, thinking her about to fall.

And when Caroline's mouth grazed his, when the soft cushion of her full lips and her warm sweet breath caressed his mouth in invitation, how could he refuse her? It was a barely-there touch, but it was enough to rekindle his senses, and when she murmured the words *proper kiss*, as she slid her arms about his neck and opened her mouth on his, it was all the permission he needed to stoop and kiss her without restraint.

They gave themselves up to a long, lingering kiss full of mutual yearning and feverish promise. A kiss that threatened to engulf them in impropriety if not for the scintilla of awareness of the world provided by Peter the Macaw's intermittent calls and a noise, Antony wasn't quite sure what and couldn't care less, similar to the teeth-shuddering screech of fabric being rent in two. The bird's distress hammered in his ears, but he did not want the kiss to end. He had waited such a long time to kiss Caroline that he was damned if he would allow a jealous raging feathered fiend to interrupt the exquisite pleasure of tasting the sweet moistness of her mouth.

Before they knew what they were about, the couple had scattered chairs in their wake as they clung to each other, lost in the passionate moment.

Peter the Macaw shrieked as if he were being attacked, caught in the silken folds of a torn damask curtain, and the two footmen standing sentry at the book room double doors so far forget themselves to see their noble employer's sister engaging in a passionate kiss with an unknown gentleman that they gingerly crept down half the length of the room, contemplating if they should take matters into their own hands, or run from the room in ignorance.

Into this dramatic scene walked the butler.

MILLER STRODE INTO THE ANTEROOM FROM THE HALL, HAVING exited the book room via an internal servant door. He was across the threshold and apologizing to Sir Antony that his lordship was unable to grant his request for an interview when the anteroom came into focus. Peter the Macaw's loud screeches of alarm had his head snapping about in the direction of the windows, and there was the large bird half way up the curtain, flapping his bright blue feathers and hanging by his black claws in the tattered remnants of the silken damask, shredded in mischief by his large black beak. By the damage done, Peter had been left to his own devices for quite some time.

If this weren't enough to set the butler's bottom lip wobbling in shocked outrage, the two footmen not at their posts but transfixed in the middle of the room like a couple of inanimate companions, were all that was needed for him to lose his composure completely. He forgot his manners. He forgot his exalted position within a great and noble household. And he so far forgot himself as to bellow, so there was every chance it was his booming voice as well as Peter the Macaw's screeches for attention that penetrated the gilded double doors leading into the book room.

His mannered apology to Sir Antony was swallowed whole as he exploded with anger.

"God Almighty! I'll wring that bloody bird's neck m'self, if his lordship don't break down those doors and do the deed! And I'll damned well wring your necks as well! What the hell are you two playing at, eh? Want to be mucking out the stables? You! Fetch a couple of the lads from the hallway. And, you! Find the Lady Caroline. No one else can get within a foot of that bloody bird without losing a finger, more's the pity! I'd wring its neck myself otherwise. What? Well! Don't both stand there gaping at me like you've seen a ghost! Her ladyship's not going to appear before me like some bloody apparition!"

"I'm here, Miller," Lady Caroline responded as calmly as she could, face flushed and a hand to her mussed hair, standing at the butler's back. She couldn't suppress a smile when Miller's feet left the ground and he swirled about to face her with a terrified expression, as if she were indeed a ghost. "I won't need any assistance with Peter, thank you.

Best see to those chairs, and see to it the doors to the book room remain closed. Lord Salt and Sir Antony are not to be disturbed."

Miller's gaze flashed in the direction of the Earl's book room. One of the paneled doors was wide, allowing uninvited access. He grimaced. Shock gave way to frustration. He had failed in his mission. Amidst the uproar, the macaw's incessant screeching for attention and his own explosive outcry, he had inadvertently allowed Sir Antony Templestowe to quietly slip into the inner sanctum of the Earl of Salt Hendon's book room, unannounced and unbidden.

FOURTEEN

The last time Sir Antony was in the Earl of Salt Hendon's sumptuous book room he was drunk, barely able to stand upright, and had received a ruthless dressing-down from his noble cousin—justifiably so. It had immediately followed his outrageous behavior at the recital, where he had not only made a complete ass of himself, broken Caroline's heart, shocked and embarrassed the Countess, heavily pregnant with her first child, and everyone in attendance, but also lost the respect and friendship of the Earl. At the time, he was too crippled with drink and cloaked in self-loathing to fully appreciate how his behavior had affected the people he most loved in the world. Sobriety and somber reflection in Russia gave him an appreciation of the devastating effect his words must have had on the Earl and Countess, and he realized with a heavy heart that it was unlikely he would ever regain their good opinion.

At the Salt House recital four years before, while in heated argument with Caroline, he revealed visiting the Countess in her boudoir alone, she in nothing more than her nightdress. Of course he did not mention that he had gone there uninvited, seeking the Countess's reassurance that Caroline was not about to become engaged to another. He was ill from a night of heavy drinking and lay prostrate on her chaise longue, head pounding and eyes shut tight to the morning light, while the Countess remained seated at her dressing table, offering him advice and reassurance. It was all innocent and very much a brother seeking the advice of a sister in a heart-to-heart. But he did not say that. Nor did he mention the Earl not only knew all about his trespass, and while furious to find him in the Countess's boudoir, had forgiven him, knowing the circumstances behind it.

Sir Antony had held up his visit to the Countess's boudoir at Caroline like some shield, to counter the arrows of her childish goading about her imminent engagement to Captain "Big-Boots" Beresford; that the war hero from the Hanover campaign was more of a man than he ever could be. Which, when he thought about it once sober, was not an unfair accusation given that a side effect of his constant inebriation in the months following his sister's incarceration was impotency. It hit a raw nerve and so he had countered with the Countess as the epitome of female perfection, and he would know that as well as her husband because he'd been privileged enough to see her in her nightgown.

Such a startling and most shocking revelation before an audience of fifty was the best source of fuel for the gossipmonger fire. The juicy morsel was swallowed whole, without a second thought to its authenticity and with no regard to the circumstances in which the revelation was uttered. By morning, Society had turned the morsel into a three-course banquet of lust, furtive frolics and dynastic self-preservation. What had been whispered behind fluttering fans and muttered behind outstretched newssheets by the Earl's political enemies, yet dismissed as mere muckraking by the majority, had, with Sir Antony's very public jaw-dropping revelations, become fact by morning. Society's female fraternity were openly discussing it with their relatives over their buttered bread and hot chocolate, while their gentlemen folk sniggered to each other across the table at their preferred coffee house.

Lady Salt's pregnancy so soon after marriage, her husband's nonchalant attitude to his beautiful wife's close friendship with his cousin Sir Antony, and Diana St. John's surprise departure for the Continent almost to the day of the announcement that the Countess of Salt Hendon was expecting the Earl's first child, was more than enough evidence to confirm the rumor Diana St. John had been weakly denying—as a loyal sister should—just before her abrupt departure for foreign climes.

The rumor everyone knew but dared not say out loud was that Sir Antony Templestowe, not the Earl of Salt Hendon, had sired the child the Countess carried—an heir for the earldom.

Sir Antony's outlandish confession made perfect sense!

For a nobleman of four-and-thirty, who had odds at White's of a hundred to one of ever producing an heir because a fall from a horse had left him infertile, to then get his Countess with child on their wedding night was as if a bolt of lightning had struck Polite Society.

How could this be when it was a known fact the Earl couldn't even get a whore with child, and not through want of trying? The question continued to swirl in an undercurrent through drawing rooms well into the Countess's pregnancy. And then, with only two months to the birth of an heir, Sir Antony's outburst provided Society with confirmation of what they believed had to be the answer: Sir Antony Templestowe had fathered the Countess's unborn child.

Well, that was cousinly love for you! Who wouldn't want to offer his services to provide the Earl with a son when it meant sharing the bed of celebrated beauty Jane, Countess of Salt Hendon? Was it any wonder Sir Antony had riled at Lady Caroline's inferences about his manhood when he had tupped a countess and got her with child upon first mount! One wondered how the Earl tolerated sharing his bride with another. Yet, all knew the Earl to be an astute politician, single-minded and hard-hearted when it came to making decisions for the good of the Kingdom. It made sense he would be the same where his own kingdom was concerned. His earldom needed an heir and if he could not provide one, then let his closest living male relative provide one for him.

Nothing to wonder at then why Diana St. John had departed for the Continent. It was common knowledge Diana was in love with the Earl. She was also heavily involved in his political life, so it was no stretch of the imagination to believe her instrumental in furthering the Earl's dynastic ambitions by offering up her brother as stallion for the Earl's broodmare. Jealous of the Countess and knowing too much, perhaps she had threatened the Earl to reveal his dirty little secret to the world? Diana St. John was made to disappear, for her health, so it was put about. But who believed that ruse?

Underscoring why his sister was made to disappear from good society, for his sordid behavior at the recital in breaking Lady Caroline's heart and airing the family dirty laundry in public, Sir Antony Templestowe was banished by the Earl to the icy wastelands of the diplomatic service: St. Petersburg.

If there was a backwater for an English diplomat's career, the Russian Imperial Court was it. That Sir Antony was sent to such a diplomatic dump, the social stagnation pool of the Foreign Department, was indication enough he was no longer on speaking terms with his noble cousin. And with his unique services as a sire no longer required, his presence in London would only be an embarrassment for the noble couple, as well as a constant reminder of the Earl's inadequacy in fulfilling his dynastic duty by the House of Sinclair and the Earldom of Salt Hendon.

That the Earl and Countess went on to have two more healthy children in quick succession after the birth of a longed-for son and heir was not thought relevant by the Earl's political enemies and those of a weak-minded persuasion. Two more children did much to quell any further undercurrent of doubt as to their true sire, but what mattered, and where the muck stuck like wet hay to the red heel of the noble buckled shoe, was the iffy circumstances surrounding the conception of the Earl's firstborn. And for that, Sir Antony knew, he would never be forgiven.

He leaned his head against the book room's closed paneled doors, to gather his thoughts and to catch his breath, heady from the passionate kiss shared with Caroline. There was something indefinable about their kiss and it left him giddy. A few deep breaths, and he trod silently down the length of the long book-lined room, he imagined not unlike a mutineer walking the plank of a ship to his demise, staying close to the bookshelves, his attention fixed on the massive double sided mahogany work table with its elaborate gold standish holding quills, pounce pot, ink and pencils, its surface covered in well-ordered piles of paper.

The Earl sat behind his desk, engrossed in reading a document.

Occasionally, he put the sheaf of papers to the work surface of the desk, picked up his quill, dipped it in ink and added his remarks in the left hand margin. Very occasionally, his attention wandered from the document and he would drop his chin to look over his gold-rimmed reading spectacles to the second fireplace. It was then a transformation took place and Sir Antony saw his friend of old. The Earl's features softened, the deep indent between his brows smoothed, and the grim set to his mouth disappeared, replaced by a smile that split his face. His smile lingered in that direction in some sort of dazed wonderment, and then, as if remembering the task at hand, he would bring his gaze back to the desk and continue reading.

When the Earl smiled, so did Sir Antony. He had never seen his friend looking so well and more content with life. Physically he was still the same bear-sized man of four years ago, still as healthy and, no doubt, as well exercised as he had ever been. He was the same as the day he had turned his back on him, except in his apparel.

At this hour, Sir Antony was surprised to find the Earl in undress. Always a stickler for correct attire at the appropriate time, whether at home or away from the house, Salt dressed immaculately, more often than not in a matching suit of frock coat, waistcoat and breeches, richly embroidered, that would not look out of place at the Opera. And he always wore powder when in town. Perhaps his cousin had employed a new valet? But that could not account for the lack of powder in the sandy shoulder-length hair tied back with a black riband, or that a deep blue silk banyan was thrown negligently over a crisp white shirt and cravat. No doubt his stockinged feet were encased in red Moroccan leather mules, which would put the finishing touch to the Earl's at-home attire. In such undress, Sir Antony knew well enough that his cousin was in no fit state to receive visitors, and thus no one but immediate family would be permitted into his presence.

The Earl's undress did not bode well for Sir Antony's trespass. Small wonder the doors to his book room remained closed. With a depressing sigh, he took this as a sign that he was no longer considered family, and thus an audience had been out of the question. Still, it did not deter him from his purpose and he put his trust in the Earl's smile. It was the only indication his noble cousin was in a benevolent mood. Yet, the Earl's mood and his opinion of him were of little importance. What mattered was coming to an agreement regarding how best to handle Diana's incarceration while minimizing scandal and averting tragedy. Keeping these thoughts uppermost, he walked straight up to the front of the massive mahogany desk and bowed respectfully to his noble cousin.

The Earl sensed a presence but did not look up.

"No means no, Miller," he said flatly, setting aside the page he was reading and removing his eyeglasses. He put a hand flat to the stack of papers that made up the document. "Take this to Mr. Ellis. Tell him to read my annotations and then to come and see me in—about an hour's time. Place the tea tray on the low table. The bottle of claret you can leave here."

"Salt."

The Earl's head jerked up. The dark eyes widened in surprise and the nobleman half rose out of his chair, a smile of recognition softening his handsome face. Sir Antony returned the smile, relief coursing through his veins, and stuck out his hand in greeting. It was on the tip of his tongue to tell his cousin how well he looked and how overjoyed he was to see him, when the light died in the Earl's dark eyes, the smile dropped into a thin, uncompromising frown, and he resettled on his chair, pulling the silk banyan tighter about his shoulders. Reaction had given way to memory, and with a small sigh Sir Antony dropped his hand to catch the riband about his neck that secured his quizzing glass.

"You look well," the Earl stated. He fiddled with his eyeglasses but kept his gaze on Sir Antony's face. "I can't see you now. Didn't Miller tell you I—"

"You're looking well, too," Sir Antony interrupted, keeping his feelings well in check.

"Now the niceties are done, have the decency to end your intrusion and take yourself off—"

"Miller had no opportunity to tell me anything; he has his hands full with a recalcitrant bird. I won't take up much of your time, but we need to talk about—"

"It can wait."

So it had come to this—talking at one another as if mere nodding acquaintances. There was a time when a day hadn't gone by that they didn't spend some part of it in each other's company. Sir Antony noted the Earl's fidgeting and it offered him a glimmer that his granite exterior encased a softer center.

"No. It cannot wait. You know it cannot; reason for my trespass; reason I am in England and not in 'Petersburg. It is the reason we need to talk about—"

"Not now," Salt said through his teeth.

Sir Antony frowned. By the Earl's action of cutting him off so quickly before he could even utter his sister's name, it was obvious he was well aware Diana had escaped her confinement. Was he that sensitive, that intractable to hearing the truth out loud? Did he hope that by ignoring her, she would just disappear? He could not believe it. Or perhaps his cousin meant to keep him ignorant of how he was going to deal with his mad sister? That he would not allow. If Salt's lack of enthusiasm at this forced reunion had wounded his feelings, his implacable arrogance angered him to the point of sarcastic bluntness.

"I won't leave this room until we have discussed what is to be done. Perhaps you have already decided what you intend to do, which wouldn't surprise me! But I have a right to know, and a right to be consulted. That you sit there half dressed in the middle of the day, I couldn't care less. What does it matter in the greater scheme of things? I'd not have cared had I interrupted you soaking in your bath! Perhaps being in your tub would've been more convenient, because you'd be a captive audience and forced to entertain my conversation!" He took a breath, put up a hand and then let it drop heavily. "This isn't what I envisioned for a reunion with you, and with—with Jane. And I will call her *Jane* in private with you, not Lady Salt, because she is a dear friend and wife of my closest cousin."

When the Earl put up his brows but said nothing, he added with a sigh of exasperation,

"Oh, for God's sake, Salt! I grant our last meeting wasn't my finest hour, but a lot of apples have fallen from the tree since then, so the least you could do is not sit there wooden-faced and pinched-nosed, as if the sanctity of your book room has been breached by a sweep! And I won't apologize for my lack of servility and I won't bow down to the Head of the Family. I had a damned uncomfortable journey to get home as swiftly as possible, without so much as a leave-taking, so no doubt I've burned my bridges in 'Petersburg. But that doesn't matter. None of it does. If it costs me my position in the Foreign Department, if it means our friendship is beyond repair, all for the greater good, then so be it. I mean to have no regrets. But there is one thing I won't do this very minute and that's leave this room until I have told you what I have arranged for my sis—"

"Miller was charged with telling you to wait upon Lady Reanay for an hour and then return here," Salt interrupted evenly, folding his arms across his broad chest and leaning back in his chair to regard Sir Antony under hooded lids. "If that is how you conducted diplomacy in 'Petersburg, by impassioned brow-beating, I'm surprised you are so well-regarded. But perhaps the Russians prefer a more direct approach; or your inability—some would dare say *recklessness*—to take no for an answer. It is all I can think of why you are being honored—"

"Honored?" Sir Antony frowned and took a step closer, his fingers, which had been tight about the stem of his quizzing glass, opening. He allowed himself to stand easy. The word *honored* completely threw him off his line of argument, as Salt knew it would.

"They mustn't mind their conversations being interrupted either," the Earl muttered, adding with the twitch of a smile as he sat forward, "Yes. Honored. Despite your inexplicable departure from the Imperial Court, the Empress has graciously condescended to forgive you, not only for not taking your proper leave of her, but also for not being present so she could personally bestow upon you the Order of St. Anna. Have you any idea at all about the order?"

Sir Antony shook his head. "None."

"It is the highest order that can be bestowed upon a foreigner. To point out fact, I am not entirely certain it has been conferred on anyone who is not a Russian. You could very well be the first, and thus set the precedent. It is usually given to Russian nobles for exceptional services to the state bureaucracy or for military gallantry. There are four grades within the order, and you, my dear cousin, are being awarded the highest grade."

"Am I? How extraordinary!" Sir Antony frowned. "What does that mean, precisely?"

The Earl couldn't suppress a huff of laughter.

"A diplomatic nightmare for His Majesty, and in turn, for me. The King requested I find a solution to the dilemma, and before the trade treaty with the Russians is signed."

"Far be it for me to cause a fuss for His Majesty, and for you," Sir Antony retorted mildly. "I'll write to the Empress and decline the honor if it—"

"You'll take no such action!" the Earl ordered, all laughter extinguished. "The signing of the trade treaty and the bestowing of the Order of St. Anna go hand-in-glove. You know as well as I, the Russians import more goods from us than they do from the French. And the last thing we want is for the French to offer Catherine more favorable terms. It is imperative the trade agreement between our two nations is signed, sealed and delivered, and if part of the deal requires you to wear a red sash and star from our Russian friends, so be it. You will accept the honor and the treaty will be signed."

"And the dilemma?"

"The Order of St. Anna in the first grade comes with hereditary ennoblement."

"Good Lord!"

The Earl pulled a face. "Just so," he murmured, adding audibly, "The dilemma is that as an Englishman, you cannot be ennobled into the Russian nobility. Yet, the Russians expect you to be rewarded by your own sovereign to the fullest extent of the honor being bestowed upon you. Not to do so would call into question their judgment. That would be a diplomatic nightmare in the making. It is a case of saving face."

"You have found a solution to this dilemma."

"I have. It will not only satisfy the Russians but it is acceptable to His Majesty."

"Naturally."

The Earl's expression was deadpan. "I own I've missed your ripostes. You always were the master of understatement."

At such praise from his former mentor, Sir Antony could not help grinning like a schoolboy. What the Earl said next dropped his jaw.

"I have the privilege of informing you that as a consequence of being awarded the Order of St. Anna by Her Imperial Majesty the

Empress Queen Catherine, His Majesty is ennobling you a Viscount. You know the formalities, letters patent and then henceforth first Viscount Temple and Baron Stowe and addressed as Lord Temple; your heir to be known as Lord Stowe. Congratulations."

Sir Antony was about to respond in the usual self-effacing manner to such congratulations when the Earl's subsequent offhand rejoinder tainted his feeling of other-worldliness at receiving such remarkable news, and deflated his elation.

"Your part in the trade negotiations between our two countries must have been quite something to behold," Salt said with asperity. "From the correspondence I have read, and the conferring of such a high honor on a foreigner, the Empress must have been most impressed with your—*skills*…"

When the Earl let the sentence hang, Sir Antony kept his gaze fixed, despite his clean-shaven cheeks darkening at the inference. It was well known at the Russian court and beyond that the Empress Catherine had her male favorites, and that her lovers were rewarded with all manner of gifts and honors for services rendered. Sir Antony had successfully avoided joining a long list of Catherine's conquests through careful and tactful maneuvering, and with the help of his mentor and friend Prince Mikhail. That the Empress had granted him high honors might confound him, but it was not his cousin's place to make snide insinuations.

"I am flattered Her Imperial Highness has seen fit to reward my efforts. But you know as well as I that such honors are often bestowed through the recommendations of others."

"Yes. Prince Mikhail Knyazhevy-Yusupov holds you in the highest regard. So does the Princess, his sister…"

Sir Antony set his jaw.

"I make no apologies for the life I carved out for myself in 'Petersburg. Not when all hope of the life I had envisioned for myself here was extinguished."

"It is the life you intend to carve out for yourself now you are home which concerns me more."

Sir Antony smiled thinly. "Oh, I very much want to discuss that with you, but not now, not today. There is a far more serious and pressing state of affairs much closer to home that you and I must deal with before I can begin to contemplate the future, kicked upstairs or not, with any true sense that it belongs to me. My one regret about 'Petersburg is that I am unable to offer the Knyazhevy-Yusupovs my humble thanks in person.

He paused when, for the second time since attempting to address him on the subject of Diana's escape from her imprisonment, the Earl broke eye contact, distracted by someone or something at Sir Antony's back. He did not have the bad manners to look over his right shoulder to see who or what it was, but it made him bristle and wonder if it was the butler with a couple of footmen ready to eject him at his noble master's nod.

"You may not be able to thank the Knyazhevy-Yusupovs in person," the Earl replied, bringing his gaze back to Sir Antony's blue eyes, "but you can thank Prince Mikhail's cousin Prince Ivan Yusupov, who arrived in London only last week, bringing your ribbon and star with him."

Sir Antony took a step forward, a hand to the mahogany desk. He knew Prince Ivan very well, they had fenced together, and been partners in games of royal tennis, but he did not interrupt the Earl.

"His Highness Prince Ivan is head of a Russian agricultural delegation," the Earl explained. "Empress Catherine is intent on continuing the policy laid down by her predecessor Peter in sending members of the Imperial Court to England for all manner of edification and cultural exchanges. I have the enviable task of playing host to Prince Ivan, who will be guest of honor at my masquerade ball. Next month a small battalion of Russian bureaucrats from their Ministry of Agriculture will visit Salt Hendon. They are keen to observe and question first-hand the agricultural practices of an English estate. Rufus Willis is chafing at the bit to play tour guide." He placed his palm on the document he had been reading. "Herein are the terms and conditions of the agreement between our two nations. I'm not convinced which is more burdensome, wading through all two hundred pages of this, or donning a feathered mask and flitting about a ballroom full of Russians. Ah, the trials and tribulations one must endure as a humble servant of the crown."

Sir Antony was digesting this information when the Earl's remark about the feathered mask and being a servant of the crown was given particular emphasis by a tinkle of female laughter.

Far from taking offence at being laughed at, the Earl's austere expression cracked into a grin. He pushed out his chair and stood, shoving his hands deep into the pockets of his silk banyan, gaze directed at the second fireplace.

"Do stop teasing Antony," the Countess playfully chided. "You gave yourself away by pretending you find a return to politics burdensome. Admit to it, my lord. The thought of entertaining a ballroom full of noble Russians, not to mention parading about with your newly-ennobled cousin in his Russian sash and star, to the envy of your political opponents, has you mentally rubbing your hands with glee!"

The Earl chuckled and came around to the front of his desk. He paused and stuck out his hand to Sir Antony.

"Must welcome you upstairs," he said, in much the old manner in which he had addressed his cousin before his banishment. He warmly shook Sir Antony's hand and briefly gripped his silken shoulder. "Apologies for casting aspersions on your abilities, Antony, but it is good to hear you earned the honor going about your daily business and not as one of Catherine's minions. Whatever my darling wife thinks to the contrary about my mentoring abilities," he said, turning to look at the second fireplace, "I will not own to it! Nor will I agree to what you propose about the upcoming masquerade, my lady. My private glee will be because everyone at the ball will be envious that you are at my side and not theirs."

Sir Antony swiveled about on the balls of his black leather shoes, and swayed, grateful he was in close proximity to the Earl's desk, allowing him to keep a hand to the polished surface to stay steady on his feet. His return to London was shaping up to be one of an hourly expectation of a speechless surprise. If he were superstitious, he would blame the loss of his talisman, now in his sister's keeping. But his life had been turned upside down and inside out long before Diana had ripped his gold locket from the front of his embroidered waistcoat.

In the space of one day he discovered his house commandeered by his unstable sister, who was hiding in full view of the world. He had also found himself in debt to the sum of two thousand pounds. He had then agreed to Caroline's astonishing demand that they share a bed before marriage. And what of his exhibition in front of servants, and one irate feathered fiend, by enjoying a most wondrous kiss with her? Finally, he had barged into the Earl's book room making demands without a thought to what lay beyond the door—now this!

Honored by the Russians and being kicked to the Lords as a Viscount by His Majesty was more than enough for one lifetime, least of all one morning call on his noble cousin.

He burned bright with discomfort at the sight presented to him at the arrangement of furniture about the second fireplace. He mentally winced at his stupidity for not realizing sooner the Earl was not alone. Small wonder the book room was off limits; why the Earl was distracted; why he kept diverting the conversation away from mention of Diana; why his responses were more civil than expected; why he had not once raised his voice when Sir Antony had all but shouted at him.

If someone didn't fetch him a strong cup of tea at once, he believed there was a good possibility he would faint, not from thirst, but from acute embarrassment.

FIFTEEN

As if in answer to Sir Antony's silent prayer, the butler and two footmen trod lightly down the length of the book room. A footman deposited a silver tea tray on the low table at the center of a group of chairs where the Countess sat, another put a Japanned wooden tray holding a bottle of claret and crystal etched glasses on the Earl's desk. The butler, once he had positioned the silver teapot on its stand and lit the warmer, went about pouring out a cup of tea for the Countess and placed the fine porcelain Sèvres cup on its saucer on a satinwood whatnot within her easy reach.

When the Earl offered Sir Antony a glass of claret and he declined, preferring a cup of tea, he showed his surprise with a light lift of his eyebrows but said nothing, exchanging a look with his wife as he joined her by the fireplace. The servants silently took their leave, Miller hovering by the tea kettle until the Earl waved him away.

The Countess was comfortably seated on a wingchair, painted cotton overskirt arranged about her and cream silk slippers upon a footstool. Her shiny black hair was in undress, piled loosely on her head and threaded with pale pink ribbons knotted with pearls, the weight allowed to fall across her right shoulder. Her pretty shell pink quilted maternity jacket was untied and gaping.

Jane had her baby son to her breast when Sir Antony disturbed the peace and quiet in the book room. With the nursery maid's help, a diaphanous silk shawl was strategically draped across the front of her gown, shielding her feeding infant from view before the trespasser realized the Earl was not alone. Still, such arrangements for the sake of protecting the uninitiated—for surely an unmarried man, any man unfamiliar with the basic needs of an infant, must be made uneasy by such an arresting sight—were in vain. While his mother was speaking, her infant son took hold of the embroidered edge of the shawl in his tiny fist and tugged, no doubt in protest at not being able to clearly see the only face in the world that mattered.

"I offer you Sam's apologies, Antony, but babies have no sense of timing or occasion," Jane said chattily, in the hopes of easing Sir Antony's shock and discomfort at discovering her suckling her six-week-old son. "Thus you find me attending to Sam's needs here in Salt's book room and not in the nursery. Ned and Beth are having their midmorning rest, which means Salt and I may have an hour or two alone, a rare occurrence these days. And if it requires I intrude on affairs of state, then so be it." She smiled up at her husband. "I am not entirely convinced being called 'a welcome distraction' is complimentary. What do you think, Antony?" When Sir Antony glanced quickly at the Earl, she laughed. "Oh, do forgive me! I should not make you choose sides so soon after your return. You may have a reprieve today, but not tomorrow."

"You scheming minx!" the Earl retorted lovingly, setting his glass of claret on the ornately carved mantel. "Antony is not five minutes in the front door and you already have him pegged as your petitioner. Ron was right. There are too many females in this house. And with Ron now at Eton, it is only fair all remaining male relatives are duly co-opted to my cause. Am I not lord and master in all things?"

"Of course you are, dearest," Jane responded sweetly, adding with a dimple, "We all say so—in your presence."

The noble couple laughed at that, sharing a private joke, and Sir Antony was strangely melancholy that there was a time when he, too, would have joined in their laughter. Now he was oddly ill at ease, and sent his gaze anywhere but in the direction of the Countess. Jane sensed this and she handed off her replete infant to his nurse to have his little back rubbed to settle his stomach, while she adjusted her clothing behind a lacquered leather screen perpendicular to the settee.

"Please make yourself a dish of tea, Antony, while I make myself presentable. I will then introduce you to the newest member of our family, who, I am quite convinced, will one day be taller and wider than his papa."

She reappeared a few minutes later, quilted maternity jacket secured, pink silk bows tied and painted cotton overskirt with its frothy under petticoats given a gentle rustle to settle its fall. If she noticed the heavy silence between the two large men in the room, that the Earl remained by the fireplace, he now with his infant son in his arms, Sir Antony still by the writing desk watching his cousin, she ignored it and said at her chatty best,

"I must offer up our apologies for our want of dress. Salt only arrived in town a few hours ago having seen Ron safely embraced by his Eton fellows. As a consequence, he has had no time to do anything but bathe and change and read that wretched document." She smiled when the Earl pulled a face. "That is not entirely true. Had the children been awake when Papa arrived, it would have been impossible for that document to receive his lordship's attention, undivided or otherwise! We would have been in the nursery. Which, by the way, is still painted blue, though the Turkey rugs have now seen their fair share of wear. Little boys *run* everywhere."

She crossed the space between the settee and the Earl's desk, a hand out in welcome, and smiled when Sir Antony came gingerly across the room to meet her. When he bowed over her fingers, as befitted her rank as countess, she pulled him close to kiss his cheek.

"You must not stand on ceremony with family," she smiled, a lump in her throat and tears in her blue eyes. "You are not in 'Petersburg now. Hopefully, the Foreign Department will allow you to stay home for some time, and not send you off to Constantinople or Kyoto or Oslo, which Aunt Alice tells me sees no sun for half the year."

She had rattled on because she feared bursting into tears of happiness to be reunited with her husband's closest cousin, and, at the time of her marriage, her dearest friend. She had not realized just how much she had craved his company until that moment. Three babies and the running of a noble establishment had kept her far too busy. With Antony home, she so wanted to believe all was now right with her world. But she knew why he had left St. Petersburg in such a hurry, and that overshadowed her joy, the look in his eyes only increasing her apprehension for the safety of her young family.

"Jane... It is quite wonderful to be home... I just wish the circumstances... Excuse me. I'm such a wretched sentimentalist," Sir Antony apologized, quickly dashing a tear from his blue eyes. He smiled down at her. "You are looking very well indeed. Family life suits you." He glanced over her mass of dark hair at the Earl, who was admiring his infant son cradled in the crook of his arm. "Both of you."

"Let me introduce you to Sam," she said brightly, taking his arm and leading him to the fireplace. The Earl turned his crooked arm to allow Sir Antony to better view his son's rosy and very chubby cheeks, dark hair like Jane's peeking out from under an embroidered white linen cap. "This is Samuel Antony Hugh Sinclair, and we would be honored if you would consent to be your namesake's godfather."

"Don't blame me for saddling you with our son's spiritual welfare," the Earl quipped when Sir Antony's wide gaze immediately flashed up at him, as if needing confirmation of the Countess's declaration. "It was his mother's idea entirely, and who am I to say no when her ladyship has provided me with three healthy children, two of them fine heirs?" He grinned at his cousin. "You'd best accept. This cherub is quite beautiful, like his brother and sister before him. And that's just not my partial opinion." When Jane squeezed his arm affectionately, he lost his roguish smile and said confidentially to Sir Antony, to tease her, "Odds are the next one might not be worthy of oils. Remember cousin Felix? He was most definitely no oil painting, or watercolor for that matter. Odd-shaped head; towering forehead."

The Countess gasped. "Magnus!? How can you say so? *All* our babies will be beautiful."

The Earl smiled at her and winked. "With you as their mother? Undoubtedly."

"Good Lord! I'd not given a thought to Frightful Felix in years," said Sir Antony. His brows contracted. "Isn't his portrait hanging in the Gallery next to Bedlam Bonamy?"

"Bedlam Bonamy…?" echoed Jane, a questioning look from Sir Antony to her husband.

Sir Antony could have kicked himself for mentioning Bonamy Sinclair, and by the scowling look the Earl threw at him, Salt wanted to kick him too. The Earl took a moment to answer his wife.

"Bedlam because poor old Bonamy's mind snapped and never repaired. Father would not hear of a Sinclair being interned in Bethlem Hospital, so sent Bonamy to a private asylum in Northumberland. He just vanished. We were never to speak of him again on pain of punishment. Mother refused to have his likeness removed from the Gallery, and so his portrait remains beside that of his brother Felix. Mother always maintained Bonamy's mind snapped when his heart was broken. The woman in whom he had invested all his feelings, and whom he hoped to marry, turned down his proposal and married another. Poor old chap never recovered. He was mad but he was also quite harmless…"

There was an awkward silence. The parallel to Diana St. John's predicament was glaring. She had invested all her emotional energy in the Earl from a young age. She had expected the Earl to marry her.

When he did not, when she finally came to the realization that the Earl loved Jane, she lost all notion of right from wrong in her quest to become the object of the Earl's singular devotion. It did not need to be said out loud, but all three, Salt, Jane and Sir Antony, were acutely aware that unlike Bonamy Sinclair, Diana was far from harmless.

Finally, Sir Antony moved time on and lightened the mood, saying with a formal bow of his head to the noble couple, "I would be deeply honored to be Samuel's godfather."

"Sam. We insist you call him Sam."

Sir Antony smiled and nodded. "I would be deeply honored to be *Sam's* godfather. Thank you… Both of you."

Jane kissed his cheek and Salt shook his hand. Sir Antony looked down at his godson sleeping contentedly in his father's large arms and marveled at such wondrous new life. Overcome with an overwhelming desire to protect, he was also gripped with a sense of urgency to see his sister's malevolence contained before any harm could be done to this infant, his brother and sister. Such dark thoughts sent him to the tea trolley before Jane caught a glimpse of his face, for surely it reflected the apprehension he felt on her behalf.

"Sam is off to the nursery, where I am very sure his sleepyhead brother and sister will soon wake and ask for their papa," Jane announced buoyantly, Salt placing their infant son into the arms of the waiting nursery maid. She fussed with Sam's blanket and, distracted, said to the nursery maid with a frown, "Have you seen Sam's unicorn rattle, Betsy? It was pinned to his blanket this morning…"

When Jane had to repeat the question, the girl snapped out of her trance-like state but could not speak, quickly averting her gaze from the handsome guest, who was pouring out tea from a silver teapot, to the sleeping infant in her arms. She shook her head so vigorously the floppy brim of her white mob cap slapped about her flushed face, which caused Jane to smile in understanding. The poor creature was out of her depth in his lordship's book room and would not recover her wits until returned to the familiar surroundings of the nursery. Locating Sam's silver rattle could wait. She had far more important matters to discuss with her dear lord and his cousin. So she sent Betsy on ahead and turned to the Earl, who was sipping his claret, and Sir Antony, who was stirring sugar into his tea, and broached the subject that was uppermost in their thoughts but which they were most reluctant to discuss in her presence.

Knowing Diana had escaped her confinement and was hiding in full view of the world provided the key to certain particulars that had been troubling Jane over the past two months. With the hours of idleness that came with an infant at her breast, she had had the leisure to ruminate: Her husband's sleepless nights, the intermittent nightmares; the furtive looks of deep concern cast her way by Rufus Willis and his wife when they thought she wasn't looking; the increase in not only the number but also the sheer physical size of the footmen at Salt Hendon, and now here in London at Salt House, so that she was literally tripping over big burly servants in passageways; Sir Antony's surprising and unheralded return from St. Petersburg. They all now made perfect sense.

It also made perfect sense that she be present at any discussion regarding what was to be done to recapture the creature who threatened the very existence of her family, and was not at all pleased at her husband's efforts, with the cooperation of Mr. Willis, and no doubt Sir Antony, too, to keep her in ignorance. Though she realized his gentlemanly efforts to shield her from the shock of Diana's escape were done with the best of intentions, where the safety and happiness of her family were concerned she was prepared to grapple any monster, or a demon taking the human form of the beautiful Diana, Lady St. John.

"Ned and Beth will have to wait the pleasure of their papa's company," she said, addressing the Earl, a glance at Sir Antony, "because something far more compelling requires our attention, does it not? I suspect Antony has fretted all the way from 'Petersburg, for the same reason you, my dear lord, have been fretting in your sleep these past two months or more."

She looked from one startled face to the other as both men exchanged a telling glance that, had it not confirmed her suspicions, would have made her smile. It was comical to see two large men wearing the same guilty expression as that of a little boy caught out putting a frog down the back of his sister's bodice. But she did not smile. In fact, she felt queasy and cold with apprehension just saying the name few had uttered in her presence in four years.

"Magnus. Antony. Something must be done, and done today, about Diana."

"You'd best let her see what she wants," the housekeeper said in a clipped tone, looking from Nanny Browne to Betsy Smith, the nursery maid with her chin pointing to the floor. "Though I don't see why your aunt needs to see you a third time when we've only been in town five minutes."

"Betsy's first six weeks with us was in Wiltshire, Mrs. McIntyre," Nanny Browne reminded the housekeeper. "And this is her first time in London. It's a good aunt who wants to reassure herself her niece is settled."

Mrs. McIntyre scraped back her chair with a huff. She was not convinced.

"Settled in too well, if you ask me, Nanny Browne. Five minutes as part of this household and her ladyship already thinks the sun shines out of Betsy's cap! If it were up to me, you wouldn't get within ten feet of her ladyship's private rooms, Betsy Smith. You'd stay in the nursery where you belong. It's as well Dicken is there to keep an eye on you."

"And her ladyship's personal maid has only good to say of her," Nanny Browne reminded the housekeeper.

After all, Betsy came under her jurisdiction. She herself might be accountable to Mrs. McIntyre but all the nursery maids were her responsibility. As for the Countess's personal maid, Nanny Browne did not have as high an opinion of Sally Dicken as the woman had of herself, but she was a good lady's maid for all that, so she respected her judgment. She gave Betsy's arm a little nudge, and said,

"All your hair under that cap, Betsy, and straighten your skirt. You want your aunt to see how fortunate you are to be employed in this noble house."

"You remind Mrs. Smith there are hundreds of local girls who'd give a good tooth to be in your position. Remind her that you have work to do and she can see you on your half day off a fortnight. Why Mr. Willis saw fit to employ a will-o'-the-wisp from Birmingham is beyond me. But Mr. Willis is steward and I'm not, so there's an end to it. Well, girl? Do as Nanny says and tidy your hair and petticoats!"

The housekeeper waited while Betsy hurriedly adjusted her petticoat, pulled the bodice flat and then shoved a handful of springy ringlets under her bright white linen cap, retying the bow so the cap was secure. When the girl stood tall, hands clasped in front and bobbed a curtsy, gaze respectfully lowered, the housekeeper was satisfied and nodded to Nanny Browne.

"An hour, Betsy," Nanny Browne cautioned. "If you're not returned on the hour, I'll send one of the lads to fetch you out of that coach, aunt or no aunt!"

Dismissed, Betsy scampered from the housekeeper's room and along the servant passageway to the door that opened out into the kitchen courtyard and beyond. At every turn there was a servant, at every door two footmen, and out-of-doors, in the kitchen courtyard with its vegetable and herb gardens, men and women were busily engaged. If they noticed her, they did not look up, but she noticed them. She also noted the gardeners tending the formal flowerbeds and raking the gravel pathways that led to a large square of bright green lawn. At its center, a fountain where water bubbled from an urn into a pond filled with carp, and here, supervised by nursery maids and under the watchful eye of half a dozen footmen, his lordship's children were permitted to play when there were blue skies and sunshine.

At the heavy wooden door set into the thick stone of a high garden wall that gave access to the outside world, two more footmen. They were larger and wider than the footmen encountered indoors, and Betsy's knees trembled with guilt when they stared down at her and asked her to state her business. Satisfied, they pulled the bolts, but before letting her out into the laneway they showed her the sliding panel in the door that allowed them to see out without the necessity of opening the door. If she did not raise her head so they could see her face under the cap, the door would remain closed to her. Understood? An obedient nod and Betsy found herself in Blackburn's mews, a lane that ran parallel to the high garden wall and doglegged around a rectangular high-walled building that was his lordship's royal tennis court.

It was at the back of the royal tennis court, in a laneway no wider than a carriage, that her aunt was waiting. By her pacing, Betsy knew she was late, and her knees began to tremble again.

"Don't waste your breath tellin' me why! Get in!" Mrs. Smith demanded and opened wide the carriage door.

Betsy scrabbled up and it was only when seated did she realize the carriage was occupied. She breathed in her ladyship's heady scent before she saw her, sitting quiet and still in a darkened corner. Light filtered in through a crack in the drawn curtain and fell on her silken lap where an ungloved hand clasped a leather glove, and a diamond winked from the pearl and diamond bracelet about her wrist.

"Tell me what you know," her ladyship purred.

Betsy took a moment to collect her thoughts. It was a moment too long. Mrs. Smith cuffed her over the ear and told her to be quick about it.

"I-I don't know much, m'lady. Just that there's a difficulty gaining entry to the 'ouse and garden."

"Difficulty?"

"There's no-no way to get in without 'em all knowin' about it; there's-there's men *everywhere*. Big men they are, too. That's why I was late. It's as tricky to get out as to get in. There's always someone askin' a question if you're not where you're supposed to be, and that's just movin' from one part of the house to the other. No one who isn't wanted gets inside the garden gate, much less the 'ouse."

"Did you bring what I asked?"

Betsy quickly removed her cap and from the top of her mop of hair carefully untangled a tiny silver bracelet, sized for an infant's chubby wrist. From the silver links dangled a silver unicorn charm and three tiny silver bells.

"It was a gift from Mr. Willis," Betsy offered unnecessarily.

Diana St. John held it up between thumb and forefinger and frowned, as if it were unclean.

"Sam don't put it in his mouth," Betsy assured her. "It's always pinned to his blanket, or his dress. Nanny Browne says the bells ward off evil spirits."

Diana St. John gave the bracelet a little shake so the bells tinkled, a glance at Mrs. Smith

"Oh dear, Mrs. Smith!" she said with melodramatic emphasis. "Now I have the bracelet, what will protect the poor dear infant when the evil spirits come?"

Betsy looked flustered but before she could speak, Diana St. John continued in an altogether different voice,

"It will do. What about the other brat—his brother? What did you bring me that belongs to him?"

"Ned don't have anything I could hide under m'cap, m'lady. There's a cloth monkey he carries everywhere, and he sleeps with it, too. But it's almost as big as Sam. And if I took that he'd scream the 'ouse down and it would be turned inside out lookin' for it!"

"You had best make certain the monkey is close at hand when he's taken from the house." Diana smiled. "We don't want the little cherub screaming for his monkey, do we?"

"We certainly do not want that, my lady," Mrs. Smith agreed. "The quieter the little bastard is, the better."

Both women snickered.

"You're not meaning to hurt the children, are you?" Betsy asked fretfully, looking from one smug face to the other. "They're not to blame. They're just babies."

"How fortunate for us they are; the smaller the better. Easy to snatch."

"Easy to shove in a sack," agreed Mrs. Smith.

"Easy to throw in the river."

"Easy said."

"Easy done."

Both women laughed.

Betsy was horrified. Disbelief made her momentarily brave.

"Babies shouldn't be punished for the wickedness of their mamma. Not even babies born on the wrong side o' the blanket! It's not their fault his lordship loves their mamma—Ow!"

"*Love*? What would *you* know of love?" Diana St. John snarled. In one quick movement she had the girl by the wrist, yanked her up off the seat and stuck her face in hers. "You lackbrained drudge! He no more loves that skinny whore as he would a workhorse fit only for the knackery!"

"Ow! Ow!" Betsy wailed, a glance at Aunt Smith who remained passively in her seat, and then into the dark unblinking eyes of Diana St. John, who held her wrist so tightly she thought it might snap. "M'wrist! You're hurting me!"

"You stick to worryin' about your own kin, Betsy Smith," Mrs. Smith advised. "What happens to bastard brats conceived in witchery is none of your concern!"

"But I seen the way he looks at her," Betsy argued, lip trembling, eyes on her aunt. "It's not witchery when *he* looks at *her* without her knowledge, is it? He's not under a spell then, is he? He can't help his'-self! He looks at her with such—with such—*love*... And he loves her children—"

A stab of pain in her wrist stopped her breathing; it was as if her hand was on fire, and then she yelped, tears in her eyes. Diana let her go with a shove and Betsy crumpled into the seat moaning, holding her limp and throbbing wrist.

"Stupid, ignorant dolt! I don't want your worthless opinion!"

Diana St. John batted the curtain aside to look out the window. She could just make out the corner of the high wall of the royal tennis court. There was a time when she sat pride of place in the spectator boxes to watch the Earl play at tennis with his male companions. Athlete that he was, he always won, and then she would host a dinner for the players and their wives... That was before he brought that skinny Wiltshire whore into his home and into his bed. Why hadn't he tired of her before now?

She had hoped in the four years she had been away from London Salt would have grown weary of a singular devotion, that he would have had a new mistress or two, even a casual liaison, any dalliance would do. To arrive at Hendon to the wretched ringing of Church bells proclaiming a second son, and this infant the Earl's third child, had made her physically ill, as had the knowledge he was the most faithful of husbands and the most devoted of fathers. She did not understand. Faithfulness. Devotion. Sentimentality. These were the characteristics ascribed to weak men, and to cowards. Her brother exhibited such tendencies, but he was a political nobody, and no Salt. It had to be witchcraft; the Earl was bewitched.

Her stalwart companion agreed that this could be the only reason such a nobleman remained constrained from exhibiting his natural tendencies, and she was prepared to do whatever Diana bade her to see the Earl freed from sorcery. Diana congratulated herself on having recognized Bertha Smith's sycophantic tendencies and lax moral fiber. From their first meeting, when the woman arrived at the castle to take up the position of lady's maid, Mrs. Smith was in equal measure awed by Diana St. John's beauty and her nobility. In less than a fortnight, the woman no longer trusted the guardian's word; by the end of the first month, Mrs. Smith was Diana's slave, willing to do whatever was asked of her.

It would be a shame to lose such a devoted servant to the gallows. But someone had to pay the price for the deaths of Salt's brats. Mrs. Smith's niece would also be implicated. The girl was a simpleton to be sure, but even simpletons were strung up at Tyburn for their misdeeds. Surely a very public hanging at Tyburn of aunt and niece would provide Salt with some redress for the tragedy of losing his family. Not that she thought he would care who was strung up. He would be mad with grief, so stricken he would be forever grateful to her for picking up the pieces of his life and setting him back on the path to political greatness—that's what truly mattered.

Diana smiled her satisfaction and let the curtain fall, returning her attention to Mrs. Smith and the nursery maid; tractable and gullible servants were so hard to come by these days…

"It's lust. That's all it is, Betsy," Diana St. John heard Mrs. Smith tell her idiot niece. "The creature who has taken her ladyship's place is a witch and she's bewitched his lordship. If you're not careful she'll put a spell on you, too! I wouldn't be at all surprised if she's done so already. That's why you're being foolishly stubborn. That's why you're not thinking of your father locked up for debt and your brothers and sisters going about in rags, half-starved. They're what's important, Betsy. They're kin."

Betsy whimpered. She stared at her tortured wrist. Blood oozed from three crescent shaped wounds where Diana St. John's nails had dug deep into her flesh. Somehow seeing those wounds made the throbbing all the more painful. She was incredulous that such a fine lady could inflict such pain. Aunt Smith might be convinced this woman was the true Countess of Salt Hendon, but with the throbbing in her wrist, Betsy asked herself if perhaps it was Aunt Smith who had been bewitched by this beautiful woman who had a black heart, or no heart at all, to want to harm the innocent.

She was young but she knew right from wrong, good from bad. She had seen enough brutality, known hunger, and watched her father be hoodwinked out of his savings by crooked business partners who had left the family destitute. The past six weeks spent in the Earl of Salt Hendon's household were the happiest six weeks of her miserable fifteen years of life, and she was beginning to understand why his lordship had thrown off this woman in preference for his mistress. Though, Betsy wondered now about this too.

It occurred to her that perhaps the beautiful and kind lady who lived with the Earl was indeed the real Countess. That made sense. After all, she was the one inside the house with her three children, whereas this fine lady who Aunt Smith told her was the true Countess remained on this side of the thick high garden wall. Why was that if she were indeed the Earl's true wife? Could Aunt Smith be so gullible? And why did this lady want to do harm to babies? None of it made sense to Betsy. She couldn't wait to return to the safety of the Grosvenor Square mansion and there she would stay. She wished with all her heart she could confide her situation to Nanny Browne, or perhaps Sam's mamma would listen to her story…

Diana St. John shook Sam's silver rattle in Betsy's face.

"Attend me! Do you know what happens to those who steal?"

Betsy nodded, a glance at Aunt Smith.

"Well? What happens?"

"You get strung up and hang from a rope until you're dead."

"That's right. You swing on a rope that chokes the life out of you until you are dead," Diana St. John repeated with heavy sarcasm. "And that is what's going to happen to you if Lord Salt finds out you stole this silver trinket from his house. Children are strung up for less."

Betsy's mouth fell open. "But—but I only took it 'cause Aunt Smith asked me!"

"Mrs. Smith has no recollection of telling you anything of the sort.

His lordship will never believe you. You'll be hanged and your family will starve to death."

"Do as you're asked. There ain't nothin' simpler," Mrs. Smith added matter-of-factly. "You don't want to be hanged for stealing and you don't want your family to starve, now, do you?" When Betsy shook her head, doing her best to hold back tears, she added with a smile, "Very well. Then it is time to return to your post, and take this with you."

Mrs. Smith held out a small flat parcel tied up with cord. When Betsy hesitated, she said with a sigh of annoyance, "It won't bite you, girl! It's for the infant."

Betsy glanced at Diana St. John who waved a hand at her impatiently to take the parcel.

"What is it?"

"A chemise," Mrs. Smith told her. "Lovely it is, with scalloped edges and fine lace trim. Make sure you dress him in it the instant you're back indoors, so it's next to his skin, under his gown."

"Why?"

"Impertinent girl! Just do as you're told!" Diana St. John demanded.

When Betsy tugged on the cord as if to untie the bow, both women shouted in unison for her to stop.

"Leave it tied until you're indoors. You don't want to have to rewrap it, and you might be asked why you opened a parcel that's not meant for you," Mrs. Smith argued, and audibly sighed when Betsy let go of the cord.

"If I discover you haven't done as you've been asked, his lordship will know you for a thief!" Diana St. John hissed.

Betsy nodded vigorously in recognition of her ladyship's threat but she found it all very strange. In one breath her aunt and her ladyship were making light about tossing the Earl's children into the river, and in this breath they were giving her a gift for baby Sam. She didn't understand but she didn't say another word. She climbed down out of the carriage, and with the package under her arm and her heart beating fast, she ran all the way to the wooden door in the garden wall without looking back.

SIXTEEN

ONCE IN THE CONFINES OF THE EARL'S GROSVENOR SQUARE estate, Betsy went straight to the nursery, though she was thirsty and needed to have her injured wrist washed and bandaged. All she cared about was being assured the baby was safe.

She found Sam crying. One of her sister nursery maids, Sukie, was doing her best to get him to drop off to sleep, rocking his cradle, but without success. His little face was crumpled and red and his arms were stiff, so he had been in distress for some little while. Betsy forgot about her injured wrist, tossed the package on the chair, shouldered Sukie aside, and scooped Sam up into her embrace. She held him against her, hand supporting the back of his head to keep his linen cap in place. She whispered soothing words of reassurance, that his Betsy was returned and he was safe, and would always be safe. Soon Sam's fretful sobs subsided and he snuggled into her neck and was quiet in her arms. She rocked him and sang him a lullaby as she paced before the warmth of the fire, her own heart beat slowing with every step.

"What's this?" Sukie demanded, holding up the discarded parcel. "Shall I untie it?"

"Leave it," Betsy replied, scowling, and then, seeing Sukie's frown, added in a more conciliatory tone, "It's nothin' special, just another gown for Sam."

"Like he don't have a dozen or more of those!" Sukie replied, no longer interested in the contents of the parcel. She dropped it back on the chair. "What's that from?" she asked, pointing to the dots of fresh blood on the back of the soft shawl in which Sam was wrapped, revealed when Betsy shifted the infant in her arms. "They weren't there before. I swear it!"

Betsy lifted her arm and saw that the wound inflicted by Diana St. John's nails had stopped bleeding but that it was still fresh. She showed her wrist to Sukie. "It's mine. See. My blood. I scraped m'wrist on the —on the garden wall, just now."

Sukie smiled crookedly. The markings to Betsy's wrist did not resemble any scrape she had ever seen. To her mind they looked like the markings left by fingernails dug deep. She knew all about those; her elder sister had done the same to her on many an occasion when she wanted her compliance. Still, she did not correct the girl.

"You don't want that scrape to turn nasty," she said with a kind smile. "I'll fetch a bandage and salve and bind it up for you, if you want?"

Betsy smiled and nodded.

"Here. Give me that shawl and I'll take it to the laundry quick," Sukie advised, over by the clothes press, "before Nanny sees them blood spots and starts askin' all sorts of questions. You don't want her thinkin' they belong to the baby, do you. That would be your job gone, whatever you said to the contrary. Don't worry. I won't tell."

Betsy carefully unwrapped the shawl and handed it to Sukie, who gave her a clean shawl in which to wrap Sam up snugly.

"I'd best get that bandage before you bleed again."

"Thank you, Sukie. I'll just rock Sam to sleep..."

Sukie nodded, regarding the younger nursery maid pensively.

"Betsy... A word of advice: Don't be telling untruths to Nanny Browne. She hates liars as much as she does thieves, and that would be too bad for you if you turned out to be one of them, or both..."

With that cryptic advice, Sukie left, and Betsy turned away to give her full attention to baby Samuel. Sam blinked up at her with big blue eyes under tired heavy lids and she smiled at his efforts to stay awake, but with every gentle rock in her arms the heavier his lids became. In that moment, staring down at the infant in her arms, Betsy was not worried at losing the good opinion of Nanny Browne. Now returned to the comforting surroundings of the nursery, she felt much braver than she had in the carriage, and cared even less what Aunt Smith and her ladyship threatened. All that mattered was this little life she was cradling.

She glanced at the discarded parcel with its cord of plain twine on the rich tapestry cushion of a wingchair. Who gave the son of an earl such a poorly-wrapped gift? It looked to have come from a poor house.

She suspected her ladyship was having a laugh at her expense, or, at the very least, wanting to dress this baby in rags as a gesture of spite against his mother.

Finally, with Sam's eyes closed, she sat with him in the wingchair by the fireplace and stared at the parcel tied up with twine. She wondered what she should do with it…

WHEN THE EARL AND SIR ANTONY REMAINED MOMENTARILY mute at the mention of Diana St. John by name, Jane went over to her husband, drew up his fingers and kissed the back of his hand before looking up into his troubled brown eyes.

"That at least solves the riddle as to why you haven't been sleeping," she said quietly, so only he could hear. "Since we've shared a bed you've always slept like a man half-dead."

"That is not my fault, Jane."

She blushed and lowered her lashes, saying with a grumble, "This isn't the occasion to fun—"

"No, it isn't," he said gently, cupping her face, thumb lightly brushing her cheek. "But you are still to blame."

"Then I am most offended it is another woman who is keeping you awake!" Jane retorted without heat.

The Earl laughed in spite of himself. He was not laughing when he said,

"What woke me in the dead of night was the thought of losing you and the children, of being alone once again in the world; that perhaps these past four years—such wonderful years—were indeed but a dream."

"My dear man, why didn't you confide in me? Why keep such a burden to yourself? Do not our marriage vows say 'in sickness and in health, for better or worse'? It is the strength we find in each other that allows us to overcome any dilemma."

Salt smiled at her choice of the word 'dilemma,' as if eradicating Diana St. John from their lives would be as easy as clearing pastureland overrun with brambles. Or perhaps that was just the impression she wished to give, to ease his mind and his conscience, for his conscience was heavy with guilt. He had been too complacent in thinking a castle in far-off Wales would keep Diana forever locked up. He should have had her transported to the colonies or a remote island off the Hebrides, or as far as it was possible for a ship to sail without falling off the edge of the known world. But he also realized that would not have stopped her, or stopped him from worrying.

"You are ever the practical optimist, my darling Jane, and I love you a thousand times for that alone. Yes, we will overcome this dilemma, and for all time," he said, resolutely. "I am determined."

He kissed her forehead, a glance over her dark hair at his cousin, who had wandered a little way down the book room to allow the couple their privacy.

"No doubt Antony wishes to admonish me for not being forthcoming about his sister's escape, though I suspect he knew of the circumstance well before Willis and me."

Sir Antony was sipping his tea at the undraped window with its view of the gardens, the flowerbeds bursting with color. He was deliberately not listening, but imagining the children running about the gravel paths and across the stretch of green lawn, laughing, without a care in the world, the high stonewall shutting out the noise, the commotion, and the evils of a city that never slept.

He was thinking that a high stone wall and an army of servants wouldn't be enough to keep his sister from interfering in the Earl's life, when into his line of sight scuttled a slightly-built servant girl, head down, face and hair obscured by a large white cap. She was heading down a gravel path leading to the garden wall. There was something oddly familiar about her. Perhaps it was the mob cap, more particularly the large loose brim that flapped up and down as she walked. Someone had told him something about a girl with a cap just like this one. But then, in the library just now, a nondescript and unobtrusive nursery maid in a similar cap had been attending to Jane's infant son; his godson. So that could account for the stab of familiarity…

He liked the idea of being a godfather, and it split his face into a grin just as he heard Salt mention his name. He lost the grin and turned away from the view, teacup on its saucer and the maid forgotten.

When the Earl repeated what he had said, Sir Antony came straight to the point.

"No. I, like you, had no inkling she had escaped. So when it happened, I was shocked, but not surprised. I am very sure she has been planning and plotting her escape since her first day under lock and key." He glanced at Jane before bluntly addressing his cousin. "Diana's put it about that she's just returned from abroad. No one doubts her story. Why would they? It's the same story we agreed upon when she was first incarcerated. You, Tom Allenby, Rufus Willis,

Arthur Ellis, and me—we swore an oath never to divulge the truth of Diana's foul deeds. I see no reason to break that pledge. None of us wants the truth known, not even by other family members. I certainly don't want Aunt Alice and Caroline to know my only sister is a murderess. Imagine their horror and incredulity. Caroline would be as furious as a bee trapped in a bottle, and Aunt Alice has already aligned herself to Diana's cause—"

"I beg your pardon," Salt interrupted, scowling. "What cause is that?"

Jane and Sir Antony exchanged a knowing look, and Sir Antony allowed Jane to explain.

"Aunt Alice has never fully recovered from St. John being taken from her when a small boy. No mother would, and so she sympathizes with Diana's loss of Ron and Merry. Well, she does not know the true reason the children were taken from their mother, so it is only natural she would. On the face of it, she has every reason to be sympathetic to Diana's plight."

When the Earl huffed his angry annoyance but said nothing, Sir Antony continued,

"And as we don't want Aunt Alice, Caroline and the wider world to know the truth, we must play along with Diana's version of events—for the time being. We cannot act, we would be foolish to do so, until we know her intent—"

"Her *intent* is to destroy my family!"

"In her obsessed mind, her intent is to see you First Lord of the Treasury by whatever means necessary," Sir Antony replied mildly to the Earl's outburst. "All that matters to her is achieving that outcome. If that means people must be swiped out of her way, and yours, then she sees this as merely a problem to solve, nothing more. Your family is an obstruction to your rise to power. She said so herself that day in Jane's sitting room." He looked at the Countess then and bowed his head. "Forgive me for recalling such a painful episode, but needs must, my lady." He returned his blue-eyed gaze to the Earl. "To achieve her goal of seeing you rise to greatness, she must first make you come to your senses. I am of the opinion she thinks you cast under a spell by your beautiful wife, that your family is a hindrance, and because she is of unsound mind and lacks a moral compass, Diana intends to destroy your family, without hesitation or conscience."

"Dear God," Jane uttered, and turned her head into her husband's chest.

"If you know where she is hiding—"

"Hiding?" Sir Antony's laughter was harsh. "Salt? You know Diana better than that! When has she ever slunk away from anything or anyone? She is the consummate female Machiavelli!"

"She is residing not half a street away, at Antony's house," Jane informed her husband, and shivered. "That is very clever of her... To hide in plain sight..."

The Earl stared down at her with surprise, before glaring at his cousin with incredulity.

"Yes, she is clever," agreed Sir Antony. "What better way for Society to believe she's been forgiven by her cousin Lord Salt, and accepted back into the bosom of her family, than to take up residence with me. She even predicted I would come hotfoot from 'Petersburg the moment I discovered her guardian was dead and she free!"

"How—How did her guardian die?" asked Jane.

Sir Antony left it to his cousin to respond, but the Earl was preoccupied with his thoughts, and by the grim set to his mouth and his hands balled into fists, they were not pleasant.

"I should have rung her bloody neck when I had the chance," he muttered, leaving his wife's side to pace the Turkey rug in front of the tapestry fire screen. He thumped the mantel with the side of his fist in frustration, upsetting the cards of invitation propped against a Sèvres vase and the rhythm of French Ormolu clock. "I should have gone into Wales and dropped her off a parapet; no one the wiser. At the very least, paid a knave to poison her!" He glared at Sir Antony. "If you think I will sit idly by now that I know her whereabouts... Knowing she wants to slit the throats of my children—"

"*Magnus.*"

The Countess staggered, and it was Sir Antony who caught and steadied her, assisting her to a wingchair closest to the warmth of the fire. With Jane settled, he quickly went to the tea trolley and made her a cup of tea. The Earl continued to pace like a caged lion recently caught in the wild.

"I will have her dead by my own hand, and tonight. She will cease to exist. We can all breathe—"

"I cannot allow you do that," Sir Antony interrupted calmly, stirring sugar into a fresh cup of tea, which he then gave to Jane. But as she still gripped the arm rests, as if forcing her body to be still, he set the teacup on its saucer on the whatnot, and on his haunches took hold of both her hands. "It will not come to that; your children are safe, your husband, too. No harm shall come to them, or you. I give you my solemn promise with my whole heart. Now drink," he added gently, placing the cup of tea in both her hands and holding it there until she nodded. "It will help settle your nerves." He smiled and winked at her. "I have already thought of the perfect gift for Sam's twenty-first birthday, but for the life of me have no idea what to give as a christening gift! You must think of something for me…"

The Earl rounded on his cousin, affronted, Sir Antony's words finally penetrating his consciousness.

"What do you mean *you* cannot allow it? Who do you think you are, telling me…? You, who have allowed her into your house, who sit at the same table with her, who share in her conversation as if all's right with the world—"

"Oh, for God's sake, Salt!" Sir Antony interrupted, exasperated. "You never were one to think rationally about Diana! You disliked her before she married St. John. You hated her as his wife, and you loathed her as his widow! And ever since she was locked up in that castle, your dreams—*nightmares*—are filled with ways of wiping her off the face of the earth! She has half the battle won if you let her consume you in this way. If we hope to beat her at her own game, we must discover—"

"Game? *Game?* This is no game! It is not some diplomatic conundrum for you to mull over a drop of port at the club! This is *my life*, the lives of my wife and children that are at stake. You know, *you know* of what that creature is capable, what she did to-to Jane, to our-our unborn child! You know she came close to killing her own son all to get my singular attention. She is a murderer of innocents, a procuress of abortifacients for others. She is a-a *she-devil* who, given a knife and opportunity, would willingly murder three little children! Do you have no feelings, no understanding of—"

"That's enough!" Sir Antony growled, furious. "Do not utter another syllable until you have taken stock of what you have just uttered. I grant you your genuine fear for your wife and children but do not—*do not ever*—question my feelings or my loyalty!"

The nobleman needed a large dose of common sense and Sir Antony was going to give it to him, whether he wanted it or not. To that end, he did the unthinkable, something so out of character for a man who prided himself on being a gentleman with impeccable manners that the Earl was too shocked to put up any resistance.

While Salt gaped at him, stunned at such an uncharacteristic outburst, mulish and immobile, Sir Antony grabbed a handful of his cousin's silk banyan and tugged him forward. And once the Earl's feet were moving, he took hold of his upper arm and marched him to the furthest corner of the book room to stand beside a library ladder. They were in line of sight of the Countess, if she turned in the wingchair and looked over her shoulder, which she did, but, if they kept their voices level, they were out of the range of her hearing every word uttered.

Salt was so unaccustomed to having his immaculate person manhandled—no one had ever attempted it—and his conversation bluntly terminated, and by the mild-mannered Sir Antony, no less, that when his cousin let him go and presented his argument, he just stood there, silent, incredulous but listening.

"Hear yourself, Salt! *Think* before you declaim in front of the mother of your children. We all know what Diana has done and what she is still capable of doing. We know she is the devil incarnate, walking amongst us, who will stop at nothing, *nothing*, so that she can be with you. She has no feelings, no soul worth saving. Jane is being brave for your sake, you oaf. Within, she must be terrified and crumbling. She has three little ones to protect—all healthy and thriving, and yours. And how do you respond to her loyalty and bravery? You advocate murder yourself!"

Sir Antony lifted a hand and dropped it again, gathering his thoughts, pleased his cousin remained silent with his hands thrust in the pockets of his banyan, face taut, but attentive nonetheless.

"My need for justice, to see Diana out of your life and mine forever, is as great as yours," he continued. "If I were conscienceless, if I had a shred of my sister's malevolence, I would have remained in 'Petersburg where I had grown accustomed to my lot. That you dare question my feelings, and thereby my loyalty, cuts to the quick. Yet I understand what prompted it, and thus will ignore it. You are not alone in this. You have friends and family who will gladly give you their support, those of us who made that pledge. But first you must stop being so bloody-minded and emotive about Diana. And you must enlist the support of those who can help you play Diana at her own game."

The Earl raised an eyebrow in skepticism.

"So simply choking the life out of her would not end my troubles?"

"I don't doubt you could and would do it. You almost succeeded four years ago," Sir Antony replied. "It provides a solution and a certain satisfaction—For all of about five minutes..." When the Earl frowned in incomprehension, he smiled to himself, but explained flatly, "Perhaps you would get away with it, too. Diana would be dead, Jane and your children safe. But you could never lay your head gently on a pillow without your dreams being consumed by what you had done, and its implications. You are too honorable a man. You would quickly realize that you, too, are a murderer, and thus no better than the murderess you killed. And your waking hours would be consumed with the anxiety, that one day your children, Ron and Merry, too, would discover what their Papa had done, what he had become. You would worry yourself sick wondering if Jane loved you as she had before you became a murderer—"

"Yes, all right! I have your mental image fixed firmly in my head, thank you!" Salt grumbled, hunching his shoulders, head momentarily turned to the bookcase. When he remained silent, Sir Antony continued,

"And if you did not get away with it, if you were caught and put on trial for Diana's murder—"

The Earl's gaze snapped back to Sir Antony, and if his close-shaven cheeks had been flushed with the embarrassment of truth in what his cousin proposed would be his life if he did murder Diana St. John, they were now purple with anger at this further, and to him, outrageous suggestion.

"No one would dare!"

Sir Antony cocked his head, regarding his cousin with a small smile, not surprised a nobleman of his rank and fortune would smart at such a scenario, yet surprised that his supreme arrogance made him so naïve to the ways of the wider world.

"You think not…? Perhaps no one of our society would dare accuse you of murder," Sir Antony replied calmly. "I realize you can only be tried by your peers. But there are only a handful of persons who know Diana for a murderess, so you tell me if there wouldn't be an outcry by the general populace to see justice done a woman, your kinswoman, killed by your own hand. Your family name, your rank and position, all would work against you. That you married for love and one of the most beautiful women in the Kingdom, who has an infant at her breast, and two other small children, whom Diana hated with a mania, provides fodder for the newssheets. You couldn't keep the crowds away from such a trial. No matter the judge and jury are exclusively your peers. The masses would welcome the pronouncement that Magnus Vernon Templestowe Sinclair, fifth Earl of Salt Hendon, is hereby charged with the willful murder of—You get the idea."

"Yes, I do. Thank you!"

"Then you must surely realize there is more at stake here than the preservation of your family's honor. During any such trial, your defense counsel will do whatever it takes to have you acquitted by whatever means necessary. I do not doubt they would use the insanity card. They would have no hesitation in airing in public all of Diana's foul deeds. You and I know there are women of our society who sought out Diana for her remedies when they found themselves with an unwanted pregnancy. Whatever their reasons for ridding themselves of an unwanted child, it was unwanted and Diana helped them get rid of it. Such sensational evidence would gain you sympathy from the bench but alienate you from your fellows; it would be seen as a betrayal of trust.

"You would be acquitted by virtue of insanity but be a pariah amongst Society. There would also be that tiny speck of doubt in the minds of your relatives and friends, if you have any left, that maybe, just maybe, you are mad. Jane and your children would be vilified, your blood and your memory forever tainted for generations. No chance of your portrait hanging in any ancestors' gallery. No one would speak your name. Is that how you see your legacy to your son and heir when he inherits your title?"

The Earl shook his head, eyes fixed on his Countess, who was sipping at her cup of tea, head turned away to the little leaping flames in the grate. He heaved a great sigh, as if defeated by his cousin's words, and took a moment to digest the consequences as suggested to him. Finally, he tore his gaze from Jane.

"What do you suggest?"

"We must include Jane in our deliberations," Sir Antony told him, avoiding the question for the time being.

Linking arms with his cousin, he walked him back to the fireplace where he picked up the silver teapot off its warming stand. There was just enough tea brewed without the need to call the butler for a fresh pot.

"Tea?" he asked the noble couple and when they declined, poured out a fresh cup for himself.

Salt refilled his wine glass with claret, an eyebrow raised at his cousin. "This newfound abstinence and preference for tea... A 'Petersburg affectation?"

"Ha! You have found me out!" Sir Antony took a sip of his tea, which was adequate but not quite up to what his sensitive palate now demanded in a brew, and added with a sad smile, "When this business with Diana is over with I will confess all... Caroline has the right to be told first..."

The Earl and Countess shared a glance, and when Jane smiled knowingly at her husband he had the feeling that again, where matters stood between Caroline and Sir Antony, he would be the last to know. As he had no wish to discuss their volatile history there and then, he returned the conversation to the problem of Diana, willing to listen to whatever his cousin was about to suggest, having no thought but murder on his mind.

"I want you to send for Tom Allenby and Rufus Willis: Tom to stay close to Jane and the children; Willis to keep a keen eye on the household comings and goings. Their arrival here will not seem out of the ordinary, particularly when you have the masquerade ball at the end of the week," Sir Antony explained. "You both must carry on with your daily lives as if Diana did not exist. You owe it to your family and children to do so, and, more importantly, any change in your routines would alert Diana and she may change her plans accordingly."

"You know her plans?" Jane asked.

Sir Antony shook his head. "Not yet. I hope to discover that from others. I have instructed a thief-taker to be her shadow. She cannot move without it being reported to me. But Diana is clever. Much cleverer than I, and therein lies my strength." He smiled wryly. "She has always been the more intelligent of the two of us. Ever since childhood, she has never let me forget it. And because of that, her self-confidence will be her undoing. While I remain the suitably stupid younger brother in her presence, she does not suspect me, nor does she think me capable of comprehending her machinations—"

"It is not true that you are not clever!" Jane argued, annoyed by his self-deprecation. "You have always been quick to understand people. You are highly sensitive to how people *feel*, which is a far superior attribute to my way of thinking than possessing an intellect that hypothesizes and strategizes or pontificates but gives no thought to another's wishes and wellbeing."

"It is pointless to argue with her ladyship," the Earl said when Sir Antony turned pink with pleasure at the Countess's spirited defense. "Jane's way of thinking is always sound. So is yours. I shall have Rufus Willis brought up to town at once. Tom has accepted his invitation to attend the masquerade ball." Salt smiled thinly. "He would not forfeit watching you squirm under the weight of your new title and sash for anything. His words—not mine! Besides, he said he wants the opportunity to beat you at a game of tennis. Although..." He looked Sir Antony up and down. "I do believe Tom will lose, and I shall forfeit fifty pounds."

"Magnus!? You did not wager against Antony to win?"

"It's your brother who stands to gain," the Earl retorted good-naturedly. He shrugged and looked momentarily sheepish. "I'd not have done so had I the benefit of seeing Antony before I put down my blunt."

"Then I shall give you the opportunity to win back your fifty on the tennis court before Tom's arrival. I need the practice," Sir Antony said good-naturedly, adding quietly, a glance at Jane, "Salt, when Willis arrives, have him look into your household. Diana stopped in Hendon the day of Sam's birth, on her way to London. As Diana does not breathe without purpose, there has to be a reason she was lurking so close to the estate."

He returned his empty cup and saucer to the tea tray then addressed the Earl.

"There is no easy way to ask this, so I shall just come out with it. I want you to invite Diana to the masquerade."

SEVENTEEN

"What?" the Earl thundered.

"Antony, how can you make such a request?" Jane asked, distraught. "You know I cannot allow into my-my *home* a woman whose only purpose in life is to-to *harm* my children!"

Salt pulled Jane into his embrace, and when she turned her head into his shoulder on a shudder, he held her closer and put up his chin at his cousin.

"You have your answer."

Sir Antony mentally sighed. He understood only too well that what he was asking of them was distressing in the extreme, but he was also convinced the course of action he had decided on was the right one, and the only way they would discover his malevolent sister's plans.

"Diana's weakness is her conceit," Sir Antony explained patiently. "She will accept your invitation because it will give legitimacy to her claims that she has returned from the Continent forgiven by you, and because such an invitation is clear evidence that you want her here. She will be so consumed with this idea, and the fact she has won a small victory over Jane, that she will let down her guard that evening in her efforts to show you how very necessary she is to your life and political success."

"That is not reason enough to allow that creature within the orbit of my wife and family. And if that is the best you have to offer in how to deal with—"

Sir Antony met his cousin's gaze without a blink.

"If you do not invite her you will create the sort of scandal you abhor. Society has welcomed her back with open arms. Society will expect her to be in attendance at the social event of the year. She is your cousin. More particularly, her brother, a newly-created Viscount, is to be honored by the Russians. Her absence will raise more questions, and needless gossip, than you are prepared to answer."

"Damn," Salt muttered through clenched teeth. He looked down at his wife. "Antony is in the right…"

Jane nodded. She addressed Sir Antony. "Why? Why now?"

"Why has Diana chosen to escape her castle confinement now and not before?"

"Yes," she replied. "Why come to London? Why not run away, go abroad? Anywhere is better than here, where she must surely realize it is only a matter of time before she is recaptured and reincarcerated?"

"Running off to the Continent to live free and in style holds no purpose for Diana. Her only purpose on this earth is to bathe in the bright candlelight of your husband's political success—"

"Dear God!" Salt spat out with a grimace. "That just makes me want to be violently ill!"

"No doubt your political opponents would feel the same urge to purge by such unadulterated adoration for the Earl of Salt Hendon," Sir Antony quipped disrespectfully, which made the Countess clap a hand to her mouth to stop a giggle. He lost his smile and continued. "Diana is utterly convinced your rise to greatness cannot happen without her assistance. Thus, while you rusticated in Wiltshire, she too rusticated in her Welsh castle, planning and waiting. And then by some means, possibly the newssheets, she discovered your intention to return to the political arena—"

"Yes, the newssheets!" Jane interrupted with a gasp, looking up at her husband, then around at Sir Antony. "Speculation on 'a Lord S-H's return to the political fray' was mentioned in several articles in *The Gentleman's Magazine* before Christmastime. And then, when Salt came to town on the resumption of Parliament, that, too, was reported on."

"Just so," Sir Antony agreed and continued. "I believe the moment Diana read in the newssheets of Lord S-H's return to the political arena she decided it was time to break free of her confinement. With Salt's return to politics, her intellect and her particular talents as a political hostess would be needed and praised."

"This is all well and good, and I won't argue with your reasoning," the Earl said flatly. "But what possible outcome do you hope to achieve, other than quelling societal gossip, by allowing her access to my home on the night of the masquerade ball, and thereby causing her ladyship great distress?"

"Better her here, under your roof and the watchful eye of your friends and servants, than lurking somewhere close by, waiting to strike," reasoned Sir Antony. "And she will strike the night of the ball, that I do not doubt. It is just the sort of grand occasion that lends itself to Diana's cunning. To everyone present it will not be any different to the balls and soirées she presided over before you were married— indeed, she did so the first few months of your marriage, too."

"So she attends the masquerade and flits about in my shadow as she was wont to do… Heaven knows, I couldn't turn my head left or right without seeing her out of the corner of my eye! What then? What can she possibly do with three hundred people and a dozen Russian diplomats surrounding us?"

"I predict she won't come near either of you while you remain within the orbit of the Russian contingent. To do so would expose the lie that she visited me in 'Petersburg, and she won't want that. And while she flits about telling all and sundry how she helped orchestrate your return to the political arena, she will be focused on keeping you within view, awaiting the opportunity to take the grand stage to present herself, convinced that once you see her, once you are both surrounded by your political friends, and given the grandness of the occasion, you will welcome her with open arms."

It was the Earl's turn to shudder, and with disgust. "Must I? I can't fault your picture of Diana's behavior, but must I welcome her with open arms?"

"If you did, it would be the first time in your life you ever did so, and she would see through your ruse!" Sir Antony quipped. "You must treat her as you always have done upon such occasions, with distance and disregard."

"Then upon your pedestal you must remain all evening," Jane said, a swift kiss to her husband's flushed cheek. "That won't be difficult; distance and disregard are second nature to his lordship."

"With great pleasure shall I remain there, but only with you up there beside me, and nowhere else," Salt responded. He glanced at his cousin. "I am more than happy to leave Antony to deal with the creature, if I can be assured you and the children will be safe…"

Jane was about to ask how precisely Sir Antony intended to deal with Diana St. John when the butler trod quietly into the room from the servant passageway. Behind him was Nanny Browne, which meant something or some little one in the nursery required the Countess's attention, so she excused herself.

With her back turned and out of earshot, Sir Antony put his hand on the Earl's sleeve to have his attention and said very low,

"Salt, I give you my word that by the masquerade night's end, you and your family will no longer be troubled by my sister. Ever."

Salt took a deep breath.

"I made that same promise to Jane four years ago, and yet here we are…"

"And I made a solemn promise before leaving 'Petersburg that I would do whatever it takes to keep you and your family safe. I mean it and I will. Whatever it takes…"

The Earl swallowed his emotion and smiled crookedly.

"What do you intend to do?"

"Plans have been put in place and I have men ready and waiting on the Continent. That is all you need know for now. Protecting Jane and the children should be your only concern."

"What about here, here in England? What plans do you have in place here?" When Sir Antony hesitated, the Earl grinned. He was not amused, nor was he convinced. "You have absolutely no idea, have you?"

"To extricate her from society with the least fuss and no scandal? No, none yet," Sir Antony confessed. "But there are three days until the masquerade…"

"And the rest of her long life, given a castle in remote Wales could not hold her…?"

"That," Sir Antony said with conviction, "was decided before I left 'Petersburg."

"SEMPER, YOU WILL BE ORANGE WITH DELIGHT TO KNOW THAT I am being kicked upstairs," Sir Antony informed his majordomo from the warm aromatic waters of his thinking tub.

It was Ralph Semper who had dubbed the linen-lined copper bathtub, brought from St. Petersburg, the thinking tub. It was while stretched out and shoulder-deep in the hot scented waters of this bathtub that his master spent time with his thoughts. It served no other purpose; daily ablutions were performed in the hipbath by the warmth of the fireplace before entering the thinking tub.

Semper took these dressing room arrangements in his stride, as he

did the attendant ritual that went with his master's tea-drinking ceremony. The silver samovar, like the copper bath, had been introduced
on the advice of Prince Mikhail, and if such devices and their rituals
kept his master from giving in to the temptation of the fermented
grape, then Semper was all for them.

He was, however, surprised when Sir Antony addressed him from
the thinking tub. Usually, it was a time when Semper and the male
servants tiptoed about the dressing room so as not to disturb their
master who, sans wig, settled back against a cushion with eyes closed,
diaphanous silk curtains pulled about the bath to keep in the heat and
shut out the world. But the curtains remained flat against the painted
wall of the niche and thus the majordomo paused in the middle of the
Aubusson rug, Sir Antony's discarded wig in one hand. He had been
about to cross to the closet, and had heard one word in five of Sir
Antony's announcement.

"An orange light on the stairs, my lord?"

"I'm being kicked upstairs."

Semper moved a little closer to the thinking tub.

"I beg your pardon, my lord?"

Sir Antony did not open his eyes. He lifted an arm, elbow resting
on the edge of the bathtub, and pointed skywards.

"Up, Semper; up to the Lords. Viscount Temple and Baron Stowe.
Lord Temple."

"Congratulations, my lord. That is *very* good news indeed. And
fitting, if you don't mind me saying so."

Sir Antony opened one eye.

"I don't mind you saying it *now*, Semper. All it means is that you
may address me as *my lord* in good conscience, which you have stub-
bornly done since we sailed up the Neva. No! Don't tell me it was
because the Russians believed an English baronet with a weakness for
embroidered silks and gold braid must be a lord."

"I beg your pardon, my lord, but I was not about to say so,"
Semper stated seriously. "I addressed you as *my lord* because their High-
nesses Prince Mikhail and Princess Ekaterina insisted I do so; and so, I
did."

Sir Antony's shoulders lifted slightly in surprise. "They did?" He
settled again, and closed his eyes on a sigh of resignation. "I miss their
company…"

Semper remained inert, waiting to see if his master intended to
offer any further insights, but when Sir Antony's arm dropped
languidly over the side of the bathtub, he scurried away to put aside his

master's wig. He did so in haste, because a great deal of noise was coming from the other side of the closed double doors, and thus he forgot to draw the curtains about the bath.

If he was not very much mistaken a fracas was taking place in the sitting room, and from the raised voices the Russian servants were involved, and there was a female. Which would explain why the exchange was heated. The female was trespassing, and as the Russians knew females were not permitted in the North wing, they were doing their best to enforce an eviction. Semper prayed the female was not Lady St. John.

The majordomo slipped into the sitting room from the dressing room with all the stealth of a snake slithering undetected through tall grass. But as his gaze was at a man's eye-level, and not on the polished wooden floor, he did not see, and thus was unaware, of the four-legged intruder who, the minute the door opened, shot through the space into the dressing room as Semper slowly closed the door on his back.

The four-legged intruder scampered across the spacious dressing room with all the confidence and boundless energy of extreme youth. Its stubby little legs scrabbled along the polished wooden floor and then the deep carpet to the fireplace where the hipbath remained full of soapy water. After an interested sniff and then lick of the splash on the floorboards, a snuffle at the pile of wet towels, it nosed and then tackled a pair of discarded silk breeches as if they were the enemy. With great effort, the four-legged intruder dragged the breeches a little way in front of the fireplace, then lost interest, finding an opponent more its size in a silk stocking. After shaking this article of leg wear to and fro to ensure it was well and truly dead, and with this spoil firmly clamped between its jaws, the four-legged intruder then trotted over to a decoratively painted niche with its two classical stools either side of an enormous bathtub. Here the stocking was dropped, as if presented, with much tail wagging, to the hand on the end of the human arm that hung inert over the side of the bathtub.

When the hand made no effort to pat the four-legged intruder for its good behavior and bravery in dealing with such a terrible foe, there was only one way to get its attention, and this produced immediate results.

Sir Antony was beginning to doze, stretched out in the hot water with its blanket of bubbles, and was well on the way to clearing his mind of his troubles—most particularly how he was to take his sister into custody with least fuss and a suitable explanation—when his hand was nudged by something wet and cold. When his fingers were licked and nibbled, he sat up, and so swiftly a great wave of water splashed the end of the bath near his toes and cascaded over the side, spilling to the floor.

He had no idea what had assaulted his hand and did not like to hazard a guess, so he took a peek over the side of the tub, both arms now immersed in the warm fragrant water. But what he saw quieted his heart and lifted his mouth into a grin. He extended his arm over the rim of the bathtub once more and offered the back of his wet and dripping hand in greeting.

"Well, my fine little fellow, where is your master?"

The fine little fellow was a black and fawn pug, just a puppy in fact, from which large protruding brown eyes stared up adoringly from out of a black wrinkled face. The pug recognized in the soft deep timbre of Sir Antony's voice, and in offering the back of his large hand to lick, a friend, and so stood on his sturdy little hind legs, front paws against the bathtub. The tightly curled tail went into a frenzy of wagging, and when Sir Antony scratched the puppy affectionately behind the ears, the pug gave his wrist a big lick of thanks.

"Oh, and you've brought me a gift!" Sir Antony said to the pug, as one addressing a small child, and scooped up his discarded stocking. He chuckled when the pug's tail wagged in response, but then made a sad face, saying on a sigh, "Thank you so very much, but unfortunately I do not have a chop bone to offer you in exchange for your efforts."

He scrunched the stocking into a ball and threw it in the direction of the fireplace where his discarded clothes were now strewn. It fell dismally short of its target. He had not meant it to be a game, but the pug had other ideas. It dashed after the stocking. Half way across the carpet the stocking lost its appeal and the pug returned to snuffling about the wet towels. Finally, it trotted back to the bathtub where it obediently sat and looked up at Sir Antony with the adoration only a dog can offer its human master.

"You are a fine little fellow but I still do not possess a bone to give you. When Semper returns I shall have him send to the kitchen..."

Sir Antony did not have the opportunity to finish his sentence, and the pug stopped listening the moment a female voice, adored by both man and beast, was heard over the ensuing din that accompanied her entrance into the dressing room. Man and beast reacted in completely opposite ways. The pug dashed towards her; Sir Antony took a deep breath and plunged under the water to hide his discomfiture beneath a blanket of bubbles.

EIGHTEEN

"You may ask it of me, you impertinent oaf, but I won't tell you my name! It is none of your concern! Now have this bearded brute put me to firm ground before I have him arrested for assault!"

Semper was not only at a loss he was lost for words. Never in all his years as a gentleman's gentleman had he ever had a female storm the male bastion of an unmarried gentleman's apartments. The Princess had upon occasion trespassed into the inner sanctum, but always when his master was wearing some sort of raiment, and because she was a princess and Russian and thus viewed servants as one did any piece of furniture, it was somehow less disconcerting.

This female, who had been discovered by one of the Russians prowling about Sir Antony's rooms in a red hooded cloak over not much else, had, upon discovery, not shown one ounce of remorse for her trespass. Granted her cheeks had turned as apple red as her fur-lined cloak, but when she was politely asked to state her name and her business, she had reacted with indignation and demanded to be taken to Sir Antony at once.

Hearing her imperious tone, if not understanding her words, and because she tried to brush past the majordomo, the Russian footman scooped her up into his arms and held her fast. It was then that the hood of her cloak fell back, revealing her tumble of strawberry blonde hair, and the Russian had a stab of memory. He had seen her before, at the soirée, as a guest in resplendent silks. Her gloriously bright hair was not easily forgotten, nor the fact his master had gone down on bended knee before her. Without a word to Semper, the Russian strode through the apartment and into the dressing room to present this female to his master, the majordomo on his heels.

No sooner was Lady Caroline's threat voiced than the Russian set her down, bowed with great courteousness and left the room, deserting a speechless Semper. He had no idea what he should do in such a novel situation. Instinct told him to do as the Russian had done and leave immediately, but there was a small part of him that felt duty-bound to remain to provide assistance to Sir Antony if he lost consciousness; his master remained submerged under the bubbles of his bathwater.

"There you are, you naughty boy!" Lady Caroline playfully scolded the pug. She scooped him up and gave him a nuzzle. "Some hero you are, leaving me to fend off the nasty men by myself!" She glared at Semper as she said this, adding with her gaze firmly fixed on the major-domo, "A bowl of fresh water and something to gnaw on would be greatly appreciated."

Semper hovered in an agony of indecision. A great whoosh and gasp for breath from the bathtub followed by the pug puppy's yap of excitement decided him. For the first time in his employ as valet to Sir Antony, he ignored the discarded clothes and towels, leaving them where they had been dropped. He bowed to Lady Caroline, and without turning to see if Sir Antony was still breathing, left the room in search of a bowl of fresh water and something to gnaw on.

Lady Caroline put the pug to the floor, and with one eye on the male attire strewn across the carpet, carefully stepped over a pair of silk breeches and a lone silk stocking, as she crossed to the fireplace. Out of the corner of her eye she saw a hipbath and a pile of wet towels, while to her right was an enormous bathtub and in that bathtub was the man she had come to spend the night with.

At the fireplace she stripped off her red kid gloves, placing these on the mantel before spreading her hands to the warmth of the smoldering coals. She was wearing a wool cloak to be sure but not very much underneath, just white silk stockings and a thin linen nightgown, and that was because her decision to visit Sir Antony under cover of dark-ness had been an impromptu one. She had spent the day in an agony of anticipation as to his reaction when she confessed all to him, and later that night tossing and turning in her bed, unable to sleep because of his kiss. The sooner she confessed and they shared a bed, the sooner they could both move forward with their lives, and she would again be able to sleep peacefully.

Mind made up, she executed her plan, despite her personal maid's squeak of horror, at the late hour, her ladyship's lack of acceptable raiment, and the fact she was visiting an unmarried gentleman's abode, all under cover of darkness. It all added up to disaster in her book. Lady Caroline remarked she had not read that particular book, swore her maid to secrecy, and scrambled out of bed. She threw on her wool cloak and took the pug puppy along for the journey. Somehow having the newest member of her animal family for company made her more resolute to confession.

The hour and the addition of the puppy certainly had the burly chairmen mentally scratching their wigs in puzzlement as the Earl's sister climbed into the Salt Hendon sedan chair parked in the entrance foyer, her four-legged companion happily sitting on her lap. It was not their place to make comment. If his lordship's sister wished to go visiting in the middle of the night, then so be it.

Sedan door emblazoned with the Salt Hendon coat of arms closed, long poles threaded and secured either side of the chair, one chairman up front, the other in the rear, and both with the leather straps across their shoulders, the sedan chair was lifted up and went out into the night air. Her ladyship was taken the short distance across deserted Grosvenor Square, along South Audley street and up the two shallow steps and into the spacious foyer of Sir Antony Templestowe's townhouse, a junior footman providing light from a burning taper for the journey on such a moonless night.

Now Caroline stood before the fire, staring into the flames, but very much focused on the fact that Antony was over her right shoulder in his bathtub. She couldn't keep the grin off her face. The anxiety that had set her heart racing on the short journey in the sedan chair, when she had questioned her outrageous actions several times and had her long-suffering chairmen stop, change direction, stop, then take up the poles again and continue, had evaporated, but her heart still beat just as fast as ever. But it was not anxiousness that caused the thudding to reverberate in her ears. It was the wicked thrill of not only having made it all the way into Antony's dressing room, but knowing that just feet away, he was naked in his tub.

In all the years she had known him, she had not so much as seen him without his cravat, and certainly never in his shirtsleeves. He was always dressed immaculately, regardless if he was playing royal tennis or rusticating in the country. In the country, even her illustrious brother cultivated a beard. Not Antony, who maintained the same sartorial standards no matter the setting. She wondered if he wore his wig while in his bath, and it was such a silly thought that it gave her the courage to turn about and face him; that and the fact her four-legged companion gave the hem of her cloak a tug with his little teeth.

She scooped up the puppy, again delaying the inevitable, but finally lifted her gaze to the bathtub. What she discovered made her blink, face devoid of her thoughts for enough seconds that the occupant of the bathtub wished he possessed gills so he could remain underwater indefinitely. Finally, when she hunched her shoulders and smiled, a fist to her mouth, as if to stop a fit of girlish giggles, owning gills was unimportant; drowning was the only option.

Bravely, Sir Antony remained upright, elbows resting either side of the bathtub, bare wide chest, wider shoulders, unshaven face, and head without covering, all on display for Lady Caroline's gleeful inspection. It was only when her gaze remained riveted to his head of thick, short-cropped auburn hair, did he feel the heat intensify to a prickly heat, not in his face but across his scalp. His head actually tingled, as if each individual hair glowed with embarrassment. And when she gingerly approached the bathtub, head cocked to one side in silent contempla-tion, eyes never leaving his scalp, he swallowed hard and said, after clearing his throat,

"I hope you realize how damnably unfair this is, Caro! I wonder at your reaction, if the situation were reversed."

"Your hair is the same color as Merry's," she remarked with surprise, ignoring his remark and his discomfort. "It would probably be just as wavy, too, if you let it grow…"

"Probably! Will you stop staring at my head as if it is malformed?!"

She smiled at his awkwardness.

"Silly. Of course I must stare at your head because I have never seen you—*ever*—without your wig." She frowned. "Come to think on it, I have not seen any gentleman of my acquaintance who wears a wig without his wig—"

"I should hope not!"

"In *any* situation," she added with a raise of her eyebrows, and when he looked away she knew he understood. She retreated to the stool at the end of the bathtub, the pug on her lap. "Not that there was ever a situation for Aldershot to remove his wig—"

"Caroline—"

"Please listen, Antony. I wasn't sure how I was going to tell you about Aldershot and me, when the situation would be comfortable enough. I've been wretched all day since you kissed me. Not that the kiss was wretched," she added hastily. "The kiss was perfectly wonder-ful, and that's why I couldn't sleep tonight, thinking about that kiss, and if, after telling you everything, you would ever want to kiss me again. So I thought why not just come and see you at once. Get the horrid confession over with. Sooner is better, isn't it?" She smiled, suddenly shy. "That you are in your tub makes it that much easier for me to tell you."

"Does it? Well, I don't want you feeling wretched and sleepless," he confessed, just as uncomfortable but somewhat placated at having his privacy violated by her admission that she had enjoyed their kiss in the anteroom as much as he had.

"Thank you. I knew you would understand."

"You don't have to tell me. I told you that earlier today. But if it will ease your mind…"

"Yes. I do know and yes, it will ease my mind." She blushed. "That wasn't the only reason I came here tonight…"

He smiled then sighed, as if disappointed, and shook his head.

"Oh dear, and now you've seen me *sans* wig, you've had second thoughts. *Damn.*"

There was silence and then they both laughed at the same time. The moment served to make them more at ease in themselves and yet suddenly awkward in each other's company.

"Quite to the contrary," Caroline confessed quietly. "The wig gives you presence, but without it you are an extraordinarily beautiful man—"

"Caro! That's—"

"—a compliment, so accept it," she said, finishing the sentence for him, adding quickly before he could interrupt again, "Now let me tell you how I came to be married to Stephen Aldershot."

"Very well. I shall listen without comment," he replied, and reclined his shoulders against the tub, warm under his blanket of bubbles.

Caroline took a mental deep breath and said matter-of-factly,

"I did something very shocking at a masquerade ball… I was more than flustered. I was *drunk.*" She stopped and took another deep breath and continued, hand stroking the pug puppy, which had the effect of calming her. She bravely looked into Antony's blue eyes and said bluntly, "I was so angry with you, with what you had said and done at the recital. I was past caring. I just wanted my innocence to be over with. I let myself be seduced. I gave my-my virginity away cheaply. At the time, I was not at all remorseful. It was not an unpleasant experience, what I can remember of it. It wouldn't have mattered had it been ghastly. I just wanted to-to—*hurt* you. Fool that I was, I didn't see that the only person I was hurting was myself!"

"Caro... Darling..."

"Please... Allow me to finish. Aldershot witnessed the entire episode. *Ferret*. He used it to *persuade* me to marry him. He agreed not to speak of what I had done to anyone, in exchange that I become his wife and provide a home for him and his sister. If I refused..." She shrugged. "He threatened to tell Salt everything. I didn't care for me. I was beyond caring. I had deliberately ruined myself and you had been sent off to 'Petersburg, forever, as far as I knew. But I did care what my ruin would do to Salt, and to Jane. I also knew that if Salt discovered who had ruined me, he would insist I marry that man, not Aldershot. Marriage to my seducer would not have been a bad match. He is due to inherit a title and is an MP my brother respects, but as a husband?" She shuddered. "Never! His morals are questionable at best, whatever his talents as a lover. So my choices were to marry a conscienceless rake, or a blackmailing fortune hunter who was not the least interested in being a man—polar opposites, in fact. God! What a muddle."

She stopped and sighed deeply, unaware she had done so. Antony's gaze never left her face.

"I could not bear the thought of Salt discovering the truth. If he had known I was drunk beyond reason and allowed myself to be seduced... If he knew the identity of the man who had taken advantage of me... Regardless of their connections and good opinion of one another, my poor brother would have been duty-bound to defend my honor and challenge my seducer to a duel. He may well have forced him to marry me! That I could not allow..."

"So you chose the lesser of two evils?"

"Yes. Yes, I suppose I did. We, Aldershot and I, let Salt believe we had been so overcome in the moment that we cast aside all propriety. Remarkably, Salt believed us, even if later he was to wonder if Aldershot was capable of being a husband in any sense, not least in the bedchamber! He really was little more than a silly boy..."

"So you married Aldershot."

"Yes. I married him." She swallowed. "But not for the reason you think. Not because I gave into his threats. Of course, that was part of the reason but... I married him because he was dying."

"Another ploy?"

"No! He had consumption. He was quite ill. He told me, not to elicit sympathy but to convince me to marry him. He said the marriage wouldn't last many years. I would then be free to marry again. He wanted his sister—Kitty—to have a home. He wanted his debts paid. He wanted the years he had left to him to be spent carefree without the worry of his sister or ending his days in debtors' prison. I could provide all that for him, and he would provide me with respectability, and if I happened to have fallen pregnant by my seducer, then the child would be born in wedlock. Of course, I hated myself twice, because had he not been dying, I may well have called his bluff with my harebrained solution..."

When Antony did not ask the obvious question, a silence stretched between them. The only sounds were the tick tock of the clock on the mantel and the crack and spit of the fire in the grate. Finally, Caroline found the courage to continue her confession.

"I had this harebrained notion that if I wrote to you, told you of my dilemma, you would rescue me. All my troubles would magically disappear. You would come home, vanquish my seducer, drop money in Aldershot's lap to make him go away, and you would marry me, even if I were pregnant by another. The spoiled child so wanted to believe that fairytale could come true, and I did, for all of one day. Then, when all my tears had dried up, and I stopped feeling supremely sorry for myself, I conveniently blamed my predicament on you. If only you had remained in England. If only you had not been drunk that night of the recital. If only! If only! If only! I so *hated* you!"

"You had good reason to hate me..."

Caroline shook her head.

"Not for what occurred at the masquerade. Not for the consequences of my actions that night, or for Aldershot, or for my life being one big muddle, and all within six months of my eighteenth birthday! All of that had *nothing* to do with you. I was not your responsibility; I was mine..."

"I wish you had written to me. I would have come home."

Caroline blinked at him and her shoulders slumped. She stared not at him, but at the pug puppy in her lap, curled in the folds of the red wool cloak, asleep, and then the tears came, big droplets splashing onto the puppy's fawn fur. She nodded, and said after a shattering sob and dashing her eyes dry,

"Yes. Yes, I know that *now*... But I did not know that *then*. I had no notion of what you thought of me after our quarrel at the recital. You said I was a spoiled child, that I had a lot of growing up to do before you would even contemplate marrying me..."

"Caro, I threw a lot of idiotic statements at your head that I now regret..."

"But about that you were right! You know you were. I was spoiled and childish. I goaded you terribly by flirting with other, lesser men, all to get your attention. Worse! I tried to make you jealous. That was an utterly childish action because all it did was push you away.

"I know what it is like to be around a childish, thoughtless, self-absorbed being. Stephen Aldershot was such a being and his behavior exhausted me. He knew I did not care a jot for him, and he certainly had no interest in being a *proper* husband. Yet, he constantly demanded my attention, as a spoiled child demands of its overindulgent parents. He loathed my menagerie. He could not bear to have any of my pets near him. He was jealous of the time I spent with them and he even threatened to have them destroyed, but as we were living under my brother's roof, it was an idle threat. Still, it did not stop his nastiness and petty jealousy."

Her green eyes opened wide with incomprehension. It still baffled her.

"Can you imagine being jealous of poor old Penny Pug or Peter Macaw or Spaniel Daniel?"

He smiled knowingly.

"No. I cannot. They are as much a part of the family as your brother, Jane and the children."

"Precisely! That's what I tried to explain to him, but he never listened. He was just as jealous of the time I spent with others as he was of my animal family. Even Kitty, his younger sister, was not saved from his tantrums. She is such a kind soul and loves animals almost as much as I do, and is so opposite to her brother in every way, you would not know them for brother and sister. In much the same way as you and Diana are as different as sweet is from sour. Oh! I beg your pardon. That was impolite, but you know I have never taken to your sister."

"You were saying about Aldershot's tantrums…?"

"He would fly into a rage if I dared to have a conversation with a gentleman in any social setting, but he rarely showed his true nature to Salt. He behaved and cowered in my brother's company. I had the most unchristian thoughts while married to that fiendish boy! It was only the fact he was indeed dying of consumption and was sometimes too weak to get out of bed that stopped me pushing him out a window! It's true!" she stressed with a watery smile when Antony chuckled. "And then, to make matters a hundred times worse, the morning of the day he died, we had a ferocious argument. He had discovered that I-I had been—*unfaithful*. But how can one be unfaithful in a marriage that was never a marriage in the true sense? And so I told him. But what set off one of his temper tantrums and sent him into an apoplexy was the identity of my-my lover…"

She looked away, unable to hold Antony's steady gaze, a gaze that gave no indication of his thoughts. He was so still in the warm water of his bath under the layer of bubbles that he looked to have been cemented in place. Yet his blue eyes did not leave her face for a moment. She sensed them on her, and she blushed, wondering what he truly thought of her after such a shocking disclosure. She took another deep breath, relieved she had finally told him, but knowing there was worse to come, though she could not bring herself to mention Dacre Wraxton by name. Just wanting to get the rest of the confession over with, she said flatly,

"I can hardly believe I chose to have a very brief affair with the very man I should have abhorred above all others. But he pursued me, wooed me, and it—happened. There is no excuse for what I did, but I was lonely and miserable and he was there. Twice, it was only twice, well, three times if you count the masquerade ball, and part of me is not sorry that it did happen because he gave me the satisfaction of knowing I was *desirable*. And then Aldershot, the idiot, goes out riding, when he could barely make it up the stairs without falling into a coughing fit, and is killed when his mount shies from a dry rock wall and he falls and hits his head! My reaction to the tragic news was one of huge relief and my immediate thought was that I was free to marry you when you returned from 'Petersburg! Am I not the most unchristian, the most selfish female you have ever encountered? Are you not hugely relieved you went off to 'Petersburg when you did? Now do you see why I had to run away from your marriage proposal?"

Antony came to the side of the bathtub and held out a hand to her. Caroline set the drowsy pug puppy to the floor and willingly knelt beside the tub. He put a hand to her copper curls and searched her tearstained face with a soft smile.

"It is time for you, my dearest darling girl, to stop blaming yourself, for Aldershot's puerile conduct, and most certainly for the deplorable behavior of the blackguard who seduced you. Having had one too many drinks is cause to *protect* a young girl from lechery and vice, not see it as an opportunity to take advantage of her. I don't give tuppence if you let him kiss you, or if, indeed, you enjoyed the kiss. He had no right to take from you what you would not have given him willingly had you been clear-headed."

"I was not drunk on the other two occasions," she naïvely countered in a small guilty voice. "I knew what I was doing then."

"And if he had been a gentleman he would have shown restraint and not allowed it to happen. It was grossly immoral of him to pursue you. He knew you were vulnerable and he used that vulnerability to his advantage. He possibly persuaded you that you'd been more than willing that first time, so what was the harm in allowing him to bed you a second time, and then a third..."

When her green eyes went wide, he had his answer. He cupped her hot face and gently kissed her forehead, his understanding smile masking the impotent rage that seethed within him to do harm to the unnamed seducer. The lothario may have escaped the point of Salt's sword, but give him a name, and he would find any excuse to force a duel and draw blood for what had been done to his sweet girl. Undoubtedly, Caroline wasn't the only innocent the scoundrel had preyed on and he needed to be stopped, Caroline's honor avenged. What she confessed next truly surprised him.

"He has asked me to marry him. Twice. I could not, and never would. But perhaps that makes him less of a-a seducer...?"

Antony did not know why, but this sliver of information only intensified his contempt for her blackguard and it was with great effort that he bottled his rage. He touched his head to hers, saying with a soft smile,

"He and Aldershot were both contemptible opportunists; neither deserved you."

"And I don't deserve *you*," she said with a teary smile, a hand to his stubbled cheek. "I have yet to meet a more perfect man..."

Antony blushed at her fierce sincerity, saying with a laugh to hide his deep embarrassment,

"Salt would have something to say to that—"

"Salt? Pshaw! He's my brother! I love him to pieces but he is pompous and far from perfect, whatever Jane thinks to the contrary!"

He grinned and brushed a strawberry curl from her flushed cheek.

"You should reserve judgment until after I have laid bare my soul. In fact, I predict you may wonder if by marrying me it is you who is entering into an ill-judged bargain. Believe me, my condition requires far more forbearance on your part, should you decide to become my wife, than my ready acceptance of what you have just confided in me. Now, please, return my dignity by allowing me to leave this tub and put on my robe."

Caroline did not move and he did not move away.

She dimpled.

"But I find you are very much to my liking stripped of your dignity," she admitted, kissing his cheek, hand sliding across his wide shoulder and down the contours of his upper arm, wiping his damp skin free of bubbles. "Must you leave your tub just yet?"

He took a moment to answer her, enjoying her warm fingers on his damp skin and reveling in the soft pinkness of her lips grazing the stubble under his jaw. He couldn't wait for them to share his bed. He could hardly believe she was actually in his dressing room, and that it wasn't all a wonderful dream. He managed to reply in a steady voice,

"If I am not to catch cold, yes, I must."

She pouted, arm going up about his neck again

"For a kiss. I shall let you leave your lovely tub, for a kiss. But it must be a proper kiss!"

He smiled, blue eyes crinkling with mirth.

"Very well. For a kiss; a *proper* kiss."

He dipped his mouth to hers; only this time there was nothing diffident in his action, nor did he draw back on a single kiss. She slid her arm about his neck and held on as he rose up on his knees in the scented water, took her in his arms and kissed her passionately. This kiss dissolved words and doubts, speech unnecessary to convey feelings. She melted against the tub and pressed herself against him, delighting in his long, lean body naked against her, wishing herself stripped of the bulky woolen cloak and thin linen nightgown so that he could caress her curves and explore her roundness.

His fingers tangled in the weighted tumble of her hair, caught up in the hood of the cloak, and he held her fast to him, wanting more. And when she gave him more, when he tasted the sweetness of her mouth, all conscious thought evaporated. Both were determined that this kiss would be enjoyed and savored without interruption, unlike their first proper kiss which was disrupted by a screeching macaw and an over-efficient butler. But determination alone was not enough to prevent the mundane from intruding on a couple whose craving for passionate intimacy was, at that moment, more necessary to them than air.

NINETEEN

THE PUG PUPPY PADDED ACROSS THE CARPET, CURLY TAIL wagging furiously and pink tongue lolling, when into Sir Antony's dressing room via the servant door stepped Semper, carrying two small Chinese patterned porcelain bowls. Behind the majordomo, three of the Russian servants went into the bedchamber with the tea trolley and silver samovar. Semper positioned both bowls on the floor before the fireplace. One contained fresh water, the other not only a nice bone of proportionate size to its four-legged diner, but also some cooked lamb cut into chewable bites.

The couple was oblivious to footfall, the rattle of trolley wheels and the tinkle of porcelain teacups. It was only when one of the Russians dared to dart a glance at the bathtub upon returning to the servant passageway and, diverted by the preoccupied couple, stepped on the heel of the footman in front of him. His fellow Russian lost his shoe and cursed into his beard as he rounded to find the lost article. The ensuing scuffle and harsh whispered conversation was enough to penetrate Sir Antony's subconscious and he reluctantly set Caroline aside, the couple taking a moment to regain a sense of time and space.

Sir Antony grabbed the pail of fresh water by the side of the bathtub and tipped it over his head, the icy stream numbing his body to sensation, serving to bring it once again under the mastery of thought. Caroline, the wet front and soaked hem of her wool cloak suddenly making her cold, scurried across to the warmth of the fireplace where she spread her hands to the radiant heat. Seeing the puppy enjoying the offerings provided by the majordomo was enough to return her equilibrium, and she sat beside the pug to watch him tackle the chop bone.

"Thank you on the pug's behalf," she said with a smile up at Semper, whose gaze remained politely fixed on the puppy. When he nodded in acknowledgment of her thanks but did not look at her directly, she returned her attention to the puppy, who was head down and tail up in the food bowl. "What a feast for you, Boots!" she cooed. "That will see you through to morning."

Caroline, like Semper, had her back to Sir Antony to allow him to exit his bath with a modicum of decorum and privacy, but such considerations were ignored when the occupant of the bathtub exclaimed with derision at her moniker for the pug,

"*Boots*? Surely you didn't name such a splendid little fellow for that buffoon Big Boots Beresford? It makes a mockery of him *and* Peter the Macaw."

"Beresford? How could you think—Well, yes! Why not?" she teased, hearing the twinge of jealous disapproval in his voice. "As soon as I saw the pug's wrinkly little face and those big brown eyes staring up at me with such adoration, my immediate thought was to name him after Beresford; a gentleman known throughout Wiltshire not only for his larger than average boot size, but, if gossip from the county's numerous haylofts is to be believed," she added, turning to face him, "is far larger than the average where it counts most—Oh my! You are—"

"Don't—"

"—*splendid*."

"—be obvious, Caro!" he grumbled with acute embarrassment over her outburst of spontaneous admiration.

But as she had no shame in fixing her stare between his long legs, or seemed to think Semper's presence an impediment to her brazenness, he sighed his defeat and gave up the attempt of maintaining propriety. Still, he managed to towel dry himself, toss aside the wet bath sheet, snatch up the silk banyan off the stool and quickly cover up his nakedness all in record time, and all under Caroline's unblinking appreciative gaze.

"I can't be the first to compliment you," she said with a pout as he joined her by the fireplace, "so my honest response shouldn't be that much of a surprise. Besides," she added from under her lashes, "I took a peek earlier."

This candid admission dropped his jaw. He was in equal measure embarrassed and pleased by her irreverence and reaction to that most intimate part of his anatomy. And if Semper had not sprung into action the moment Caroline had turned to face the bathtub, dashing about collecting up the discarded clothes strewn across the floor, no doubt to hide his own embarrassment, it was on the tip of his tongue to make a quip that at least her eyes were finally somewhere other than riveted to his close-cropped head of auburn hair. Strange, that even with his body covered, in Caroline's company he still felt completely naked with his head uncovered. He itched to grab the silk embroidered nightcap Semper had placed beside the banyan, but he left it, reasoning that once they shared a bed—he most definitely did not make love wearing his wig—what was his head without its wig in the grand scheme of their life together?

"My dear Lady Caroline," he said in a tone he hoped was authoritative, though he could not control his smile when she looked up at him with wide-eyed expectation, "you invade my dressing room with a pug named after a buffoon—"

"I did not say so. You did. In truth, it was Beth, my baby niece, who gave pug his name, because he is always running off with one of her silk boots. She pronounces it *booffs*. Every time Beth sees the pug she giggles and calls out 'Booffs! Booffs!' So Boo*ts* it is."

"I am pleased to hear it. But as much as that story is delightful, it has not diverted me from wondering if, when we are married, you intend to make a habit of peeking into your husband's bathtub?"

"When we are married I shall have my own dressing room, as you well know, my lord, but that won't stop me sharing your lovely bathtub, when invited to do so, of course. And you will invite me."

He put up an eyebrow as if to quell her belligerence.

"Will I indeed?"

"Yes. And although I do believe in a husband and wife having separate private apartments, I do not believe in separate beds. Jane and Salt share a bedchamber, and so shall we."

"Shared with an assortment of animals, no doubt," he said under his breath, and was heard.

"Of course. Viscount Fourpaws sleeps at the foot of Jane and Salt's bed, or did until Merry decided she needed the company." She frowned in thought. "Or perhaps it was Fourpaws who decided to sleep with Merry after Jane and Salt started having babies? I must ask..."

"Please. Don't," he stated, slipping on a pair of embroidered mules before joining her by the fireplace. "The sleeping arrangements of others do not interest me."

He leaned against the mantel, hands in the pockets of his banyan and watched her feed the pug the morsels of lamb, her long mane of bright copper curls tumbling over her left shoulder and brushing the floor. He wanted to carry her off to the bedchamber, to pick up where they had left off at the bathtub. However, he curbed this very natural desire and took his thoughts to the waiting samovar full of hot water and his ritual tea-making. Tea and confession first, and then to bed…

"They cry a lot when they are new," Caroline offered. "Babies. Human babies cry *a lot*. On balance, and please do not repeat this to my brother or to Jane, I prefer my animals."

"You always have."

"Yes. But I thought once Jane and Salt had their babies, I might change my opinion. I do love them all, and will love the ones still to come, and I particularly enjoy Ned and Beth, now they are walking and talking and we can play games together. I'm sure I will love Sam just as much when he is a little older, too. But… I am not so altered at being made an aunt that I do not love my animals just as much, if not more, than before Salt had his babies. Is that wrong of me?"

"It is not wrong to be truthful. But it would be wise not to convey these feelings to the doting parents. I have yet to meet Ned and Beth. I was introduced to Sam today, and though I have a very limited knowledge and experience of infants, he did present as a well-looking baby."

"Yes. He is. He reminds me of one of those fat cherubs painted on the ceiling of the ballroom. All he requires is wings and a tiny bow and arrow."

"He does indeed! I have heard it said that females who are not so enamored of babies become entirely different beings once they have one of their own to have and to hold."

She wrinkled her freckled nose. "Do you expect me to have lots of your babies?"

He had made the comment in a general sense, not meaning to highlight her doubts about her feelings for babies and children in general, so the studiousness of her enquiry coupled with screwing up her little nose at the idea caused Antony to give an involuntary bark of laughter. His grin remained when Semper, having just walked through from the bedchamber, heard Lady Caroline's question and immediately tripped over his own feet. Thinking he was helping move an awkward conversation in another direction, but realizing later he only made the situation even more embarrassing, not only for Semper but for all, Sir Antony said to Caroline,

"It is not an expectation I have thought deeply about. That is not to say we won't have—um—lots of babies. What I expect, and have known for a very long time, is that married life with you means sharing our home with an assortment of friends, furry, four-legged and feathered. And I have always been comfortable with that arrangement. After all, you would not be you without your menagerie. We both share a love of animals. As to babies and children… I confess to not allowing myself to think about that aspect of our married lives which results in babies…"

Caroline frowned, not entirely pleased with this admission. She passed the pug his bone, which he had dropped into the bowl but seemed unable to grip again with his little teeth.

"Did you not—Did you *never* think of us *in that way*?"

"I could not allow myself to think of us *in that way*."

"Could not? Not *ever*? Not even on my fifteenth birthday when I kissed your cheek and told you I was going to marry you?"

"Certainly not! You were only fifteen."

Caroline shrugged a shoulder in dismissal.

"That is not a reason."

"It is when I am eight years your senior!"

"Perhaps you did on my seventeenth birthday?" she coaxed. "It was a particularly hot month. Remember? It was so hot I went swimming in the lake most days, and you came to stay, and you and Salt were out riding one day and caught me stretched on the steps to the summerhouse in my wet chemise. Surely you remember *that*?"

Sir Antony wiped a hand across his face with eyes closed. Of course he remembered. He remembered how the sodden chemise clung to her every luscious curve. How her hair when wet, went a dark ruby red, and that it fell in dripping coils to her thighs. That it was only the fortuitous placement of two of those coils that provided coverage for her nipples. He had stared without blinking at her curvaceous loveliness until his eyes dried of moisture.

He refrained from commenting.

"Of course you must! I was about to wade back into the lake, when Salt tossed me the bath sheet, droning on in his brotherly way about never swimming in the lake without my governess present. He made me promise to wear my hideous bathing gown over my chemise, and have at least one of the footmen by the lake, because if I got myself into difficulty there would be no one about to shout out for help and I would drown. Of course I wasn't listening, even though I pretended to be contrite. The entire time Salt was being brotherly at me I was smiling on the inside because I knew you were staring at me. You did not blink once! Admit to it!"

"You fumbled about with that bath sheet, making no attempt to cover yourself," Sir Antony grumbled. "You purposely stood there in all your glory knowing I was staring at you! I'd have had to be born without male parts and no natural inclinations not to stare at you! And you knew it! Teasing a man like that is nothing to laugh at, Caro! God, I had a damn difficult time sitting comfortably in the saddle after that!"

Caroline smiled her satisfaction. "So you *did* look at me. You did look at me *in that way* so you must have thought about us together, nak—"

"Yes! Yes! All right! I'll admit to it that once," he confessed to cut her off.

"Just the once? That is not very romantic."

"Romance has nothing to do with it!"

Caroline pouted and then said cheekily, "I've often thought of us together in bed, naked. I can't be certain, but I am very sure, which is almost the same as being certain, the first time I imagined us naked together was just before my fourteenth birthday—"

"Good—God!"

She giggled at his stunned expression and more so when she undid the large button of her damp cloak and let it fall from her shoulders. Sir Antony took a step forward, to grab the cloak, but Semper was there first and was quick to catch the heavy garment before it fell and smothered the unsuspecting puppy happily gnawing on his bone.

He had forgotten his majordomo was still in the room. He tried to continue to forget he was still in the room.

"You're in your nightgown!"

"Silly! Of course I am," Caroline replied mildly. "I was in bed when I decided to make this visit. You didn't expect me to be fully clothed at this time of night, did you? That would have taken *hours*. No, please don't wrap that wet thing about me again," she ordered when he snatched the cloak from his majordomo. "Make me a hot cup of tea and I shall be warm again. Besides," she added, skipping off towards the open double doors she presumed led into the bedchamber, "there's always the bedclothes to snuggle into... It's this way...?"

Sir Antony rolled his eyes to the ornate ceiling, shoved the cloak back at his majordomo, who had stuck out his arm to receive it, face devoid of his thoughts, and was about to follow the love of his life into his bedchamber when she came scurrying back to fetch the pug puppy. She scooped him up with profuse apologies for leaving him behind, and was about to pick up the chewed bone when Antony took the bone from the pug and stuck out his hand for the puppy.

Caroline hesitated.

"Boots has never been left alone before. To point out fact, this is his first time away from his brother and sister—"

"Brother and sister?"

She nodded.

"I have found good homes for two of Penny Pug's litter, and I am keeping Boots, whatever Salt says to the contrary, because he is the runt of the litter. So that leaves me with two..."

He smiled at her concern.

"I am sure you will find good homes for them. If not..." He shrugged. "I have no objection to two more joining your animal family, if that would ease your mind..."

Caroline ran up to him, threw her arms about his neck and kissed him. "Thank you! Now I feel very much better."

"That said," he added gravely, though his mouth twitched to smile, "I'm perfectly willing to share my house, but not the bedchamber with your menagerie. I like my sleep, and so must you..."

"Jane and Salt share their bedchamber with—"

"What your brother and his wife, or any other couple alive, do in the privacy of their apartments is not important. I am only interested in our bedding arrangements."

Caroline cocked her head in thought. "But when we have babies—"

"—we shall revisit my edict." He caressed a long thick strand of copper hair that fell over her left shoulder, saying softly, "Perhaps you would rather return to your own bed..."

That settled it. After giving Boots a nuzzle, she reluctantly handed the puppy to Semper, who had just returned from dumping the wet cloak on a footman in the servant passageway. If he hadn't been asserting his position as master in his own home, stern expression fixed in place, Sir Antony would have laughed to see his majordomo recoil at having his immaculate person defiled when the puppy promptly licked him across the chin.

"Semper, perhaps Mrs. Semper would do the Lady Caroline the supreme kindness of caring for Boots until her ladyship returns to Salt House—"

"—in the morning," Caroline interrupted.

"In minutes, if you don't take yourself off to the bedchamber!"

"How unromantic you are!" Lady Caroline threw at him with a pout, but did as she was told when Sir Antony pulled a face and looked struck down with embarrassment. She was gone less than a minute when she poked her head around the door, tumble of fiery red hair sweeping the floor.

"I apologize in advance for his puddles!" she called out, interrupting Sir Antony's murmured conversation with his majordomo. "Boots doesn't have any manners—yet!"

"Thank you, my lady. I am confident Mrs. Semper will manage splendidly," Sir Antony stated without turning round. When there was no cheeky comment in response, he could not help himself and glanced over his shoulder. Of course she was still there, smiling at him. He silently mouthed the word "go".

Caroline put up her chin and looked defiant. When he raised an eyebrow, she reluctantly did as she was told, but not before poking out her tongue.

LADY CAROLINE'S ARRIVAL AT SOUTH AUDLEY STREET UNDER cover of darkness went unnoticed and would go uncommented on by the inhabitants of Westminster; all were within doors and sleeping at such a late hour. With the lack of a full moon and fog hanging low over the rooftops, even the adventurous were disinclined to wander the streets without good purpose. If the drunken gentleman on horseback or the weary seller with his empty wheelbarrow ventured to notice the sedan chair, neither was sufficiently bothered to recognize that the coat of arms emblazoned on the black lacquered panel under the curtained window belonged to the Salt Hendon earldom.

There were those, however, who were alert to all possibilities and did have purpose. Two hatchet-faced associates of the thief-taker employed by Sir Antony and reporting to Ralph Semper lurked deep in the shadows on the opposite side of the street, coats pulled up around their ears and hats low on their brow to stave off the cold night air. They were the night watch, in place to keep an all-night vigil on the Templestowe residence.

The day watch had spent daylight crisscrossing the environs of west London following a carriage occupied by Lady St. John, her companion Mrs. Smith and, for a time, Lady Dalrymple. Mr. T had advised the night watch he was confident that after such an eventful day, Lady St. John and her companions would not be setting foot outside the premises that night. Thus the associates allowed themselves to close an eye and get a few hours' sleep in a doorway. The arrival of the sedan chair with a liveried linkboy carrying a flaming taper to light the way had the associates nudging each other awake.

They watched the chairmen negotiate the sedan chair up the two shallow steps and across the threshold, admitted into the wide foyer by the porter. The door was shut on the cold night air, and the linkboy disappeared with his taper down the steps to the servants' entrance below street level. An hour ticked by, and then another, and just as the associates began to wonder if the occupant was spending the night, the sedan chair emerged from the townhouse, carried by its burly chairmen, the liveried linkboy scurrying up the servant steps with his taper relit to again lead the way.

The associates observed with only mild interest as the chairmen carried the sedan chair back the way they had come, disappearing into the darkness, the flame of the taper hazy in the mist.

What they could not know—the unsuspecting chairmen and linkboy were just as ignorant—was that the occupant of the sedan chair who departed the premises was not the occupant who had arrived at the townhouse two hours earlier. Wearing a fur-lined red cloak similar to that worn by the Lady Caroline, and confident the chairmen would not know one red cloak from another, a female came sailing down the curved staircase, hood pulled up over her coiffure and head bent to conceal her face. She was seated inside the chair and had pulled the door closed before the porter had rallied the dozing chairmen from the powder room under the staircase.

Without a word spoken, the chairmen lifted up the poles and transported the sedan chair back to Grosvenor Square. Admittance to the Earl of Salt Hendon's house by a sleepy porter under the vigilant eye of two burly footmen was a mere formality. The front door bolted on the world and the servants, who knew the meaning of the word *inconspicuous*, opened the sedan chair door before returning to their posts for the night, the female given the privacy to exit in her own good time.

Four years had come and gone since Diana St. John had been within the walls of this illustrious establishment, so she took a moment to breathe in the rarefied air. With smug satisfaction, she recalled the layout of the house. Every opulent room with its tasteful decoration and furnishings, every wide corridor and candlelit vestibule, was burned so deeply into her mind's eye that, if required, she could find her way blindfolded.

What disturbed her, and had eaten her up in her captivity, was that she was unfamiliar with the suite of rooms she most needed to know intimately, if she were to successfully carry out her plan of wiping the Countess's offspring from the face of the earth. No matter how many vivid dreams she had of Salt House, of her presiding over it as if she were indeed its mistress, none of her dreams were ever of the nursery. She had only ever visited that most hateful of spaces the once, and that on sufferance. The existence of a nursery at Salt House consumed and tormented her in her incarceration, for it represented the Earl's future, a future without her.

Still wearing her red wool cape, its hood up over her hair, Diana St. John made her way to this most hateful of places.

TWENTY

"WHEN YOU SAY YOU ARE A *HABITUAL* DRUNKARD, DOES THAT mean you are drunk *all* the time?"

Caroline was leaning back against the polished headboard of Antony's bed, having made herself comfortable amongst the down pillows, fine linen sheet and embroidered coverlet drawn up to cover her crossed legs. In her lap was a small lacquered chinoiserie tray that had upon it a saucer and a small plate with discarded lemon slice and a silver spoon. The porcelain teacup she held in two hands, and sipped at the hot sweet brew from time to time while they talked.

"I was. I was drunk all the time," Sir Antony replied to her solemn enquiry. "I may not have appeared so, but I cannot recall a day when I did not drink beyond what was necessary."

"But everyone drinks."

"Not the way I did. Not all day, every day. Not to the point where you cannot recall what you did that morning, least of all the day before!"

"And now you do not drink at all?"

"I do not drink anything that has been distilled, fermented or that can intoxicate."

"Nothing of that kind—*ever*?"

"Not a drop."

"So what do you drink?"

He smiled and lifted his porcelain teacup.

Caroline frowned. "Just tea? Nothing else?"

"Oh, you'd be surprised what there is to drink that does not contain spirits: Tea, coffee, chocolate, cordials, distilled water… And then there is Prince Mikhail's special wine."

"Special wine? What is so special about it?"

"I should say it is the bottles that contain the special wine that make it special. It is not actually wine in the bottles," he explained, "merely flavored distilled water. I have a dozen of the bottles in my cellar. When required, I drink only from those bottles. It is a neat trick that allows me to indulge with my fellows without actually drinking wine."

"When will you be cured?"

He hesitated to respond and took his time to add and then stir half a teaspoon of sugar into his tea, finally leaving the tea trolley to sit on the edge of the bed near her. He felt battered and bruised, and the tea, his second cup, helped to quiet his heart, which was beating too hard in his chest. He had laid bare his soul, confessed his drunken past, all of it, to Caroline, and she had listened without comment, as he had asked her to. Naturally, she now had questions that needed answers, and the one question, the question she had just asked him, was the hardest of all to answer. It required that he tell her what was in store for their future. He prayed she would still say *yes* to marrying him. Would she consider sharing her life with a habitual drunkard any better than being married to a consumptive narcissist prone to temper tantrums?

He reached out and took hold of her hand and looked into her green eyes. Best to be direct—how else could he tell her?

"There is no cure. I will be a drunkard for the rest of my life."

"But… You do not get drunk anymore. You have stopped drinking…"

"That does not mean I do not want to drink, or that I won't get drunk in the future," he explained. "The craving is always with me. It never goes away."

Caroline frowned. "How do you know it won't go away? How do you know that you can't just have one small drink and stop?"

"A habitual drunk cannot stop at just one drink. It is all or nothing."

"But… How do you know? Perhaps it will go away?" she asked hopefully. "Mayhap one day you will wake up and you will no longer have the craving?"

He shook his head.

"Caro, listen to me. It is important you realize what I am, and that this is how it will be every day… This is how it will be for us, if you do marry me. Remember I told you about how His Highness Prince

Mikhail helped me when I was at my lowest? He was able to help me because he, too, is a habitual drunkard. He recognized in me the same signs. He allowed me to see to what depths a drunkard will stoop, all to find the next drink. He paid a high price before he came to his senses and realized that if he did not stop drinking he would be dead, and before his sons were out of leading strings!

"One night he was found frozen in the streets. His heart was barely beating. His frostbite was so severe, surgeons had to operate. Two fingers from his left hand and three toes from his right foot went black and turned gangrenous, so they had to be removed. But he was thankful to be alive. He did not want me to suffer a similar fate before I came to my senses. He convinced me to accept his help and counseling, and so it is to Misha—His Highness—that I owe my life, this new life I now lead. He has managed to control his craving for alcohol for almost a decade, which is a feat in itself, but not without the support of his wife, his sister, and the vigilance of his minders."

"Minders?"

"Servants trained to be on the alert for signs of weakness. If their master lapses, they have his written permission and full pardon to lock him away until he regains mastery of himself and over his cravings. It is a drastic measure, but it is effective."

"You have such servants, such minders, too?"

"Yes. Five of the Russians who came with me to England are highly trained, trained to watch me, to watch for signs of weakness, and if I lapse, to act, and act swiftly. They have the same written permission and full pardon should they decide it is necessary to lock me away against my will. They will treat me and care for me until such time as I am fit company for others. No one must interfere with the treatment…"

"You mean your wife and family must not interfere."

"Yes. Have no fear; I cannot be locked up on a whim. All five must agree the treatment is necessary. One cannot act without the others, and four cannot act without the fifth. Caro, you must understand, as surely as night follows day, there will come a day when I will lapse. The compulsion is at times unbearable, but so far I have managed to control my craving."

Caroline squeezed his fingers. "I think I understand… I do not like the idea of you being locked up, of needing *treatment*. And I will fret terribly until you are well again, but I would never interfere in what is best for you…"

He kissed her hand. "Thank you."

"The bearded footmen who brought the tea trolley to the saloon… The one who picked me up and brought me to your dressing room… They are your minders?"

"Yes." He smiled thinly. "I had hoped that despite being Russians, they would blend in to my household dressed in livery." He gave a laugh. "Little did I realize that five minutes out of 'Petersburg and they threw away their razors. The wearing of beards is forbidden in 'Petersburg by Imperial decree but the rest of Russia ignores the edict. I cannot force them to shave, nor would I want to. Facial hair, it seems, is part of their natural way of life. So I shall be the only English lord with hirsute footmen!"

"Oh, I think they look splendid with their beards. It lends an exoticism to your household." She dimpled. "You should dress them in a different livery to the other footmen. Give them gold braid and colored stockings. Make them special. Make them appear as your household guards. Which, if you think about it, is what they are. They certainly look the part, being so wide and tall. And when we travel from one Continental embassy to another, we will be talked about, if for no other reason than our bearded household guard. We may even start a fashion for hairy footmen!"

"So my kisses meet with your approval? Or was it something else in particular about my person which decided you to accompany me on my next posting…?"

She kept her lashes lowered, though she could not stop the heat glowing in her cheeks. "Your kisses make me tingle—"

"Do they?"

"—all over. And the something—"

"Something?"

"—the something in particular is not what you think! Though what I will say about that *other* particular something is that you don't need my compliments, because I am certain there are other women, with far more experience, who have praised you without exaggeration."

"Praised me? About my short-cropped hair?" he responded with a feigned questioning frown.

"Your hair?" It was her turn to frown. "Do you let other women see you without your wig? No! Do not answer that! It is not my business, it is yours, and I—"

"—will be the only woman from this day forward who will have that privilege. You seemed inordinately pleased with my natural head of hair, so despite the urge to want to cover my exposed head with a cap in company, I have not, for you."

"Oh! Oh! Yes! I was—"

"The particular something you were referring to is my scalp *sans* wig?"

"Yes! Of course!" she said in a rush, more flustered than ever.

When he smiled and winked more color rushed up into her face realizing his playful ruse. She smiled, not at all made uncomfortable. In fact she was surprised to find herself overwhelmed by a sense of complete happiness. For the first time in many years, gone was the uncertainty and heartache. She was content and with contentment came an awareness of how comfortable she felt propped up against soft downy pillows in Antony's bed. She imagined this was how it would be when they were married. She wanted to snuggle down under the covers with his arms and body wrapped around her to fall into a deep satisfied sleep. Sleep. She suddenly realized she was very tired, for it must be well into the small hours of the night.

Yet there were a few questions remaining to be asked, and she wanted him to answer them now, while he was comfortable sharing confidences. He had been so candid about his affliction, something of which she had been totally unaware, and it had provided her with answers to past behavior that was so out of character for the Antony she knew and loved. She admired his bravery at opening up his soul to her, and because he had done so, because he was her best friend and she loved him, it was only right that she share his burden.

"Tell me about the tea," she asked quietly. "Is that what helps stop you wanting to drink those substances that harm you?"

"It is the ritual that goes into the making of the perfect cup of tea that helps me overcome my craving," he explained. "Every time I make a cup of tea I follow a precise set of steps. Each step closer to the perfect cup of tea is a step away from wanting a glass of wine, or that drop of brandy."

"Yes. I can see how you become absorbed in the ritual. How you make your tea is very calming," she replied with a smile and stifled a yawn.

He grinned. "Is calming another word for boring? Am I sending my lady to sleep?"

"No! Don't fun!" she pouted. "It's late and I'm sleepy…" She put aside her teacup to lie back amongst the pillows. "I like the way you make your tea. I like watching your ritual. I watched you today in the saloon and you followed precisely the same steps now as you did then. Every little detail is the same. For example, the handles of the teacups are all angled to the left, while the spoons rest on the saucer on the right."

He smiled. "You are observant. Ritual is what helps me maintain my sobriety. There are other aspects of my life to which I apply ritual. It all helps to distract me, allowing me to concentrate on what is most important in my life."

Caroline snuggled under the covers and looked up at him with a coquettish smile. "Am I important in your life, my lord?"

He put up an eyebrow. "Need you ask?"

"Of course. I will never tire of hearing you say it."

"Do you know who finally stopped me drinking?"

She shook her head, though she tensed with anticipation of his answer.

"Misha opened my eyes and gave my compulsion a name. He made me come to terms with what I really am, to stare myself in the looking glass and say *I am a habitual drunkard*. But I still had to *want* to turn my life around, to have a reason to change, to change for the better."

"Tell me," she murmured. "What was your reason?"

He answered without hesitation.

"You, Caro. I wanted to be able to ask you to marry me with a clean heart and a clear mind." He huffed. "I managed to do that, even if I made a muddle of the delivery."

She shook her head, tears in her eyes.

"No. No. You said it beautifully. You asked me to marry you as I always dreamed you would. It was perfect. I was the one who spoiled it for you—for us—*I* made a muddle of it!"

He looked down at her hand in his, and said with a note of sadness, "I made the decision to stop drinking before I knew you had married Aldershot. When I discovered you were the wife of another, that you could not be mine… I almost gave up. I seriously considered being drunk for the rest of my life preferable to living a sober life with you married to another."

"Oh, Antony, *no*."

"But then I realized that if I could not remain sober for my own self-esteem, what sort of man was I? I feared that if I reverted to my drunkard ways and returned to England to find you happily married, possibly with children, I would never control my addiction."

"But you have returned, and I am no longer married, I have no children and you are in control, so there is no reason for you to be fearful, is there?"

He smiled at the note of optimism in her voice and hopped off the bed. He picked up the little lacquered tray holding their empty teacups, and stood looking down at her for a moment.

"I realized something else while staring into that looking glass... A life lived without sharing it with the one you love is a life only half lived..." He made her a quaint little bow of the head. "Please excuse me for a moment while I clear away the tea things..."

He took his time, stacking the clean plates, rinsing the teacups and the silver spoons with hot water from the samovar, and then carefully wiping the items dry before returning each to their allotted places on the tea trolley. The used sodden tea leaves were tipped into a tall porcelain jar with fitted lid, and the two teapots rinsed and replaced on their respective stands. He next cleaned the blue and white porcelain tea strainer and set it aside, before wiping his hands dry on a towel that he then folded and returned to its hook affixed to the side of the trolley. Confident the tea service was ready and prepared for his next cup of tea, he left the tea trolley and returned to his bed.

Caroline was sound asleep. He knew she would be. He had taken his time, time enough to make certain that try as she might to stay awake, she would not be able to fight her need to close her heavy eyelids and fall into a deep sleep. With his hands in the pockets of his silk banyan he watched her. He still found it hard to believe Caroline was in his bed, that it was her bright red hair that tumbled across his white linen pillows.

Earlier, when he had first come through to his bedchamber after depositing Boots the pug with his majordomo, his overwhelming urge was to throw off his banyan, help Caroline out of her thin nightgown, toss her naked onto his bed and kiss her all over. He would make love to her as many times as she desired; prove to her he could make her happier than any other man alive. Instead he had curbed his overwhelming desire and calmly made them both a cup of tea.

It wasn't that the confession and the late hour had drained desire. He was no less desirous of making love to her; his body offered him stark evidence of that. It was something less tangible but no less real to him. Was it pride? Honor? Self-conceit? Whatever name it went by, it demanded he remain true to his code of gentlemanly conduct. Maintaining his honor was as important to him as breathing. Without it he was no gentleman. He would not cheapen the ultimate intimate experience between a couple in love that should begin on their wedding night and not before. And so he tenderly brushed a long curl of silken red hair from Caroline's cheek, softly kissed her forehead, tucked her up properly under the coverlet and retired to his dressing room. An uncomfortable night spent on his chaise longue was a small price to pay for a clear conscience and untroubled sleep.

He woke two hours later, bathed in a cold sweat, dreaming, not of his adored Caroline asleep in his bed in the next room, but of his sister, and he knew with depressing certainty he would never have the life he dreamed of with Caroline until Diana was dealt with, once and for all time.

Earlier that day, his sister had snatched from him the invitation to attend the Salt masquerade, eyes glittering with triumph. She proudly showed the gilt-edged card to Lady Dalrymple and Mrs. Smith. Not surprisingly, conversation throughout dinner and later, over coffee and macaroons in the Etruscan Saloon, was all about the masquerade ball, from what to wear, to who would be attending and the need to spend the few days leading up to the ball engaged in fittings for their costumes and visiting their friends also on the guest list.

Sir Antony had sat back in a gilded wingchair in the Saloon with his cup of tea, the silent male audience of one to these animated female discussions. He could have been a ghost upon an ethereal visitation, his presence forgotten. It mattered not. In truth, he was glad to be ignored. It gave him the latitude to watch his sister and, selfishly, imprint this memory of her: Beautiful and animated, brimming with excitement, consumed in the harmless pursuit of costume and mask.

Finally, he went off to his rooms overwhelmed with sadness. The invitation had begun to serve its purpose. Diana was lulled into a false sense of confidence as to her place in the Earl of Salt Hendon's affections, for surely the invitation indicated forgiveness.

It was while undressing and his bath made ready, that he formulated a plan for Diana's incarceration. With the help of his Russians, and Mr. T and his associates, he intended Diana to "die" the night of the masquerade. A heavy narcotic and finding her unconscious at the bottom of the stairs would lead Society and unsuspecting family members to believe she had fallen and broken her neck. There would be a funeral but no body. Only with her death could her children mourn, the family name be saved from ignominy, and life go forward. In truth, his sister would spend the rest of her days in the remote Russian wilderness from which the only escape was death.

However, he now had a better plan, thanks to his tête-à-tête with Caroline, he submerged in his bathwater and she seated on the bath stool at the end of his tub. He had listened and reacted to her heartfelt confession of her life since his departure for 'Petersburg with what he thought was equanimity and restraint. Just beneath this veneer, he seethed. Anger simmered and boiled up into fury as she poured out her heart, her deep shame and feelings of unworthiness to be his wife. He knew he was ultimately to blame for the four years of heartache she had suffered, and so most of the anger was self-directed, but he was not to blame for her loss of innocence at a public masquerade. He knew where to direct culpability for that. Although she had not said his name, it had not taken much deductive reasoning to conclude her seducer and her lover were the same man, and that man was none other than Dacre Wraxton MP.

He had a great desire to choke the life out of the rakish Wraxton, or at the very least pink him with the point of his sword and draw blood. However, the diplomat in him devised a much better scheme that would not only deal with Dacre Wraxton, but his sister, too. Society loved scandal and none better than one dripping with lasciviousness. Wraxton and Diana would run away together to the Continent, his sister would then subsequently die, perhaps by drowning on the Channel crossing, and Wraxton would write to Lord Salt with this tragic news. So Society would think, particularly when Dacre Wraxton disappeared at the same time as his sister. Sir Antony could not care less where Dacre Wraxton spent his exile, as long as it was a hundred miles distant from Caroline. He had every confidence the rakish MP would fall in with his plans. If not, a duel would soon change his mind.

Confident this plan would work, he was determined to put his sister out of his mind for the few hours of sleep left to him. He plumped the cushions, settled again as best he could on a chaise that did not sufficiently accommodate his length, thoughts on the love of his life snuggled up in his bed, and stared into the glowing embers in the grate until he fell asleep.

<h1 style="text-align:center">TWENTY-ONE</h1>

Diana St. John smiled at her own cleverness as she made her way to the nursery. She traversed the main staircase and passageways without rousing the suspicions of the footmen dozing at their posts in the lit alcoves she passed on her way to the third floor. She was so confident of not being caught that she threw back the hood of her scarlet cloak to better see her way around the interconnecting rooms. A smoldering fire in every grate and two candles burning in mirrored sconces in each room, provided warmth and a warm glow.

The children were fast asleep in their little beds. The nursery maids who watched over them during the night, should a little one wake and need resettling, were asleep on trundles or in chairs in each room. That there were no doors on the rooms aided Diana St. John's ease of movement from one bedchamber to the next. She did not linger in any room but one. It was the bedchamber of two small children, a boy and a girl. Both were deep in an untroubled sleep on their backs, so she was able to get a good look at their little faces, cheeks flushed with warmth and brows smooth and unworried. The boy had a mop of blond curls and the Sinclair coloring; the little girl, not much more than an infant, had a head of black ringlets, round cherry red cheeks and an angelic visage that had a great look of her accursed mother.

It was at the boy Diana stared longest. If she possessed a scintilla of motherly affection it was all for him, because he greatly resembled his noble father. But the moment passed just as quickly for this golden-haired boy had usurped her son's place as heir to the Salt Hendon earldom, and that left a bitter taste and a resentful hatred. Not for much longer would this firstborn son be assured of his noble legacy, and that made her smile.

She glanced about the large room with its pretty gilded furnishings in pale blues and pinks with matching curtains, the fireplace with its safety screen, and at the plush carpets. A nursery maid was curled under a coverlet asleep in a chair. How simple it would be to set fire to the curtains. How long would it take before someone smelled burning textile, before the room was engulfed in flames, before the children suffocated in the haze of smoke? Yet, she resisted the urge because she could not allow herself to be implicated.

She needed to be seen as a savoir in the eyes of the Earl, to be his only comfort when the time came for his family to perish in an inferno. And the perfect opportunity had been handed to her in the form of the masquerade ball. She almost squeaked her glee aloud at having received an invitation from Salt that very afternoon. Surely it meant his wife's hold over him was waning, for she would never agree to a rival's presence, and that was no surprise. Three children in quick succession would have faded the skinny whore's looks. A man of Salt's appetites required fresh, willing females to cater to his needs, any number of which she would supply once reinstated to her rightful position by his side.

With a legitimate reason to be in the house on the night of the ball, what could be simpler than disappearing to allow Mrs. Smith access to the house? She would set the fire, the Countess alerted that her children were in peril, and the entire family locked up with no escape from smoke and flame. Diana would rescue the Earl of Salt Hendon's heir, only for the boy to die in her arms, despite her best efforts to revive him. Rescuing the boy would be tangible evidence of her devotion to the Earl; that the boy had died in her arms after every effort to save him would not be seen as her fault. She could hardly wait for that moment to arrive.

Not tonight.

Tonight she had come to collect what the useless niece of Mrs. Smith had been too cowardly to pry from the chubby fingers of this golden-haired child. She found the cloth monkey tucked down the side of his mattress by his pillow. According to Mrs. Smith's niece, this absurd toy, a cloth doll that was supposed to resemble a monkey with a grinning face and dressed in a yellow shirt and short trousers, never left the boy's side. Such overindulgence would not have been tolerated in her household. Her children were only permitted objects that had a practical or educational purpose, for how could children become well-behaved obedient beings if they were allowed to indulge their childish caprice? This monkey was another manifestation of that creature's unsuitability as Countess of Salt Hendon, and it, too, would burn to ashes with the rest of the Earl's family. But for now, she needed it. The monkey was necessary to coax the boy into her arms and away from his nurses and his parents, and the flames engulfing the nursery.

With the cloth monkey in her possession, she was ready to return to her brother's townhouse in the manner she had left it, in the sedan chair, and without rousing the suspicions of the chairmen. For how else would the Lady Caroline return to Salt House none the wiser to the misuse of her mode of transportation and her servants? Shoving the cloth monkey under her cloak, Diana turned to leave and was confronted with a tall adolescent girl in nightgown and stockinged feet in the passageway, blocking her exit.

It was her daughter, Magna.

"Mama, that's Ned's monkey," Merry said in a thick drowsy voice that indicated she was not awake. "Did you like my painting of Peter the Macaw? He's a special bird…"

After a forced separation of four years, a mother's natural instinct would be to rush to her child, to hug her, to kiss her, the need for physical contact overwhelming all other considerations to reassure the child they were loved and greatly missed. Not Diana. She was gratified to see her daughter in such good health, but the girl could not have chosen a worse time for a family reunion. That was to come later, with the Earl and Ron present, not before. She simply did not have the time to indulge the girl in her half-awake state. So with an arm about her thin shoulders, she coaxed Merry back to her bed. Asleep, Merry readily complied, and crawled under the covers.

"Goodnight, Mamma," Merry said sleepily, settling her head on the pillow. "Granny and me… We are coming to call…"

Diana patted her shoulder, waited a few moments and was gone.

WHEN MERRY ASKED AFTER HER MOTHER AT THE BREAKFAST table the next morning, the Earl and Countess stared at one another in surprise. It was the first time in six months she had mentioned Diana. The only logical explanation, and one Merry readily accepted when she recounted what had happened the previous night to her Uncle Salt and Aunt Jane, was that she had had a dream.

"It was a dream, Aunt Jane," Merry reassured herself, putting the silver butter knife on the plate. She offered Beth her last slice of bread and jam, which the little girl eagerly accepted, and looked from the Countess to the Earl, who were both attending to her, and then back at the Countess. "Ron told me once that if you want to dream about something or someone, that should be the last thought you have before falling asleep. It's never happened to me before now. And I have never wanted to dream about Mamma because that would only make me sad…"

"That's quite understandable," agreed the Earl.

Merry nodded and let her gaze drop to the blue and white patterned plate, saying in a small voice, "I don't want to see her…" She looked to the Countess. "I don't have to see her, do I?"

"I'm sorry, Merry, I wish I had power over your dreams."

Merry shook her head. She turned to the Earl.

"I wasn't supposed to tell, but you said we should not have secrets if it makes us uncomfortable keeping them…" When the Earl nodded, a swift glance at his wife, she continued, a little more confidently. "It was to be a surprise for Mamma. Granny is taking me to see her today. I said yes, but I don't want to see her without Ron and without you, Uncle Salt… Granny says we must go alone," she added in a rush. "She says I must keep the visit a secret, but I don't want to go. And I don't like keeping secrets!"

"No *she*crets!" Ned declared from his cushioned seat beside his father, mouth half full of bread and egg.

"And no speaking with our mouth full of food, Ned," Jane mildly chastised her firstborn, though she was grateful for the outburst because it considerably lightened the mood and elicited a watery giggle from Merry.

"Mamma is right, Ned. But thank you for your contribution," the Earl replied gravely, and though there was laughter in his eyes, he was thunderous beneath that Lady Reanay was foolish enough to attempt to go behind his back. "Thank you for confiding in us, Merry," he said gently. "I gave you and Ron my word that if the time came to be reunited with your mother it would be in my company, and only if you wished it. I don't break my promises."

Merry nodded, her relief palpable. She frowned. "Granny will not be pleased with me…"

"You may leave Lady Reanay's feelings to me," the Earl stated, nostrils aquiver.

"I am certain that once your uncle *gently* explains to your grand-mother how uncomfortable you feel about such a visit, she will understand," Jane reassured her with a smile and looked to her husband. "Is that not so, my lord?"

Salt unlocked his jaw and inclined his head. "Be assured, my lady, that I shall be *very* gentle."

"Was that all you dreamed, Merry?" Jane asked in a light tone, attention seemingly on cutting a piece of bread and butter in two.

"I dreamed about my watercolors of Peter the Macaw," Merry replied, suitably diverted. "Which one I would give to Uncle Tony. Kitty says Uncle Tony was very taken with Peter when he met him yesterday." She addressed the Earl. "Will Uncle Tony be coming to call soon? I so wish to see him! Perhaps he would prefer a portrait of Penny Pug…?"

"I think your Uncle Tony will treasure whatever painting you decide to give him," Jane said. "And not only because you have a talent for drawing, but because he loves you and has missed you greatly while he was away in 'Petersburg."

Merry nodded with a smile. "Yes. He always told me so in his letters—about missing me—and that he keeps every one of my watercolors in a special folio." She frowned. "Perhaps I will give him a watercolor of Peter… But I've painted *much* better portraits of Penny Pug. Peter is more colorful—"

"—and a lot louder," the Earl complained with an exaggerated sigh he knew would have his niece giggling. "I'm surprised you didn't say it was a bad dream when it was about that blue feathered fiend! I dream about Peter *all* the time."

Merry's brown eyes went very wide.

"Do you, Uncle Salt? *Truly?*"

"Yes! I dream of having him *removed* from my anteroom!"

"Uncle Salt! How could you?"

"To—to—Timbuktu!"

"Tim—*bucket!*" Ned chimed in.

He proceeded to show everyone about the table his wide-open mouth as proof he was not eating and talking at the same time. When his little sister squealed her delight to see her big brother's gaping mouth of pearly white teeth and clapped her sticky hands, Ned opened his mouth wider, if that was possible, and for further effect, stuck out his tongue.

"Thank you, Ned. Now close your mouth, please," his mother stated quietly.

The Earl and Countess exchanged a suppressed smile at the antics of their firstborn, and both were on the point of laughing. Merry giggled behind her hand. Ned did as he was told, loudly, and pushed out his bottom lip with a sly sideways smile at his little sister, proud to have made Beth squeal at the breakfast table. He went back to eating his egg.

"Uncle Salt, Cousin Caroline will never allow Peter to be moved from your anteroom. *Everyone* but *you* loves him!"

"There! You said it, Merry! *My* anteroom. Not Caroline's anteroom. *Mine*," the Earl retorted, pretending offence. He looked to his wife. "Did you hear that, my lady? I am beholden to a blue-feathered fiend whose screech can be heard as far away as-as—*Bristol*."

"He only screeches at you, my love," Jane replied mildly, a smile exchanged with Merry. She wiped her little daughter's chubby cheeks and sticky fingers free of jam. "There! All clean, Beth!" she said with a wide-eyed smile and kissed the palm of her daughter's chubby hand. She put a silver feeding cup of warm milk into her daughter's little hands and looked round at the butler. "What is it, Miller?"

A liveried footman had trod up the length of the morning room, careful to avoid tripping over a discarded toy drum, an assortment of painted wooden pull-toys, and two silver whistles on corded ribbons, and spoke near the butler's ear.

"The article in question, which has been the subject of a thorough search of all appropriate rooms, has still not been found, my lady," the butler intoned to the Countess, without inflection but with a sidelong glance at Lord Salt's heir.

"Thank you. Please tell Nanny the nursery maids are not to fret. It will appear somewhere. I am sure of it, and in the most unlikely of places, too."

"Very good, my lady," the butler replied, and with a nod sent the footman off to the nursery with this directive before turning to another footman, silently in attendance, to have him replenish the silver urn with boiling water.

Salt set down his coffee cup on its saucer and looked across the table at his wife, after a glance at his eldest son, whose whole concentration had returned to dipping one leg of a bread soldier into the half shell of a soft-boiled egg as his father had shown him. Salt had cut the rectangular strips of bread half way up their centers to give the soldiers two legs, making it more difficult, and thus time consuming for an almost four-year-old, to dip one leg at a time into the soft yolk. Unlike most boys his age, once engaged in an activity, Ned showed a great capacity for sticking at a task, something of which his father was secretly very proud. This activity had added purpose: To keep his son's mind from wandering to the inexplicable whereabouts of his favorite toy companion, Mr. Monkey Mischievous, known by the entire household simply as Monkey.

"No luck?" Salt asked Jane lightly.

"None."

"Perhaps it is for the best that it remains l-o-s-t," the Earl offered brightly. "Having your firstborn breeched and weaned of his t-o-y m-o-n-k-e-y five months before his fourth birthday is not such a bad thing, is it?"

Jane was not appeased, nor was she fooled.

"Teaching your son to paint breakfast soldiers with yellow egg trousers is all very well, but *this* state of affairs is not something to brag about at White's, if that is what is meant by that grin. This is one wager you will lose. It is not such a bad thing if it happens naturally. Breeching was a necessity. He is far too active to be in skirts. But as to the other—" She stopped herself, shrugged a shoulder and smiled at her husband's hopeful grin. "When you look at me in that way I know I am being far too serious for my own good! Admit to it. You like breakfast soldiers as much as Ned!"

"Ah! My secret is out! Ned," he added in a whisper at his son's ear, "Mamma knows my secret." And to the Countess, "They are excellent bread soldiers, you will admit."

Jane smiled. "Yes. Most excellent bread soldiers, my lord."

"See, Ned! Mamma agrees," Salt said with a wink at his wife and pretended to steal one of the fingers of bread from his son's plate.

"No, Papa! They are *my* soldiers. You must make more soldiers, *p—lease*."

"I know where Monkey is," Merry offered.

Ned's head snapped up and he wiped away the blond ringlets falling into his brown eyes, eyes that were suddenly very round with interest. "Monkey? Does Merry know where Monkey is hiding?"

"Monffey! Monffey!" Beth called out from her highchair, watching her brother jump up and down on his seat.

"Monkey! Monkey!" Ned chanted in reply, losing all interest in bread soldiers dipped in warm runny egg yolk.

The Earl and Countess shared a moment of collective eye rolling before glancing at Merry and having the same thought: They had forgotten a twelve-year-old was more than capable of knowing the words the couple spelled out in front of their young children.

"Ned will be very grateful to know you have Monkey safe and sound."

"I'm sorry, Aunt Jane, I don't have Monkey," Merry apologized. "I just know Monkey's whereabouts."

"You would be doing my entire household a great service, Merry, by revealing where Monkey has run off to," the Earl said, holding to the back of his son's fine linen shirt to stop him toppling off his cushion. "And before Ned manages to snap a chair leg."

"Mamma has Monkey," Merry said matter-of-factly, picking up her porcelain mug to finish off the last drops of her hot chocolate. When the Earl and Countess exchanged a startled glance and then stared at her mute, she added simply, "I saw her take him from Ned's bed last night, and put him under her cloak." She frowned, head to one side. "So if I saw Mamma take Monkey... I remember particularly she was wearing a red cloak... And Monkey is missing... Does that mean I wasn't dreaming...? Oh, Aunt Jane! You've spilled your tea!"

The very idea that Diana St. John had somehow managed to enter her house, worse, been to the nursery and in her children's bedroom, had Jane trembling with dread and she lost the grip on her teacup. It couldn't be true. Surely, Merry had dreamed her mother's trespass? But if Monkey was missing, and Merry had seen the beloved toy in Diana's possession...

The teacup bounced and shattered at the Countess's feet, sending shards of porcelain under the mahogany breakfast table, and splashing tea to stain the hem of her pink silk day gown and matching silk shoes.

Merry's bad dream had become Jane's nightmare.

NOT FIVE MINUTES LATER, JUST AFTER MERRY WAS FETCHED AWAY by Kitty to help sort through a trunk full of old masks to find suitable ones for her and Lady Reanay to wear to the masquerade, Sir Antony poked his head into the breakfast room.

"Good morning, Salt Hendon family!" Sir Antony said with false cheeriness. "Please excuse the intrusion. I need a word with one of your nursery maids—wears a frilly cap with an overlarge flapping brim. Without delay, if you please."

TWENTY-TWO

Some two hours earlier, Sir Antony was shaving by the light streaming through his dressing room window. A footman tilted a gilt-framed hand mirror at just the right angle and height to allow maximum light to illuminate the stubble growth to his master's chin and jaw. A second footman held a blue and white patterned porcelain bowl full of hot soapy water into which Sir Antony dipped his sharpened blade free of lather. He was in his stockinged feet and buff breeches, bare back presented to the room. The rest of his ensemble lay across the upholstered chaise where he had passed a restless night. The morning's chosen silk frock coat hung on a peg. The day's wig was dressed and waiting on its porcelain wig stand at one end of the dressing table. Here Semper was rearranging items from his master's tortoiseshell and silver shaving box so he could set out the buckles required for breeches, stock and shoes, as well as the requisite accoutrements for his master's pockets: Gold watch, fobs, tortoiseshell etui and enameled snuffbox.

Rinsing the shaving blade, Sir Antony said over his shoulder, a jerk of his bare head towards the bedchamber, "Lady Caroline got away this morning…?"

"Yes, my lord. Her ladyship said not to wake you. She and the pug puppy departed just on first light, before the chambermaids were up to reset the fires. Your lordship can be assured that no one saw her leave," he added confidentially, because his master's blade remained poised over the soapy water. "And even if they had, no one in this household would own to it if questioned."

"Semper… Semper, I—"

"There is no need to explain, my lord," the majordomo interrupted hastily, unnecessarily fiddling with the arrangement of tortoiseshell combs in the shaving box. "Her ladyship spent the entire night in your bedchamber, alone, while you slept on the sofa in here."

"Is that what her ladyship told you, or is that what you believed happened, or is that your response to the below-stairs gossip?"

The majordomo looked affronted.

"I beg your pardon, my lord. I thought, as a gentleman—"

"Yes. Yes, Semper, you thought correctly! That was unfair on you. I apologize. Put it down to lack of sleep. Still, lack of sleep gave me time to ponder the future. You will be delighted to know that when this horrid business regarding the Lady St. John is done, the Lady Caroline and I will immediately marry, and spend our honeymoon in Ireland. I won't impose on your own visit to Mrs. Semper's sister, but it would make sense for us to travel across together. I have a second cousin in County Wicklow. Lives in a massive stone pile with acres of topiary dotted with statuary. Owns the local landmark, a waterfall. He's presently Governor of Virginia, or is it Maryland? Point is, he's not there and the estate is. We'll take the Russians and an assortment of household staff and the various domesticated animals her ladyship can't leave behind or she'd spend the entire time fretting for their welfare. When you've done visiting relations in Dublin you and Mrs. Semper must join us there."

Semper made Sir Antony a quaint little bow of the head.

"Thank you, my lord. On behalf of Mrs. Semper and myself, may I wish you all the happiness in the world. Mrs. Semper will be doubly delighted."

When he next rinsed the shaving blade in the porcelain bowl, Sir Antony said, "Thank you, Semper. Why will Mrs. Semper be doubly delighted?"

"Mrs. Semper had the privilege of being introduced when her ladyship collected the pug puppy. If I may say so, they got on famously. If not for the necessity of her ladyship returning to Grosvenor Square, they would've conversed till breakfast."

"Ah. You must thank Mrs. Semper for taking care of Boots for the night."

"It was no bother, my lord. In fact," the majordomo added with an unconscious sigh, "Mrs. Semper took a great liking to the puppy—a *very* great liking… The thing of it is, my lord… Of course, I stressed to Mrs. Semper that I would seek your lordship's permission…"

Sir Antony turned his right cheek to the sunlight and skillfully shaved his heavy jaw free of stubble. "Permission for what, Semper?"

"However, I'm afraid your permission may be just a formality when all is said and done," Semper apologized. "Lady Caroline and Mrs. Semper have arrangements in place that I dare not interfere." He grinned sheepishly. "Marriage gives a man another perspective."

"I am certain it must," Sir Antony replied, carefully shaving one sideburn and then the other. He patted dry his clean-shaven face with a towel and turned to his majordomo, waving away the two attending footmen. "These arrangements...?"

Semper carefully set aside the shaving blade. It would need sharpening before returning to the shaving case. He fetched Sir Antony's fine linen shirt, saying evenly, "Mrs. Semper and I have become the proud parents of a pug puppy, brother of one Boots. Name to be decided upon delivery, my lord. That is, if your lordship will permit the adoption and doesn't mind the interference of a pug below stairs..."

A deep chuckle came from within the shirt as Sir Antony threw it over his head. Tucking the voluminous folds into his breeches, he was still chuckling and shaking his head as he buttoned up his falls. "Not five minutes in my house and the minx is setting up a menagerie!"

"I did warn Mrs. Semper the arrangement was wholly dependent on your lordship's approval, and not to get her hopes up."

"I would never dare to presume to call Mrs. Semper a minx," Sir Antony interrupted quietly, buttoning his shirt, all laughter subsided.

Semper's eyes widened and he stuttered. "Of course—of course not, my lord!"

He handed his lordship his cravat to arrange to his satisfaction.

"Have you decided on a suitable costume for the masquerade ball, my lord? There is the costume you wore to Prince Ivan's Bacchanalian Revels? The frock coat in puce embroidered with grape vine, with the—"

"I have. I will attend this masquerade ball as something far more exotic," Sir Antony informed him. "I have a frock coat with matching waistcoat and breeches of blue silk with gold buttons and heavy gold trim to buttonholes, cuffs and white lapels, such as military types parade about in when wanting to show off. You remember it, Semper? I can't recall why I decided it would suit me..." He shook his head, adding with a grin, "But I do believe such a striking ensemble is just the thing to complement the lovely red sash and Imperial Cross I will receive earlier that morning in the presence of His Majesty."

"Is there a particular military personage from the pages of history you wish to impersonate at this ball, my lord?"

Sir Antony pulled a face

"Military personage? Hardly. Besides, Lady Caroline is not interested in people, Semper. I'm going as me. Well, me as a bird, a feathered fiend, in fact. Big, blue and golden..." Sir Antony reflected for a moment. "Sad eyes..." Then roused to say with a smile, "His name is Peter, Peter the Macaw, and my outfit will be as splendid as his feathers!"

Semper sensed Sir Antony thought his costume a very clever idea indeed, so he controlled his features and said in all seriousness, "Then may I suggest a feathered mask appropriate, my lord?"

"Feathered? Perfect! White and black should do nicely. As to this puppy... You've probably gathered from your conversation with Mrs. Semper, her ladyship's primary concern is the welfare of domesticated animals, hers and others. Your adoption of one of Lady Caroline's pug puppies, if it is truly what you and Mrs. Semper desire, and you have not been overly persuaded into this adoption by her ladyship—"

"No, my lord! Never. Mrs. Semper is very keen to take on the rearing of a puppy, and as Mrs. Semper's happiness is paramount... I was left uneasy, however, as to the introduction of this animal into your lordship's household..."

"Good gracious, Semper!" Sir Antony replied good-naturedly. "One small puppy will not make a speck of dust difference to my household once I am married and inherit Lady Caroline's menagerie as my own. Which brings me to something else I pondered while wide-awake at three in the morning. Once I am married there will be a great many changes to this household—so many, in fact, that you will no longer be capable of juggling the dual roles of valet and majordomo. So what I propose is that you confine yourself to the tasks of running my considerably expanded household as its majordomo, with suitable remuneration, naturally."

"Thank you, my lord. That is very generous of you. Mrs. Semper will be pleased."

"She'll be ecstatic when you also inform her the position comes with its own apartment in the south wing. Unfortunately, you won't be able to take possession until Lady St. John and her conniving female companion have vacated the premises." Sir Antony sighed as he plucked at the folds of his cravat. "That, God willing, is only days away... One of the Russians can be trained up to be my valet. I want you to decide a suitable replacement as soon as possible and make a start on showing him what's what so he can accompany us into Wicklow."

"Nikolas, my lord," Semper said without hesitation. "Nikolas would be the most suitable of the Russians. And again, thank you, my lord, for the consideration."

"You're very welcome, Semper." Sir Antony sat at his dressing table to have his wig fitted and looked at his majordomo's reflection, "Now to the more tiresome but necessary business at hand. Tell me what Mr. T relayed to you this morning…"

Semper enlightened Sir Antony about his early-morning conversation with the thief-taker Mr. T and the comings and goings of Lady St. John and her party of the day before. All seemed mundane and in order until Semper mentioned a peculiar late-night occurrence involving the Lady Caroline's sedan chair, adding with a frown,

"It was not Mr. T's night watch who informed me of this strange event, but Randal the porter. It seems her ladyship's sedan chair made a quite separate journey to and from this house, without her ladyship."

"The chairmen took an empty sedan chair somewhere then returned here? What the devil for? Are they taking coin on the side; hackney chairmen in secret?"

"As to that, my lord, I could not say. It was rather odd, to say the least, except when I tell you that the sedan chair was not empty. I believe the chairmen *thought* they were conveying the Lady Caroline to and fro…"

Sir Antony waved a hand and Semper stepped back from tying the black bow of his master's wig, Sir Antony swiveling on the dressing stool to face his majordomo.

"*Believed?* Who was it in the sedan chair?"

"Lady St. John, my lord. She was able to dupe the chairmen because she wore a red cloak similar to that owned by Lady Caroline."

"Where was she off to? No! Don't answer that. I can guess."

"I do not know for what purpose, but I do know her ladyship returned here within an hour; so Randal informed me."

"My porter seems to know a good deal about her ladyship's comings and goings," Sir Antony mused, eyes narrowed. "Is he, too, employed by Mr. T?"

"No, my lord. I thought as you do, and also wondered how Lady St. John knew the Lady Caroline had come to call at such a late hour *and* what she was wearing."

"Get rid of the fellow! He's obviously hedging his bets, running tales between Lady St. John and your good self."

Sir Antony sighed and stood, closing his eyes briefly before turning his back so Semper could shrug him into a waistcoat of pink and green striped silk with matching covered buttons, embroidered with sprays of honeysuckle and bees on pockets and lapels.

"God knows what she was doing at Salt House… The only good to come of *that* news is she returned here within the hour… I trust the news from Mr. T is less startling."

"I wish that were so, my lord," the majordomo answered with real regret. "Yesterday, the carriage carrying Lady St. John stopped at a particular residence on Windmill Street off the Tottenham Court Road."

"Tottenham Court Road? But that's practically in the country!"

"Yes, my lord. Mr. T was surprised Windmill Street had a name at all, such is the lay of the land out that way—all open fields and dirt tracks. But there is a tavern and a freestanding residence set in its own grounds, and this was the establishment Lady St. John's carriage drew up outside."

"Possibly the only house on Windmill Street."

"Yes, my lord. And there is good reason for that," Semper replied with a frown and continued on with relating the events as told to him by the thief-taker. "Mrs. Smith went to the servants' entrance of this particular residence in Windmill Street where she spoke to one of the inhabitants who, by her drab clothing, looked to be a domestic. Mrs. Smith disappeared inside the establishment, but was gone from view for less than five minutes, whereupon she reappeared and returned to the carriage."

"I presume Mr. T thought this—exchange, meeting, call it what you will—exceedingly underhanded?"

"He did, my lord. Forgive me for not mentioning Mr. T's observations earlier but you had a razor to your throat… The establishment Mrs. Smith visited is a smallpox hospital."

"Good—God! No wonder it is in the middle of nowhere!"

"Just so, my lord."

Sir Antony returned to his dressing stool.

"Why visit a smallpox hospital…?"

"As to that, my lord, Mr. T and one of his associates are presently making a call on the domestic with whom Mrs. Smith had words." Semper permitted himself to give a lopsided grin. "I am confident we shall know the answer to your question in a very short while indeed."

"Excellent. Any other news?"

"After calling upon the smallpox hospital, Lady St. John's carriage was followed to a laneway at the rear of Lord Salt's Grosvenor Square house, where it remained stationary for some time."

"What a hectic round of social calls!" Sir Antony murmured sarcastically and stuck out one foot then the other to allow the majordomo to affix the polished leather latches of his black shoes with diamond buckles.

"It was while the carriage remained stationary in the laneway, Mr. T observed a young domestic from Lord Salt's household exit the garden gate at the back of the establishment and disappear into the laneway, whereupon, at the invitation of Mrs. Smith, who was pacing the cobbles, she entered the carriage. Approximately twenty minutes later, this domestic exited the carriage."

"Man or woman?"

"Neither, my lord. A girl, and from her clothing and the overlarge cap with its frilly wings that hid her face, Mr. T surmised her to be employed in a very junior capacity..."

"Did she have an overabundance of hair?"

"As to that, I could not say, my lord," Semper replied, startled by such a question.

"*In white muslin mob cap hidden away,*" Sir Antony recited, "*Flap, Flap, Flap, the frilly fringe would not obey. A servant wench of abundant hair in disarray...* Good Lord! Why hadn't I made the connection earlier? I saw her in the garden... Mr. Wraxton saw her at Hendon in company with Mrs. Smith and Lady St. John... She must be in my sister's pay; or Mrs. Smith's, which is one and the same! I wondered how she would find a means to get inside the house..."

"The domestic re-entered the Earl's premises via the garden gate," Semper started to explain but was cut off. "She had in her possession—"

"Not her! My sis—Lady St. John," Sir Antony said brusquely, heart beginning to race. He had a deep foreboding about this girl and her involvement in his sister's mischief making. He stared at Semper without really seeing him. "Mr. T is well-prepared for the night of the masquerade?"

"Yes, my lord. Everything is in hand. Mr. T has his instructions and your letter for the authorities, should he and his associations be questioned about their activities on the night. He has also employed a dozen strong-armed and reliable men who would be willing to abduct His Majesty, given the gold coin you have offered them for their services."

"Good. Did you say this maid had something in her possession?"

"When she exited the carriage, she was carrying a small parcel."

Sir Antony snatched up his personal accoutrements and shoved them in a deep frock coat pocket. "I'm off to Salt House, to have a word with this supposed *servant girl*. When Mr. T has something to tell you about his interview at the smallpox hospital, you know where to find me…"

"My lord? Sir Antony!" Semper called as his master strode purposefully from the dressing room. "You've forgotten your pocket watch…!"

Sir Antony took in the activity in the Salt House breakfast room as he tentatively crossed the threshold, having shooed aside the officious under-butler, whose offer to announce him went unheeded. A footman was down on his hands and knees collecting up remnants of what appeared to be a shattered teacup. A second was clearing the table of breakfast things. The butler was giving directions to a third, no doubt to fetch a maid to mop the floor of milky tea. But what stopped Sir Antony in his tracks was the Countess's stricken look. She was up out of her chair, a hand to the table, as if to keep herself upright, seemingly oblivious to everyone and everything around her.

The Earl tossed aside his napkin, and within three strides was at the foot of the table, the Countess in his arms just as she went limp. A little girl in a high chair was straining to look under the table and squealing with delight at a boy with golden ringlets who had scampered between the chair legs to better view the mess left by Mamma's smashed teacup.

"Antony! Thank God you've come!" Jane burst out, grabbing Sir Antony's silken sleeve when he came straight up the length of the table.

He saw Jane was trembling and shot a concerned glance over her dark hair at her husband, wondering what had caused the normally self-contained Countess such distress that she had dropped her teacup. Salt was about as responsive as a marble statue, though the fact he was holding his wife and ignoring all else about him spoke volumes.

"What is it, Jane?" Sir Antony asked gently. "How may I be of help?"

"She was here. Here in our house! She-she was in my children's *bedchamber*. She took—Merry saw her… Thank God Merry came upon her… I hate to think what she meant to do—Magnus! Magnus, *you* said she couldn't gain entry to this house. You said our children would be *safe*. But they aren't safe, are they? They aren't safe *anywhere* while that-that *witch* roams free. Antony! Antony, you must *do* something! *You* can stop her!"

"She gained entry using a sedan chair and disguised in a red cloak."

This simple statement was all it took to trigger the Earl's pent up fury, anger he had carefully bottled in consideration of his wife and the fact his children were present. As it stood, Diana's escape from her castle confinement had made him question his judgment, and now, with her menacing trespass of his home he felt a thoroughly derisory head of his house. His inadequacy was further exacerbated hearing his wife seek the help of his cousin, as if she had abandoned all hope in his abilities to protect her and their children. Sir Antony's seemingly flippant statement was the final straw.

"What the—the *bloody hell* does it matter how she got in or what she was wearing? Didn't you *listen* to anything of what was said? The bloody woman was in the nursery, for God's sake! I don't know why I let you convince me you could handle her! Ha! Your incompetence in allowing her to gain entry to my house—in a *bloody chair* no less—you might as well have opened the bloody front door yourself and welcomed her in!" Salt gave a fuming huff of dismissal. "I don't know why I put my trust in you. What a bloody God-awful *mess* you've made—"

"I beg your pardon?! *My* bloody mess?" Sir Antony retorted, temporarily forgetting his manners and his mission in coming to Salt House unexpected and unannounced. "You're the one who locked her up, threw away the key, and then stuck your head under a carpet for four years! You may not have wanted her in your bed but you certainly did nothing to stop her running your life! She stroked your ego and you let her! Always telling you how bloody clever you were! How you would one day be First Lord of *bloody everything*!"

"I won't stand here listening to your tripe—"

"Enough! That's enough from you both. Magnus! Antony! Take stock. That woman's evil is working to divide you! We cannot be at each other's throats if we are to have any chance against her. If she truly is a witch, she is peering into her cauldron this very moment and cackling to see her malevolence at work. And for pity's sake, remember your manners!"

It was Jane. The strong, quietly unflappable and ever optimistic Jane had returned, all traces of fear and anguish dissolved. But it was not her husband's explosive outburst or Antony's equally furious reply that had vanquished her fear and snapped her back to her true self. It was her little daughter's crying and the rush of motherly instinct to quell her baby girl's fears and need to soothe the little red and crumpled tear-stained face. Beth was so frightened by her Papa's uncharacteristic blast of anger that in her young mind her Papa had turned into an unrecognizable bad-tempered giant.

Hearing her little daughter's howls of fright, Jane instantly scooped her up and held her tight, all other considerations pushed aside. She murmured words of comfort and reassurance that all was right with her world, and her Papa was not an ogre and loved her very much.

As for Ned, he had rarely seen his father angry. It was only on the odd occasion when he did something so exciting his heart would race, which his father called *dangerous*. Such as the time he climbed all the way to the top of the library ladder, because he wanted to capture a robin red breast that had flown in through the open window and was perched on the carved wooden lintel of the bookcase. Or when he had stretched out his net too far at the lake's edge to catch up one last tadpole and had slipped and fallen into the cold water. But this anger was much more ferocious, and although he was scared, he wasn't going to be a baby about it like Beth. So instead of cowering under the table, he poked his head up and rested his chin on the padded seat of his mother's vacated chair and gazed up at his father in trembling awe. He'd never seen Papa's face so red. It opened his brown eyes very wide and sunk his little shoulders out of sight.

Sir Antony was the first to come to a sense of his surroundings and humbly apologize. He bowed to the Countess who held her daughter in her arms; the little girl exhausted of tears, her head nestled on her mother's shoulder, a thumb in her mouth. He then stuck out his hand to the Earl, who instantly took it in a firm clasp.

"She may not have achieved her object, thanks to Merry's interference," Sir Antony said evenly, "but trust Diana to upend your household, upset your wife and children, and get you to blow steam out of your cravat! Not to mention make me feel as small and as useful as a gnat!"

"Apologies," Salt grumbled, feeling utterly foolish, particularly for losing his temper in front of his children. He bowed to his wife. "I crave your forgiveness, my lady." He smiled at his daughter and son, Ned clambering up onto his mother's chair the instant his father smiled, and said with a sad shake of his head, "Papa was very naughty to get so angry with your Uncle Tony. Yes, this is him," he said in response to Ned's cautious side long glance at the man with the big chin who was as tall as Papa, "the Uncle Tony from 'Petersburg you have heard Merry talk so much about. Uncle Tony and Papa were very silly doltheads and we deserve to fall hard on our *rumps* for losing our manners. I hope you will forgive us—"

"Papa! You said *r-rump-s*," Ned exclaimed, shoulders hunched with excitement to hear an adult, his father no less, say a word he had been told repeatedly was not a nice word to use in polite company; nor was he to shout it at his sister, even if it did make her laugh.

"Did I, Ned?" the Earl replied with surprise, a surreptitious roll of his eyes at Sir Antony and then a conspiratorial wink at the Countess before looking back at his son as if he could not remember ever having said such a vulgar word. "Did Papa say the word *rump*? How remiss! I must tell Uncle Tony that in our house *rump* is quite a vulgar word, but not quite as vulgar as *bottom* or *buttock*, which we never say in company. Do we, Mamma? The polite thing to do is not to mention our *rump*, *bottom* or *buttock* ever. Not in front of the servants and most definitely not in polite company. It is not a pleasant topic of conversation. So I do apologize to all present. To Miller and James and Jeffrey and-and—"

"Meg," the Countess offered, when the Earl had no idea as to the name of the maid mopping the floor.

"Thank you, my lady. Yes, and Meg," said the Earl, a nod to his wife. "But most particularly to Mamma, and Uncle Tony."

Ned took a look about the room at all the adults, servant and relation alike, and his mouth dropped open at his father's use of three words he was expressly forbidden to utter, ever. A swift glance up at his mother and he caught her smile, which she tried hard to suppress, and with a cheeky grin he dared to blurt out those three words, which had the Earl covering his ears as if to block such vulgarity from his hearing.

Salt then scooped up his son and ran around the sunny room, careful to avoid the footmen still clearing the table, and Miller, who had a watchful eye on a maid mopping the floor. Returning to the table, he tipped Ned upside down, as if about to set him down head first on Jane's chair, his squealing son's blond ringlets just brushing the blue patterned damask covering. Finally, Salt righted him and held him for a moment to settle any dizziness, his little son laughing and giggling, all fear at his father's burst of anger extinguished.

Beth sat up in her mother's arms, watching her father's antics and laughed along with her brother. She flung wide her arms to Papa for him to lift her high in the air and run around the table as he had done with Ned, which he did, much to her great delight. The end of Beth's flight coincided with the appearance of two nursery maids, who took the children by the hand and out to the garden for their morning playtime. Beth and Ned were happy to go off with a kiss and a wave from their parents, both again in charity with their father.

A silence followed the exit of the children, and the contingent of servants ushered from the morning room by the butler, who also excused himself because there seemed to be a minor servant disturbance requiring his intervention.

"You were not exaggerating," Sir Antony said to the Earl. "They are beautiful children. You are blessed—"

"—with a beautiful and level-headed wife," Salt responded with a smile and kissed Jane's forehead. "I don't know what came over me," he murmured. "To shout in front of the children in that unforgivable way..."

"We are all simmering pots of nerves to think Diana so easily gained access to the nursery... I still don't know how she did so, and I won't be able to sleep tonight, knowing she can! Perhaps we should put the children's beds in our bedchamber until after the masquerade...?"

"I hope it will ease your mind, in a small way, to know that Diana's trespass was not due to the lax practices of your servants. You misread my response earlier," Sir Antony explained. "Diana gained entry to your house by seizing upon a unique opportunity; she would not have been able to do so under normal circumstances."

The Earl and Countess waited for him to explain, all wide-eyed interest, and Sir Antony gave them a measured and heavily-edited version of events of Caroline's visit to his townhouse of the night before, adding sheepishly, because it was an outright lie, and because Jane was looking at him intently, a strange half-smile curving her mouth,

"You know Caro—always fretting over her animals. No sense of time or occasion when there is an animal to save, feed and house. She couldn't sleep, so just had to discuss a home for Boots the Pug's brother with the Sempers."

"How like her to go off in the middle of the night without a thought to her welfare or reputation, or a thought for others, all for the sake of a blasted dog!" Salt retorted, swallowing Sir Antony's story whole. "A soldier could be dying of his wounds, and it would be the horse shot out from under him which Caroline would prefer to nurse back to full health! God knows where she inherited her mawkish affection for the animal kingdom. It's certainly not in the Sinclair blood!"

"No. But perhaps it is in the St. John blood, or the Allenby blood...?" Sir Antony suggested lightly.

It had not been his intention to divulge what he knew about Caroline's true parentage, confirmed in the strictest of confidences by Tom, but it had just come out. And now that he had voiced it, he wasn't about to let Salt brush the matter aside. Besides with no servants present, not even the hovering butler or a footman or two at the doors, it was the perfect and possibly only opportunity to do so. Jane's soft smile alerted him that she knew well enough to what he was referring, and the fact she held fast to her noble husband's arm was all the encouragement he needed to say his piece.

"I will say this once, now, and then bury it for all time. Caroline's parentage doesn't matter a flea's hair to me. She will always be a Sinclair and your sister in my eyes and the eyes of the world. I have known almost since the day you married, when I first clapped eyes on Tom's mother at the ceremony. Caroline bears a striking resemblance to the Allenbys. None of the Sinclairs are so curvaceous, and that magnificent mane of fiery hair is a St. John trait. Caroline is St. John's natural daughter; her mother, Tom's aunt who died in childbed." He smiled crookedly. "Don't blame Tom for telling me the truth. He did so because he knows I love Caroline. I won't let it bother me, if it doesn't bother you both. We three and Tom are the only ones who know and nothing need ever be said again to anyone…"

"Good. Let's leave it there," the Earl replied in a clipped voice by way of acknowledgment of the truth of Sir Antony's words, as he pulled needlessly on the points of his crumpled oyster silk waistcoat, a heightened color to his cheeks. Yet, a glance at Jane and the wash of tears in her eyes and he stepped down from his pedestal to add with a dry swallow, "She—Caroline—she has St. John's green eyes… Her preference for saving the Animal Kingdom must be an Allenby trait…"

"Well that explains why Tom is Caro's partner in the rescue of abandoned and abused animals," Sir Antony said, deftly returning the conversation to a more comfortable and less controversial subject. "I gathered from Tom's letters he is enjoying a newly-established menagerie on his estate. Well, that is what it is now. All those large animals saved from baiting rings and mismanaged menageries, and which are unable to be housed domestically are crated up and shipped off to Tom…"

"Yes, that's true," Jane answered brightly, a counterweight to her husband's continued uneasiness. "We took Ned and Beth to see Tom's menagerie, did we not, Salt? It has become something of a talking point for locals and travelers alike. At last count, he had two zebras, an ostrich, a handful of large African cats, and Ned's favorites, any number of monkeys in their special enclosure. Oh, and there is an elephant Caroline has teasingly named Magnus."

"Ha! Ha! The minx!" Sir Antony laughed, and shut his mouth tight when Salt glared at him.

"When I give my blessing to your marriage with Caroline, you'll promise on oath not to encourage her waywardness," Salt grumbled. "An elephant named Magnus indeed!"

Jane kissed his cheek. "I think it a perfectly majestic name for a big handsome brute—and for an elephant." She smiled at Sir Antony. "And you won't make Antony promise any such thing. Truth be told, Caroline will co-opt Antony to join her and Tom in her quest to rescue every forlorn four-legged and feathered creature in this kingdom."

"I don't doubt it! Now, my lady, Antony, you must excuse this brute. I have a mountain of papers requiring my signature that will please Ellis no end. He may even allow me to escape the library for a game of tennis before nuncheon... If you are up for it...?"

"Oh yes, you must stay to nuncheon," Jane insisted, adding her voice to that of her husband, spirits much restored and lifted by the restoration of the friendship between these two big men who had once been the best of friends.

"Willingly, if my time were my own," Sir Antony replied with a sigh of regret. "I desire nothing more than to beat you at tennis, Salt, then join you, my lady, and the family for nuncheon, but I must decline. Diana and I are promised to Lady Porter's with those of her set who are invited to your masquerade ball. No doubt the conversation will be all about our costumes and masks."

"How can you maintain the façade?" Salt asked with disgust.

"With great fortitude and because I must. For you. For Jane. For your children. For Caroline. For all our futures. I have set myself the task of sister's keeper, and I will maintain the façade of doltish younger brother until such time as Diana is in my custody, Society none the wiser to her evil." Sir Antony smiled crookedly. "You forget, I am a diplomat, after all, and dissimulation is my weapon of choice."

Salt goggled at him. "I do believe you will be an ambassador one day."

Sir Antony smiled and made him a bow. But when he straightened the smile was gone and he said seriously,

"It is not my place to tell you how to run your household or your nursery, so you must excuse me if this thought has already occurred to you. But given Diana visited your nursery, it must somehow figure in her plans."

"You think Diana went to the nursery to reconnoiter?"

"I do, and suggest that on the night of the masquerade the children be moved to the royal tennis court gallery. Make a special treat of it. In the smallest of the four crates Miller is keeping for me, until I can present you with my gifts, there is a magic lantern and several boxes of plates that will keep them amused and occupied for most of the night. I will send Semper around later today to show a footman how to work it."

"Why the tennis court?"

"It is a wide-open space with nowhere to hide and there are only two points of entry. With footmen in place, it cannot be breached. With three hundred people in the ballroom on the night, and people to'ing and fro'ing to the refreshment rooms and card tables, it would be an easy thing for Diana to slip away upstairs and no one the wiser, not even the servants, who will be distracted attending to guests."

Jane squeezed Sir Antony's silken sleeve.

"Your idea is an excellent one, and the children will love to see the magic lantern. Thank you. Now you must excuse me as Sam will be wanting his Mamma, and then I am to join the ladies in Lady Reanay's apartments to discuss our outfits for the masquerade. No! You may not enquire as to what we are all wearing," she said with a dimpled smile at the Earl when he lifted his eyebrows in inquiry. "You shall see on the night, and not before! Oh, Antony, was there a purpose to your visit, not that you need one. You are most welcome any time. Shall I have Caroline fetched? When she was not at breakfast I supposed she had overslept…"

The mention of his godson brought Sir Antony hurtling back to his purpose in coming to Salt House. While he had no wish to disturb the household's equilibrium, he had to discover and expose the agent who was working for his sister inside the Earl's house, whatever further distress this caused the Earl and Countess. He asked Jane if he might accompany her to the nursery and see for himself where his godson slept. It would give him the opportunity to ask her in private about the girl in the overlarge mob cap and her position in the household.

What he and Jane discovered when they arrived at the nursery astounded them both.

TWENTY-THREE

Betsy was sobbing. She was sobbing so hard her eyes and nose were running and every muscle in her thin body ached, twisted up with anguish and fear. The thin handkerchief in her tight fist was wet through, and so was the lap of her petticoat. She had lost the use of speech and could only shake her head over and over to the same questions put to her by the housekeeper, the large frill of her cap flapping about her wet face like a pair of swan's wings. She was seated on her trundle bed in the corner of the room off Sam's bedchamber which was crammed with the necessary paraphernalia required to clean, dress and make comfortable the infant of noble parents. The housekeeper and Nanny Browne were standing over her, and behind them was the dour-faced Miller; the nursery maid Sukie cowered with a whimpering Sam cradled in her arms.

Sir Antony could not believe his eyes, or his luck. He gave a start and took a step backward and stood in the doorway as Jane bustled into the room. The girl sobbing on the bed had to be the flap-flap girl of Hilary Wraxton's poem. Surely, no one else in the Salt Hendon household wore such a startling mob cap. He wondered what had caused her such distress and patiently looked on as Jane took matters in hand. He was soon to find out.

Jane could not believe her eyes either. She picked up her infant son and smiled down at him, gave him a big kiss and tickled his nose with the end of hers then handed him back to the nursery maid. She instructed her to take Sam through to the playroom where he would not be within hearing range of such distress; she would be with him very soon. One quiet word at the butler's back and not only did Miller turn about, but the two senior females of her household domestic staff fell apart and down into tight-lipped curtsies.

"Good Gracious! Betsy? Whatever is the matter?"

"My lady, I beg your forgiveness for this most unnecessary and unsatisfactory disturbance but—"

"Thank you, Miller. I wish to speak with Betsy," Jane said firmly. "What I ask of you is to have tea fetched to the playroom, and tell Dicken to lay me out fresh petticoats and a pair of shoes." When the butler just stood there and exchanged a look with the housekeeper, she added with a note of imperiousness, "I beg your pardon, but was there any part of my request that was unintelligible?"

"No, my lady. Very good, my lady," the butler replied tonelessly with a nod, and took himself off, determined to have a word with his lordship if the little thief wasn't shown the gutter before sunset.

Sir Antony could not help a smile at Jane's confident dismissal of the senior servant of the household, every inch of her slender frame a countess, and he silently watched proceedings unfold, aware that it might be some time before the nursery maid was able to answer his questions, such was her distress.

"My lady, if you only knew what this-this—*wicked* and *ungrateful* creature has done!" the housekeeper blurted out. "She is a-a *thief* and a-a *liar* and should be shown—"

The word *thief* was enough to rouse Betsy from her melancholy stupor. She was up off the bed and threw herself to her knees at the Countess's feet before she could be stopped, going so far as to grab the delicate silk embroidered hem of Jane's petticoats in two fists.

"I'm no thief! I'm no liar! I-I—It ain't true!" Betsy blubbered, looking up into Jane's face. "You must believe me, my lady! Please, my lady! *Please.* I'm none of those nasty things! I don't want to be hanged! Don't let his lordship have me hanged!"

Momentarily stunned by the girl's actions and her terrified plea, Jane was slow to react. The housekeeper mistook this reaction for revulsion at having her person handled by a menial, and a lowly nursery maid at that, and she grabbed Betsy by the upper arm and tried to haul her up and away from the Countess.

"Get up! Get up, dolt!" the housekeeper demanded, tugging at Betsy's arm. "Nanny Browne! Grab her other arm!"

"No! no! I love baby Sam!" Betsy wailed, holding fast to the Countess's petticoats. "As God is my witness, my lady, I'd never do anything to harm him! Never! You know I love baby Sam! I made you that promise! Remember? You must remember!"

"Sam? What has this to do with Sam?" Jane asked, suddenly fearful for her infant.

"How dare you address the Countess before being spoken to! How dare you assault her ladyship!" the housekeeper hissed in Betsy's ear, continuing to tug on the girl's thin arm. "You have no place in this household, no place at all after what you've done!"

"Betsy!" Nanny Browne whispered in the girl's other ear, a tight hold on her upper arm, "Stop this at once. You are only making matters worse for yourself. Own to it and you may have your life spared."

Jane looked down at Mrs. McIntyre and Nanny Browne, both women with a tight grip on Betsy's thin arms, all sense of decorum and place cast to the winds. A temporary madness had taken over her household, but she was determined it was not going to overwhelm her. She was also determined that Betsy would have a fair hearing. She remembered a time when she herself had been treated as less than nothing by those in a position to know better, demonized and vilified, with no voice of her own and no one to champion her cause. She had been so helpless and alone in the world. A steadfast self-belief and an ingrained optimism that her life would one day be just as she imagined it, married to the man she loved and with a family of her own, had kept her spirits from flagging into perpetual melancholy.

This poor creature who gripped her petticoats as if her life depended on her word had no one in the world and no prospects, and so had every right to her terror. Jane was not about to see her dismissed without giving her the benefit of the doubt, and that meant talking to her without the presence of others.

Yet, four years as Countess of Salt Hendon had opened Jane's eyes to the myriad of layers to a nobleman's grand establishment and what constituted a well-run household, one of which was the pride and satisfaction the servants of a nobleman, particularly the upper servants with whom she had daily contact, derived from being valued members of the Earl of Salt Hendon's household. Thus she could not dismiss outof-hand the opinions of her housekeeper or her Nanny. They deserved a fair hearing, too, even if she had given Miller his marching orders. But the nursery was not the butler's domain, and she was certain Mrs. McIntyre and Nanny Browne would tell him so, whatever his dominion over these and all servants below stairs. What she was also

certain of was that her two most senior female servants would be mortified by their behavior when they came to their senses, not only because
of the way they had behaved in her presence but also because it was in
the presence of Sir Antony, a guest to the house and thus an outsider.

"Mrs. McIntyre. Nanny. Please unhand Betsy and show my guest
some common civility," Jane commanded quietly. "Sam's godfather, Sir
Antony Templestowe has come to see for himself where his godson
spends his days with his brother and sister when he is not with me."
When both women slowly rose up, brushed down their petticoats and
bobbed curtsies with chins down, she smiled to herself, but added with
a sad sigh, "I am only sorry his lordship had to bear witness to a
common brawl. I assure you, Sir Antony, that in all my days, I have
never seen the like before! And in the nursery, too, which, thanks to
Nanny, is normally a place of happiness and calm for his lordship's children. I can only think there must be something odd about the tea
today."

"My lady, I cannot apologize enough for having caused your ladyship and-and—Sir Antony such distress," the housekeeper murmured,
stricken with acute embarrassment. "I assure your lordship that this is
not the usual manner in which matters are conducted in his lordship's
house. As her ladyship rightly says, it is a most unusual occurrence
indeed…"

"Most unusual," Nanny Browne threw in because she felt she
should add something. She looked at the Countess and then down at
Betsy who had let go of her ladyship's petticoats but who still cowered
at her feet. "Thank you, my lady, for your kind words about the nursery. I do my best for their little lordships and her little ladyship."

"I know you do, Nanny, and Lord Salt and I cannot praise you
enough," the Countess replied. "Mrs. McIntyre? I am sure you will
agree that it would be best to leave this small domestic matter to
Nanny. You must have a thousand more important matters to oversee,
what with the masquerade ball the day after tomorrow…?"

Jane let the sentence hang, hopeful the housekeeper would see
sense. The woman nodded, curtsied, then silently took her leave, a
quick worried glance exchanged with Nanny Browne, something Jane
ignored.

"Nanny, when Betsy has washed her face and tidied herself, and has
had a few moments to recover her wits, please bring her through to the
playroom. Sir Antony has a few questions he wishes to put to Sam's
nurse, which," she added with a kind smile, "I am certain you appreciate take precedence over this little incident…?"

Again, Jane let the sentence hang, and as had happened with the housekeeper, Nanny Browne bobbed a curtsy, a furtive glance at the tall handsome gentleman in the fine candy-striped silks.

"Of course, my lady. I shall send Betsy through to you directly."

Sir Antony remembered well the nursery playroom that stretched almost the width of the house, and it made him smile, despite his trepidation at what the interview with Betsy might reveal. The familiar blue-painted walls and the marionette theater up against one wall were as he remembered them, but the scattering of toys littering the carpet, and the small pile of paintings in the fist of a child across the surface of a child-sized table that had four small chairs drawn up to it, were new. How times had changed for the better in this house, and he intended to do everything in his power to ensure they continued that way.

"Merry is not the only budding artist in the family I see," he said, lifting a corner of one of the parchments. "A dog. A bird. A cat?" He held up a parchment that had a dark painted center and on this dark center was a crudely painted white blob with four thick brushstrokes radiating out from one side and many thinner strokes in relatively straight lines from another part of the circle. "Or perhaps it is a portrait of Viscount Fourpaws all grown up?"

"Indeed it is his fluffy lordship. And a most fabulous guess, Antony! Or was it the whiskers that informed you?"

Jane laughed behind her hand, seeing her son's efforts at emulating his cousin Merry's exceptional drawing talents for what they were: Special to her but nothing out of the ordinary to the larger world. She retreated to the window seat, where Sukie was cradling a restless Sam. With her infant back in her arms, she dismissed the nursery maid, asking her to fetch Betsy, and hoping the girl was ready and willing to be interviewed.

"I must warn you, Antony, there is a great likelihood Sam will demand his midmorning feed before your interview is concluded, a circumstance I can do little about."

"You must not apologize for what is the most natural thing in the world," Sir Antony said with a gentle smile. "And this is a nursery… Ah! Here is the tea." He went about making the cups of tea as best he could, and as his ritual demanded. "I must warn you, too, my lady—

"Jane. It has always been Jane between us…"

"Yes, yes, so it has." He smiled and placed Jane's cup of tea on the window seat between them. "Jane… I must warn you, the questions I need to put to Betsy will disturb you. I only pray her responses are what we both need to hear. I don't want to think the worst. I want to believe that by some miracle of common sense or serendipity, all is as it should be in this wonderful little corner of your world."

"I have a foreboding that in some inexplicable way Diana is involved."

"Yes. But I do not think it inexplicable. I believe we shall find that it has all been very carefully planned. What we must put our trust in is something that Diana is incapable of understanding but which you and I believe is indubitable."

"And that is?"

Sir Antony smiled crookedly, a heightened color to his lean cheeks.

"It is something Diana sees as a major flaw in my character. Most definitely a weakness in a male... And she despises you for it because it makes Salt love you all the more." He put his teacup on its saucer and met Jane's blue eyes. "It is the capacity for love to conquer all—to conquer evil. Betsy called out that as God is her witness she loves baby Sam. That is what shall ruin Diana's diabolical scheming. It simply would never have occurred to her that Betsy would not do her bidding, that a girl of no family and little prospects would cross her—that Betsy has a good heart."

Jane baulked.

"Diana sent Betsy to this household to do her bidding; a poor girl of fifteen—to spy on us? Goodness me! I do not disbelieve you. What must she have over the poor child to make her want to do such a dreadful thing? Betsy hasn't an evil bone in her body."

"Yes. That's what I believe, too, now that I have seen the girl."

"Do you think there are other servants in this household in your sister's keeping?"

"I could not say, but I do not believe so. That is, unless you have employed other household servants since my sister's escape from Harlech?"

Jane shook her head.

"Good. I just hope young Betsy has remained steadfast and not weakened under my sister's constant haranguing. Believe me, I know how easy it is to give in. Diana is an implacable force of nature when she wants something. She made my childhood an absolute misery. Ah! Here is my godson's nurse now."

"Come forward, Betsy," Jane said with a smile.

Betsy did as she was told, slowly, gaze to the floorboards, her ever present mob cap with its wide brim shielding her face.

"Do me the favor of removing your cap, Betsy, so that Lady Salt and I may see your face."

Betsy did as Sir Antony asked of her and a great mass of wiry curls sprang out and around her face, the curls dropping no lower than the lobes of her ears so that it appeared as if a bowl had been place over her head and her hair cut around it. On anyone with straight hair such a haircut would have made them appear ugly but because Betsy's hair was so curly, it rather suited her. Sir Antony and Jane had never seen the like before, so much so that Jane asked,

"Who cut off your hair, Betsy?"

It was not a question the girl was expecting, and she gave a start.

"I won't lose my position because of my hair, will I, my lady?"

"It is not your hair that concerns us, Betsy," Jane replied kindly. "Though you must not be so self-conscious about it in future. Having such short curls is quite pretty."

Betsy's eyes lit up and she smiled nervously, the cap unconsciously screwed up in her hands. The compliment also loosened her tongue and made her feel at ease.

"Do you truly think so, my lady? Me da, he cut it off. He said it got in the way. That I didn't need it, as no boy was going to look at a skinny wench like me anyways, and as I had no prospect of marrying what was the use of it?" She shrugged. "Nanny Browne says it will grow again in time."

"And so it will... Betsy, Sir Antony wishes to ask you a few questions. I know you will give truthful answers."

"Yes, my lady. Yes, I will! I don't tell lies! I told Nanny Browne that, and Mrs. McIntyre, but they—Sorry, my lady..." She glanced at Sir Antony, adding in a rush, "I don't tell tales neither!"

"Well, Betsy, you may have to break that rule this once because it is a tale I wish you to tell. A truthful tale," Sir Antony said mildly. "But first, there is a very pressing question that requires an immediate answer."

"Yes, sir?"

"Nanny? Is there something urgent that has caused this intrusion?" Jane asked, interrupting Sir Antony's questioning when Nanny crept up the room, an unfamiliar gentleman at her back. She was about to enquire as to the gentleman's identity when Sir Antony shot to his feet and went to meet the stranger.

"Semper?"

"Please excuse the intrusion, my lord," the majordomo apologized, not a blink in the Countess of Salt Hendon's direction, and still slightly out of breath. He had run all the way from South Audley Street, the muck to his shoes and his windswept hair testament to the urgency of discharging his errand. "I need a private word—*now*."

Sir Antony nodded to Nanny Browne, who reluctantly departed, and he took Semper a little way down the length of the room, out of earshot of the Countess.

"You spoke with Mr. T?"

"Yes, my lord, I did."

"He was able to persuade the domestic of the establishment in question to divulge the particulars of what transpired with Mrs. S?"

"Yes, my lord, he was very *persuasive* and the domestic forthcoming."

"And?"

"The information is distressing to say the least…"

Sir Antony felt a prickle of sweat break out across his scalp.

"Go on! Go on!"

"The domestic told Mr. T that Mrs. S was very particular in her wants, and that it was some days before the object could be obtained, and then secreted away and given to Mrs. S—"

"Well? Well? Semper! For God's sake, just spit it out!"

"Yes, my lord. The domestic gave Mrs. S the object wrapped up in a parcel. This parcel matches in size and shape the one the nursery maid was seen carrying under her arm when she left the carriage."

"And in this parcel, Semper? What was in it?"

"An article of clothing, stripped from the still-warm body of an infant recently deceased, along with its mother, from, as you can rightly surmise, the smallpox. The domestic told Mr. T that the dead infant's outer garments, shoes and cap were not wanted. Just the plain chemise, that which is worn next to an infant's skin—"

"Good—God, how diabolical," Sir Antony muttered. "That scoundrel Amherst has a lot to answer for!"

"I beg your pardon, my lord? Amherst…?"

"Never mind that lunatic! I have my own to deal with!" Sir Antony rallied and gripped his majordomo's shoulder. "Thank you for coming so quickly."

"I thought time was of the essence, my lord."

Semper dared to glance over at the window seat where he let his gaze linger a moment on the beautiful young woman cradling an infant, and at the nursery maid standing mutely to attention before her. Recovering his wits when he heard his name for a second time, he bowed and left the nursery with as much dignity as he could muster,

Sir Antony striding back to the window seat to say to Betsy without preamble,

"You were given something yesterday. A parcel. Mrs. Smith gave you a parcel. Where is it?"

"Please, Betsy. Don't cry. You must be brave and tell Sir Antony what he wants to know, and be truthful."

Betsy nodded vigorously and dashed her moist eyes.

"Yes, my lady. I will. I will be truthful! I was truthful with Nanny Browne. I told her I did what I did because I had to. I didn't want to steal Sam's rattle but Aunt Smith said if I didn't, me da would never get out of debtor's prison."

"You took Sam's rattle?" Jane asked before Sir Antony could, such was her surprise. At least she did not need to ask the maids to keep searching for it. "What did Mrs. Smith want with it?"

"I don't know, my lady! I don't know why I was to do any of the things they had me do! It made no sense to me at all. Please. You must believe me!" The tears were back and she glanced at Sir Antony before saying to the Countess, "Will I hang for it? Mrs. McIntyre says little children get strung up for stealing a lady's handkerchief!"

"No. You won't hang, Betsy. That I promise you."

"The parcel, Betsy?" Sir Antony prompted. "What did you do with the parcel?"

Mention of the parcel again set Betsy off into a convoluted explanation that made no sense.

"It wasn't right what they wanted me to do! I told Nanny Browne, I didn't care if I got into trouble for doing it, I just had to do it! I had a feeling in m'bones, you see. A feeling that told me what I had to do. And it wasn't what they wanted me to do."

"That's just it, Betsy," Sir Antony said with extreme patience. "It is what you did with it, or didn't do with it, that concerns us. What did you do with the parcel?"

Betsy looked from the Countess to Sir Antony as if it was self-evident. And as both showed not the slightest twinge of getting angry with her, she took a deep breath and told them.

"I brought it into the house as I was asked to do but it just didn't feel right to me and so I let it be, and when I got up this morning, before I came down to your ladyship's bedchamber to fetch Sam to change him into a clean chemise after his first feed of the day, I put the parcel to the flame." She pointed to the large fireplace with its white painted overmantel and tapestry safety screen on the other side of the room. "I put it in the grate over there. I waited and watched until it was well alight, so no one could pull it out again. I wanted it to burn until there was nothing left to show for it, but then I had to fetch Sam, and it made some smoke and one of the footmen had to open a window, and that's when Nanny Browne was told. There must have been something of it left in the grate… All the nursery maids were blamed for it, but it was me and I didn't want anyone else to get in trouble."

When Sir Antony put his face in his hands and let out a great sigh as he crouched before her, Betsy cowered, thinking he was about to berate her as Mrs. McIntyre and Nanny Brown had done. But in the next instance he stood tall and ran a hand over his face and smiled at her, so she took a step closer.

"I did the right thing, didn't I? To put it to the flame?"

"Yes! Yes! You did, Betsy! Thank God for that! Thank God for you, Betsy! Well done. Burning that parcel was the only thing to do with it!" He had a sudden thought. "You didn't open it first, did you?"

She shook her head. "No, sir. I saw no reason to do so."

"Good girl! Do you know what was in the package?"

"Yes, sir, I do. A baby's undergown. It was for baby Sam. Aunt Smith told me. She said it was a gift. But the parcel was tied up with a bit of dirty old string and it didn't look the sort of wrapping for a gift for a noble babe. It would be cloth tied up with silk ribbon or a velvet pouch, wouldn't it? That was what the silver rattle was given in, wasn't it, m'lady?"

"Yes, Betsy. That is so."

The girl nodded and continued, the more time she was permitted to explain herself, the more confident she became, particularly with such a receptive and attentive audience.

"They said I had to dress Sam in the gown, and when I had me doubts, they did this to me to convince me otherwise." She showed Sir Antony and Jane her bandaged arm. "The true Countess of Salt Hendon is not a very nice lady for all her finery. I don't care what Aunt Smith says otherwise, or how badly she says the true Countess has been treated. I've never had it so well in all my life as I have here in this house. I've been treated very kindly by your ladyship. My bones told me that there was somethin' wicked about such a gift. And so I knew, I knew in my heart what I did with the parcel was the right thing to do, whatever they say will happen to my family back in Birmingham!"

Jane and Sir Antony shared a look.

"I beg your pardon, Betsy," Jane said, incredulous. "The *true* Countess of Salt Hendon?"

Betsy nodded again. "I don't know her by any other name. Aunt Smith says she calls herself something else in good company until the time comes when she can claim back her husband—"

"Claim her husband?"

"—from you, m'lady. He who shares your bed and has given you children, even if he can't give you his title, because he loves you, not her."

Jane clapped a hand to her mouth. She didn't know whether to laugh at the girl's ingenuous explanation or cry because she was certain that in her insanity and self-delusion that is precisely what Diana believed, no doubt reinforced in her years of captivity.

Jane's action and Sir Antony's subsequent frown made Betsy blurt out, as if she was disbelieved,

"As God is my witness, everythin' I've said is the truth, m'lady. I tried to tell Nanny Browne everythin' from the beginnin', but she says I made it all up to get m'self out of trouble because I burned the parcel. She says it's all a fairy story, but it isn't! You must believe me, m'lady!"

"No, Betsy, it is not a fairy story, although I do hope it will have a happy ending just like a fairy story," Jane said with a smile, returning her pinkie to her son's mouth. "And I do believe you."

The nursery maid's vehement plea coincided with Sam's wail of need. When Jane had clapped her hand to her mouth in surprise, she had unconsciously pulled her little finger from her son's mouth. He had been sucking on it in the vain hope of receiving nourishment. He was now not content with that ruse and let his mother know in no uncertain terms his demands must be met at once or his wails would get louder.

"Shall I fetch a shawl, m'lady?" Betsy asked, a glance at Sir Antony, and at Jane's nod, she rammed the cap over her curls and scuttled out of the room.

"You really must get her a new, smaller cap, Jane. Perhaps one with a pretty blue bow."

"It is the least I can do for her, believe me! Good Gracious!" Jane exclaimed when Betsy was out of earshot. "Is it any wonder the poor creature was accused of being a liar and a thief? That poor, dear girl. What hold must Diana and that Mrs. Smith have over her to try and get her to do such dreadful things?"

"I have no idea, but it seems to involve her father and her siblings. I am sure Betsy will tell us. And when she does, I will assure her that we will do everything in our power to correct the mischief caused by Diana and that dreadful creature who does her bidding."

"I have the greatest feeling of dread, but yet also of wondrous relief. I can't explain it. But I am very sure Salt and I are in Betsy's debt for burning that parcel."

"You can have no idea just how much. Sam is upset enough, so I don't want to upset you both. It can wait for another day. Suffice disaster has been averted because of the feeling in Betsy's bones!"

He returned the empty teacups and saucers to the tea trolley by the door and went to inspect the fireplace where the parcel had been put to the flame, back to the window seat. He did not expect to find any remnants of its contents, but he prodded the ashes with the brass poker as if he were searching for something, all to give Betsy the time to return with the shawl and Jane the grace to undo the lacings and adjust her maternity bodice to accommodate her infant son's demands. Before he returned to the window seat, he walked the length of the long room and stood at the furthest window with its view of the gardens. There was no sign of the children, so perhaps they were on their way up to the nursery.

The absence of Sam's lusty cries and Betsy fussing about Jane signaled he could safely return to the window seat, but first he went to the tea trolley and made a cup of milky sweet tea in the remaining clean teacup. He then grabbed one of the children's chairs and placed it before Jane and had Betsy sit upon it. He then surprised the girl by handing her the cup of tea. He returned to his corner of the window seat, where he plumped a cushion and settled himself, long muscular legs crossed at stockinged ankles and arms folded.

"Betsy, I want you to tell Lady Salt and me everything there is to tell about you and Mrs. Smith and the lady you know only as the true Countess of Salt Hendon. Don't spare any detail and don't worry. Everything you tell us will go no further than these four walls. I shall now close my eyes, but I am very much awake and eager to hear every word of your story. Shall I start you off? Once there was a girl called Betsy..."

"It's Elizabeth, sir. But Betsy is what I've always been called. My ma named me after her ma, and she was named after her ma who lived..."

Sir Antony smiled to himself. It was going to be a very long story indeed... But what did that matter? The smallpox-infected chemise was burned, his godson was safe, and as he had foretold, Diana had not calculated on the power of love to conquer all. He prayed she continued in her ignorance and supreme arrogance, unaware of what awaited her the night of the masquerade until the moment of capture. He hoped he could maintain his façade of civility in her company long enough not to throttle the life out of her beforehand, causing the sort of newssheet sensation he was desperately trying to avoid.

Two days later, as he stepped up into the carriage to join Diana and Lady Porter for the short drive to Salt House for the masquerade, he caught his sister's spiteful retort, and it took supreme effort of will not to leap across the seat and do just that, and the evening not yet begun.

TWENTY-FOUR

Sir Antony settled on the upholstered carriage bench next to Lady Porter, diagonally opposite his sister. He carefully avoided stepping on the hems of the voluminous silk petticoats of either lady, although he couldn't avoid the gathered-up yards of gold embroidered silks of Lady Porter's Jacobean costume, despite the wide panniers being concertinaed to accommodate travel in such a confined space. With the steps folded up and the door closed, he gave a knock with a gloved knuckle on the wooden panel above the upholstered headboard, and the carriage set to for the short journey to Grosvenor Square for the most anticipated masquerade ball of the Season.

He had heard Diana's spiteful remark about the Countess of Salt Hendon but chose to ignore it. Fluffing out the delicate lace ruffles at his wrists, he took stock of his sister in her masquerade costume. She had chosen an Elizabethan-themed outfit. Her upswept auburn hair was tightly curled, her face powdered, cheeks rouged, lips a cherry red, all framed by a magnificent Elizabethan ruff that encircled her neck. Constructed for the ball of the thinnest parchment, veneered with beeswax mixed with other ingredients to give it a high sheen, it complemented her red taffeta gown. From her ears dripped a pair of diamond and garnet earrings, and at her décolletage was a matching necklace. Her outfit had cost him a small fortune. But it was a tiny price to pay, given it had kept her preoccupied right up until the moment the carriage pulled up to take them to Salt House.

Before leaving for the ball, he'd had a last word with Semper about arrangements for later that evening. His valet-in-training, Nikolas, shrugged him into the blue silk and gold brocade military-style frock coat that completed his costume as Peter the Macaw, and as he stood before the long looking glass appraising his outfit, he enquired if everything and everyone was in place for when the time came for him to give the signal for Diana's recapture. This would occur at the end of the evening, as the guests departed in the small hours, when people milled about the entrance foyer of Salt House saying their farewells, and carriages were coming and going. He and Diana would climb into his carriage, Lady Porter shown home by sedan chair, and leave Grosvenor Square heading north, not south and drive up North Audley Street. The carriage would turn left into Tyburn Road and head out of the environs of Westminster. A carriage carrying Mr. T and his associates would follow, and a second carriage was waiting to meet both carriages at the turnpike.

There was a cottage near the turnpike, possibly lived in by the collector of tolls. Sir Antony did not care to know. All he cared was that Mr. T had secured its use and the selective blindness and loss of hearing of the cottage's occupants. In this cottage, Diana would be stripped of her finery and put into a rough linen gown, her ankles and wrists manacled. She would be rendered speechless by a scold's bridle. A frightening instrument, but as necessary and as justified as the manacles for a cold hearted murderess—a monster who had tried to infect a newborn infant with a smallpox-ridden rag.

Once the prisoner was bundled into the second carriage, Sir Antony would hand over a letter of instruction and half what was owed Mr. T and his associates. The rest of their payment would be forthcoming once his sister—he would never call her that after tonight—was transferred to her Russian handlers, those intrepid souls taking her deep beyond the Ural Mountains. The last he ever wanted to hear of the prisoner was by letter, from her jailer at the settlement at Beryozovo.

And what would Society make of this second sudden disappearance of Diana, Lady St. John? The inspiration for that had popped into Sir Antony's bare head while soaking in his thinking tub. Such a necessary luxury, his thinking tub. The details he had mulled over while making the perfect cup of tea. He had taken his cup of tea to the walnut writing table in the sitting room off his bedchamber. Here he sat with a scarlet silk banyan covering his nakedness and composed a news piece to be published in the morning's newssheets. It would be anonymous. Written on fine parchment, the red sealing wax offset, clumsily imprinted with the intaglio seal in his signet ring, so as not to identify the sender. Yet, delivered by a liveried footman, the proprietors could not fail to print the interesting news as fact, not hearsay. It only remained for Sir Antony to persuade the second party named in the missive to cooperate, and he didn't doubt that gentleman's support when he confronted him at the masquerade.

As for Mrs. Smith…

Diana had descended the stairs to the entrance foyer in all her Elizabethan finery with a secret smile of satisfaction curving her painted mouth, no doubt in response to last minute instructions given Mrs. Smith for her next dastardly deed. Sir Antony responded with one of his own lovely smiles as he admired her gown, knowing that at that very moment, four of his Russians were bundling Mrs. Smith down the backstairs and out into a waiting hackney bound for Bethlem Hospital. Mrs. Smith would spend the rest of her days in Bedlam, a certified lunatic. It was more than she deserved. But Sir Antony had taken a modicum of pity on the woman for being duped. Besides, anyone who could be so slavishly devoted to such an evil creature as his sister had to be insane.

Returning his mind to the immediate present, Sir Antony yet again curbed the desire to choke the life out of his sister but decided that, as this was their penultimate carriage ride, he should allow her a momentary glimpse beneath the surface of his urbane exterior to see the brother she did not know in the least. If nothing else, it would provide him with a temporary release of tension and a mild satisfaction.

"Jenny Dalrymple invited to one of Salt's masks?" Diana St. John scoffed, opening out her red silk fan to flutter air across her low décolletage. "My dear Lady Porter, you and I know poor Jenny is not fit for decent company. She would only be an embarrassment to Salt. It was quite right of his lordship not to invite her. No doubt if the guest list had been entrusted to the Wide-Eyed Stick Insect, who knows what sort of riffraff would bump our shoulders!"

"That red ribbon and star suits you very well, Sir Antony," Lady Porter said with a smile, thinking it prudent to change the topic because in the four years Diana St. John had been absent from London she had made several visits to Salt Hendon at the invitation of Lady Reanay and had gotten to know the young Lady Salt; she liked her very much. "What order did you say it was?" she added, with a vagueness she hoped hid the fact that she knew well enough the answer to her own question.

"The Imperial Order of St. Anna," Diana answered before her brother could part his lips to respond. "Bestowed by the Russian

Empress at her discretion. I was rendered speechless when told my little brother was to be given such an honor, and he the first foreigner too!"

"That is because you do not know me," Sir Antony said flatly.

Diana shrugged a shoulder in dismissal and pulled aside the velvet curtain to look out the window. "What is there to know…?"

"An audience in the royal drawing room is quite something to behold," Lady Porter continued, as if brother and sister had not spoken. "Their Majesties in all their finery… The long-suffering ladies-in-waiting in those outdated mantuas that were the height of fashion when my mother was a young girl… That red sash is quite splendid, Sir Antony—oh! Or is it Lord Temple now, or does that come later? I do apologize. My mind is not what it used to be…"

Sir Antony doubted that very much. Lady Porter was known in polite circles as a very shrewd matron who never let a piece of gossip pass her by, be it gossip from her drawing room or about those below stairs, her servants and those in the employ of others. He had no idea why she was being deliberately vague but decided to play along with her little charade.

"I believe I should not be addressed as Lord Temple until the Letters Patent have been prepared and my new title gazetted. That is of small importance. It can all wait until Lady Caroline and I return from our honeymoon in Ireland."

"Ireland? Honeymoon? Oh, so a date has finally been settled between you and Lady Caroline? What simply wonderful news, Sir Antony! I congratulate you both. Isn't it, Lady St. John?" Lady Porter said with a sigh of satisfaction. "Oh dear! Are you perfectly well, my lady?"

Diana St. John was making a choking sound, a gloved hand to her rapidly rising and falling bosom. She brought herself under control and said contemptuously,

"My God, Antony! You cannot—you *cannot*—be serious? You are given the highest honor the Russians can bestow upon an Englishman and are made a viscount by our sovereign, and you instantly throw away the opportunity to marry a great heiress by shackling yourself to a penniless widow?"

"I am marrying a great heiress, but Caroline's dowry never entered my mind."

Diana St. John slowly lifted her eyebrows as if she knew vastly more on the subject than he did; this was nothing new to him.

"I have it on the best authority that Aldershot frittered away every penny of Caroline's dowry."

Sir Antony resettled on the upholstered seat, not a blink at his sister's thin smile of superiority, long fingers fiddling with the collection of gold fobs dangling from a thick gold chain at his waistcoat pocket. He allowed himself to look smug.

"There is no higher authority than Lord Salt in this matter, and he hasn't spoken to you in four years."

"Oh I do hope Lady Caroline still has part of her dowry. Her marriage to that petulant boy was not a happy one."

"Indeed it was not, my lady," Sir Antony replied to Lady Porter. "Fear not. Lady Caroline still has her dowry, every penny of it. Salt made certain the thirty thousand pounds was buried in legalities until Caroline reached her twenty-fifth birthday, or married me, whichever came first."

It was news to Diana. She screwed up her mouth. She hated second-hand information almost as much as she hated her brother's self-satisfied grin. She pretended a moment of deafness and returned to staring out the window, her gloved hands gripping hard the sticks of her fan, which she had closed with an annoyed flick of her wrist. Well! He certainly wouldn't be smiling when she emerged from the smoke of the burning nursery, the golden-haired child limp in her arms. Ha! No one would be smiling *then*. Salt would talk to her *then*. Oh, he would talk, talk to her for hours *then*.

Sir Antony held his feathered mask up to his face and said, to goad his sister, "So you see, my dear Lady Porter, I am finally marrying the woman I love, who just happens to have a dowry fit for the bride of Croesus. The notice will be in the newssheets tomorrow, but I crave you will keep this piece of news to yourself, though you do have the satisfaction of being the first to congratulate me."

Lady Porter smiled. Diana did not and kept her profile to him until the carriage slowed, joining a long line of carriages waiting their turn to drive up to the entrance of Salt House to deposit their excited occupants. It was just as Lady Porter was being helped down the carriage steps by a liveried footman, Diana ready to ascend after her, that Sir Antony noticed the unusual tassel ornament dangling from the closed sticks of his sister's fan. He had never seen a baby rattle before and would not have known one had it been shoved in his face, and this fan ornament looked to be nothing unusual to the untrained eye: A little silver ornament of a unicorn and three tiny silver bells all hanging from a fine silver chain.

However, Sir Antony was very attuned to such a silver ornament because it matched the description of his godson's stolen rattle, given him by Betsy over her cup of tea. Such an embellishment to Diana's fan would go unnoticed by everyone and be of significance to no one, except the one person Diana hated with every beat of her blackened heart: Jane, Countess of Salt Hendon.

Sir Antony did not doubt that Diana gained some sort of warped satisfaction in having in her possession the silver rattle belonging to Jane's infant son. It was a talisman of her superiority and intelligence, a trophy of sorts, much like the skin of a bear or a lion proclaims the mastery of the hunter over the hunted. And he was certain his sister had brought it along to the masquerade to taunt the Countess. He doubted Salt would be able to identify the ornament as belonging to his infant son, but to the fretful mother—to Jane—the rattle would shine out like a lighthouse beacon, as obvious and as dramatic as a twenty trumpet salute.

Diana would flaunt it, but slyly, making certain Jane saw the rattle at every opportunity, knowing the Countess was powerless to say a word or cause a scene over something most would consider unworthy of comment, or disbelieve the Countess that Diana St. John would have in her possession an insignificant object belonging to another, an infant at that.

Sir Antony was having none of that, and so he put a stop to his sister's planned cruelty before she had a chance to inflict her mental torment.

Furious, he grabbed Diana's upper arm before she could take the gloved hand held out to her by a liveried footman, and pushed her back onto the carriage seat. Before she knew what was happening and could get her bearings he snatched for her fan and with one hard tug broke the rattle's little silver chain.

"No you don't," he growled, shoving the silver rattle in a waistcoat pocket. "This doesn't belong to you. It belongs to my infant godson, a babe, an innocent babe you tried to infect with the smallpox!"

"Dear me, Antony, what has come over you?" Diana said with practiced amazement. She slowly brushed out the folds in her petticoats, all to regain the upper hand. She carefully avoided all mention of the rattle. "Parents inoculate their children all the time with the smallpox in the hopes of making them immune. Putting the brat into a diseased chemise is surely less cruel than scratching pus under such lovely soft skin?"

"Good God! If you think I'll swallow that twaddle—!"

Diana blinked across at him, as if he were the one speaking nonsense. Sir Antony had to concede she was a remarkably good actress. Either that, or in her insanity she was convinced that her alternate explanation was just as valid and believable.

"It was a gift," she enunciated, as if speaking to a half-witted child. "Is it my fault you and the Stick Insect choose to consider it differently? I suppose that lackbrained nursery wench lost the small card that went with the package...?"

The card was new to Sir Antony. Betsy had certainly not mentioned any card. He did not believe Diana, and decided it was not worth his time arguing with one who was criminally insane.

Diana tapped her brother's silken knee with her fan and said with a frown of concern, "What you need is a glass or two of champagne and a large brandy. That will quell your temper and put you back in charity with the world. Since you have foolishly decided to limit yourself to tea and cordial you've become the most bad-tempered fellow imaginable. I have an excellent notion! Once we are indoors, you should immediately take yourself off to the refreshment rooms where you can join the other inebriates, and drown your sorrows at having a sister who is so much cleverer than you'll ever be. Let's not keep the other carriages waiting, there's a good little brother."

She shook out her petticoats and prepared to leave the carriage, but Sir Antony stuck his arm across the doorway and filled its space so that she could not exit, and those outside on the cobbles could not see what was taking place in the carriage. He looked into her brown eyes and held her gaze, and when he spoke his voice was flat and thus far more effective than had he shown her his fury.

"Let me assure you that once this night is over, I will have no further contact with you in any form. You can also be assured that my life, married to Caroline, and as part of the Salt Hendon extended family, will be a joyous one. I will distinguish myself in my chosen career and if I am fortunate enough to be remembered for my efforts, then so be it. Though, I would rather be remembered for being a gentleman, and as a loving husband and father. You will not be remembered, in fact you will be forgotten, a footnote to the family tree. If your children do recall you upon occasion, it will not be with love or fondness, and you will never be spoken about. The rest of your life will be miserable, but that was of your own making, and misery is more than you deserve, you wicked, *vile* creature."

Without expecting a response, he turned and stepped out of the carriage, put up his gloved hand to help her alight, folded her arm over his and offered his other arm to Lady Porter, who was patiently waiting for them to join her. They then merged with the throng on the pavement filing into Salt House. Sir Antony's handsome face was again in repose and he managed a smile as he admired the guests dressed in their exotic and quite fanciful costumes, from Roman senators and Turkish sultanas, to Merry Monarchs and Medieval maidens, everyone in animated conversation and brimming with excitement and laughter to be attending the ball of the season.

Diana dared to blink up at her brother and wonder if she had not had a mild faint brought on by her tighter than usual corset lacings. Perhaps her brother's speech had just popped into her head of its own accord, certainly not by his initiative. Yet, that could not explain his demeanor. She had never seen her brother so self-possessed and certain of his place in the world. It had to be his costume, the military frock coat, or was it the red sash across his waistcoat and the Imperial star upon his right breast that gave him such an air of confidence? Or was it the fact he was to be made a viscount? She could not work it out. She could not work *him* out.

Not since those early days locked up in Harlech Castle, when she had questioned her actions for the briefest of moments, did her arrogant self-belief slip ever so slightly from her shoulders. But it was not enough to stop her believing that the path she trod was a righteous one. The plan she intended to carry out that very evening with the help of the stalwart Mrs. Smith was the only recourse left to her to make Salt come to his senses. What did one tiny little silver rattle matter, when, under her skirts, was hidden the golden-haired child's toy monkey. Her plans for the second son may have been thwarted, goading his mother the skinny whore also, but she was in no doubts that when the time came, Salt's eldest son and heir, the boy that was the future of the Salt Hendon earldom and all that it stood for, would come running into her open arms, and that would be the beginning of the end for his parents.

SIR ANTONY RAISED HIS FEATHERED MASK AND PEERED THROUGH it to slowly look the Earl of Salt Hendon up and down. He gazed at the curled toes of his silk slippers, then at the dark blue and gold sash wrapped about the waist of a pair of billowing ivory silk pantaloons, and which held to the Earl's hip an ornate-handled scimitar. Up Sir Antony's gaze went, to the white silk shirt over which was a long open waistcoat covered in gold braid worthy of any military uniform. He finally fixed on the dark blue and gold silk turban atop his lordship's noble head. Pinned center front was a large brooch of a single sapphire surrounded by diamonds that he did not doubt were genuine sparkling gems, worth a sultan's ransom.

"Good God, Salt! Let me guess: You are the Pasha of Persia; Terror of the Turks; The Emperor of Ethiopia, mayhap? No! Don't tell me! I know. You're the King of Constantinople!"

Salt eyed his cousin with barely-concealed resentment, nostrils aquiver.

"Very good, but no. I am the Sultan of the Ottoman Empire, and you, like all those under my roof, are a mere vassal!"

"As are the multitude of ladies of his harem," Jane announced, appearing at her husband's side, blue eyes bright with mischief. She held his arm and looked up at him lovingly. "He makes a wonderful sultan, do you not think so, Antony?"

Salt winked down at his wife with a smile, again in charity with the world, although he privately agreed with Sir Antony's veiled estimation that his costume was outlandish to say the least. Truth be told, it was the prospect of Jane in a diaphanous Turkish costume that had him agree to attend his own masquerade dressed as a sultan, when his first thought was to dress as a Plantagenet king.

"Harem? I would have thought that circumstance of a Sultan's life you would not countenance in the least, my lady," Sir Antony said, bowing over Jane's outstretched hand, mask dropped to his side.

His admiring gaze swept over the Countess dressed as the female counterpart of her husband, in light blue silk pantaloons and matching silk bodice without stays which was heavily embroidered in silver thread, a row of small silver buttons down its center. Over this two-piece outfit was an open, knee-length translucent robe of the finest shimmering silver. Her raven hair fell to her waist, threaded with pearls and covered with a veil of the same shimmering material as the open robe. But it was at the sapphire and diamond tiara that he stared. Or was it a sarpech, because this most glittering head ornament held the veil in place, encircling the Countess's head and sitting flat against her forehead, one perfect drop pearl dangling from its center.

Jane blushed at Sir Antony's fixed stare at her head ornament. "It is lovely, isn't it? A gift for our fourth wedding anniversary, and a neck-lace, but I thought it well-suited to my Ottoman attire." She glanced up at her husband. "I am yet to find a suitable gift in exchange…"

"You have given me three precious gifts already, Jane," Salt said, smiling down into her eyes. "I hope there are more to come…"

Sir Antony glanced at the Earl, who returned to surveying the silken and bejeweled crowd gathering under the blaze of the magnificent candelabrums that lit up the ballroom as bright as the noonday sun, and said to goad him,

"It is a truly magnificent and most worthy gift, my lady, so perhaps you are the Sultan's Number One Wife after all. Then again... You could be a captured slave girl who has taken his fancy and he is enticing you with such trinkets. If you require rescuing—"

"She is not, and she does not," Salt stated loftily, gaze remaining on the crowd. "Her ladyship is indeed His Turkish Majesty's Number One and only wife. Although," he added, unable to stop a smirk, "if anyone requires rescuing... I do, from my own harem!" He looked Sir Antony up and down. "If the overabundance of gold braid and buttons on that frock coat means you're dressed as some military hero, then perhaps you can offer His Turkish Majesty your assistance to escape the clutches of his harem?"

Sir Antony laughed and shook his head. "Sorry, dear fellow. I'm as far from the military as it is possible to be, despite the deceptive appearance of this costume. But I'll keep you guessing as to who or what I am until I've seen Caro." He glanced about the ballroom, and then at the noble couple. "Point me in her direction and I shall take my leave of you. By the by," he said in an undertone, although with the incessant chatter all about them it was unlikely he would be overheard, "your unwanted guest is in company with Lady Porter, dressed as, I am not certain which, Queen Bess or her prisoner Mary of Scotland. Her partner in all things dastardly has, given the hour, become acquainted with her new abode at Bedlam." He smiled into Jane's troubled blue eyes. "It will all be over soon enough. Try your best to enjoy the evening..."

Jane nodded, catching her lower lip with her teeth.

Sensing his wife's apprehension, Salt caught up her hand in his and held it surreptitiously at his side, hidden in the silken folds of his pantaloons lest Society think him mawkish, and said to lighten the mood,

"I have no idea where my dearest sister is hiding, but hiding from me she must be, because the idea of giving me a harem was hers, was it not, my lady?"

"I shall own to it for Caroline," Jane admitted, dimpling, once again at ease, particularly with her hand in her husband's warm comforting clasp. "And I am not breaking any confidences, Antony, when I tell you it was Caroline who suggested the females of the Salt Hendon household all dress in Ottoman attire and present as Salt's

harem, which we did, without Salt's knowledge. You can guess the face
Salt showed us when we descended upon him in the Yellow Saloon
before making our entrance into the ballroom."

Sir Antony laughed. "I have a good mental picture of his scowl!"

"You truly should feel for my position," Salt grumbled. "I am vastly
outnumbered and could do with all the male support I can get!"

"And yet it was Ron who gave Caroline the idea…"

"What?" This was news to the Earl. "An act of treason by my
second in command cannot be tolerated. When he returns home from
Eton—"

"You heard him say it at the breakfast table one morning," Jane
interrupted. "That the Salt Hendon household was overrun by females,
and that he was pleased not to be the Sultan of the Ottoman Empire
with his harem, because nothing could be worse than being surrounded
by a hundred gabbing women! You almost choked on your egg when
Ron said the word harem, as if a twelve-year-old boy should not know
the meaning of the word!"

"He shouldn't," Salt stated at his most stiff-necked.

"I am very sure *you* did," Jane said bluntly. "And that you held
vastly different feelings on the matter to Ron!"

Salt's brown eyes crinkled at the corners. "You are an incorrigible
wretch, my lady," he whispered at his wife's ear, "and I will have my
way with you later. For now this Turkish Terror must behave himself."

Sir Antony, who had dropped his quizzing glass on its silk riband,
after a quick survey of the ballroom to see if he could find Caroline,
was about to again ask her whereabouts when at the Countess's
shoulder who should appear but her step-brother Mr. Tom Allenby,
and beside him the steward to the Salt Hendon estate, Mr. Rufus
Willis.

"Tony! Tony! Egad! You're a sight for sore eyes, my dear fellow!"
Tom Allenby exclaimed and not only took the hand Sir Antony held
out to him in a warm clasp but embraced him as a long-lost brother.
He stepped back and surveyed Sir Antony from muscled calf to broad
chest and grinned. "Lady Caroline said I wouldn't recognize you, and I
didn't! I'll wager you'd give Salt and me a run for our money on the
tennis court!"

"And soundly beat you both!" Sir Antony smiled. He squeezed
Tom's shoulder. "It is such a delight to see you again, I cannot tell
you… Your letters to 'Petersburg… Such a comfort…" He quickly
turned to politely acknowledge Mr. Willis with a nod, fearing sentimentality would be his undoing. He suggested to the Earl, "If Mr.

Willis is up for a game, what say he and I soundly beat you and Tom in the best of three, tomorrow?"

"Three?" Tom snorted. "Salt and I will take you on in the best of five!"

"Steady on, brother!" the Earl quipped. "Under all that red sash and gold braid I'll wager Antony has more muscle and sinew than you and I combined."

"I would be honored to be your partner, Sir Antony," Rufus Willis said with a bow. "Racquets at forty paces it is, my lord."

It was then that the Earl noticed the costumes worn by his brother-in-law and his steward. Both young men were dressed in pantaloons, billowing silk shirts and wore small turbans; and upon their feet were curled toed slippers.

"I will beg no one's pardon and change the topic of conversation from tennis to enquire as to why the two of you are also dressed in Turkish attire?" When Tom Allenby and Rufus Willis shared a look full of humor, lips firmly pressed together to stop from bursting into laughter, Salt rolled his eyes. "Don't say it; another of Caroline's ideas. What are you? The chief eunuchs of my harem?"

Everyone in the small party laughed, and loud enough that those around them immediately halted their own conversations to turn and listen in on what had amused the family members surrounding the Head of the House of Salt Hendon, the only family member who seemed not to have got the joke.

"What did I tell you, Jane? I knew Salt would discover our costumes without either of us having to say a word!"

Sir Antony was about to add fuel to the harem fire when out of the corner of his eye he spied the gentleman who was the subject of the anonymous missive he had sent to the newssheets. He excused himself and looking neither left nor right, shouldered his way to the alcove where the gentleman had cornered a pretty young thing. He could only guess from her white feathered mask and accompanying feathered wings attached to the back of her white silk bodice, that she was dressed as a swan.

The swan was pleased at the interruption, and when Sir Antony politely asked for a moment of the gentleman's time, alone, the girl readily took herself off. A hovering footman enquired if either gentleman would care for a glass of champagne. Sir Antony waved the servant away. Dacre Wraxton grabbed for a second glass. Something in Sir Antony's blue eyes told him his nerves would require alcoholic fortification.

TWENTY-FIVE

"'Twas not my idea, my dear fellow," Dacre Wraxton drawled before Sir Antony had uttered a syllable.

Sir Antony wondered what the man was driveling on about. His knight costume of gray knitted chain mail tunic and bascinet without visor over which was a shiny tin heraldic breastplate, a small sword and knitted gloves, was no doubt supposed to make Dacre Wraxton appear a mighty medieval warrior. In truth, he looked more court jester than court protector. Sir Antony would not have been surprised if the man had knocked knees but did not have the bad manners or inclination to find out. Instead, he took up his quizzing glass and followed Dacre Wraxton's hand that held the champagne flute as he raised it to his lips. It was then that he saw what was pinned to the sleeve of his tunic. A brooch. Not just any brooch. His brooch. It was the gold brooch containing the painted miniature of Caroline which Diana had taken from him while seated at the clavichord.

Sir Antony let fall his quizzing glass on its riband and stuck out his palm.

Dacre Wraxton immediately unpinned the brooch and gave it to him.

Sir Antony thrust his feathered mask at him to hold. He then carefully pinned the brooch to the front of his waistcoat, over his heart, readjusted his frock coat, stretched his neck and snatched back his feathered mask. With his back to the crowded ballroom and oblivious to the incessant chatter and laughter, he waited for Dacre Wraxton to provide an explanation as to how he had come by a brooch that did not belong to him.

"You can guess whose idea it was that I wear the thing on my sleeve! Ha! Some joke! I said I wouldn't do it. But she can be very persuasive... Downright nasty, to point out fact—Apologies! She is your sister—"

"Not any more she isn't."

"I couldn't fault her line of argument," Dacre Wraxton continued as if Sir Antony had not spoken. "I wish I could but—Anyway, I didn't mean anything by it, dear fellow. So no harm done and now we can carry on with our—"

"Harm?" Sir Antony growled and took a step closer. "I don't give a damn what sordid piece of filth Diana managed to drag out of the sewer about you that had you whimpering for her to keep it to herself. And I understand perfectly she can twist and turn her knife in an old wound, and so hard that you'll do just about anything to stop her. But what I will never understand or forgive is your pathetic need to prey on the vulnerable and the innocent. What sort of man are you that you derive pleasure from seducing drunken girls who are not much older than children? It's not as if you have deficiencies to hide from experience; you are capable of satisfying a woman between the sheets—"

"That's spreading the butter a bit too thick! I may own to being many things, but there is one thing I'm not and that's deficient between the sheets!"

"That's what I just said."

"Ah! So you did! Apologies. Impossible to hear over the din. There must be two hundred or more souls trying to figure out each other's fancy dress. Who did you come dressed as? What famous General? That Russian sash and star add a certain imperial splendor—"

"You haven't answered my question..."

Dacre Wraxton dared to look sheepish. He shrugged. "Boredom?"

When Sir Antony's face darkened, Dacre Wraxton realized he was not in a party-going mood but perfectly serious, and he became petulant.

"Look here, Templestowe," he argued. "I don't force m'self on them. I'm no rapist. They could always say no; most never do. Besides," he added, unable to resist a smirk, "why have tomorrow's soup when you can be first to dip your crust in fresh broth?"

"You're a disgusting maggot, Wraxton," Sir Antony sneered, grabbing a handful of Dacre Wraxton's tunic and shoving him hard up against the painted paneling. He was now beyond caring who saw or heard their altercation. "You knew she was drunk. You knew she was vulnerable. You should have done the gentlemanly thing and put her in a sedan chair and sent her home! You couldn't even step up and offer her your name after you ruined her; you allowed a silly little boy to do that for you! God, you're a pathetic excuse for a man!"

"Pathetic? Me? I wasn't the one staggering about from one social event to the other, a miserable drunkard! That's what she called you. Did you know that? And that's what you are—*were*—four years ago, before this miraculous transformation," Dacre Wraxton spat back, bravely pushing Sir Antony off. With manly pride at stake, and a modicum of truth on his side, he looked Sir Antony in the eye with an arrogant upward tilt of his chin. "She wanted it, just like all the others. I didn't raise her petticoats. She did that for me, and with a giggle and a come-hither look in her green eyes. What man with blood in his veins would refuse such an invitation from a pretty little redhead? Only a drunkard dolt such as yourself!" He came a step closer and dared to push a finger into the broad hard chest. "I'll tell you something else... She was ripe for the picking. If it hadn't been me, it would have been some other fellow; she was that desperate to give away her innocence, desperate for anyone to have it but you! Better it was me—someone who could show her a good time *and* keep his mouth shut—"

"But not his breeches up! Knowing her state of mind, what you did is doubly despicable."

"You're just peeved you weren't first. I can understand that," Dacre Wraxton conceded magnanimously. "But I didn't disappoint her. Far from it! She came back for more. Did she tell you? While married to that milksop Aldershot she committed adultery with Yours Truly. Not once but on two separate occasions. I didn't force her into my bed. I didn't force her to enjoy making love. She did that on her own initiative, and a damn good time we had between the sheets, too!"

"And that is the only reason I won't kill you..."

Dacre Wraxton misinterpreted Sir Antony's flat statement for a sardonic quip and with a grin raised his glass of champagne in a toast. "Happy to be of service. Should make your bridal night all the more enjoyable, her knowing a thing or two about connubial pleasure. And I wouldn't be breaking a confidence if I told you you're in for a treat. She's damnably responsive. Has the most voluptuous little body, and when it wriggles—"

Sir Antony pinched Dacre Wraxton's mouth hard between his fingers; the man's eyes bulged.

"Listen very carefully, if you want to live. You have a choice. I have a great desire to run you through here, but I have enough manners left in my pinkie to offer you one of two options. I will remove my hand before I crack your jaw, and you will listen without comment. Understood?"

Dacre Wraxton nodded, eyes wide with fright, not only because of the searing pain in his jaw, but because he had never heard the large gentleman speak with such suppressed rage.

"This is what you will do to ensure I don't stick your worthless carcass: When you leave this alcove, you will go to Lord Salt and immediately resign as MP for Hendon. You will not say why or give a paltry excuse. You will just do it. You will then take your leave and go directly to your place of residence. Once there you will write out a formal letter of resignation of your parliamentary position and offer the name of a suitable candidate for your replacement: Mr. Thomas Allenby of Allenby Park, Wiltshire—"

"Isn't he—"

"—Lady Salt's brother? Yes. You will then have your man pack a portmanteau for France—"

"France? *France*? I'm not going to France!"

Sir Antony took a step closer and Dacre Wraxton backed further into the alcove, if that was possible, his shoulder blades through his knitted tunic scraping up against the paint.

"Listen without comment, Wraxton, or meet me tomorrow morning in the mist of Green Park, sword in hand. I guarantee you'll be shivering, and not from cold…"

Dacre Wraxton opened his mouth to make further protest, but when Sir Antony showed him he was deadly serious, left hand dropping to the ornate hilt of his dress sword, just visible under the skirts of his frock coat, Wraxton's eyes went wide and he shut his mouth tight.

Just as Sir Antony suspected, Wraxton was an inveterate coward. His instincts as to why the man's younger brother Hilary kept a chamber pot with the family crest painted in the bowl proved right. Hilary might be a foppish poet with a penchant for wigs made from the most outrageous materials, but one thing he was not was a coward. No wonder then why he had no respect for his elder brother.

"You are going to France, and for an extended period," Sir Antony continued. "I don't have a preference where you take yourself after that. You may wander the Continent from Paris to Athens for all I care, but one thing you will not do is set foot on English soil again until such time as my firstborn is two years old." Sir Antony's mouth twitched into a smile. "You had best keep abreast of the births, deaths and marriages column in the English newssheets. By my reckoning, your sojourn away could be for as little as three years. Unfortunately I cannot offer you a finite number. No matter. Once you leave here I don't care what happens to you, only that it happens abroad." He smiled thinly. "And don't try and creep back across the Channel when my back is turned. I have people employed to keep an eye on you, and they report to my majordomo. Oh, one last detail—"

Dacre Wraxton regarded Sir Antony under hooded lids with shoulders slumped. He knew there was no point trying to wheedle his way out of such an arrangement. He carried a sword but he had no skill with a blade, and as the only exercise he took was frolicking in a bed with a willing nubile female, he knew he would be cut down within minutes of any encounter with Sir Antony's weapon of choice.

"There is no need to threaten me," he interrupted. "I will avert mine eyes from your intended and will have no further contact with her, verbal or written."

Sir Antony grinned. "That is a most excellent idea and is to be immediately executed. But it was not what I needed to tell you. The reason for your immediate departure, and the reason you will tell all and sundry whom you meet, and of course always in the strictness of confidences, is that you eloped with my sister to the Continent—"

Dacre Wraxton lost his grip on his champagne glass. "Dear God, *no*."

Sir Antony caught the glass, which was empty, and deftly set it on a silver tray held by an attentive and eagle-eyed footman hovering at his shoulder. He almost felt sorry for the man, and he clapped a hand to the slumped sloping shoulder.

"I should leave you to your misery, but I cannot in good conscience tell you an untruth. Diana won't be fleeing to France with you. It is a ruse, but one you will abide by. That you eloped should suffice as the reason for your absence from London. Once on French soil, for your purposes, my sister died at sea, washed overboard by a rogue wave."

Dacre Wraxton eyed Sir Antony shrewdly.

"I wondered when you would come to your senses and realize she is many slices short of a full loaf. There is the rumor Salt packed her off to the Continent, much as you're doing the same to me, because her mind snapped when he married another. But my suspicions about her mental stability go way back. St. John also had his suspicions, and not long after he married her. He and I were friends at Eton, and in a far more intimate way, if you understand my meaning, than his friendship with Salt. I confess that to you and no other, only because Diana discovered that interesting tidbit about her husband and me and used it to sinister effect."

"I do not doubt it."

Dacre Wraxton heard the note of sympathy in Sir Antony's voice.

"Dear St. John. If he had not died of the smallpox when he did, I'm very sure she would have found a way of hounding him into an early grave…"

He made Sir Antony a bow of farewell, saying with a huff of laughter, "Be assured, I will welcome the birth of your son and heir with much rejoicing. Adieu, my lord."

Sir Antony inclined his powdered head in farewell and stood aside to let the man pass. He watched him be swallowed up by the perfumed laughing multitudes strolling the length of the ballroom in preparation for the first of the dances, then took up his quizzing glass and scanned the crowd for sight of the love of his life. Lady Caroline instantly appeared out of the silken throng, as if she had been watching him for some time.

She, like Jane, was dressed in a costume fit for the harem of an Ottoman potentate, in ornately-embroidered slippers, pantaloons of chocolate brown and mint green striped satin, and a bodice of chocolate brown velvet, cut low at the décolletage and made decent by the strategic draping of a translucent fichu of shimmering silver. Upon her head was pinned a small silk turban that matched the fabric of her pantaloons. She looked every bit a harem beauty, and he was certain that if the real Sultan of the Ottoman Empire clapped eyes on his Caroline, she would instantly be his favored jewel. But it was at her bright flaming hair that he stared. It was pulled over one shoulder and fell unrestrained to her thighs, tied loosely half way down its length with a mint green satin ribbon entwined with pearls.

He wanted to pull her into his arms and kiss her. Instead, he smiled and bowed with a flourish over her hand in greeting. When he straightened, she grabbed the upturned braided cuff of his frock coat and, with a cheeky smile, disappeared with him behind an eight-paneled tapestry screen.

The tapestry screen hid a small comfortable room where there was a chaise longue, several chairs about a low table, a washstand, and on a japanned side bureau a row of ornate silver ewers full of iced water, and a tray of glassware. In a far corner there was a dressing screen, and off to one side of this, two chairs drawn up to a small table that had upon it a seamstress's serviceable *nécessaire* containing the sewing items required to repair rips and sew on dangling buttons. On the small table there was also a polished wooden box holding the cleaning products required for the removal of the wax that dripped from the candelabras onto the guests' embroidered silk and velvet costumes. By the entrance to this quiet haven from the multitudes two footmen stood to attention, ready to assist any guest requiring a moment's reprieve from the noise and the heat of the ballroom or who needed their expert repair services.

Upon seeing the Lady Caroline in company with the gentleman with whom she had shared a passionate kiss in the anteroom off the Earl's book room, one of the footmen nudged his counterpart and both took themselves off to stand guard on the other side of the tapestry screen.

Alone together, Caroline threw her arms about Sir Antony's neck and commanded he kiss her, to which he readily acquiesced.

WHEN SIR ANTONY HAD THE INCLINATION TO SPEAK, HE SAID, arms about Caroline's waist, looking down into her upturned flushed face, "You're not wearing stays."

"Silly. Harem girls don't wear boning. Well, at least, that's what Aunt Alice says. She is our resident expert, having been to Constantinople." She sighed. "It is so liberating!" Then giggled. "And just a little bit naughty." When he did not respond she cocked her head. "I thought you would like me this way..."

Like it! His scalp prickled with suppressed desire. The thinnest layer of silky satin separated his flesh from hers, and hers was so intoxicatingly curvaceous he could hardly think straight. He swallowed and found his voice.

"Dressed like that, it's no small surprise why the Ottomans keep their women locked up in harems away from other men. I think it for the best if this is the first and last time you wear such a costume to a masquerade." When she scowled, he pinched her chin. "But I would be very pleased if you wore your fetching harem outfit in the privacy of our home—just for me... You see, mostly I am a very congenial sort of fellow, but not where you are concerned. To tell a truth, I find I am inordinately possessive. I do not like the idea of other men looking at you with desire. I want you all to myself—always."

She touched his shaven cheek. "You will—*always*. I never want others to-to come between us, for others to interfere in our lives. I love you with my whole heart, and would hate myself if ever I were a *disappointment* to you..."

So she had been surreptitiously observing his alcove conversation with Dacre Wraxton and worried now what that maggot of a man may have revealed to him. He would never tell. Not liking to see her apprehensive and miserable, he said, smiling into her eyes, fingers gently entwined in a long silken lock of her fiery mane,

"That, my darling girl, will never happen. I, too, love you with my whole heart. I cannot say it enough. Soon I will be able to show you just how much…" He opened his frock coat and to reveal her brooch pinned to his chest, just above the red sash. "This token of my devotion will have to suffice for now. I have never been without it since you gave it to me, and soon, I will never be without you."

Caroline's eyes widened and she gave a little sigh of relief.

"Oh! You do have it! I thought—I thought I saw it—Never mind!" She dimpled and changed the subject, a hand to the gold buttons and brocade of his wide lapel. "As for your splendid costume, my lord, the only creature who should not see it is Peter. You will surely make him jealous. He thinks he is the only macaw in my life!"

"Ha! Best Peter the Macaw see me for what I truly am—a rival for your affections." He picked up his feathered mask and held it up to his face. "Semper will be very pleased his efforts were not in vain. Now, my love, as much as I would prefer to remain cozy with you here, we best rejoin the guests before the Pasha of Persia sends out his eunuchs to find us."

"Eunuchs? What is a eu—eunuch?"

Sir Antony swallowed. A good question for her to ask, but not one to be answered there and then. He forgot that though she might be a widow, Caroline was only two-and-twenty and had led a very sheltered life under her brother's roof.

"Not a topic the Pasha would approve. I'll tell you when we are married."

"You will tell me, won't you?" she asked, eyes narrowed.

"Of course. You can ask me anything once we are married and I will tell you honestly. My word on it."

This satisfied her and she said with a grin,

"Pasha of Persia? I call him the Sultan of Glum! You laugh, but that is what he is, ever since he saw the females of his household dressed in Ottoman outfits. He was all very pleased to see Jane in pantaloons but I wish you could have seen the look of disapproval he pulled when told Kitty, Aunt Alice and I were part of his harem. Deep down, he's always been such a straight-line walker!"

"And a good thing, too!"

She smiled cheekily, very pleased with herself. "Wait until he sees Tom and Mr. Willis!"

Sir Antony chuffed her under the chin.

"He has. He gave them the same gloomy reception."

Caroline's smile instantly disappeared. She frowned.

"Is there something or someone bothering him of late? He hasn't been himself for weeks… I thought it was because he was worried about Jane and her third lying-in. He is always moody and preoccupied just before a baby is born. That surprised me because when there is first news of a baby on the way, he goes about with a grin on his face for days!"

"I can only imagine it is because childbirth is a very scary experience—for both parents."

Caroline pondered this and then said, startling Sir Antony, "Yes, for us, it is. Animals are so much better at it than we are." Adding seriously, "Is it Diana's return from the Continent that is bothering him?"

"I believe you are right. Diana has always had the power to make your brother testy. And now she has returned, he worries she means to interfere in his life."

"As only she can!"

"Yes, as only she can, and will. Which is even more reason for us to rejoin the masses, to offer the Sultan of Glum our support." He kissed her forehead. "Will you do me a great favor? Keep an eye on the children."

"Jane has already asked me to do so. I promised to look in on them every hour. Though why Jane and Salt saw fit to move the entire nursery to the tennis court…"

"Oh, I am sure the children are enjoying themselves hugely," Sir Antony said lightly. "With all the excitement in the house over the past few days leading up to this masquerade, and now the ball tonight, it will give them a sense of involvement. Particularly for Merry, who at twelve years of age must be wishing she were able to dress in pantaloons and join in the fun, and not be stuck with three children under the age of four as company. If Ron were here with her, perhaps she would feel differently."

Caroline tried to suppress a knowing smile, but Sir Antony caught the look in her eye and knew she was up to something. Sometimes he wondered if he knew her better than she knew herself.

"Out with it! What have you and Merry concocted between the two of you? Don't tell me you've disguised her in costume and she is somewhere close by?"

Caroline's lips parted but she said nothing. She was not going to be the one to give her cousin away. Aunt Alice was also in on the scheme.

"Out with it, Caro! What have you done with Merry?"

"Why should you think I—"

"Because you did the same at the Hunt Ball when you were fourteen. Don't think Salt and I didn't know you had dressed yourself as a page boy and were lingering in the Gallery with the musicians watching proceedings!"

Caroline gave a sigh at a remembrance.

"Salt could not have cared less had the house been burning down around his ears! All he cared about was dancing with Jane. Who could blame him? She looked so beautiful in her gold satin gown... I might have been only fourteen, but I saw the way he looked at her and knew, even then, that he was in love with her. He'd been looking at her that way for a month or more! He still does, when he thinks no one is looking at him. I remember thinking then I wished you would look at me that way."

"Caro, you were only fourteen. If I'd looked at you at all, in *any* way, Salt would have had me gelded there and then, and I'd be the one wearing the eunuch costume!"

Caroline giggled. "So that's what a eunuch is!" She kissed his flushed cheek. "Wishes do come true. You do look at me that way —*now*."

"Caro, darling, please tell me if Merry is out there amongst that lot. It is very important."

Caroline pouted. "It will be much more fun for her if she thinks she isn't being observed."

"I dare say it would be, if she didn't have Diana for a mother. But she does, and if Diana knew Merry was in costume, flitting about the ballroom, she might create the sort of scene your brother abhors. You know she will blame Jane. So please—"

"Oh! Yes! So she will. We—Aunt Alice and I—we didn't think of that. Of course Diana will blame Jane, and cause a scene. It is just the sort of nonsense Diana thrives on. But I'm afraid it might be too late to do anything about it. I left Aunt Alice talking with Diana to find you..."

TWENTY-SIX

"Oh? Is she truly here, here at the ball?" Diana asked with feigned breathless surprise, turning full circle to look about the crush of guests because the large Elizabethan collar encircling her neck precluded her from looking over her shoulder.

She had her back to the crowd and was talking with Lady Reanay, whom she had spied in conversation with Lady Caroline, Lady Porter and a group of matrons by the open sash window, sipping champagne and exchanging the latest gossip. She had watched Caroline cross the room to an alcove where her brother Antony was in conversation with someone out of her line of sight. With Caroline gone, she made her move and joined the party, Lady Porter and the three women quick to see she wanted a private word with her turbaned mother-in-law. Two minutes of conversation and she had the old woman telling her what she wanted to know without the least need to exert any influence; silly old fool.

"You mustn't say a word to Salt! He is already out of charity with me for my attempt to take Merry to visit you. He was pleasant but firm in his refusal but I could see he wanted to bawl me out." Lady Reanay shivered recalling that unpleasant interview, and looked at Diana with a small smile. "You always did look your best in red, my dear. And that ruff, so majestic! I once wore a—"

Diana wasn't about to let her change the topic.

"He can hardly object to me seeing my darling daughter with a hundred onlookers present," she interrupted. "I promise not to say a word, or give her away. If I could just *see* her... Please, my lady. You know what an *agony* it is for a mother to be denied access to her own child!"

Lady Reanay was in a misery of indecision. She had made the Earl a promise she could not forfeit, and yet she understood only too well the distress of which Diana spoke. She had also promised Merry not to reveal her truancy if she kept to the small alcove between the refreshment rooms and the ballroom, where she could watch the guests, resplendent in their costumes, as they sauntered back and forth from room to room. As all the liveried footmen and pageboys were wearing black facemasks, in keeping with the masquerade theme, no one would be the wiser to Merry's identity.

What neither Caroline or Lady Reanay had envisaged was the vigilance which Nanny Browne and her nursery maids and sundry staff were keeping over the Earl's children. When Merry did not return after being permitted to watch Lady Caroline dress for the masquerade, Nanny Browne sent one of the nursery maids to scour the house to find her, and to not return until she had Miss Merry firmly by the hand. When the nursery maid returned in tears after an hour, Nanny Browne decided to involve the housekeeper, and on it went until the truancy came to the ears of the very servant in whose trust Merry had been placed.

When the butler had a word in her ear about this state of affairs, Lady Reanay almost lost her turban, such was her jolt of surprise. What Miller confided played straight into Diana St. John's hands. The old lady put a bejeweled hand to her pearl beaded bodice and taking a deep breath said to Miller,

"We will keep this to ourselves for the time being. Send word to Nanny Browne that she has been found—oh! And that his little lordship has also been located and is safe with Miss Merry. I will seek out Lady Caroline and she can—"

"Perhaps I can be of assistance, my lady?" Diana interrupted. "After all, I am here, and Caroline could be anywhere. By the time we find her, Magna and—?" She glanced at the butler with alarm, then said to her mother-in-law, "Pardon me, my lady, but who is this little lordship keeping company with my daughter?"

Lady Reanay squeezed Diana's arm.

"No! No! You mustn't think that!"

She pulled Diana by her full length sleeve towards the window, fearing to be overheard, but with the quartet playing and the masqueraders ever boisterous, it was difficult for Lady Reanay to raise her voice to be heard at all.

"Edward—Lord Lacey—*Ned*—the Earl's eldest son, has bolted from his nurse. He is quite a handful, and reminds me so much of his papa when he was the same age—too intelligent by half and just as naughty. Of course with that beautiful face and those golden ringlets he looks like an angel, so he could get away with strangling a cat and no one would think he had done such a wicked thing. Not that he would ever be so cruel. He is very gentle with Viscount Fourpaws, and with any of Caroline's animals, particularly her darling little pug dog. He is not a wicked boy, just curious, as little boys are wont to be when bored. I just meant—"

"I understand what you mean," Diana said through her teeth, losing all patience with the old lady's ramblings. She made a quick recover, and to hide her intense irritation made a show of fluttering air across her mother-in-law with her fan, and said to the butler, who still hovered, "Have a glass of wine fetched for her ladyship, and a chair. But before you go, tell me what I may do to help recover my daughter and Lord Lacey and return them to the safety of the—nursery...?"

"Not the nursery, my lady. The children are spending the evening quartered in the gallery of his lordship's tennis court. But it is to the nursery it seems his little lordship has indeed gone. I fear he is still obsessed with the whereabouts of his sleeping companion."

"Sleeping companion...?" Diana St. John asked, pretending ignorance.

"Mr. Monkey Mischievous," Lady Reanay told her as if it were common knowledge that was the name given to Ned's cloth monkey.

When a footman presented her with a chair, and another handed her a glass of wine, Lady Reanay quickly sat and gratefully sipped at the wine. Events threatened to spiral out of control if Ned and Merry were not fetched at once from the vacant nursery, and before Salt came to hear of it. She was certain her heart was beating too fast.

"It was one of the footmen who informed me that his little lordship was seen making his way up to the nursery alone," the butler continued when Diana waved a languid hand for him to continue. "I took the opportunity of asking Miss Merry to leave her position in the alcove to fetch and return him to Nanny Browne. I reasoned his little lordship would do as Miss Merry asked of him, and as she herself is now required at the tennis court, both would be back where they belonged."

"A wise plan," Diana St. John praised the butler.

"Thank you, my lady. However, they have not returned promptly to the tennis court and so I fear that perhaps his little lordship has turned his truancy into a game and is playing at hide-and-go-seek with Miss Merry."

"I do believe you may be right, Miller," Lady Reanay agreed. "Ned does love to play games, and he may well be hiding from Merry. Oh dear, this is all so distressing…"

"Are there any servants in that part of the house tonight?" Diana St. John asked the butler.

"No, my lady. All the nursery staff are at the tennis court, and the footmen who usually service those private rooms are being used here, in the public rooms on account of the masquerade."

"So the entire nursery is empty of servants and family?"

"Yes, my lady."

"The nursery maids and the children are being kept—where did you say…?"

"They are spending the night at the tennis court, my lady. A treat for the children…"

Diana nodded gravely. Mentally, she was quickly revising her plans. She had hoped to stage her tragedy in the nursery. She so wanted to see those apartments burned to cinders, and their occupants along with it! Mrs. Smith and two hired ruffians should, at this hour, be awaiting her outside the garden gate in the mews. They had enough combustible rags between them to burn down Westminster Hall, and she had enough gold coin in her bodice to bribe the gatekeepers.

What now that the precious offspring had been moved to the tennis court? Perhaps the change of venue would also work for her plans? After all, the royal tennis court had a door that opened straight onto the mews, so easier access for Mrs. Smith and the ruffians. If both doors could be bolted, and enough smoke generated to fill the gallery boxes, and with the general pandemonium that ensued with a fire, there was every chance the occupants would either be trampled to death or asphyxiated… Perhaps it was worth the risk… She had not schemed and dreamed for all these years to abandon her plan over one small detail.

It only remained for her to coax the golden-haired child to return to the tennis court, then have the Countess sent for on some excuse… Perhaps to say goodnight to her children? If she was told one of them was fretting, she could not fail but attend to its needs…

"I will of course inform his lordship of—"

"No! No, Miller! Don't do that!" Diana St. John snapped. She quickly brought her features under control and said with grave concern, "There is no need to disturb Lord Salt. I will go to the nursery and return my daughter and the boy to the safety of the tennis court."

"Diana, I do think Miller is in the right of this. We should inform Salt," Lady Reanay argued, which caused the butler to hover in indecision and Diana to clench her fists tightly to suppress her anger at being contradicted in front of a menial. "Caroline and I will be in enough trouble for allowing Merry to attend the masquerade… But that is as nothing when Salt learns his heir has managed to escape his nurses and is playing truant in a deserted nursery! Dear me! The man is likely to tear the place apart and the servants too! I dread to think what her son's disappearance will do to poor Jane…"

"Which is even more reason to keep them in ignorance, and allow me to fetch him," Diana enunciated with a tight smile. "You can see that Lord Salt is deep in conversation with His Russian Highness." She stared at the butler with an imperious lift of her eyebrows. "Do you wish to be the one to interrupt his lordship in the middle of what could well be a very delicate diplomatic discussion, and to give him such disturbing news that his son and heir is missing?"

The butler shook his head without knowing it. Lady Reanay peered across the sea of costumed guests to where the Earl and Countess in their Ottoman attire were chatting with Prince Ivan and a number of the Russian contingent, who had come to the ball dressed as bejeweled versions of seventeenth-century French courtiers, in high red heels and elaborately full-bottomed powdered wigs. All were smiling and at their ease, and when the Earl threw back his turbaned head with laughter at something Jane said in response to the Prince, her heart sank and she could no more have Miller inform the noble couple their little son was playing truant as cut off her own hand.

"Lady St. John is right, Miller. We must keep this to ourselves, for now, and hope that Ned is under Miss Merry's care." She looked up at her daughter-in-law. "Thank you for your kind offer, my dear. If you would be so good as to go up to the nursery so that we can all breathe easy again; I know Salt and Jane will be grateful."

"I will send a footman with you, my lady."

"No! No, that will not be necessary," Diana St. John stated firmly. "I presume the sconces are lit, so I do not need light. Besides, if Merry does not have the boy in hand, and he sees a male servant with me he may think himself in trouble and not come out of hiding." She smiled sweetly at Lady Reanay. "Have no fear, my lady. Once I have the boy returned to his nurses, I will send word and perhaps the Countess would then care to visit her children to see them safely tucked up for the night? Surely that will allow everyone to breathe easy, his lordship included?"

"Oh yes! That is an excellent notion, my dear," Lady Reanay agreed. "If Jane and Salt were to visit the tennis court—"

"No need to bother Lord Salt," Diana counseled with a smile. "I should hate for the boy to perhaps mention to his father he was playing in the nursery, all alone and without supervision. You did say he has a naughty streak…"

Lady Reanay almost choked on a mouthful of wine.

"Good Gracious! Heavens! It would be just like Ned to think it a great lark and tell his Papa of his adventure. How disastrous! Of course you are right again. I shall have a quiet word to Jane, once you send me word, and I know she will somehow manage to slip away without Salt any the wiser."

"Of course if anyone asks after me—if Salt were to enquire as to my whereabouts—you need only say I am getting a breath of fresh air in the garden…"

Lady Reanay smiled and nodded. "Of course, my dear. I shall do that."

She watched Diana St. John sweep away in the butler's wake, several powdered heads turning to rake their gaze over her grandiose Elizabethan gown of red silk with its surprisingly large ruffled collar, that gave Diana the appearance of offering her beautiful head with its elaborate coiffure on a serving platter.

Lady Reanay was just starting to feel her heart rate return to its normal rhythm when, not five minutes later, Lady Caroline came up and asked if Merry had returned to the tennis court. It took her five minutes to unravel the story to Caroline, who then went off in pursuit of Diana. And then Sir Antony sauntered up, a cup of tea in one hand and a chair in the other, and sat alongside her. He was looking very pleased with himself and Lady Reanay did not have the heart to inform him of recent events, that is, until he casually inquired where his sister was to be found. He could not see her amongst the dancers, and she was not part of the costumed crush in the refreshment rooms, well, not in the one he had frequented to fetch a cup of tea.

Lady Reanay tried to delay the inevitable in the hopes Diana would send word Merry and Ned were returned to the tennis court, and Caroline was there too, before she had to explain matters to Sir Antony. So she said casually,

"That frock is most impressive. Are you a military personage, Antony?"

"No, Aunt. I am a bird. A macaw, in fact."

Lady Reanay's eyebrows lifted with surprise. Sir Antony chuckled at her inability to hide her incredulity.

"Do you know, Caroline has promised a pug puppy to the Russian prince," she continued, her astonishment no less acute at this piece of information. "The fellow positively overwhelmed us with his enthusiasm for Caroline's gift! You'd think she had offered him a ruby the size of a duck's egg!" She shrugged a shoulder. "One wonders if he was being polite, as he was when I mentioned Diana's visit to 'Petersburg. He nodded politely but looked at me with an odd, blank expression that it was obvious he had no idea who I was talking about. I remember Diana telling me specifically that she had met Prince Ivan in 'Petersburg. I did not meet Prince Ivan in 'Petersburg, so it surprised me, as it did the Prince."

"Prince Ivan spends most of his year in Moscow. Diana could not have met him. And that is why you did not meet him, either. But I do believe his enthusiasm for a pug puppy to be genuine. The Russian nobility can't get enough English goods, and pug puppies bred in England are very highly-prized items on the lists given to Russians visiting England by wives, daughters, and mistresses." He set the teacup on its saucer. "How clever of Caro to think of such a gift. Though I suspect she was more concerned that the puppy go to a good home, than the impact of such a gesture on His Highness."

Lady Reanay regarded her nephew pensively.

"I trust everything is now settled between you and Caroline...?"

"Yes. Everything is settled." Sir Antony could not help smiling broadly. "I am—*we are*—very happy."

Lady Reanay let out a small sigh of satisfaction, tears in her eyes, and patted his silken knee.

"Oh, that is *such* good news, such *very* good news. Salt will be pleased. Everyone will be overjoyed. Now, if you could just get your sister married off again and settled..."

"Where is Diana?" When Lady Reanay threw up her hands, as if in defeat, Sir Antony frowned. "You did not betray Merry to her, did you, Aunt?"

"Betray? But... Antony, Diana is her mother and has a right to—"

"No. No, she does not," he enunciated. "Diana has no rights."

She looked at her nephew for a good five seconds, saw that he was deadly serious and let out a little sigh. "Oh dear...Oh dear..." She put a hand to her cheek, desolate. "You and Salt will be so angry with me..."

Sir Antony controlled his anxiety, though his fingers went cold, and said patiently, "Please, Aunt, tell me from the beginning…"

Lady Reanay managed to explain all about Merry's attendance at the ball. She managed to tell him about Ned's truancy. Both made her nephew smile. She was even able to tell him that Caroline had gone off to the nursery, too. But as soon as she started to explain how Diana had offered to locate Ned and Merry, Sir Antony lost his smile and stopped listening. Up off his chair, he thrust his teacup and saucer at a footman and rudely strode off while his aunt was mid-sentence, to be swallowed up by the animated crowd making its way through to the refreshment rooms.

Lady Reanay was so taken aback by her nephew's uncharacteristically rude behavior that she choked on a breath, and then coughed so hard she was sure she was having a heart attack.

Kitty Aldershot and Mr. Tom Allenby had finished their first dance together and he was escorting her from the dance floor when they noticed Lady Reanay in distress. A footman was hovering over her, and she had a hand to her chest. The young couple quickly went to her aid just as a small group of guests were forming a semi-circle about her chair.

Kitty Aldershot sat on the chair vacated by Sir Antony and took hold of Lady Reanay's hand while Tom Allenby had a footman fetch a glass of cold water. Neither spoke and waited for Lady Reanay to regain her composure. The small crowd of onlookers, seeing her ladyship now recovered sufficiently to sip at the glass of water, took a step away, but remained near enough to return should the old lady go into a fit.

"Is there anything we can do for you, my lady? Perhaps take you for a walk in the gardens. The fresh air—"

"Thank you, my dears, but no. I will be myself directly." She smiled at Kitty and then looked at Tom Allenby who was on his haunches beside her chair. "So pleased you were able to come up to London for the ball, Mr. Allenby." She glanced at Kitty. "I hope you mean to spend a few weeks with us…"

Tom's smile was bashful, her meaning well understood. He gingerly looked across at Kitty Aldershot and when she met his gaze for the briefest of moments and smiled, he found himself growing hot in the face.

"Would you care for another glass of water, my lady?" he asked, not daring to look at Kitty again. When Lady Reanay shook her head, he asked, not to pry but because the look exchanged with Miss Kitty Aldershot had made him nervous and happy in equal measure, "Did I not see Sir Antony here with you just a moment ago… And Lady Caroline…?"

"Oh dear! Oh dear!" Lady Reanay groaned and out came the story yet again of Merry's masquerade as a page boy, Ned's truancy, and Diana's kind offer to fetch them both from the nursery, and how not only had Lady Caroline gone off to the nursery, but so had Sir Antony. She had no idea as to why and she was now worried that there would be a fuss and it would all come to the attention of the Earl and Countess, and for some reason she believed she would be blamed for it all. And then it happened again! She was in the middle of lamenting the whole episode and Kitty was offering her assurances that she could hardly be blamed for the actions of others, when Tom Allenby made her and Kitty Aldershot a curt bow, and without another word strode off in the same direction as Diana St. John, Lady Caroline, and Sir Antony before him.

Lady Reanay and Kitty Aldershot exchanged a look of astonishment.

"Thank goodness you are with me to witness the strange behavior of the family, Kitty dearest," Lady Reanay said with relief. "No one would believe me otherwise!"

MERRY AND NED SAT QUIETLY AT THE SMALL TABLE IN FRONT OF the fireplace in the nursery playroom, drawing by the glow of the fire. A maid, who had been busy cleaning out all the grates in this particular part of the house, took pity on them drawing in the gloom of one taper and rebuilt the fire. With the coal well alight, she placed the tapestry fire screen before the fireplace to protect the children from an errant spark. As soon as she left them alone, Merry dragged the screen out of the way and brought the little painted table and chairs closer so they could feel the warmth and the bright orange glow would illuminate their respective drawings in progress.

Ned promised that after he had completed one drawing, Merry could take him back to the tennis court. Merry took him at his word and so they sat, Merry's page boy mask discarded on the carpet alongside Ned's nightcap, both content and busy with charcoal and crayons, both agreeing not to show the other what they had drawn until each was satisfied with their respective works of art. So absorbed were they that they did not feel the presence of a figure hovering in the shadows close by.

Merry was the first to complete her drawing and she held it up under her chin for Ned's inspection. She had drawn what Ned had come to find in the nursery but which remained lost. He could not sleep without Monkey, so he told Merry, and so she had drawn his sleeping companion, telling him that perhaps he would sleep if he had a likeness of Monkey to put under his pillow. She had given the cloth monkey in her drawing a bigger smile than he actually had, but it was a very creditable likeness of the lost toy.

"Do you like him, Ned?" she asked.

"Monkey Misch-*ievous*! Is that for Ned's pillow?

"Yes. For your pillow. See, he is smiling. He misses you, but because he is smiling, he must be having a good time wherever he's run off to. What a naughty monkey!"

Ned put out his hand and Merry gave him the drawing.

"He's not having a good time," Ned pouted, peering closely at the drawing. "He has the bestest time with Ned." Then he smiled at Merry before again inspecting the drawing. "I like your monkey, Merry."

"I'm pleased you do. Do you want to show me your drawing now?"

Ned nodded and placed Merry's drawing of his companion on the floor by his nightcap. He picked up his drawing and put it under his chin and held it there. He peered down at it as best he could, to see if it was the right way up, and satisfied, he pushed the bright yellow curls out of his eyes and looked up at Merry with a grin. He was very proud of his drawing. It was of Ned and Monkey holding hands in the garden. Merry could tell this because there was a large flower the same size as the two smiling stick figures with their stick fingers touching. One stick figure had ears on the top of its head and a long tail, and the other wore short trousers.

"Oh, Ned! What a lovely drawing of you and Monkey in the garden!" Merry gushed. "When you show Mamma and Papa, they will say you are the best drawer in all the world!"

The little boy grinned at such praise, shoulders hunching with delight. But no sooner had he made eye contact with Merry across the table than he was distracted by something lurking in the shadows over her left shoulder. He blinked, and at first he leaned across the table, trying to make out what it was in the darkness, such was his curiosity.

Merry saw his distraction and looked over her shoulder, swiveling on her chair. As she did so, Ned let out the most piercing scream imaginable. It caused her to topple backwards and fall to the carpet.

Ned screamed and screamed and could not stop. His brown eyes widened in terror and his little face went white. He pushed back his chair so hard that what happened to Merry happened to him. His chair toppled and he fell to the carpet. Such was his fright that the bump to his head and jolt to his bones did not register. He scrambled out of the chair, wide terrified eyes locked on the monster as he pushed backwards on his bottom, little legs working back and forth along the carpet, propelling him as fast as he could go, away from the thing that terrified him. He could not stop looking at the thing as much as he wanted to look anywhere but up at it.

He tried to put as much distance as possible between him and the monster but very soon his head hit up against the wall and there was nowhere else for him to go. He could not move. He could not look away, and he kept on screaming.

Floating towards him was a head. It had no body. The head floated on a big white cloud and it was coming straight towards him. The head's face was painted white with spots of red on each cheek. It had wide wild eyes that stared at him without blinking, and blood dripped from its ears. There was sparkling blood and snowflakes in its tight curly hair, and its red mouth was painted in an evil grin. And when the head without a body that floated on a cloud opened its red-painted mouth and spoke to him, Ned covered his ears with his hands, closed his eyes tight and screamed even louder.

TWENTY-SEVEN

Merry picked herself up off the carpet, disorientated and befuddled. But Ned's screams snapped her to the present. She saw the head on its floating white cloud, but she also saw the dark red Elizabethan dress beneath. Another, closer look at the painted face, with its garnet drop earrings and coiffure of tight curls littered with diamond and garnet headed pins and she recognized her mother.

"Mamma? Mamma, what are you doing here?"

"Magna, get him to stop screaming in that dreadful way!" Diana St. John snapped. "Stupid boy! Anyone would think he'd seen a ghost!"

"Perhaps he does think you're a ghost, Mamma," Merry offered timidly, hovering in indecision.

She wanted to scoop Ned up and tell him everything was all right, but she had a very bad feeling that everything was not all right, and so she hesitated, not knowing what she should do.

Diana St. John went over to Ned and beamed down at him with her very best smile, one she thought welcoming and warm. "Hello, Lord Lacey—

"It's Ned. No one calls him that. Aunt Jane says—"

"Oh spare me what *Aunt Jane says*," Diana St. John mimicked.

Again, she smiled down at Ned, who now had his eyes shut tight with his hands clamped firmly over his ears. He was still screaming.

"Ned! Ned!" she shouted, and lifted the top layer of her silken petticoats to reveal beneath a large embroidered pocket secured by ties around her waist. She shoved a hand in the pocket and pulled out Ned's cloth monkey. "Look what I have, Ned! Ned!"

"That's Ned's Monkey!" Merry exclaimed, eyes round.

"Yes! Yes! Now get him to stop screaming and open his eyes so he can see his wretched toy!"

Merry was about to do as she was told when Lady Caroline appeared in the doorway.

"Diana? Merry? What is going on here? What's happened to Ned? Why have you got Ned's monkey?"

Merry was so happy to see her cousin Caroline that she did not to do as her mother ordered. Instead, she burst into tears of relief and ran into her cousin's open arms.

"We were drawing a picture," Merry explained tearfully. "We didn't mean to be such a long time. Just one picture and then we were returning to the tennis court. Promise."

Caroline gave Merry a warm hug. It wasn't from Merry she wanted answers, and with an arm about Merry, she came further into the playroom with every intention of picking up Ned, who was now sobbing, great aching sobs that stopped his breath.

Diana crossed in front of her, blocking access to the boy.

"I will deal with him, if you please, Caroline," Diana St. John said at her imperious best.

Caroline gaped at her but made a quick recover.

"You will do no such thing! Ned doesn't know you from soap! Truth told it was seeing you in that ridiculous ruff that scared him witless. Now stand aside!"

Diana did not move; Caroline took a step closer.

"Diana? Caroline? May I be of assistance?"

It was Sir Antony and he tried to keep the timbre of his voice neutral and light.

"Uncle Tony!"

Merry broke from Caroline and ran up to Sir Antony and threw her arms around him, cheek pressed to the front of his waistcoat. "I'm so *happy* you are home. So *very* happy."

Sir Antony hugged his niece. "Merry? Or is it a pageboy who dares to call me uncle?" he teased but kissed the top of her head. "I'm so very pleased to be home, too," he said quietly. Before Merry could reply, he said to Caroline, "My lady, it's time Merry and Ned were returned to the tennis court."

"I was just about to—"

"If you would just pick up Ned and bring him over to me," Sir Antony said in a soothing voice.

Caroline frowned, a quick look at Diana and then back at Sir

Antony. It was in that small hesitant frown that Diana saw her chance. She flung the toy monkey away, swooped on the sobbing boy and scooped him up.

"Caroline! Come here!" Sir Antony demanded stridently, and when Caroline did as he ordered he put Merry into her care. "Take Merry away from here—*now*."

"I don't understand—*Tom*?"

"Please, do as I ask," Sir Antony demanded, and on hearing Tom's name, he swiveled on a foot to say to him, "I'll deal with this. Take Caro and Merry away."

Tom Allenby did not hesitate. With a nod to Sir Antony, he took Merry by the hand, put an arm about Caroline and ushered them both from the room before Caroline had a chance to even turn and dispute Sir Antony's directive.

Caroline's hesitant frown, Sir Antony's demand, Tom turning up in the playroom and then taking Merry and Caroline away, all happened within seconds of Diana snatching Ned. What she intended to do with him, Sir Antony had no idea. All he did know was that his sister was not sane, and thus anything was possible. With Caroline and Merry out of the away he could now concentrate on freeing the little boy.

"Shall I pick up the monkey?" he asked, slowly crossing the room to the little table scattered with drawings and paper, where the toy monkey had landed, sprawled across the back of one of the overbalanced little chairs.

With both arms holding tight to the sobbing boy, Diana backed away from her brother, thoughts racing as to what she could do now, with her plans in disarray. It was all the fault of her stupid daughter, and her interfering redheaded cousin with her green eyes that had always looked at her with suspicion, and reminded her of someone she had once known but could not now remember. If she could just get the boy outside, to the gardens, to the garden gate... Mrs. Smith was waiting for her... If only the brat would stop his blubbering... All those years planning her return to Society... All those hours dreaming of how it had been and would be again with Salt taking her advice and guidance... Dreaming of his wretched family and that skinny whore dead... Her plans could not end here. Not now. Not when she was so close to having them fulfilled.

"Ned? Ned, here is your monkey," Sir Antony said soothingly, holding out the cloth toy, extending his arm just far enough to show the boy his toy but not so close that Diana could snatch the toy from him. "Lady St. John found your monkey. Did you not, my lady?"

Diana nodded. "That's right. I found it. He can have it if he stops crying like a baby."

Sir Antony nodded as if he agreed with her and did not move any closer because if Diana took another step back she risked setting her petticoats aflame, she was that close to the fireplace. He went down on his haunches so the little boy could see him clearly. Ned was now whimpering, hands hanging loose but eyes shut tight.

"What's that you say, Monkey?" Sir Antony said, holding the cloth monkey to his ear. He saw Ned open one eye, and pretended to have a conversation with the toy, as he had done with his niece and nephew's toys, when they were about Ned's age. They had thought it a great joke and laughed and laughed to see their Uncle Tony talk to their toys who never said a word in reply. "You wish Ned to stop crying so you could say hello? Well, we all wish that, Monkey." He put the Monkey to his ear again. "What's that? You think Ned is crying with happiness to see you? Truly? Well I don't know about that—"

"You are making yourself ridiculous!" Diana spat out. "That rag can't speak or hear—"

"He can! He can! He wants Ned!" the boy shouted, suddenly animated. "Let me go! Let me go!"

"Stop it! Stop and be still, you little beast!"

Sir Antony straightened and stood tall.

"Diana, put the boy down," he demanded flatly. "There is no point to this anymore. There is no one waiting to help you outside the garden gate. Mrs. Smith has told me everything and she is now in irons in Bedlam. You are friendless. You are powerless. Your scheming is at an end. Put. Ned. Down."

"I don't believe you! I won't! You must do as I say or I will—I will —" Diana looked about wildly, the boy slipping as he struggled in her arms. "I will throw him in the fire!"

"Diana. I will use force. Put. Ned. Down."

"Monkey! I want Monkey!" Ned screamed, flailing in the head monster's arms, tossing his head from side to side, body twisting this way and that as he tried desperately to free himself.

Strong little legs released from the confines of his ankle length linen nightshirt that was now bunched up around his waist, he kicked out wildly and kicked out again. He felt the grip on his arms loosen and with one arm finally tugged free he lashed up and out. His fist connected with the head monster. He had thrust his arm back so hard that all of a sudden his other arm was free, too. He was free. He fell through the air and dropped into the waiting arms of the nice man who was friends with Monkey; he remembered seeing him at breakfast when Papa had said rude words out loud and made him laugh.

He felt safe with the nice man with the kind voice, safe from the head monster and the head monster's screams and growls. And when frightening noises filled the nursery and were loud and terrible he scrambled to throw his arms around the nice man's neck and bury his face in his soft neckcloth. The nice man gave him Monkey to hug and he cuddled in, eyes shut tight, as he was whisked away, out of the nursery and into the passageway, away from the head monster's piercing screams.

Half way along the passageway, he was placed in the arms of another. Ned dared to open his eyes and discovered Uncle Tom smiling at him. Such was his relief to see a most beloved face that he threw his arms around his neck and hugged him tightly. As Uncle Tom carried him away to safety, Ned clutching Monkey's arm in a tight fist and swinging him against Uncle Toms' back, he watched the nice man who had rescued him run back into the nursery to do battle with the screaming growling head monster.

When Ned had struggled to be free and lashed out, his fist connected with Diana's face. She was hit so violently between the eyes that she reeled. In shock, she instantly opened her arms and dropped the little boy.

Disorientated, and in a moment of blindness, she staggered, tripped against the fire screen and fell. With the large heavy ruff a weight about her neck, she could not stop the momentum and she landed in the fireplace, face first, inches from the hot coals in the grate. The ruff broke her fall, but wedged in the grate she could not move and the ruff held fast. The intense heat of the fire began to sear her flesh and she screamed for help. Panicked, she thrashed about, trying to find anchorage within the fireplace to hold firm to pull free. When that failed, one hand tugged at the ruff, fingers frantically grappling with the hook and eye closures, but they would not release and so the ruff remained fixed in place. The more she panicked, the more her fingers fumbled, and still the ruff would not release.

The heat was now unbearable.

Her frantic attempts to be free of the ruff and escape the fire fanned the coals into new life, and the waxed paper ruff suddenly ignited. In an instant, a river of flame whipped around the ruff, engulfing her head. The flames leapt and danced and her elaborate coiffure of waxed and pomaded curls was also soon ablaze with the same ferocity. Within seconds the ruff collapsed to ash and Diana's face dropped into the glowing coals.

SIR ANTONY RUSHED BACK INTO THE NURSERY TO THE unbelievably shocking sight of his sister burning alive. Grasping her petticoats he dragged her free of the fireplace, to the carpet, and turned her on her back where her body continued to convulse with pain and shock, arms and legs flailing of their own accord. The sound of air being sucked down a seared throat in an effort to breathe was truly hideous, and her face and hair were still alight. He dashed to the window and with an almighty tug, ripped down a curtain. This he threw over her upper body to extinguish the flame. Just as he did so, her body convulsed one last time, went rigid, and then fell limp and still.

He removed the curtain to a gruesome sight. The once beautiful face was burned out of all recognition. The fine nose was an indefinable charred blob. Where there had been lips, the flesh was blistered exposing teeth in a final grimace. Both hands were red and blistered. Diana had died a hideous and agonizing death, and he had been powerless to prevent it.

He held her lifeless hand and wept.

WHEN HE FINALLY FOUND THE STRENGTH TO COVER HER CORPSE with the curtain, Sir Antony reminded himself that this creature was not his sister. Diana had died a long time ago. Perhaps her mind had been slowly dying of reason since before her marriage to St. John. He did not know, and now it did not matter. This creature was no longer tormented by demons, nor could it inflict torment on others. It was at peace. He was at peace, and certainly the Salt Hendon family could now live in peace. He could not feel sadness or regret at her passing, only in the manner of her death. If he felt anything it was a huge relief, and with relief came renewed hope and optimism for the future. Tomorrow was a new day and a new beginning. The first day of the rest of their lives…

TWENTY-EIGHT

Sir Antony had expected to wake on the first day of the rest of his life brimming with cheerful optimism, but all he felt was the stubble on his chin. He wasn't particularly cheerful either. After dealing with the immediate aftermath of his sister's death and all that entailed, the masquerade was over, with only one or two guests taking their leave at the ungodly hour of four in the morning. Thankfully, none of the guests were wise to what had occurred in the nursery and he had decamped to the tennis court to spend the night in one of the gallery boxes on a makeshift bed.

He reasoned that three hours of restless sleep on a hardened surface could account for his mood. He had slept in waistcoat and shirtsleeves, the red sash of the Imperial Order of St. Anna forgotten about his neck, now wrinkled, he hoped not beyond repair. He removed the sash, straightened his clothes and washed his face in the porcelain bowl with the water from a matching pitcher, put at his disposal by an attentive servant. Leaving off his frock coat, and hearing voices and laughter out on the tennis court, he gingerly poked his head through the netting to the wondrous sight of the Salt Hendon family having a picnic breakfast.

The net that usually stretched across the court had been removed and in its place on the tiled flooring was a scatter of carpets, and upon these carpets were a scatter of silken cushions, and upon these cushions reclined various family members, helping themselves to the variety of breakfast foods to be found on the platters under silver domed covers.

Still dressed in their Turkish masquerade costumes of the night before, the Earl, his Countess, Lady Caroline, Kitty Aldershot, Tom Allenby and Rufus Willis presented as if at an Ottoman banquet. Merry was there, still in her pageboy outfit, and the Earl and Countess's three children. The baby was nestled in the crook of his father's arm, and Beth sat in Kitty's lap giggling at the antics of Boots the pug puppy, as he wrestled the string of a discarded wooden pull toy. Ned was in his nightshirt and silk banyan, running barefoot around the perimeter of the carpets holding Monkey high above his head, as if he were flying a kite, seemingly recovered and unaffected by his frightening ordeal of the night before.

Making up the complement was the Earl's secretary Arthur Ellis, and of all the guests to be found at the Earl's breakfast picnic, Hilary Wraxton. Dressed as a courtier from the time of Charles the First, Sir Antony did not want to hazard a guess what material constituted the poet's full-bottomed wig of tight curls. He appeared to have an entire black lamb's wool fleece draped over his head, made all the more glorious sprinkled with tiny bows in all colors of the rainbow.

"Hey Ho! The macaw has awoken! Come join us while there is still food to be had. Miller. Pour his lordship out a nice hot cup of tea."

Sir Antony jumped the barrier at the Earl's hearty invitation and Lady Caroline scrambled up from her cushion to meet him. She grabbed his hand and kissed his cheek good morning.

"Please, Caroline, you should not come near me while I am in this deplorable state." He gratefully accepted the cup of tea a footman offered him and sipped. "Certainly not before I have had the first cup of tea for the day."

She dimpled, saying so only he could hear, "Are you telling me that when we are married, we won't be spending the entire night together?"

He replaced the teacup on its saucer, an eyebrow raised.

"You will have to push me out of the marital bed."

She smiled sweetly and led him to the breakfast banquet.

"You needn't be embarrassed by your whiskers. Salt is thoroughly unpresentable," she said so all could hear. "He practically has a beard! And I have never seen Tom or Mr. Willis so disheveled. Mr. Wraxton is the only respectable one amongst us. Oh, and Jane. But Jane *never* looks ruffled. None of us have been to bed, as you can see."

Sir Antony had seen. Yet, it had not registered with him that because everyone was still in their masquerade outfits, they had stayed up all night.

"There seemed little point in retiring for the night when the children were due to wake in a matter of hours," Jane explained as Sir Antony took his place on a cushion between Caroline and the Earl.

"So we made a party of it," Tom added, passing Sir Antony a bowl filled with fruit. "Did we wake you?"

Sir Antony took an apple and shook his head. He then noticed his aunt was not one of the party.

"Lady Reanay perfectly well...?"

"Yes. I sent her to bed," Jane explained. "The physician gave her something to sleep. The—events—of the evening greatly unsettled her..."

"Booffs! Booffs!" Beth called out, jumping up and down on Kitty Aldershot's lap, a chubby finger pointing in direction of the pug puppy.

This considerably lightened the mood, and everyone watched Boots the pug puppy struggle to remove his round head from under one of the domed silver lids. As the pug puppy attempted to back his way out of his dilemma the domed lid went with him, which had everyone laughing. In the interval that saw Lady Caroline rescue the puppy and the footmen fuss with removing the platter, the Earl took the opportunity to have a private word with Sir Antony, who was quietly chomping away at his apple.

"The local magistrate came to call an hour ago. He is satisfied with Bennetts'—the physician's—verdict of accidental death. She will be buried without fuss, and quietly—today. Everyone has been informed, Merry too. Tom has offered to fetch Ron from Eton. I suggest a private memorial service in a day or two ..."

Sir Antony nodded, surprised by the constriction in his throat, and not from the apple, that made it impossible for him to speak. The Earl sensed this, and he, too, was overcome with emotion. Taking a moment to find his voice, and clearing his suddenly dry throat, he gave his cousin's hand a squeeze and said,

"Antony... *Tony*, I cannot—I cannot imagine what you went through... What you witnessed... Bennetts told me the extent of her injuries... Horrific. He is of the opinion she probably died of a heart attack, brought on by the shock suffered by such burns. Tom told me the rest... I—Jane and I—what we owe you... You have given us—*all of us*—a reason to embrace the future..." He gripped his cousin's shoulder. "I'm so pleased—so *very* pleased—you've come home."

Sensing there was a lull in the laughter and activity, the Earl rallied and looked up to find Merry waiting patiently to speak with him. He put out his hand to her. "Dear me, for a moment I mistook you for a junior footman, Merry!"

"Junior footman?" Sir Antony questioned, entering into the spirit of the Earl's good-natured teasing. "How many junior footmen do you employ with waist-length hair?"

When the Earl pretended to think about the question, Merry giggled and said, "Silly Uncle Salt!" She glanced at Sir Antony, and asked quietly, "May I please be permitted to ask Uncle Tony the question about the boxes now?"

"Ah, yes! The mystery of the boxes! More correctly, the crates that have been blocking up poor Miller's pantry." Salt nodded at Merry, who asked her question.

"Are the contents of those crates over there for us, Uncle Tony? May we open them now?"

"Two questions I am more than happy to answer *yes* to," Sir Antony replied, tossing aside the apple core amongst the remnants of breakfast. "With Uncle Salt's permission, now is the best time to have them opened and the gifts distributed. But I shall need two gift fairies to deliver my gifts to the correct recipients. Do you think you and Miss Aldershot would do us the honor of being the gift fairies?"

"Monkey and Ned want to be fairies too!" Ned demanded, rushing up to stand beside Merry.

"An elf, mayhap, Ned. Only girls are fairies," Salt told him.

Ned made a face pondering this, and looked over at his mother. She was smiling. He shook his curls at his father. "No, Papa. Monkey and Ned will be fairies with Merry."

"Why not," Sir Antony agreed. "The more fairies the merrier."

Ned beamed and taking Merry's hand skipped behind Kitty to the far side of the tennis court where three footmen were busy opening and removing straw packing from three large crates.

Lady Caroline held Sir Antony's hand, and the rest of the picnickers sat up on their cushions in anticipation of what the crates would reveal. Miller had a footman help the children carry several larger items across to the carpets, while another footman put into Kitty Aldershot's arms a pile of smaller articles. All were wrapped in cloth and tagged, and the gift fairies did an excellent job of distributing the parcels to the name listed on the tag; Merry reading the names to Ned, who then was given a parcel to hand to the respective recipient. This worked well until Ned heard his own name read out, and all thought of helping Merry vanished in the excitement of opening his gift; this, his father helped him do.

Everyone was engaged in unwrapping their gifts, but not so self-absorbed that they did not fail to hear the little boy's huge intake of breath, and then look up to see the astonishment in the roundness of his eyes as he beheld a stick pony, and not just any stick pony. This one had a lush mane and a leather bridle, and at the end of the stick, two wheels painted in gilt. With the stick pony came a blue velvet cape trimmed with silver spangles, a silver and gold-leaf helmet with plumes, a matching shield and sword, and a pair of red leather boots. When dressed, Ned would look—not that he had any idea what one was—every bit a Roman centurion.

The others were no less thrilled with their gifts. Beth was given a doll dressed in a silk damask gown, and there was a miniature tea set complete with silver teapot and porcelain cups to share. Jane received the adult version of the same, a lemon yellow porcelain tea service from the Russian Imperial Porcelain Factory in its own special case. Caroline, Jane, Kitty, and Lady Reanay all received a folding fan with ivory sticks and mother-of-pearl inlay, every one with a different painted pastoral scene in the manner of the artist Boucher. Wrapped with each fan was a Sèvres porcelain bonbonnière, the little sweet boxes the shape of the head of an exotic animal. There was a nécessaire for Caroline, the tortoiseshell toilette traveling case complete with ivory combs, brushes, perfume bottles, traveling beakers, utensils and a silver etui manicure set. Just what she required to go traveling the Continent with Sir Antony.

Tom was very pleased with a set of quills and a porcelain standish, standard equipment for any gentleman who had a great many letters to write. If this cryptic remark by Sir Antony raised the Earl's eyebrow, Sir Antony chose to ignore it. Arthur Ellis could not believe his good fortune to be gifted a pair of shoe buckles he could never hope to purchase himself, and a Parisian embroidered ivory silk waistcoat.

Mr. Rufus Willis wondered if he had unwrapped someone else's gift by mistake when he opened a velvet-lined box to discover a silver fob watch and chain. But when he turned it over and saw his initials elaborately engraved on the backing, he was lost for words. A similar watch with his initials engraved awaited Ron when he returned home from Eton. The steward was also given a small wooden box. He was not to open it now. It was for Mrs. Willis: A Sèvres porcelain chocolate pot with matching chocolate cups and dishes.

There was even a gift for Hilary Wraxton, who was delighted with a set of quills. With it came a rather odd-shaped porcelain receptacle decorated in the Chinese manner, which at first glance looked to be a vase for holding flowers. It did not take the poet many minutes to realize its more practical function, and he quickly wrapped it up again lest the ladies take too much interest in it, a nod and a tap to his temple at Sir Antony.

"Up there for thinking, Antony! Up there for thinking!" was all he would say, a smug little smile splitting his face.

For the Earl, a gold snuffbox covered in diamonds and precious gems. On the inside of the lid was a miniature portrait painting of his beloved Jane. The miniature was one of two he had commissioned and when only one was delivered, he had wondered at the whereabouts of the second. The Countess had remained suitably vague on the subject. Now he knew; she had sent it to Sir Antony to have it set in the snuffbox. He stared down at the precious object for a good five seconds, too overcome to speak, and then, at the Countess's gentle inquiry, passed her the snuffbox to admire.

Another gift for Caroline and she pried open the lid of a velvet-lined box to discover not one but three leather and velvet collars studded with diamonds and set at intervals with tiny silver bells, mistaken by the others to be bracelets, but she knew better. She threw her arms about Sir Antony's neck and kissed him heartily, further astonishing everyone by scooping up Boots and having Sir Antony put the smallest collar about the puppy's neck.

This made Salt laugh and shake his head.

"I should counsel you not to overindulge her, but you will anyway," he said to Sir Antony, and to goad his sister.

Caroline opened her mouth to make a retort but closed it in deference to Merry who, after distributing the gifts, was now able to sit and open her own gifts from her Uncle Tony. Both were what she had always dreamed of having, and never thought she ever would, despite telling her uncle in one of her letters that she hoped one day to have a paint box and easel of her own. She not only received a paint box full of every paint imaginable, there were paint brushes, porcelain mixing pots, and palettes, a fold-away easel and parchment.

It was the second gift that set the ladies ooh-ing and aah-ing and the gentlemen smiling with indulgence.

It was a beautiful doll, twenty-three inches in height, with poseable limbs and lovely smiling porcelain features. She had a head of waist-length real brunette hair to dress, and a wardrobe of the latest gowns and petticoats in silk damask and velvets from the workshop of a Parisian couturier. There were linen chemises, whalebone stays, pairs of embroidered pockets to tie on under her gown, stockings and garters, and a set of cane and velvet panniers. She had five pairs of shoes, two miniature folding fans, a purse, an umbrella, fichus, shawls and three hats, a pocket book, parasol, and a chair to sit upon. Most surprising of all, she also came with three little wigs of real hair to powder and dress. All the dolls' clothes and accoutrements fitted into a polished wooden armoire that was no less spectacular, with drawers and a space for the doll to live when she was not being dressed and played with. It was the most wondrous gift, and one any woman of fashion, not least a girl almost thirteen years old, would love to own.

When Merry stopped hugging her Uncle Tony and thanking him, she skipped over to the assembled nursery maids and Nanny Browne to show them her beautiful doll and her accessories. Nanny asked if she had a name in mind for her doll, and Merry replied Antonia, in honor of her Uncle Tony. At about the same time, baby Sam began to fuss in his father's arms, and as Jane was busily engaged in watching Ned ride his pony, Beth having migrated to her lap to show her mother her beautiful doll, the Earl looked about for Sam's nurse.

Betsy was there in an instant, and as she took Sam into her arms, Sir Antony caught her eye and smiled up at her. She smiled back and retreated, but not before Hilary Wraxton made a startling discovery.

"Antony! Oi! Antony!" he demanded, finger wagging at Betsy's back. "By God, there she is! There she is! The mob cap girl!"

Conversations stopped in an instant. However, as Sir Antony remained perfectly calm, and it was Hilary Wraxton making the pronouncements, after a small pause, conversations resumed as if the poet had not spoken.

"Yes, Hilary," Sir Antony replied calmly. "Perhaps, at some later date, you may care to recite your poem to Betsy. And when you publish your slim volume of poems, you will dedicate that particular poem to Betsy Smith—your muse."

Hilary Wraxton's eyes glazed as the idea took hold. "My muse… Yes. Yes! Betsy Smith… My muse…"

"His brother has run off abroad with Jenny Dalrymple," Salt mentioned casually.

"Has he? With—Lady Dalrymple?" asked Sir Antony, mildly interested.

"Yes," the Earl replied, a sly glance at Sir Antony whose features remained perfectly composed.

"It's not what I had in mind, but given the events of last night, it will do," Sir Antony mused, and said nothing further.

Rufus Willis stared at Sir Antony, astounded, then blinked at his noble employer.

"Dacre Wraxton? *The MP for Hendon*? Run off? Run off with Lady Dalrymple?"

"Came up to me at the ball, apologized and resigned as MP," the Earl told him. "Said I would have it all in a letter today." Salt pursed his mouth, adding, another glance at Sir Antony, "I received the strongest impression his speech was rehearsed... Or that someone else rehearsed it for him and he just spat it out. What is vastly more interesting is that he gave me the name of a suggested replacement for his seat in the Commons. Mentioned that would be in his letter, too."

"Tom will make a capital and most diligent Member of Parliament," Sir Antony stated.

"I never mentioned Tom by name."

"I know that," Sir Antony replied adroitly.

Tom Allenby looked about, and realizing the Earl and his cousin were talking about him sat up straight. "Me? Me an-an *MP*?"

"I also know that Tom, while furthering the cause of Hendon and his mentor Lord Salt in the House, will have causes of his own to further..."

"I will?" Tom asked with a blink.

"Don't be coy, Tom. Caroline told me all about your interest in the emancipation issue. And then there are the rights of animals—"

"The rights of *animals*?" Rufus Willis repeated, incredulous, a worried glance at the Earl.

"Come now, Mr. Willis," Sir Antony said. "Surely you have had your fair share of Lady Caroline's lecturing on the suffering of the fox during the hunt. And I am very sure you have, in your small way, assisted her ladyship with the relocation of those larger animals she rescues from their cruel owners and sends to Mr. Allenby at Allenby Park?"

"Well—er—yes," Rufus Willis admitted truthfully.

Tom Allenby's eyes suddenly shone and he looked to Sir Antony for confirmation.

"As an MP I could put a bill before the House seeking a ban on the cruel and unusual practices of those establishments that keep animals for sport and—"

"Don't get ahead of yourself, Tom," the Earl advised. "I marvel at your ability to orchestrate and manipulate at will," he said to Sir Antony. "The sooner you are made an ambassador, the better for England's relationship with its neighbors across the Channel."

"I have no vested interest other than Caroline's happiness."

"I cannot argue with that," the Earl quipped, a sidelong glance at his sister who was tugging at Sir Antony's sleeve to get that gentleman's attention.

"I do love the nécessaire, and the glorious gifts for my puppies, for which I thank you most heartily, but what of *the* gift?" Lady Caroline asked in an under voice. "Do you not have a *special* gift just for me…?"

Sir Antony did not take her hint. He did indeed have a betrothal ring, set with rubies and diamonds, and a gold wedding band to match, but he pretended ignorance. He said in all seriousness,

"I can think of no greater gift than my everlasting love and devotion."

Lady Caroline blinked at him, and blushed. "Of course! Of course that is the most important gift of all but-but—"

Sir Antony could not have been happier to see her contrite. He cut her off, saying with continued practiced ignorance,

"Oh? Do you mean the Special License your brother keeps in the drawer of his desk which has our names upon it?"

Lady Caroline's eyes sparkled.

"Do you, Salt? Do you have a Special License for Antony and me?"

The Earl glanced at Sir Antony, frowning, wondering how his cousin knew. "Yes. I do. But how did—"

"Then we can be married at once!" Lady Caroline declared. Swept away with her enthusiasm, she looked to her family, who were now listening to the conversation, and said happily, "Merry will be flower girl, and Kitty my bride's attendant. Tom must be Antony's best man, as Salt is to give me away, and Jane—" She looked at Jane with contrition. "You do not mind if Kitty attends me, do you, dearest?"

"I am more than happy for Kitty to do so," Jane replied. "And of course Salt must give you away." She glanced at the Earl and said, tongue firmly in cheek, "I can't promise his mood, but I can assure you that the Sultan of Glum will be in a vastly better frame of mind than he was the day he married me!"

"Jane! That is unfair and cruel," the Earl grumbled and flushed.

No one spared his feelings; everyone laughed heartily.

"What will you wear, Caroline?" Kitty asked.

It was a simple enough question, but it had the ladies instantly alert and soon in discussion on which of Caroline's many robe *à la française* gowns would be most suitable, or if she should have an entirely new gown made for the occasion. As the conversation threatened to be constant and unflagging, with Hilary Wraxton offering up suggestions on required accoutrements for this bridal gown, Sir Antony anchored the discussion before it set sail into the uncharted waters of choice of fabric, color and suitable trimmings.

"To say I am delighted by your joyous enthusiasm for such an event, my darling, would be an understatement," Sir Antony drawled. "But you forget perhaps that were this grand event to take place, it cannot be for at least two months."

Lady Caroline was startled.

"*Two months?*"

"Six weeks would be prudent," Salt stated. "And if the ceremony is a small family affair on the estate, and the honeymoon conducted somewhere out of the way—"

"Ireland."

"Capital choice," Salt agreed. "Then no one would raise an eyebrow of objection if Antony's period of mourning were not the requisite six months."

"*Six months?*" Lady Caroline gasped the words, incredulous. She shot a glance about at the now silent group lounging on cushions and said what none of them dared voice openly. Her bitter disappointment made her uncaring for the feelings of others. "She hardly deserves six days of remembrance given her treatment of her children and her brother—"

"Yet, out of respect for her children, and her brother," the Earl stated evenly, "we shall do what is right and proper."

There was a deafening silence and then Lady Caroline nodded and shuddered in a great breath. "Yes. Of course. Forgive me. I am being selfish and uncharitable."

"Six weeks will give you time to have the perfect ensemble made," Jane offered quietly. She glanced at Sir Antony. "And for your future husband to set his house in order. There are a great many adjustments to make when one marries, and even more when a husband inherits his future bride's family."

Everyone knew the Countess referred to Lady Caroline's animal family. The Earl, to goad his sister out of her petulance, slapped Sir Antony's back and said with a laugh,

"Huzzah! At last I can get rid of that bloody bird!"

"*Magnus.* The children," Jane hissed.

"*Buddy* bird!" Ned repeated as he climbed onto his father's lap, a quick glance up at his father and then at his mother before grinning at the assembled company who were unable to stifle their laughter.

"Glad that's settled," Salt said with satisfaction and ruffled his little son's golden curls. "You can be Aunt Caro's ring bearer and wear a velvet suit and—"

"Pardon, Salt, but nothing at all is settled," Sir Antony stated as he got to his feet and brushed down his sleeves. Out of the corner of his eye, he watched Caroline struggle up, too, Tom being of assistance. He must really put his foot down at her wearing Turkish garments in public. As for having her hair undressed down her back, never mind she was still wearing her fetching little turban; that was for their private apartments only. "It is all very well to have a Special License in your drawer, but what is the point of it when it is quite useless to me under the present circumstances?"

"What do you mean?" Caroline demanded in a whisper, standing before him. "Present circumstances?"

He tried hard to suppress a grin and flicked her under the chin.

"You must agree that for one to be able to marry, a betrothal must come first."

She looked up with head angled, and said with a smile, "You have asked me to marry you."

"You have yet to give me an answer."

She caught at his hand. "Ask me again," she whispered. "Now."

Sir Antony went down on bended knee before her, took from his pocket a small velvet-covered box, opened it to reveal a ruby and diamond betrothal ring, and for the second time in less than a week solemnly asked Lady Caroline to marry him. This time, she answered him without a second's hesitation.

"With all my heart, yes!" she responded, choking back tears. "A-a *hundred* times—*yes*."

With the betrothal ring secure, Sir Antony swept Lady Caroline up in a fierce embrace to the applause and cheers of congratulations of their family.

Never one to miss the opportunity of a captive audience, Hilary Wraxton jumped to his feet, ready to declaim. Hands shot out in the poet's direction to halt the recital before it had begun, objection voiced in the strongest possible terms with children present. This exertion was for naught. A flick of the lamb's wool wig, and Hilary Wraxton burst into recitation of his *Ode to a Belated Betrothal*, the newly-betrothed couple sealing their mutual happiness with a passionate kiss, oblivious to the aural pain and suffering of the Earl of Salt Hendon and his harem.

. . .

BEHIND-THE-SCENES

Explore the places, objects, and history in *Salt Redux* on Pinterest.

www.pinterest.com/lucindabrant